A PENGUIN MYSTERY

DEATH WITHOUT COMPANY

Craig Johnson is the *New York Times* bestselling author of the Longmire mysteries, the basis for the hit Netflix original series *Longmire*. He is the recipient of the Western Writers of America Spur Award for fiction, and his novella, *Spirit of Steamboat*, was the first One Book Wyoming selection. He lives in Ucross, Wyoming, population twenty-five.

By Craig Johnson

The Longmire Series

The Cold Dish

Death Without Company

Kindness Goes Unpunished

Another Man's Moccasins

The Dark Horse

Junkyard Dogs

Hell Is Empty

As the Crow Flies

A Serpent's Tooth

Any Other Name

Dry Bones

An Obvious Fact

The Western Star

Depth of Winter

Also by Craig Johnson

Spirit of Steamboat (a novella)

Wait for Signs (short stories)

The Highwayman (a novella)

Stand-Alone E-Stories

Christmas in Absaroka County
(includes four stories, also in *Wait for Signs*)

Divorce Horse (also in *Wait for Signs*)

Messenger (also in *Wait for Signs*)

CRAIG JOHNSON

DEATH WITHOUT COMPANY

PENGUIN BOOKS

PENGUIN BOOKS

An imprint of Penguin Random House LLC
375 Hudson Street
New York, New York 10014
penguin.com

First published in the United States of America by Viking Penguin,
a member of Penguin Group (USA) Inc., 2006
Published in Penguin Books 2007

ISBN 978-0-14-303838-2

Printed in the United States of America
37   39   40   38   36

Set in Dante MT Std

For Dorothy Caldwell Kisling (1930–2005)
for whom I still look when I laugh

ACKNOWLEDGMENTS

A writer, like a sheriff, is the embodiment of a group of people and, without their support, both are in a tight spot. I have been blessed with a close order of family, friends, and associates who have made this book possible. They know who they are and, as the tradition goes, you can never thank a good cast too much. Thanks particularly to Lilly and Glenn, the dairy princess and the crack shot.

Many thanks to Susan Fain for the philosophic and legal counsel and for the weekly Fain File and to Ana Echavarri-Daily for the clarification of Euskara, the Basque language. Donna Dubrow for a lot more than just the use of the *Presence Suite* and Ned Tanen for the Sunday drives in the desert and the prune milkshakes. Susan Miller for reading half-written novels and saying she fully likes them. Marcus Red Thunder and Charles Little Old Man for circling the wagons, because I only feel safe when I'm surrounded by Indians and books. Sheriff Larry Kirkpatrick for not making fun of me when I didn't recognize a 10–54 (livestock in the road) and Richard Rhoades for the intensive ballistic testing on gallon water jugs. Erin Guy for the Web site and phone messages and Joel Katz for the Absaroka Sheriff Department logo and for watching the detectives.

To Gail Hochman, superagent, who always has the correct word and is the fastest talker in New York and that's saying a lot. Ali Bothwell Mancini, my editor in arms, who always has a sharp sense of humor and fresh ammo. To Kathryn Court, whose steady hand charms me, and to Clare Ferraro, who hides when I come to Manhattan and probably for good reason. Sonya Cheuse for finding lodging for Lucy and knowing that three fingers in Wyoming is a long way.

Eric Boss, Viking Penguin sales rep of the year for the mountain and plains region, who taught me how to say things like *It's a character-driven piece* with a straight face. Scott Montgomery, the only one brave enough to swim when we could have just had Jim walk across the Tongue River Reservoir. To Sharon Dynak and the Ucross Foundation for not taking what I wrote about the foundation seriously and Bonita Schwann for not putting a yellow-truck hit out on me.

Thanks to Robert B. Parker, Bob Shacochis, Dan O'Brien, and Buck Brannaman for the kindness of words; you've always got a tumbler of Pappy Van Winkles in Ucross. To the Independent Booksellers Association for making *The Cold Dish* a Booksense pick and to the Independent Mystery Booksellers Association for making it a Killer pick.

For Judy who, like the stars, wonders if she shines brightly enough and always does.

A life without friends means death without company.
(Adiskidegabeko bizita, auzogabeko heriotza.)

—BASQUE PROVERB

DEATH WITHOUT COMPANY

1

"They used fire, back in the day."

What the old cowboy meant was that folks who were inconsiderate enough to die in the Wyoming winter faced four feet of frozen ground between them and their final resting place.

"They used to build a bonfire an' allow it to burn a couple of hours, melt through the frost, and then dig the grave."

Jules unscrewed the top from a flask he had pulled from the breast pocket of his tattered jean jacket and leaned on his worn shovel. It was 28 degrees outside, the jean jacket was all he wore, and he wasn't shivering; the flask probably had something to do with that.

"Now we only use the shovels when dirt clods roll into the grave from the backhoe." The tiny man took a sip from the flask and continued the throes of philosophic debate. "The traditional Chinese coffin is rectangular with three humps, and they won't bury you wearing red 'cause you'll turn into a ghost."

I nodded and did my best to stand still in the wind. He took another sip and didn't offer me any.

"The ancient Egyptians had their essential organs removed and put in jars."

I nodded some more.

"The Hindus burn the body, a practice I admire, but we cremated my uncle Milo and ended up losing him when his top came loose and he fell through the holes in the rusted floorboard of a Willy's Jeepster on the Upper Powder River Road." He thought about it, shaking his head at the ignominious end. "That ain't where I wanna spend eternity."

I nodded again and looked off toward the Big Horn Mountains, where it continued to snow. Somehow bonfires seemed more romantic than construction equipment or Willy's Jeepsters, for that matter.

"The Vikings used to stick 'em afire on a boat with all their stuff and shove out to sea, but that seems like an awful waste of stuff, not to mention a perfectly good boat." He paused, but continued. "Vikings considered death to be just another voyage and you never knew what you could end up needing, so you might as well take it all with you." The jackleg carpenter turned his ferocious blue eyes toward me and took another sip in honor of his ancestors, still not offering me any.

I buried my hands in my duty jacket, straining the embroidered star of the Absaroka County Sheriff's Office, and dropped my head a little as he kept on talking. I had seen Jules on a professional basis as a lodger at the jail when the nephew of the previous sheriff, and deputy of mine at the time, had picked him up for public intoxication and had beaten him. I had in turn beaten Turk, much to the dismay of my receptionist/dispatcher Ruby, and then turned him over to the highway patrol in hopes that a more structured environment might do him some good.

"The Mongols used to ride the body on a horse till it fell off."

I sighed deeply, but Jules didn't seem to notice.

"The Plains Indians probably had it right with the burial scaffolding; if you aren't up to anything else, you might as well feed the buzzards."

I couldn't stand it anymore. "Jules?"

"Yep?"

I turned and looked down at him. "Do you ever shut up?"

He tipped his battered cowboy hat back on his head and took the final swig, still smiling. "Nope."

I nodded my final nod, turned, and tramped my way down the hill away from the aged cottonwood at the fence line, where I had already worn a path in the snow. Jules had been there on my three previous visits, and he knew my pattern.

I guess gravedigging got lonely.

You can tell the new graves by the pristine markers and the mounds of earth. From my numerous and one-sided conversations, I had learned that there were water lines running a patchwork under the graveyard with faucets that would be used in the spring to help soak the dirt and tamp the new ones flat but, for now, it was as if the ground had refused to accept Vonnie Hayes. It had been almost a month since her death, and I found myself up here once a week.

When somebody like Vonnie dies you expect the world to stop, and maybe for one brief second the world does take notice. Maybe it's not the world outside, but the world inside that's still.

It took about ten minutes to get back to the IGA in the center of Durant where I had left my erstwhile deputy to shanghai prospective jurors for the local judicial system. I rolled into the parking lot, scratched my beard as I parked, and looked at the plastic-wrapped bundles of wood priced at two for seven bucks that were stacked at the entrance of the grocery store. We had been forced to act as the Absaroka County press gang about eight times during my tenure as sheriff, which itself had taken up almost a quarter of a century. The jury wheels used by the county were chocked so full of outdated records that a large percentage of the summonses were returned undeliverable, and the ones that did get where they were supposed to go many times got ignored. My advice that we simply put occupant on the things was dismissed out of hand.

I looked at the handsome woman at the entrance of the grocery store with the clipboard in her hands. Victoria Moretti didn't like being called handsome, but that's how I thought of her. Her features were a little too pronounced to be dismissed as pretty. The jaw was just a little too strong, the tarnished gold eyes just a little too sharp. She was like one of those beautiful saltwater fish in one of those tanks you knew better than to stick your hand into; you didn't even tap on the glass.

"Of all the shitty things you make me do, I think I hate this the most. I have an undergraduate degree in law enforcement, I've forgotten how many hours toward a masters, graduated from the Philadelphia

Police Academy in the top five percent. I had four years street duty, two field commendations . . . I am your most senior officer." I felt a sharp jab at my midriff. "Are you fucking listening to me?"

I watched as my highly capable and awarded deputy accosted a middle-aged man in a barn coat, copied down information from his driver's license, and informed him that he needed to get over to the courthouse pronto or be faced with contempt of court. "Well, there's another notch on my Glock."

I watched as the hapless shopper balanced his purchases and wandered off to his car. "Hey, there are worse places for a stakeout, at least we've got plenty of supplies."

"It's supposed to snow another eight inches tonight."

I looked over at the neatly shoveled driveways. "Don't worry. You can go in and flush them out, and you can do some last minute shopping." I was tapping on the glass and getting my tarnished gold's worth. "How many more talis jurors do we need?"

"Two." She searched the automatic glass doors behind us. Dan Crawford stood at the far register, registering his annoyance at our official abuse of his customer base. She looked back at me. "Talis jurors?"

"The process started in this country with the Boston Massacre. They pulled spectators out of the courtroom gallery to serve as jurors during the trial of a British soldier. It's from the Latin, meaning bystander. You're Italian, you should understand these things."

"I'm from Philadelphia, where we vote early and often, and everybody on the jury has a vowel on the end of his name."

I looked off toward the mountains west of town and at the broiling darkness that seemed to be waiting behind the range. I couldn't help but think that it would be a nice evening to sit by the fire. Red Road Contracting had promised to have my triple-walled flume put in by last weekend, but so far all they had done was cut an opening in my roof the size of a large porthole. They said the firebox that mounted to the ceiling would cover the hole, but for now the only thing between the inside of my snug little log cabin and the impending great outdoors was ten millimeters of plastic and some duct tape. It wasn't really their fault. The coal-bed methane outfits were paying close to twenty dollars an hour, roughly twice what general contracting paid anywhere on the high plains, so Danny Pretty On Top had signed on with Powder River Energy Exploration and had left Charlie Small Horse to pick up the slack.

"How about I go in and flush 'em out?" she said. I looked down at her. "I just want to get back and shoot your dog if he's shit in my office again."

I had suspected an underlying motive. The beast did; it was true. I hadn't had him all that long, and he had decided that rather than go to the trouble of going all the way to the door and having Ruby let him out, he would just wander across the hall and unload in Vic's office. "He likes you."

"I like him, too. But I'm going to shoot him in the ass if he leaves another little package for me."

I sighed and thought about how nice it would be to go back to the warmth of my office. "Okay, go ahead." It was like turning loose the dogs of war; her eyes grew cold, the mouth curved lupine, and she turned and disappeared.

If it did snow tonight, the whole county would be thrown into a frozen panic, court would be canceled anyway, and my little department would likely be stretched to the limit. Jim Ferguson was only a part-time deputy and Turk was already gone to the highway patrol, so Vic pretty much made up the staff; but we had a potential candidate for Turk's job. He was a Mexican kid who had finished up at the Wyoming Law Enforcement Academy, had elected to begin his career in Kemmerer, and then had moved to the state's maximum-security prison. After two years there, it would appear that he had changed his mind and was looking for rosier pastures. He was supposed to drive up from Rawlins in the morning for an interview, but I wasn't holding out much hope. He would have to gun it over Muddy Gap at 6,250 feet through the Rattlesnake range and then up the basin to the foot of the

Big Horns and Durant. It was a five-hour trip on dry roads and, looking at the mountains, that didn't seem possible. It appeared as though we were going to get our third heavy snowstorm since fall: the first had tried to kill me on the mountain, and the other I had enjoyed from a stool at my friend Henry Standing Bear's bar, the Red Pony.

It was just after Thanksgiving, and we had consumed the better part of a bottle of single malt scotch. When I woke up the next morning, Henry had already pulled a couple of leatherette chairs in front of a double fifty-gallon drum stove. I slipped off the sleeping bag and swung my legs over the side of the pool table on which I had fallen asleep and tried to feel the muscles in my face. He had hauled his bag with him and sat hunched over the stove. I watched as steam blew out with my breath, and I scrambled to get the down-filled bag back around me. "Heat's off."

He turned his head, and the dark eyes looked through the silver strands in the black curtain of his hair. "Yes." I joined him at the stove in my socks. The floor was cold, and I regretted not slipping on my boots. "Do you want some coffee?"

"Yep."

"Then go and make some. I am the one who built the fire."

I found the filters and the tin of already ground coffee on the second shelf of the bar. I had lots of little bags of expensive beans that my daughter had sent me when she was a law student in Seattle. Cady was now a lawyer in Philadelphia, and I still hadn't gotten around to getting a grinder. Henry Standing Bear had a grinder. The Bear had a vegetable mandoline, and I didn't know anybody else who had one of those.

I started the coffee, hopped back over to the fire, and grabbed my boots along the way. The windows had begun to freeze on the inside. "How come the water hasn't frozen?"

"Heat tape."

I pulled my boots on and gathered the sleeping bag back around me. "You out of propane?"

"The heater never works when it is really cold."

"That's convenient."

"Yes, in the summer it works perfectly."

We sat there for a while, the homemade stove just beginning to warm the northeast corner of the little building or at least the sixteen inches between it and us. I yawned and watched as he yawned, too. He was studying me again. We hadn't talked in the last few days; there had been too much to say. We watched as the bottom barrel began to tic and grow red.

"Dena go to that pool tournament in Vegas?"

"Yes."

"Is that a good thing or a bad thing?"

"I have not yet decided."

It felt good there with that strange feeling of being in a public place without the public. I was going to have to call and check in, but it was still early on a Sunday, our slowest day of the week. I was avoiding it, mostly because I would get caught talking to Lucian. He had a few strange ideas about some goings on out at the Durant Home for Assisted Living and had become a kind of Absaroka County Agatha Christie. I told him that if anybody shortened the span of any of the occupants they wouldn't be robbing them of all that much, and he reminded me that he would be happy to take me by my mutilated, half-century old ear and march me around the block. Ever since I had hired the retired sheriff as a part-time dispatcher on weekends, he had been gathering his salt.

I looked out through the haloed light of a high-plains winter at the falling snow with flakes the size of poker chips. I had had inclinations that it was going to be a winter to remember, and so far I had been right. The day before Thanksgiving, Cady had been trapped at the Philadelphia airport; she had been trying to get back to Wyoming for a surprise visit. I hadn't been feeling well and, after getting through one of the toughest cases of my life, she could tell. Cady had called, filled with tears and frustrated fury at a two-fold snowstorm that had grounded planes on both the eastern seaboard and in Denver, the hub to our part of the world. They had assured her that even if she did make it there, she would be spending the holiday at DIA. We talked for an hour and forty-two minutes. She was laughing that heartfelt laugh of hers by the time we were done, the one that matched her deep rustic voice, and I felt better.

"Dena says she is moving to Las Vegas."

"Really?"

"Yes."

The coffee was done, so I pulled the sleeping bag up a little higher on my shoulders and towed it over to the bar with me; I must have looked like a giant praying mantis. I poured myself a cup and got the heavy cream the Bear kept in the bar refrigerator. I added the cream to his and dumped in what I considered a reasonable amount of sugar, dropped a spoon in, and carried it over to him; I figured the least he could do was stir the thing himself. I handed him the Sturgis mug and sat back down. "Things could be worse."

"And how is that?"

I took a sip of my coffee for dramatic effect. "You could have been dating a murderer." I watched as the big shoulders shifted, and he stared at me. It felt wrong, saying it like that. It was disrespectful of somebody I still cared a great deal about. "I guess everybody's a little nervous about talking to me, huh?"

His eyes were steady. "Yes."

"I'm okay." He didn't say anything. "I am."

"Yes."

I shook my head and looked at the stove. It was warming up a little in our corner of the world, so I shrugged the bag down off my shoulders. "Are you going to say anything in this conversation besides yes?" I quickly added. "Don't answer that."

The wind pushed against the wooden sides of the old Sinclair station that Henry Standing Bear had converted into the Red Pony bar. We were on the border of the Rez, and the wind was older here. I listened to the voices of the Old Cheyenne as they screamed from the northwest and disappeared toward the Black Hills. I had had some delusionary episodes during the first really big snowstorm of the season, at least that's what I had decided to label them, but I kind of missed the Old Cheyenne. They weren't all I missed. I let the bitter taste of the coffee hold there in my mouth for a second. It wasn't anybody's fault; I was running under radio silence. My friends had spared me the crippling depth charges of understanding and, worse yet, advice, but I was going to have to come up for air; Henry was a good place to start.

"I don't think I'm going to date anymore."

"Yes." He took a sip of his coffee and nodded along with me. "It is not like women are any fun to be around, that they are soft, that they smell good, or that they . . ."

"Shut up."

He nodded some more. "Yes."

We had a wide-ranging conversation about Vonnie; we talked about love, fate, and everybody's inability to truly leave the past behind. It had been an ugly little case with two young men and one beautiful woman dead and, after four years of self-pronounced isolation, I had gotten my head and heart handed to me.

All Henry had said was yes. I guess that's when the valves opened, all the used air expended into the atmosphere, and all the fresh poured in. He made me run in the snow later that afternoon, and I have to admit that it felt pretty good.

Vic got two more and added Dan Crawford to the list for good measure. She handed me the clipboard after she had climbed in and shut the truck door. "Here, His Majesty's dutiful servants for the day." She leaned forward, and I watched as her slender neck tilted to look through the top of the windshield at the stony clouds that were bricking away the sky.

"What're your plans for tonight?"

She looked at me, and I noticed the small, etched, smile lines at the corners of her mouth. "Why?"

"You wanna go over and visit Lucian with me?"

The little lines quickly disappeared. "I'm washing my hair."

"He always asks about you."

"He always asks about my tits."

I did have ulterior motives. With her along the previous Tuesday, Lucian had been so distracted that I had won every game. "Maybe you should look at it as a visit to Pappy Van Winkle?" The only thing I really had going for me in persuading her to come was her taste in expensive bourbon, which was in ready supply in Room 32 at the Durant Home for Assisted Living.

"I can buy my own bourbon and not have to be ogled by that fucking old pervert." She shifted her weight and fastened her seatbelt. "I've got to tell you, as nights on the town go? That one was pretty lame. I haven't had a time like that since my grandfather took me to a vacant lot on South Street to drink wine and play bocce ball with his cronies." She looked at me. "I was six and a shrewd judge of a good time."

The little lines reappeared as she laid an arm along the door and looked out across the hood of the Bullet. I glanced down at the hand resting on her leg and noticed that she wasn't wearing her wedding band anymore. She and Glen had come to a parting of the ways back in November; he had gone to Alaska, and Vic was still here, thank God. She had turned down respective offers to flaunt her honor, service, and integrity with the Philadelphia Police Department, where she had worked before, and the Department of Justice's Federal Bureau of Investigation. She was that good. Instead, she was the undersheriff of the least populated county in the least populated state in the union, with an option to have my job come November.

I blinked, refocused, and became aware that she was looking at me. "What?"

"I asked how you were doing these days."

"Good."

She waited. "You know I am available on a professional consulting basis for fucked-up relationships, right?"

"I've got your card."

～～

By the time we got to the office behind the courthouse, the smallest traces of snow had begun drifting down in a nonchalant manner. This one thought it could fool us by starting out slowly. There were times in Wyoming when you needed to know where to park your car so you could find it in the morning.

I followed Vic and paused to scan my doorway for Post-its as she stopped and gathered her mail from Ruby's desk. The dog raised his eyes, looked between the two of us, and then settled the five-gallon bucket-head back on his paws.

Vic nodded as she shuffled through her mail. "Yeah, I'd keep a low profile if I was you too, shit head."

I had inherited Ruby from Lucian. Fierce as a bobcat and as loyal as the Swiss, she kept a neon blue eye toward my moral development. She was sixty-five, going on thirty. I cut in quickly, before the real fighting started. "Post-its?"

Ruby continued to pet Dog. "Somebody dumped a bunch of garbage and an old refrigerator out at Healey Reservoir."

"Let me guess who found that." Our resident fisherman and part-time deputy, the Ferg, kept us up to date on all the fishing holes in the vicinity.

"He says they left some of their mail in the garbage bags, so he's gone over to the trailer park near the bypass to have a little chat with the suspected offenders. Oh, Rawlins called to confirm his interview tomorrow."

"The Mexican kid?"

She turned. "He doesn't sound Mexican."

"What does he sound like?"

"Just different." She went back to her screen. "Lucian called to make sure you were going to be there tonight. Are you being mean to him? He usually doesn't call to confirm chess night."

I picked up some of the general delivery stuff, flipped through the latest police garment catalog, and thought about replacing my duty coveralls. "He's been weird lately."

"How?"

I decided to keep my old pair and closed the catalog. "Just odd, like he's got something on his mind." I tossed it into the wire wastebasket and started toward my office. "Does that kid know that it's going to snow ass deep to a nine-foot Indian tonight?"

Her eyes drifted up to look at me over the computer screen. "Does your Native American friend know you use such descriptive terms?"

I paused at my doorway. "Where do you think I get 'em?"

"Where is the Bear these days?"

The women in my life always asked about Henry; it was irritating. "He's up on the Rez in the basement of some defunct Mennonite church." I leaned against the doorjamb and thought about what I would do if Ruby ever retired; I would have to retire, too. "They found a couple of old hatboxes full of photographs that the Mennonites must have taken a long time back."

"Mennonites on the Northern Cheyenne Reservation?"

I shrugged with one shoulder. "It didn't take."

"Sounds like a treasure trove."

"He's cataloguing and annotating something like six hundred photographs.

Her eyes returned to the screen, and the soft tap of the keyboard resumed. "That should keep him out of trouble for a while."

I missed Henry but figured he'd get back in touch when he got the chance. He was like a warm Chinook that blew in when you least expected it. I scratched my beard. "Anything else?"

Her eyes returned to the screen. "We're putting together a petition to get you to shave."

My desk was relatively clear for a Tuesday, and Santiago Saizarbitoria's file was on the top of the nearest pile. Santiago Saizarbitoria. What did she think, he was Norwegian? I didn't think the kid was going to make it, but I had ten minutes of the taxpayer's time to kill, so I flipped the manila file open and looked down at the cover sheet. I hadn't ever spoken to him. Ruby had gotten the application via priority mail with a letter of introduction and a résumé. All of the contact since then had been done by e-mail on Ruby's computer. I didn't have a computer; they wouldn't let me have one.

Vic would be responsible for half of the interview, which would probably resemble revenge for the Inquisition. If the kid was lucky tomorrow, he'd spend the day at the Flying J truck stop in Casper, go home to Rawlins, and continue his career in corrections.

He was married, and his wife's name was Maria. They had no children, and his starting salary had been $17,000, 18 percent less than the nationwide average. He was twenty-eight, five feet nine inches, weighed 183 pounds, and had dark hair and eyes. He obviously had a facility with languages; he spoke Spanish, Portuguese, French, and German. I would have to check on his Cheyenne and Crow.

I flipped to the back page and locked eyes with the two-by-two photo. Swashbuckling. I guess that was the first strong impression that I had of the young man Vic had already tagged as Sancho. He was a handsome kid with a Vandyke that gave him a rakish and mischievous musketeer quality. He was thick and looked strong, although his features were fine. I always concentrate on the eyes, and these were sharp with just a little bit of wayward electricity in them. I had the suspicion that not much got by Sancho and what did was viewed with quiet irony.

If we were serious about him, we'd have to call Archie, the chief of police in Kemmerer, and then the man who was his supervisor in Rawlins. He had lasted two years in the extreme risk unit in the high security ward at the state's penitentiary. That told me something. We are for the dark, indeed.

Whenever I read an application, I always found myself wondering what my answers to the questions would be. What impression would I have of myself, and would I hire me? I hadn't had to fill out a form when I had gone to work for Lucian: he hadn't had one.

We had been sitting at the bar in the lobby of the Euskadi Hotel on Main Street. It was late on a Friday night and Montana Slim sang

"Roundup in the Fall" through his nose on the jukebox, and we were the only ones there. Lucian preferred the Euskadi, because the bar didn't have any video pong games or customers, in that order. It was late October, and I had a new wife and thirty-seven dollars in a checking account.

"So, you were a cop over there in Vietnam?"

"Yes, sir."

I had caught him in midsip. "Don't call me sir. I ain't yer daddy, far as we know." I watched him hold the glass tumbler and look at me from the corner of a webbed apex of sundried wrinkles and the blackest pupils I'd ever seen. He was about the age I am now; I thought he was ancient. "Is it as big a mess over there as I think it is?"

I thought about it. "Yep, it is."

He sipped his bourbon and carefully avoided the wad of chew packed between his lower lip and gum. "Well, ours was probably just as bad. We just didn't have enough sense to know it." I nodded, since I didn't know what else to do. "Seems to me with this Vietnam thing, you get yourself into trouble fifteen thousand miles from home, you've got to have been lookin' for it." I nodded some more. "Drafted?"

"Lost my deferment."

"What the hell'd you do that for?"

"Graduated."

He placed the cut-glass tumbler back in the small ring of the paper cocktail napkin and nudged it toward Jerry Aranzadi, the bartender, whom I did not know at the time.

"Where from?"

I took a sip of my Rainier and hoped my bank account would last through the interview. "University of Southern California." He didn't say anything. "It's in Los Angeles."

He nodded silently as Jerry refilled his glass with at least four fingers. "Two things you gotta remember, Troop." He called me Troop for the next eight years. "A short pencil is better than a long memory, and you get to buy me my chew 'cause I'm a cripple." The last part of the statement referred to his missing leg, which had been blown off by some Basque bootleggers back in the fifties.

"What brand?"

I closed Santiago Saizarbitoria, placed him carefully on the surface of my desk, and made myself the promise to remember the rube kid with the funny haircut who had sat in the Euskadi Hotel bar and wondered what the hell he was going to do if the old man sitting next to him said no.

"I'm going home."

I looked up from the surface of my desk to my deputy. "What's it doing outside?"

"Snowing like a bastard." Despite the fact that she was leaving, she came in, sat down, and folded her jacket on her lap. She nodded toward the file. "Is that Sancho?"

"Yep. What do you think?"

She shrugged, "I think that if he's got a pulse and a pecker, we put him on patrol." She continued to look at me. "What are you going to do about dinner?"

"I don't know, maybe go down to the Bee." The Busy Bee was in a small concrete-block building that clung to the banks of Clear Creek through the tenacity of its owner and the strength of its biscuits and spiced gravy. Dorothy Caldwell had owned and operated the Bee since Christ had been a cowboy. I ate there frequently and, due to its proximity to the jail, so had our infrequent lodgers.

"I bet she's gone home."

"I'll take my chances. If worse comes to worse, I can always catch the pepper steak over at the Home for Assisted Living."

She made a face. "That sounds appealing."

"Better than a plastic-wrapped burrito from the Kum and Go."

"Boy, you know all the hot spots, don't you?"

"I have been known to show a girl a good time, yes."

After Vic and Ruby had gone, the beast ambled in and sat on my foot. I was second string, but it was still good to be on the team. She was probably right; with the impending storm, Dorothy had most likely headed home for the night. I weighed my options and settled on a chicken potpie from the jail's resources. Dog followed me as I rummaged through the minirefrigerator and pulled out the freeze de jour. We didn't have any occupants, so I took my steaming little tin into holding cell 1 and sat down on the bunk with a can of iced tea. Dog curled up at the door and looked at me. I had taught him that begging was all right if it was done from at least six feet away.

There were no windows so I could ignore the mounting snow outside, but the phone that began ringing, I could not. I sat my half-eaten chicken potpie tin on the bunk and answered the extension on the wall of our kitchenette. "Absaroka County Sheriff's Department."

"Is this the goddamned sheriff?"

I recognized the voice. "Maybe."

"Well, if you ain't him then somebody better go out and find the simple-minded son of a bitch and tell him to get his ass over here. I ain't got all night!" The phone went dead with a loud crack as the cradle on the other end absorbed the impact, and I stood there listening as my potpie was devoured.

I had talked Lucian into coming on as a part-time dispatcher on weekends, and I think he enjoyed it, but I would be the last one he would tell. He drove the rest of the staff crazy, but Dog liked him and so did I. I took the pie tin and threw it into the trash along with the plastic spork and my empty tea. I headed for the office to grab my coat; Dog followed.

Vic was right. By the time we got outside, it was snowing so hard that you couldn't see across the street to the courthouse. I squinted against the sting, tugged at my hat, and took in the vague halos of the arch lights that ran the distance of Main Street. There was only one car, and it was parked about halfway between the Busy Bee and the Sportshop. The dog halted beside the truck and turned his nose into the wind with me. I opened the door and watched as he climbed across and onto the passenger seat. He turned and looked at me, waiting for me to climb in, but I looked back at the parked car. He stretched across the seat and settled in for a short nap, knowing full well what I was going to do before I did.

I walked down the slight grade to the parked vehicle, careful not to slip, stooped down, and wiped the snow from the front plate of the maroon Oldsmobuick: state plates, county 2, Cheyenne. I looked around at the storefronts, but the only one that showed any signs of retail life was the Euskadi Hotel bar where the Rainier and Grain Belt beer signs softly glowed in the two tiny windows.

Except for the Christmas decorations, the bar at the Euskadi hadn't changed much since Lucian had hired me there all those years ago. The jukebox was still there, playing an unintentionally ironic version of Sinatra's "Let It Snow, Let It Snow, Let It Snow." There was an ornate burl wood bar and bar back along the right side, whose ancient mercury mirror was tarnished and faded in its attempt to hold on to the glory of the age and it reflected the blonde at the bar.

I pushed my hat back to its best Dashiell Hammett advantage and felt the slick of melted snow slide down between my shoulder blades and my sheepskin coat. As entrances, I'd made better.

"Hello, Sheriff." Jerry Aranzadi was still the full-time bartender. A small man with a stooped back and black-rimmed glasses, his narrow shoulders hunched as he scooped into the cooler and popped the cap on a Reindeer beer before I could stop him. It was at times like this that I wished my habits were a little more exotic. "What brings you out on a night like tonight?"

I sat a few stools down as Jerry placed a paper napkin on the bar along with the bottle of beer. He knew all my patterns, even the one about sparing the glassware. "It's chess night."

I took a sip of my beer. She didn't look at me but seemed absorbed in what looked to be an Irish coffee. He gently patted a hand in front of her cup to get her attention. "Miss Watson, this is our sheriff, Walter Longmire."

I always try to hold on to the first impression I get of a person; usually it's a feature, but with her it was the energy that was there, an animation that couldn't be concealed by age, fatigue, or alcohol. Afterward, I noticed that she was just plain beautiful, with large, frank blue eyes and well-defined lips. "Sheriff, this is Maggie Watson, and I bet you can't guess what she does for a living."

"Ms. Watson works for the state." I took a sip and looked back at both of them. I really enjoyed watching those big blue eyes widen as they looked at Jerry and then back to me. I guessed mid to late forties; outdoorsy, and always had been from the face, nicely weathered to perfection. She had an athletic build, probably a skier. "The plates on the car outside. 'Elementary, my dear . . .'" The eyes narrowed. "Bet you wish you had a nickel for every time somebody said that."

"You have no idea." She had a nice voice, too. It was soft, but also strong and with just a touch of a southern accent. "State Treasury Department." She smiled a sly smile and took an elegant sip of her coffee. "Unclaimed property project manager."

It was her turn to look self-satisfied. "We don't see many of those up in these parts." I nodded and looked over at Jerry. "Can't say we've seen any at all."

It got a laugh that was melodic but short. "I restore the contents of abandoned safe-deposit boxes to the owners or rightful heirs." She sat her mug down and gave me a sharp look. "At least I was, till I got stranded."

I thought about it for a moment, then felt duty call and sat the almost full beer back on the bar. "Gimme your keys, and I'll start it for you. I think we can get you a room, if we move quickly. Motels get to be at a premium when the weather gets like this." I tried to pay Jerry, but he just waved me off.

Back at my truck, Dog greeted me with a terrific yawn and confirmed my thoughts about his concern for my welfare while I was gone. I cleared the accumulated snow with the windshield wipers and turned on the cautions on the Bullet's light bar. A vague feeling of sadness always came over me in the presence of the lights: too many seatbelts that were unfastened, too many bald tires. I pulled in front of her car, snagged the long-handled scraper from under the seat, and pushed the majority of the snow off her vehicle onto the covered street. An hour from now, the car would have been a permanent addition to Main. She came running out and jumped in. She was taller than I thought, or else she just didn't sink into the snow like I did. "Follow me and drive in my tracks, okay?"

She nodded, and I closed the door.

She dutifully made the illegal U-turn and followed me back up the hill and around the courthouse as we slowly made our way toward the mountains. The red glow of the Log Cabin Motel's neon wasn't far and, if worse came to worse, she could walk to all the banks in town from there. I pulled up to the office and got out, ignoring the NO VACANCY sign.

I ushered her to the porch and rang the buzzer on the intercom, pulled her in a little closer to the building, and blocked the majority of the wind with my back. She smelled really good. There was no response to the buzzer, so I pressed my thumb against the button and held it there. After a moment, an angry voice screeched at us through the yellowed plastic intercom. "No vacancy, can't ya read?" There was no more talk but presently a gaunt individual in a threadbare plaid bathrobe appeared around the counter in the tiny lobby and unlocked the door. "Jesus, Walt, what are you doing out in this?"

I ushered Maggie in before me. "This lady needs a room."

I took the key from Willis's wife, Erma, and trudged off into the snow to turn the lights and heat on in one of the cabins at the end of the short lane. It would be a cozy little place but, as I told her, the temperature wouldn't get above forty for about twenty minutes.

"I don't know how to thank you."

"Well, if you come up with any Declarations of Independence in any of those boxes . . ."

"It's doubtful, but I could buy you lunch."

~~~

The trip over to the Durant Home for Assisted Living didn't take all that long, just a couple of blocks of backtracking. When I got there, there was an EMT van waiting at the main entrance, not a completely novel experience at the place but still a little unsettling. The doors were closed, but it was still running and the amber lights made racing, yellow ghost-wolves that darted across the brick surface. I pushed the doors of the building open, only to be audibly driven back by Fred Waring and the Pennsylvanians singing "Ring Those Christmas Bells" at an ear-piercing volume; most of the residents at the home were deaf as fence posts. Dog followed me in. As we went past the Christmas tree behind the abandoned front desk and rounded the hallway leading to Room 32, a slight sense of panic began to set in. The door was ajar as we approached, and I quickened my step, but the place was empty. The chess set was out on the folding table, and it looked as though Lucian had already consumed the better part of a tumbler full of bourbon. Dog looked around with me and followed as we quickly made our way out of the room, back down the hallway, and again toward the front desk.

The Pennsylvanians were still singing as we turned the corner. I caught a glance of the EMT van pulling away, but my attention was drawn to a white-clad attendant. He was being held against the far wall by what I knew to be the strongest grip in the county.

I took the direct route behind the counter, which turned out to be something of a mistake in that my legs got tangled with Dog and the hammer of my .45 snagged the lights on the fully decorated tree, lurching it from the wall in a short spark of holiday exuberance.

It took both hands and all the weight I could leverage to tug Lucian's hand free from the choking assistant whom I recognized as Joe Lesky. "Well, it's about goddamned time." He rolled off me against the far wall and pushed himself up with his arms; he glared at Joe who was massaging his throat and coughing as Dog, who had escaped unscathed, continued to bark.

"Shut up!" Dog stopped and went over and sat beside Lucian as if nothing had happened. I was not so forgiving. I pushed the tree off me. "What the hell is going on around here?"

It was mostly directed at Lucian but, after a coughing fit, Joe was the first to respond. "Mr. Connally was interfering with the transport of a departed client." He coughed some more and leaned against the opposite wall.

"I want the room behind me sealed up as a crime scene, and I want a full autopsy arranged immediately."

I stared at him as he looked at the battle-weary tree that lay between us. "Lucian, have you lost your mind?"

It was a bad time for Joe to talk, but he didn't know that. "Sheriff, I was explaining to Mr. Connally that we couldn't hold the body of the deceased without the permission of next of kin."

He wouldn't look up from the tree. "You got it."

I disconnected the electric light string from my holster and gave the tree one last kick for holly-jolly good measure. "Lucian, you can't."

The dark eyes came up slowly, and the world was swallowed. "Hold your peace." He looked old just then; small, old, and tired, as I had never seen him before. His eyes returned to the dead lights of the tree. "She was my wife."

2

Room 42 at the Durant Home for Assisted Living had been locked off, and the body of Mari Baroja was now waiting for the medical examiner from the division of criminal investigation.

In Room 32, two old widowers were sitting over a forgotten chessboard and were looking off into the distance in so much of a Dickensian fashion that it could have been an illustration by Phiz. The exposed punt in the twenty-year-old bottle of Pappy Van Winkle's Kentucky Straight Bourbon Whiskey sat in the middle of the contained golden sea: tempest in a teapot, lightning in a bottle, or the muse contained.

Dog was already asleep on the only sofa he was allowed to sleep on.

I kept expecting the thick glass to loosen itself from the bottom of the bottle and float to the surface. Maybe I expected it to sail up through the extended neck and dance about the room; it was, after all, the season for miracles. Maybe that was what I was waiting for, something to jog us loose like the punt in the bottle, something that would allow me to approach the black king sitting across the battlefield, a man up until tonight I thought I knew.

"You have to talk or move or I'm going to fall asleep."

He didn't move. "Fall asleep, then."

I had opened with the Queen's Indian Defense, Petrosian Variation, a move I had neither the skill nor the determination to prolong, but Lucian liked to ponder it when I tried.

I didn't consciously fall asleep; it's just that the chair was soft and comfortable, the room was dark and warm, and maybe it was the protection of those black eyes that reflected the blinking of the silly lights. Those eyes were not looking into the small darkness outside the double-paned windows; they were looking farther and to a place about which I did not know. There was nothing that would overtake us tonight that those eyes would not see, nothing that would not deal plainly with a king not in his perfect mind.

I must have slept longer than I thought. I didn't remember waking up, and maybe that's what he had intended by starting to tell me the story while I was asleep. I remember hearing his voice, low and steady, coming from some place far away, "After the war. Her family were Basquos from out on Swayback, Four Brothers." He paused to take another sip of his bourbon. "My gawd, you should have seen her. I remember lookin' over the top of Charlie Floyde's '39 Dodge when she came out on the porch. Her hair was black and thick like a horse's mane." He stopped with the memory; the only other sound in Lucian's apartment was the scorched-air heating. His two rooms weren't any different from any of the others in general design, but they had all the style and mass of the Connally ancestral furnishings. I shifted my weight in the overstuffed horsehair chair and waited.

"It was summertime, and she had on this little navy blue dress with all the little polka dots. The wind held it against her body." It took him awhile to get going again. "She was the wildest, most beautiful thing I'd ever seen in my entire life. Hair, teeth . . . We sparked that whole summer before her father tried to break it up in the fall. They wanted to send her away to family, keep us from each other, but it was too late."

I looked at him, and the night in my head seemed darker. "We used to tremble when we touched each other. She had the most beautiful skin I'd ever seen. I would forget from night to night. She wasn't like American girls; she was quiet. She'd speak if spoken to but only then. Short, soft replies . . . Basque. There was a part of her that I knew I couldn't get at, ever. It wasn't hostile or intentional, but it was there, like this life apart from us. Maybe she just knew." He stared at the chessboard. "The Basquos have an old proverb, 'a life without friends means death without company.' " He sighed. "We ran off together, got

as far as Miles City and snagged a justice of the peace off his hay field
to come in and marry us." He snorted a short laugh. "His wife played
the foot-pump organ, and he stood there in his rubber, shit-caked
boots readin' the words." He took another sip, and I listened to the ice
in his glass. "They caught us a little north of there. It was her father
and three Basquo uncles." He paused again, and I became aware that
my eyes were open and he was looking at me. "Hell of a rumpus." He
reached across and took my hand, rubbing it under his hat along an ancient ridge that ran from the crown of his head to behind his left ear.
He let go and resettled his hat. "One of the uncles finally went back
and got a tire iron."

That was two run-ins with Basques that I knew about, this one and
the other with some bootleggers where he'd lost his leg. "They sent
her away?"

He worked at something caught in his teeth, or maybe his jaw still
wasn't ready to call that one even. "Annulled us and married her off."
He placed an elbow on the arm of his tooled leather chair and cupped
his chin in his palm. "I'd see her father and them uncles every once in a
while in town, even after I was sheriff. They didn't say anything, and I
didn't say anything right back."

"When did you see her again?" It took awhile for him to reply, and I
had the feeling I was getting in further than he wanted. It didn't matter; when I had sealed Room 42 and had the EMTs stow her at Durant
Memorial, it had gotten official.

He was staring back into the dark reflection of the glass. "About a
year ago, a friend of mine said there was a woman over in the far wing
who asked about me, new woman. I went over, and it was her."

"Must've been quite a shock."

"Humph. She had a little house down in Powder Junction. I guess
that's where she'd been livin'."

I edged up in my chair a little. "Lucian, why is it I've got her room
sealed up and her waiting on a table over at the hospital?" His eyes
swiveled to mine and stayed there. "All I'm saying is that an absentee
husband of a three-hour marriage that was annulled more than fifty

years ago is going to be a hard press as next of kin." I rubbed my hand across my face, tried to straighten my beard, and continued to look at him. "Lucian, you have to give me something to go on before the children and grandchildren show up and start making my life miserable." I waited. "You've got to give me something more to work with here."

"You don't trust me?"

I let it sit there for a while. He wasn't being rational, and it might take a few moments for him to recognize it. I went through the file cards on Lucian's outburst and came up with fear of the unknown and frustration with society and the system, mixed with an ingredient I'd never seen in him before, love. Lucian in love; it was hard to summon up.

His eyes shifted back outside, and I could tell a little shame was lurking there. "You have the ME down at DCI do a general, then you come back here and we'll talk some more."

When I got back to the front desk, the tree had been placed back in its original spot; it was minus a few ornaments, and I noticed the lights weren't working. Nat King Cole was now singing in German, giving the place an international flavor it sorely needed.

I figured Joe Lesky was one of those people that fill the gap of human misery, doing their best to make everybody's lives a little better; about my age, with dark hair and dark eyes, he looked like he might have a touch of Indian, but all the time spent inside must have taken a lot of it out of him.

I leaned against the counter, and Dog sat on my foot. I glanced back over at the tree. "How's the patient?"

He leaned back in his chair and looked over his shoulder at the abused conifer. Some of the arms looked as if they were signaling aircraft. "I don't think there were any family heirlooms lost, but I still can't get the lights to work."

"You don't happen to have the file on Mrs. Baroja?" He slid the folder on the counter toward me. "I had it out for the EMTs."

"No arguments?"

"You're the sheriff."

"That's usually why people argue with me."

With the advent of modern CPR techniques, organ transplants, and life-support systems, home field advantage was shifted from the heart and lungs to the brain. In an unprecedented agreement between both lawyers and doctors, the terminal indicator of the grim reaper's touch is now the point when all cerebral function has ceased and is deemed irreversible. Brain dead.

For Mari Baroja, the bell tolled at exactly 10:43:12 P.M. Chris Wyatt and Cathi Kindt were the attending EMTs. Six attempts at resuscitation were made, standard for this kind of incident, and a code 99 was radioed to the hospital. Wyatt went for the electric defibrillator paddles, and the woman's body arched five more times like a head of rough stock on rodeo weekend. They canceled the code, and they canceled Mari Baroja.

"I'm sorry, Sheriff."

I looked past the file and down at Joe. "Hmm?"

"Did you know Mrs. Baroja?"

"No." I rubbed my dry eyes. "No, I didn't."

"She's gone on to a far better place."

I nodded. "Did you?"

"Did I . . . ?"

"Did you know Mrs. Baroja?"

He thought for a moment. "Not really. I think she was very quiet. Most of the clients are asleep during this shift."

I smiled a little smile, far better places withstanding. "You know Lucian, don't you?"

He rubbed his throat and shrugged. "Everybody knows Mr. Connally. He's a legend."

I looked back at the file. "I think Mrs. Baroja just might have been a legend, too." I closed the folder and handed it back to him. "Can you make some copies of this for me? It'll save me the official harassment later today."

"Sure."

"Who found her?"

"Jennifer Felson. Mrs. Baroja must've hit the nurse's button in her room."

"Anybody else visit her last night?"

He was starting off with the folder but stopped to point. "I'm not sure, but you can check the guest register."

I flipped the handcrafted quilted book to where I could read it, scanned the names, and looked for any more Barojas. There was only one: Lana Baroja had signed in at 7:10 and left about an hour later. There were also a couple of Loftons who had gone to Room 42 less than twenty minutes before Lana. I could go there and do a little poking around. I looked at Dog, and Dog wagged.

I laughed. "Let's go get the butler that did this."

It honestly didn't look like a murder case. It looked like a lonely room where a vibrant and beautiful woman had been warehoused to finish up her days. There is no allowance for murder, no curve in which we judge the value of human life on a chronological sliding scale no matter how I had teased Lucian. I owed Mari Baroja. I'd never met the woman, but she was from Absaroka County, and she was mine.

There was a crucifix above the bed, which was the only decoration on the walls. There were a few personal items, and a quilt, a Bible, and a few letters from some law firm in Miami. I figured I'd get to the letters later.

There were seven photographs, all in antique silver frames. Some of the pictures were so aged that their emulsion had adhered to the inside surface of the glass. The oldest looked to be one of what I was willing to bet were the four short brothers, all on short horses. They were thin and hard-looking men, and I'm sure the wind whistled when it cut around them; they appeared as if they were carved out of ironwood. I thought about that fight north of Miles City and was glad I wasn't there for that particular apocalypse.

The next was of a man, I believe the fourth horseman on the end, along with a woman whom I assumed was his wife. They looked dour and righteous, so I moved on. The next photo was that strange color that only seemed to exist in the fifties, like real color wasn't good enough. There were two small girls in summer dresses and barrettes, seated on a doorstep. They looked happy but like they had to be. They both had long dark hair, and the one on the right was looking off to the right.

The next was a young air force officer circa mid-sixties who looked vaguely familiar. He was a lieutenant and battle-awarded, with a green and yellow ribbon bar that told me it was Vietnam. There was a sad quality to the photo, and he didn't seem to fit with all the others; he was blonder, and the eyes just looked different. The next set of photos was lying on the floor amid a pile of prescription medicines and a hardbound copy of *Pride and Prejudice*. I opened a reader-worn Bible and found a handwritten note in Basque that read, *"A ver nire aitaren etxea defendituko dut, otsoen kontra."*

I kneeled by a partially wrapped dish of what looked and smelled like almond cookies. I was hungry and was tempted to tamper with the evidence but instead picked up the next framed photograph. It was a group shot of the Baroja family. The vantage point of the camera and the distance made it hard to pick out the individuals, but the brothers were there with their wives and a priest. I thought I could make out the two little girls having grown and acquired husbands, but the lieutenant wasn't there.

The last was the most recent and was of a woman in maybe her late twenties who looked embarrassed in a chef's jacket and hat. It was the only one that had official printing along the bottom, which read CULI-NARY INSTITUTE DU BASQUE, BAYONNE, FRANCE. She had short wisps of jet-black hair that were pulled back and behind the ears, revealing wide-set dark eyes steeped in facetious sarcasm. I liked her already, which was good, because when I turned she was standing by the door.

It was a simple statement. "She's dead."

I stood and looked at Dog, who was looking at her. Some guard dog. When I looked at her again, she was looking at the carpeted floor down and to the left. I took a step toward her, but her eyes didn't move. I went ahead with my educated guess. "Ms. Baroja, Lana Baroja?"

She hadn't changed much since the cooking school photo, thinner, maybe a little more tired looking. She had on a full-length quilted coat that was just shy of purple and a red stocking cap that matched neither the scarf at her neck nor the gloves on her hands. She wore high-top waterproof boots, and I was thinking it was a good thing she could cook, because the career in high fashion wasn't working out. I looked at her again and felt bad about the judgments I was levying on someone who had lost someone very dear. "I'm Sheriff Walt Longmire, and I'm very sorry. I've got Mrs. Baroja over at Memorial."

"You've got her?"

It was just a turn of phrase unless you were listening for it. "Yes."

"Can I see her?"

Here we go. "There are just a few formalities we need to take care of concerning the late Mrs. Baroja."

"Formalities?"

"I'm afraid that your grandmother's death was specifically unattended with a declaration of death registered by the emergency medical technician, but we're going to need a formal certificate from the attending physician indicating that the death was due to natural causes secondary to old age." I thought it sounded like I knew what I was talking about.

"Or?"

She had spotted the flaw. "Or, if circumstances are complicated, a coroner will be asked to rule on the cause of death."

"Complicated?"

"Mitigating circumstance that might lead us to believe that an autopsy may have to be performed." I watched her for a moment, but she didn't flinch. "Right now, we're talking hypothetical formalities, but I'm sure you would want to know why it is your grandmother died." She was silent. "Could you tell me who your grandmother's doctor was?"

"Bloomfield."

Isaac. "I'll get in touch with him." I had pulled my trump card and gotten some interesting responses. I took another step toward her. "Why don't you go home, and I'll give you a call later?"

"All right." She started to leave.

"Ms. Baroja?"

"Yes?"

"You could give me your phone number. It would save me having to look it up."

She came back and gave it to me, smiling a sad and covered smile. "I'm sorry."

I reached out and lightly touched her shoulder. "No, I'm sorry. This has been a clumsy conversation at a very inopportune time. I understand your grandmother was a wonderful woman."

"Really?" I had been waiting for the facetious sarcasm, and here it was in spades. "And where did you hear that?"

The early morning sun was still a thought as I crunched across the parking lot. Dog snapped at the falling flakes and crow-hopped in a wide sweep toward the truck. When I stopped to stare at him, he barked at me. I continued to stare, and he continued to bark, ready to play. His eyes were all wild from the exertion, and his tongue unrolled from the side of his mouth. I really had to give him a formal name some day.

After a little frozen difficulty, I jarred the door open and watched as Dog left snow-dappled tracks across my seat on the way to his usual spot. I had to get some seat covers. I climbed in and pulled the door shut, fired her up, and looked down at the manila folder in my lap, at the stuff of which legends were made. I flipped the defroster to high and watched as my breath spun across my chest and scattered as it hit the paperwork that Joe had given me. The blowers on the heater started leaching warmth from the engine, and the windshield slowly began to clear.

As I pulled onto route 16 and took a left, I could see Lana Baroja walking along the sidewalk like a mobile quilted teepee. I wondered mildly where she lived, then wondered where she worked this early in the morning. She had scribbled two numbers on the back of the folder at my side. I could have offered her a ride, but it seemed like she was anxious to be away from me. You get used to that kind of response from people when you're in this line of work.

It looked like the plows had already made a pass or two, which meant that the little apex of downtown Durant was clear. I pulled off behind the courthouse and parked in my spot. Dog followed me into the office. I tossed the file onto my desk so that I wouldn't be tempted to read it and continued into the holding area and cell 1. We only had two, but I tried not to use cell 2 or the jail downstairs because it wasn't my pattern and, if something happened, no one would know where to find me. Dog jumped up and stretched out on the other bunk, and very soon we were both asleep. I don't know if it was the quick once-over I had given Mari Baroja's room or Lucian's words, but it was dream filled and didn't leave me particularly rested.

There was a house, just a little saltbox out along one of the spurs and ridges of the Powder River. There were arroyos that cut back along the foothills that headed for the Big Horns, and there were owls in the stunted black oaks and cottonwoods. It looked like the place I'd been to about a month ago, a place I didn't want to go back to again. The house stood empty and deserted, desolate against a dark purpled sky. A screen door on rusted hinges slapped shut in the framework, and the windows were missing or broken; barren, empty eyes that stared out blindly. There was an old barn and a warped calving shed that leaned away from the wind. The missing slats looked like piano keys set on edge and, having grown tired of playing the same old song, had decided to quit.

It was a place of tangible dreams that could be touched like fingerprints and felt through the raised and weathered grain of the wood; whorls and swoops of passion and loss, of qualified success and absolute defeat. I was not alone in this place. There was a woman there with her face turned toward the mountains, the northwest breeze pulling at her dark hair like long fingers and pressing a threadbare, polka dot dress against her loins. She had strong calves planted a shoulder's width apart, and she wore no shoes. Her hands held a silk scarf around her shoulders that was fringed and of an old world print, like nothing I'd ever seen before.

After a moment, she raised the scarf above her head. She held it there for an instant and then released it. I watched as it raced across the buffalo grass, where it snagged on a gnarled stub of sage and then disappeared. When I turned back to her, she was looking at me. Her eyes were like the black glass of last night and, as she moved past me toward the little house, she did not pause. I could see the delicate quality of her features, the careful shape of her lips. *"A ver nire aitaren etxea defendituko, otsoen kontra."*

I tipped my hat up. Ruby was standing at the open cell door, Dog already having left his bunk to stand beside her. "Rough night at the Home for Assisted Living?"

I let the hat fall back over my eyes. "You wouldn't believe me if I told you." As she turned, I called after her. "I might need DCI on the horn; it's possible I'm going to need an ME for a general autopsy toot sweet."

She was back with the coffee, toot sweeter. "It really must have been a rough night."

I sat up, pushed my hat back on my head, and took my old Denver Broncos mug. "Thanks."

"Sooooo?" She was petting Dog's head, which rested on her knee, and was carefully sipping hers from her own Wall Drug mug, which proclaimed 5-cent coffee.

"Ever heard of any Barojas?"

I watched the binary computer in her eyes calculate an area the size of Vermont, divide it in a swift grid pattern, and locate the appropriate square. "Basque, down on Swayback, Four Brothers."

"That's them. Ever heard of Mari Baroja?"

She paused for a moment too long, and her eyes avoided me. "No."

I sipped my coffee and let it go. "Then you missed your chance."

"Does she have a granddaughter who just opened a bakery here in town?"

I yawned and covered my mouth with the cup. "We have a bakery in town?"

She continued to stroke Dog's broad head. "What do you mean by might need a coroner?"

"Lucian thinks there might be some funny business going on." I took a sip and looked at the snorting pony sticking out of the orange D. "Ruby, what do you know about Lucian?"

She thought for a moment. "I think he is a good man. I think he gets too caught up in the romance of things." She raised an eyebrow. "You want to know about the romances of older men, ask a younger woman." Her eyes stayed steady but then broke back to Dog. She crossed her legs and patted the bunk beside her. Dog was curled there in an instant. It took a while for her to gather her thoughts or decide to share them. "I was twenty-eight years old and between marriages when I came to work for Lucian." I watched as she smiled, and the years unwrapped. She was like that; age would not pause for Ruby, since she would not pause for it. "I was quite a hottie back then." I laughed, and she started to rise.

I reached out and took her hand. "I was laughing at the word choice. Where did you get the term hottie?"

The neon blue lie detector was scanning me for signs of falsehood. "Your daughter."

"I thought so." I held on to the thin hand and ran my thumb over the web between her thumb and forefinger. "I've got news for you, you're still a hottie." She actually blushed and pulled her hand away. "So, old Lucian cut quite a wide swath around these parts, huh?"

"Yes, he was very dashing for a man with one leg."

"Did you know he had been married?" Big blue. It was the second time today I'd used surprise to get a look at the woman I was talking to. "I'll take that for a no." Ruby was the poster child for unflappable, so it was fun to watch her take flight for a change. "He was married to Mari Baroja."

"When?"

"For about three hours back in the late forties. Or about as long as it took for her daddy and three uncles to catch them, take her, beat the hell out of Lucian, and annul the whole thing."

"Well, I'll be." I waited for her to make the connection, and it didn't take long. In the meantime, I listened to the soft ticking of the radiators outside the cell. Our jail had originally been one of the tiny Carnegie libraries. It had been erected behind the courthouse at the turn of the century, the last one. Red Angus, the sheriff before Lucian, had shrewdly appropriated the red granite building and had converted it. "She's the one that Lucian wants the autopsy done on?"

"Yep." We sat there looking at each other.

"Did you tell him you'd do it?"

I had been hoping that the conversation wasn't going to go in this direction; the last thing I needed was Ruby's help in backing myself into an ethically nonneutral corner. "Maybe."

"Are you absolutely sure there is no reason for an autopsy?"

I groaned and leaned back against the wall with a thump, a few dribbles of coffee sloshing up and running down the side of my mug. I wiped the bottom on my pants. "Of course not, but I am also not absolutely sure that there is a reason for one."

She took my coffee cup and started out of the cell. "Then you'll know after you have one."

"Is it still snowing?"

She looked down the hallway to the windows out front. "Yes."

"Then the whole thing is academic, because no one from DCI is going to make it up here in this snowstorm."

She wasn't looking at me, and she wasn't going to. It was one of her techniques for getting me to do what she considered to be the right thing. "You can get a medical examiner from Billings." She disappeared around the corner, and the dog followed her.

I thought about the old sheriff. I thought about how Ruby had just lied about Mari Baroja. I thought about what I didn't know, about how I knew the anecdotes but, perhaps, not the story.

When I got to my office, my steaming cup was full and resting at the center of my blotter, and the red light on line one was blinking from Cheyenne. I picked up the receiver and punched the angry little button. There was the commensurate pause after I explained the situation. "You're kidding."

"Nope."

"Things must be really slow up there in the hinterlands."

I leaned back in my chair and tossed my hat onto my desk. It landed beside the mug. "I guess I'm going to need a general autopsy."

"Do you want us to call Billings?"

I noticed Ruby standing in the doorway. "Well, it's a blizzard, and we're kind of short on personnel." I nodded, and she brought the note over.

"I'll see what I can do, but I bet they're going to want you to transport." I hung up. The note said we had an accident near the highway at the access road. It was a bad spot where the curve of the road and a stand of cottonwoods concealed the approach from the I-25 off-ramp. "I'm going to go out there and cut that stand of trees down myself."

I reached out, picked up my hat, and twisted it down on my head. I looked up at the old Seth Thomas clock that had served the last four sheriffs of Absaroka County, a sum of almost a hundred years. It was just mornings like this that it felt like all hundred were mine. It was 7:47 A.M., and I guessed the citizenry wasn't staying home after all.

Ruby was on the phone but cupped her hand over the receiver and looked up. "Another one at Fetterman and 16; I'll call Vic and tell her to go directly out there."

"Does it sound serious?"

"Fender bender." The phone rang again, and she frowned at it.

"Call the Ferg and tell him he's full time until further notice."

〰

It was like walking into a snow globe and, since I had parked the truck, it had gained another inch. Dawn was lingering, but there was a faint blush back toward the hills and, with the glow of the streetlights, the whole place was starting to look like Bedford Falls.

It didn't take long to get to county road 196, and it didn't take long to figure out what had happened. The best news was that all the participants in the vehicular altercation were alive, well, and arguing on the side of the road. I flipped on the light bar and pulled the Bullet over to the opposite side so that it would be visible from both directions. There was an older Chevy Blazer that I knew belonged to Ray Thompson, and a newer little Japanese SUV that had number 6 plates, Carbon County. There was one of those new-fangled racks on the top of the Nissan, and it had a bumper sticker that read, IF YOU DIE, WE SPLIT YOUR GEAR. Hello Santiago Saizarbitoria. He looked just like his photograph, only now he looked irritated. "Hey, Ray. This guy run into you?"

"Yer damn right."

Ray's wife was next, and I figured they must have been on the way to dropping her off at the school cafeteria where she worked. "Came out of nowhere, flew around that corner and ran right into us."

Saizarbitoria was about to explode when I put a gloved hand up to his face. "Just a minute." I took Ray by the shoulder and steered him away from the vehicles and over to my side of the road. I checked in both directions, but there hadn't been any traffic since the wreck. "Ray, I wanna show you something." I walked him behind my truck and over to the stop sign where the two roads converged. "Ray, these are your tracks, the ones that slide all the way through the intersection."

"That's not . . ."

"You can see from the tire marks that your vehicle didn't stop at the sign, and you can also see from the point of impact on both vehicles that you went through just as he passed. Maybe in all the excitement you just didn't notice." He didn't say anything else, just looked at the tracks and fumed. I waited for a while myself, as the blue and red light flickered over the smooth surface of the snow. "In a situation like this, it's going to come down to who has his vehicle under control, and you didn't. Now, I'm going to get my camera and take a few shots of these tracks so that if there are any questions later on, we've got answers. But my advice to you is to go over there, apologize to that young man, and get out your insurance card."

By the time I'd taken the pictures, they were all grouped around the hood of the Blazer. I copied down information from both drivers, only partially listening as Saizarbitoria told the older couple that he was here for a job interview, and they wished him well.

The Blazer would continue to the school even though I doubted that there would be any, but the little silver SUV wasn't going anywhere. Ray had hit right at the wheel well, and the left front was pretty much pushed into the engine compartment. I radioed in to Ruby after we got in the Bullet and arranged for his vehicle to be brought over to Sheridan where it could be repaired.

I also asked about Vic.

Static. "She's at Fetterman, and the Ferg's out on Western where one of the snowplows took out a mailbox and got stuck turning around. By the way, you got your coroner from Billings."

"King Cole is driving down here in a snowstorm?"

Static. "You've got to keep up with Yellowstone County politics; Fast Eddie was replaced last November. The new kid's name is Bill McDermott, and he's very earnest, so be nice to him."

"Yes, ma'am." I turned to the sad young man beside me, pulled off a glove with my teeth, and extended a paw. "Walt Longmire, welcome to Donner Pass. You got anything in that car you're going to need?"

"Everything."

I watched as he climbed out and crossed, looking both ways. Fool me once . . . He gave the impression of being a lot bigger than he was. As I watched him dig a satchel bag, a Meeteetse Cowboy Bar ball cap, and a cell phone out of the car and walk back over, I would have sworn he was six feet.

I continued filling out the accident report. "So, what's the plan?"

"Excuse me?"

"You and your wife. I'm assuming you have a plan for this interview?" I broke the scenario down. "If this goes well, what happens next?"

"Oh." He nodded and quickly jumped in. "If things look good, we were planning on coming back over the weekend and taking a look at houses." He looked past me at the crumpled metal of the Nissan.

"So you're in for the long haul?"

"Sir?"

"Looking for a house? A place to raise kids?"

"Yes, sir." He waited a respectful moment before asking. "You married, sir?"

I folded up my report book and stuffed it behind the four-wheel shifter. "I used to be. She died a number of years ago." I sat there and looked out the window until the image of myself as a romantic figure quickly became ludicrous and faded.

"I'm sorry."

I turned and looked at him to see if he was real and, at that instant, I came to two conclusions about Santiago Saizarbitoria: that he had been brought up right and that he had a heart. He was halfway to being hired. He was wearing a black fleece jacket, and one of the tumblers fell into place. I looked at him the way you size up a pot roast at the grocery. "You're a climber?"

He smiled and looked at his watch. "Damn."

"Why are you looking at your watch?"

He sighed. "Because my old chief bet me twenty bucks that you'd make me and every motivation I had in less than an hour."

Archie Pulaski was the chief in Kemmerer, and we had been known in years past to terrorize the Law Enforcement Academy and surrounding bars in Douglas. "You should know better than to bet with Poles in this part of the world." I fastened my seatbelt and watched as he automatically fastened his. "What else did Archibald have to say?"

"He said you were the best sheriff in Wyoming, and that if I was smart I'd keep my mouth shut and maybe learn something."

"Yep, well . . ." I put the truck in gear. "Archie drinks." I pulled out onto the county road. "I've got a deal for you." It wasn't a question, and he looked at me. "How about I put you on for seventy-two hours, then we sit down and decide whether it's working out or not?" I would have thought, with his background, that he wasn't a gambler, but he didn't hesitate and I started thinking that he was here for another reason.

"Yes, sir." He was quiet for a moment. "By the way, how much does the job pay, sir?"

"Eighteen percent more than the job you've got now, and don't call me sir. I ain't your daddy near as we both know." It was twenty-three years in the coming, but it still felt good.

3

I was enjoying the usual. *"Coronea custodium regis."* He looked at me blankly. "I bet you can figure it out." I negotiated the last chunk of biscuit back into the spicy gravy with my fork and lifted it into my mouth.

"Keeper of the king's pleas?"

I looked at Dorothy, and we both looked at him. "Who says the values of a classical education are lost?"

I watched as the woman who kept me alive by operating the only café within walking distance of the jail refilled my coffee cup. "You did, just last week."

"Richard the Lion-Hearted established these guys as a sort of tax collector. They were in charge of keeping track of convicted felons and their property, which was confiscated in the name of the king." I laid the fork back on the empty plate. He was about to finish the same amount of the usual that I had, and I was impressed.

There wasn't anybody else in the little café, so Dorothy's attention was exclusively on us. "And the difference between a medical examiner and a coroner?"

She was reaching for the coffee pot, but I shook my head. "A medical examiner is trained, a coroner is elected." The phone rang, and I watched as Dorothy reached to get it. "The last coroner up in Yellowstone County got into a little trouble back in the midseventies." I went on. "Eddie Cole used to get paid about a thousand bucks an inquest, and it was only when four bear attacks one weekend came up with a victim of the same height, weight, and coloring that King Cole got into a little hot water."

When I looked back, Dorothy was holding the phone out to me. "Very agitated deputy for you."

I handled the receiver like it was loaded. "Hello?"

"Are you enjoying your breakfast?"

I pulled the earpiece a little away from my temple. "I was until now."

"We just got a report here at the office of some very angry individuals over at the old folks home, and now we've got those same individuals over at the hospital. I have been informed that this is one of your little fucking deals, so I would advise you to get your ass over there as fast as it can waddle." The line went dead.

I looked at the two of them. "Gotta go."

When I dropped Saizarbitoria off at the office with his bag, his cell phone, and his ball cap, I had the feeling I was sending him off to school. I warned him that all the training at the state pen wasn't going to be of any use to him in there. He seemed undaunted. I told him to make friends with Dog because Harry Truman was right, but I don't think he got it.

I stood up straight as I approached the reception desk at the hospital, something I rarely did in everyday life, but height came in handy in times of conflict. I could count on three hands how many physical altercations I had been in since I had become sheriff, but no matter what anybody says, size helps.

I walked between the two people at the desk and loomed over Janine, whom I had a special fondness for whenever I remembered that she is Ruby's granddaughter. "Janine, you've got a situation here?"

She shrugged at the two on either side of me. "Yes."

He wasn't yelling when I turned to look at him; he was a good-looking fellow in a studied western way, fifties and trim, with an oversized cowboy mustache and dark hair, about average height. I was willing to bet that his haircut cost forty dollars and that, boots, hat, and leather coat notwithstanding, he wasn't a cowboy. "Do I know you?"

He was taken a little aback but was attempting to get a verbal footing. "Lyle Lofton, I'm an attorney in Sheridan County."

A lawyer, great; the tall thing didn't work with lawyers. "Jeez, Lyle, I thought I was going to have to throw some people in jail for public disturbance." I turned to the woman. She was in her fifties as well—lean, tall, dark, and a little strained. With her collection of neck scarves and turquoise, I was willing to bet that she wasn't a cowboy either, but you never know. "Is this your wife?"

"Kay, this is Sheriff . . ."

I was glad she didn't put out her hand; I didn't want to risk being bruised by the bracelets. "Where is my mother?"

I paused for a moment. "If you are speaking of Mrs. Baroja, she's being held in an attempt to ascertain a certificate of death from the attending physician, Dr. Bloomfield. And a possible coroner's report as to the cause of death." I made a mental note to call Bloomfield and cover my ass with as many doctors as it would take to hold off the lawyers.

"She was seventy-four years old." I looked at the red splotching at her neck.

She was ready to blow again, so I figured I'd get it all over with at once. "It's a standard procedure in deaths such as your mother's where there may be concerns of reasonable suspicion."

"Suspicion of what?"

I went ahead and dropped the bomb. "Foul play."

She put a fist on her hip and looked at me with about as much jangling accoutrement and audacity as we could both stand. "The woman smoked three packs of cigarettes a day." I waited, because I was sure there was more. "You know, we hear stories in Sheridan about how backward this place is, but until now I never really believed them."

I smiled as the feathers brushed the inside of my chest like they always do when I get irritated. "Well, I'm glad we've been able to live up to everybody's expectations." I was always ready to smile when I was winning and, lawyers or not, they couldn't stop me from doing what

I was doing today. Unless my coroner was pumping nickels into the slot machines at the casino on the Crow reservation, I would be done by tomorrow. Lawyers always held domain over tomorrow; it was their gig. I looked back to her as she stared at the rug. "I'm sorry, I know."

"You're damn well going to be."

We all watched as she marched out of the place. I turned back to Lyle, who pursed his lips and silently followed her out. I leaned my elbows against the counter and watched as they whizzed by the glass doors in $50,000 worth of non-Sporty, non-Utilitarian Vehicle. She was driving.

I tipped my hat back on my head. "How you doin', Janine?"

"Better, since you arrived."

"Any word on my coroner?"

"He got here about a half an hour ago."

I found the room with a plastic sign over it that read SURGERY 02. I was just about to push the door open when I remembered what it was I was walking in on. I had been present for too many general autopsies. With as many as two MEs from DCI and a district attorney to boot, I sometimes chose not to participate. Three weeks ago, I had sat in one of these very chairs and spared myself the inevitable outcome of Vonnie's. I had a dark feeling that forensic pathologists didn't look at the rest of us the way the rest of us did.

I had forgotten to ask Janine if he had arrived alone, but all I had to do was knock on the door and walk in. I knocked on the door and opened it about an inch or two. "Mr. McDermott?"

"Yes?"

It was a young voice, a little hesitant, and not what I was expecting. I stared at the door handle in my hand as the strong smell of formaldehyde and hospital antiseptic overpowered everything. "Walt Longmire, I'm the sheriff here."

There was a pause. "I'm almost finished with this part. I'll be out in about five minutes."

I closed the door and walked to the nurse's desk. There was a coffee pot steaming on the back counter, but nobody was there, so I picked up the phone, dialed nine, and the office. As it rang, I thought about my inability to go in and witness yet another autopsy. Maybe it was because it was Mari Baroja and I had already summoned up a romantic image of her, maybe it was memories of Vonnie, but you spared yourself what you could.

"Absaroka County Sheriff 's Department."

"I'd like to report my holiday spirit as missing."

She laughed. "I was just writing your Post-its."

"How's the new kid doing?"

"He's wonderful. How can we keep him?"

"Well, we've already disabled his vehicle."

"Lenny Rowell's uniforms were still in the supply closet. They're a little loose on him, but he doesn't seem to mind. He's out with Vic right now." Her voice got low, even though I knew there wasn't anybody else in the office. "I think she's on her best behavior. Well, as best as she can be. Walt, where are you?"

"I'm still here at the hospital, waiting on the results from Mari Baroja's autopsy and making a little list . . ." I became aware of someone standing behind me, so I pushed off the counter and turned to face Bill McDermott. He was a medium-sized young man with sloped shoulders and a haircut like a blond Beatle, from their Liverpool days. He was probably in his thirties, with a childlike face that carried an innocence that was only partly diminished by one of the bloody gloves still on his hand. Bill was evidently a part of the new order of coroners who were qualified medical examiners. I had a suspicion, however, that Mr. McDermott had not been elected. "I've got to go." I hung up the phone and looked at the altar boy. "Mr. McDermott, I presume?"

He nodded a bashful smile, looked at my gun belt, and then my star. "Hello, Sheriff?"

I moved around the desk. I was thinking that a little distance between us might help put him at ease. "Bill, why don't I buy you a cup of coffee?"

He didn't respond but watched as I poured us a couple of Styrofoam cups full. "Is there any cream?"

I offered him one of the powdered packets from the tray and was relieved that he peeled off the glove and dropped it into a waste can marked with a red biohazard sticker. He took the packet, tore it open, and dumped it into the cup. I took a sip of my coffee. "Yellowstone County has dropped the coroner system?"

"Yes."

"The king is dead, long live the king."

"Both puns intended?" He looked at my blank face and continued. "He's dead. I did the autopsy on Eddie Cole. It's how I got the job."

"How'd he die?"

He took a sip of his coffee. "Suicide. He had an old Cadillac in his garage. Just climbed in, started her up, and took a nap. He left a note."

"What'd it say?" I had to ask.

"'When you perform the intermastoid incision, make sure the front quadrant is large enough for the frontal craniotomy. Most beginners make a hash of the thing.'"

"Professional to the last." I nodded toward the operating room. "What've we got in there?"

He lowered his cup. "Caucasian, female, approximately mid- to late seventies, lifelong smoker, and the scars. I've just finished the thoracic-abdominal incision, exposed the pericardial sac, and took a blood sample."

"Excuse me, but did you say scars?"

"The ones on her back." He looked at me as if it were something I should have known. "A mass of scar tissue. It looks as though they were administered over a period of time."

I unconsciously stiffened. "Administered?"

Bill nodded again. "Someone routinely beat the woman at some point in her life." He looked at his coffee and swirled the tan liquid in the cup. "Probably with a belt, whip, or riding crop, something of that sort."

I was a little shaken with that revelation. "What else?"

"Slight discoloration of the tissues and blood, but the type is what's interesting. Was she Basque?"

I nodded. "We have a pretty large population from the turn of the last century; sheepherders mostly."

"I thought so. The blood type, O with an RH-negative factor. Extremely rare, but 27 percent of Basques have it."

"Cause of death?"

"I haven't really gotten that far, but I'm betting that it's a standard myocardial infarction or cerebral vascular situation."

"That simple?"

"The numbers don't lie. Out of five hundred thousand cases of sudden death each year, three hundred thousand are cardiac arrests following heart attacks. Considering her age, use of tobacco, genetic predisposition . . ." He thought for a moment. "Well, I'm far from being finished, and who knows what else we might find before the day is done? I like to do a thorough job." He finished his coffee and dropped the cup into the biohazard container with the gloves. I agreed with his diagnosis and tossed mine in, too.

When I got out to the truck, there was another inch of snow, but there were a few streaks of sunshine. I gave the sky my darkest warning look to try and help out the little patches of blue but was only rewarded with a big fat flake in the eye. I climbed in and radioed Ruby. "What number Fetterman is Isaac Bloomfield's office?" I waited as she looked up the number.

Static. "431."

"Thanks." Ruby hated using the radio, but I had told all of them I would only get a cell phone if they let me have a computer; so far, we were at a stalemate. The plows were out, and I watched the blinking yellow lights as I passed. The route up to the mountains looked clear, and I hoped that nobody would take it as an invitation.

The day hadn't been as bad as I had thought it would be, so far. I started thinking about Cady, the fact that she was going to be here this weekend, and that, so far, I hadn't gotten her anything for Christmas. She had been difficult to buy for as a child, and the situation hadn't gotten any better as she had blossomed into womanhood. I would have to enlist Ruby's help as a covert operator. Ruby enjoyed being a mole, but we were sadly lacking in haute couture. I wondered if I had any catalogs waiting for me at home. I wondered when I might get home. I wondered if the plastic was holding or if there was snow in the living room.

I thought about Mari Baroja as I navigated to the doctor's office. I thought about who would do that to the woman, who was responsible. The most obvious culprit would be the husband. I didn't even know his name or if he was alive or dead. Her personal physician was a good place to start, though. I had seen Doc Bloomfield at the hospital a couple of weeks ago when he had given me the final checkup after my adventures on the mountain, but I hadn't been at his office in a long time.

It was on the corner with a convenient parking lot you could approach from both sides. There was a 1971 silver Mercedes 300 SEL parked next to the steps that I knew belonged to the doctor, but there were no other vehicles, so he was probably free to speak to me.

It was warm in his waiting room, and I watched the clown fish in the saltwater tank as Isaac brewed us two cups of green tea. I had said no, but he insisted. There was music softly playing, Handel, Suite No. 1 in F, and I believed we were at the Andante. It was one of Dorothy's favorites. Visiting Doc Bloomfield was like visiting your grandfather about ten years after your grandmother had died or the cleaning lady had quit.

"How is the knee?"

I watched as his glasses revealed the multiple folds that did their best to hide the glint in his hazel eyes. I took my mug and glanced down at the pale, ghostly green numbers tattooed on the inside of his right arm where he had rolled up his sleeves. "Good."

"How is the shoulder?"

I took a sip, and it tasted like kelp. "Good."

He continued to examine me. "Hands look good; how is the ear?" I turned slightly and took off my hat so that he could see for himself. "Looks good." He continued to study me. "You've grown a beard?"

"Yes."

"I don't like it."

"Nobody does."

I broached the subject of Mari Baroja. He seemed genuinely moved by her death and stared at the faded print of the carpet. I studied the side of his face; his eyes were sharp with a little too much to contain. A thumb and forefinger came up, pushed the glasses onto his forehead and pressed into the sockets, rubbing emotion away. His features were strong, and it was like watching a roman emperor at the fall; I should be so lucky at that age. I waited a respectful amount of time. "Did you know her well, Isaac?" He didn't respond, so I asked again.

He didn't move, the fingers still in his eyes. "She was not a happy woman. I think she had many disappointments in her life." He took the hand away, readjusted his glasses, and turned to look at me through the imperfect world of the lenses.

"Can you give me some idea as to the cause of death?"

I waited as his eyes went back to the floor, then to me. "Walter, do you mind if I ask you a question?"

"No."

"Why are you so interested in this woman's death?"

That set me back. "Why shouldn't I be?"

He actually reached out and patted my knee. "Even with the beard, you are a very young man."

I was flattered, I think, but still didn't know what to make of his response. "What's that supposed to mean?"

"She was an old woman who was tired of living."

"Are you telling me that this was a suicide?"

His eyes sparked hard for a moment. "No, that is not what I am telling you." He withdrew his hand; the skin was transparent, and I watched as the blue and red protruded in the fists at his lap. "I think she was tired and gave up."

"You knew her pretty well?"

"She was my patient for more than half a century."

I took a sip of the tea out of habit and immediately regretted it. "What can you tell me about the scars?" He looked at me blankly. "The ones on her back?"

He raised his head and nodded. "She was involved in an automobile accident a number of years ago."

"An automobile accident?"

"Yes."

"The scars couldn't have been the result of some form of abuse?"

He turned and looked at me again, the picture of questioning disbelief. "What would lead you to think that?"

"The Yellowstone County Medical Examiner."

His eyes widened. "You sent her to Billings?"

"No, he's here. His name is Bill McDermott, and he's over at Memorial."

"Walter, it was Mrs. Baroja's expressed desire that there be nothing done to her remains other than what was legally required."

"Well, it's gotten a little complicated."

"Who did you say was doing the autopsy?"

I sat the tea down on the magazines stacked at the table behind me. "New fellow by the name of Bill McDermott. He's a licensed ME." I waited for a moment. "So, you and Mrs. Baroja discussed the possibility of her death?"

He seemed less excitable now. "I discuss the possibility with all my patients. I try to be truthful with them, no matter what the circumstance."

I leaned in. "Isaac, it sounds like you had a lot more responsibilities than that of family practitioner. Is there something you want to say to me?"

I waited as he took a deep breath and noticed, not for the first time, how small the man was. "I lied to you just now."

"Yep, I know." He looked at me again. "It's something I'm pretty good at spotting."

"You realize, of course, that due to the physician/patient privilege I don't have to tell you anything."

"Yes." We listened as the little pumps bubbled fresh oxygen into the fish tank; Handel joined the minuet. "You want to tell me about the scars first?"

He sighed. "Charlie Nurburn, her husband."

I nodded and then stopped. "I don't know him."

"He was from the southern part of the county, near Four Brothers."

"Middle fork of the Powder; not much out there."

"Used to be a few little homesteads and an old coal mine." I looked at the thick yellow nails as his fingers tightened at his kneecaps. "I used to run a clinic down in Powder once a week, Saturday mornings, back in the late forties, early fifties."

I leaned back in the overstuffed chair and unbuttoned my sheepskin coat. "She was one of your patients then?"

"Yes. I delivered her two children and . . ."

"Three children?"

He paused for a moment. "Yes, I always forget about David, but I didn't deliver him. I wasn't practicing yet." I waited. "She didn't come in about the beatings."

"What then?"

"Latent syphilis."

I rubbed my hands across my face. "This guy sounds like a real charmer. How long were they married?"

"Long enough."

"Jesus." I looked at Isaac again. "Where is he?"

"Gone."

It seemed like there was more. "Dead?"

"I'm not sure. Just gone."

"When?"

"Years ago." He waited for a moment, and his eyes stayed steady with mine. "It's probably better that way, don't you think?" I didn't say anything. "You can understand my being circumspect concerning her situation."

"Yes." I wondered about all the individuals wandering around out there who were in serious need of the administration of a dreadful ass-kicking and weren't likely to get it. "Why the response to the autopsy?"

"I thought she'd been through enough, and it was her expressed wish that her body not be disturbed any more than it already had. She was very religious." It was a sad smile this time. "What does Mr. McDermott have to say about cause of death?"

I waited a moment and looked at Isaac, allowing myself the blurred vision of the living hell that he had endured. Lucian said that he had been one of three survivors of Nordhausen, a subcamp of Dora-Mittelbau for inmates too sick or weak to work in the tunnels of Dora. Nordhausen was a *Vernichtungslager* or extermination camp where starvation was the simple but effective measure. To make matters worse, on April 3, 1945, it was bombed by our air force. Since it was in-stalled in concrete hangers, we thought it was a German munitions de-pot. A great number of the prisoners were burned alive; a week and a half later, when the 104th Infantry Division liberated Nordhausen, they found three thousand rotting corpses and three survivors. One of them was Isaac Bloomfield, and he weighed fifty-seven pounds.

I always thought that there was a reason why the old man was able to keep going; maybe it was because, as long as he was alive, he was a re-minder. "Cardiac arrest. Any history of heart problems in the family?"

He chuckled to himself with a wistful quality. "Oh, Walter, there are nothing but problems of the heart in families such as this." He continued to smile. "I suppose cardiac complications due to prolonged exposure to syphilitic infection; that, and I believe that Mrs. Baroja took solace in a number of lifelong vices that did nothing to prolong her existence."

"So there isn't anything suspicious about her death that you can think of?"

"I don't think so." He studied me a little longer than I was comfort-able with. "Is this disappointing to you?"

I wondered how much he knew about Mari Baroja and Lucian and suspected that it was more than he was willing to admit. "No, that's the one odd thing about this job. You're always willing to turn work away." I looked down at my uniform, the badge, and the .45 at my hip. It didn't take much imagination to see the distance that they put between myself and most people, let alone Isaac. Nice people with uniforms, badges, and guns had once told him they were doing things for his own good, his own safety, and his own welfare. Next thing he knew he was being carried out of a reinforced hanger with three thousand dead people. If I were Isaac, I wouldn't let me in the same room as me. "What do you know about the children?"

"Everything. Carol, Kay, and David."

"I'm assuming David is dead?" I thought back to the sad-eyed lieutenant in the photograph in her room. "Vietnam?"

"Yes." His eyes softened a little. "That was your war, wasn't it, Walter?"

"Don't blame me, I didn't start it." I allowed my mind to play over the photograph again. "I'm trying to think if I knew him."

"He was quiet." He said it like I wasn't. "Mari had a cousin, a priest, I believe."

"Here in town?"

"He was not a priest here, but I think he retired here . . . If he's still alive."

The priest in the family photograph; this would take a little following up. I thought of the picture of the little dark-haired girls on the stoop. "Both of the twins are lawyers?"

"Yes."

I changed the subject to the only other Baroja I knew who wasn't a lawyer in an attempt to pick up my spirits. "I understand that one of the grandchildren has a bakery here in town?"

"Yes. Lana was David's daughter. She is the only grandchild. The twins both have had miscarriages, probably as a result of the hereditary syphilitic condition." It took a while, but his face brightened. "The bakery is a wonderful place. Have you been there?"

"No, but I'm going there next." I patted my stomach. "I'll take a baker over a lawyer any day of the week."

"You must try the ruggelach, it is the best I have ever tasted."

As we were leaving, I asked him if he would go by and formally identify Mari Baroja to save the family the grief. He said that he would, and I asked him if he wanted to turn the music off. All he did was lock the door behind us and ask, "Why?"

I watched as the silver Mercedes without snow tires made its way up Fetterman taking a right on Aspen and thought about a man who had escaped the concentration camps and now drove a German car. The Hun be damned.

I thought the snow had stopped, but it had just satisfied itself with a finer version of delivery. If I squinted my eyes and looked away from the breeze, I could still see the clandestine little flakes ganging up on me. "Okay, so where is this damned bakery?"

Static. "You're supposed to say, 'Base, this is Unit One, where is this damned bakery?' Over."

It had taken forever to get her to use proper radio procedure, and now I wasn't sure I was happy with the results. "It's still snowing, and I haven't bought my soon-to-arrive daughter anything for Christmas. Have you listened to the weather?"

Static. "More snow. Over."

"Wonderful. Any ideas about Cady?"

Static. "I'll work on it, and the bakery is next to the small motor repair place next to the creek. Over."

"Unit One to Base, thank you. Over."

Static. "That's much better."

The bakery was on the back street, as Ruby had described, next to Evans's Chainsaw Service, something I was going to need if I ever got my wood-burning stove into operation. The building had been a gift store that had been boarded up for a couple of years. She had pulled off all the old plywood and replaced it with new wood that sported a jaunty red with gold trim. A handpainted sign hung over the entrance between the two bay windows extolling, in a florid script, BAROJA'S BAKED GOODS, as simple as that. Baskets of baguettes and fresh loaves spilled out of carefully arranged displays along with bottles of wine and full pound wedges of exotic cheese. I stood there on the sidewalk and looked up the street to the *Durant Courant*'s sign just to convince myself that I was still in the county seat. How could I have missed something like this?

I climbed up the steps and pushed the beveled glass door open to the soft tinkling of the attached bell and was immediately assaulted by the smell of vanilla. I pulled my pocket watch out and consulted it as to lunchtime; we concurred that it was early but acceptable.

I looked around, but there wasn't anyone to be found. I had seen places like this in Denver, Santa Fe, and Salt Lake City, old buildings that had been partially restored but left with a rustic appeal. The red brick walls were exposed on the inside, and the pressed tin ceiling glowed a fiery copper. The floors had been sanded to the original planks, and their distressed quality was preserved in industrial grade polyurethane. There were shelves along the left side of the narrow building that were loaded with all sorts of gourmet goods in assorted bottles and boxes. The counter level had small wicker baskets filled with recognizable Basque baked goods that ran the gamut from black olive bread to Norman loaves. There was a large white porcelain display cooler that held all kinds of cheeses and complicated charcuterie. There were French posters on the walls, lithographs of what I assumed were advertisements for nineteenth-century liqueurs, and an old wooden display case that held a surprising number of antique corkscrews and wine accoutrements.

In the back were two country French tables surrounded by time-worn mismatched chairs, and an upright cooler that held rows of wines and beers that I had never seen before. My attention was drawn to a collection of dark gallon jugs at the bottom. I kneeled down and inspected one of the labels; it read, UNPASTEURIZED BEER FROM THE SPARKLING GEM OF THE HIGH PLAINS, WHEATLAND MERCANTILE, WHEATLAND, WYOMING.

There was a jackalope wearing a tuxedo and a monocle on the label. "You have got to be kidding."

I listened as footsteps approached from the stairwell that I assumed led to the basement. I stood and turned toward the doorway as Lana Baroja appeared, covered in a fine patina of sweat and flour. She still wore her snow boots, but the purple quilted long coat had been replaced with an apron full of doughy handprints, and her hair was now in a French twist. I was getting the feeling that Lana, with her flushed face and darting eyes, was a character in search of a French author. The eyes lost their spark when she recognized me. "I find it very hard to believe that you have a microbrew from Wheatland."

She placed a fist on her hip and cocked her head. "You'd be surprised at what all I've got in here." She walked past me and behind the counter. "I'm the best kept secret in Durant, not that it's doing my bank account any good." She straightened her arms and leaned against the counter. "I assume you're here because you have some news for me?"

I looked at the cases and tried to spy the item that Isaac had recommended. "Arugula?"

"Excuse me?"

My courage was fleeting. "Something like arugula?" She continued to stare at me as if I were an idiot. "Dr. Bloomfield's favorite?"

She looked at me through a finely arched black eyebrow and very long lashes. "Ruggelach, a traditional Hanukkah pastry, crescent-shaped, filled, and made with a cream-cheese dough?"

"That would be it."

"As opposed to arugula or rocket, an aromatic salad green with a peppery mustard flavor?"

"I'll take both."

"I only have the pastry."

"I'll take that then."

She smiled and wagged her head; she was enjoying herself. Most people did when it was at the sheriff's expense. "You're sure?"

"Anything but." As she slid back the door of the glass case and extracted a plate of the delicate pastries, I reassessed my thinking about Lana Baroja. There was something old world about her, a practical quality that superceded the popular beauty of the day and drew its warmth from the earth rather than the air. She turned back around from the opposite counter and placed a small waxed bag in front of me. I looked at it. "It's a gift."

"For what?"

"Caring about my grandmother."

I nodded. "Thank you." I studied the little sack and thought about Mari Baroja. "Did she bake?"

"Yes." She looked at the little white bag, and it was obvious to both of us that it was symbolic of something important and tactile that was being passed between us: it was a contract. "Whenever we visited from Colorado Springs she would bake things with me." The dark eyes came up. "I guess that's how I got started."

"Your father was at the Academy?"

She brought her palms up from the counter. "Air force."

"He died in Vietnam?"

"Yes. I didn't get much of a chance to know him. Did you?"

I thought of the sad-eyed young man. "No, but I know a guy a lot like him. How about your mother?"

She stared at me for a second. "She's still in Colorado Springs; her, a mean little shih tzu, and Jesus."

I nodded. "I see."

"What did Dr. Bloomfield say?"

I leaned a hip of my own against the counter. "He said that your grandmother had heart complications due to a chronic condition, and the medical examiner from Billings seems to concur with the prognosis so far."

"So far?"

I started for the door; things had gone so well I didn't want to spoil them. "We should have a death certificate by the end of the day."

"It really isn't fair, you know?" I stopped with my hand resting on the brass handle. She still leaned against the counter with her arms folded, staring at the worn surface. "Just when you get to the point where you can enjoy them, they're gone."

I thought about it. "It's that way sometimes with children, too."

She continued to stare at the wood and extended a finger to trace the grain. "I wouldn't know."

I paused for a moment more. "On the subject of family, what can you tell me about your grandfather?"

The finger stopped. "He was a prick, and he's dead."

I was relieved but tried to hide it. "He's dead? Do you know how he died?"

The dark eyes looked straight at me and blinked only once. "Surely you know. Lucian Connally killed him."

4

I told the ladies at vehicle registration to punch up Charlie Nurburn on the DMV computer and show me what they had or I was going to set fire to the place.

It didn't take long for them to tell me zip, so I asked them how far back the data went. They asked me how far back I wanted to go. The ladies at vehicle registration were like that. After all the years of abuse at the hands of the local citizenry, they had developed the finely honed tact and manners of Russian wolfhounds. I asked for the forties, and they came forth grudgingly with nothing. I asked for the fifties, and they eventually showed me that Charlie had registered a 1950 Kaiser but had failed to pay taxes or registration a year later. He had also failed to have his driver's license renewed. There were no further records to date. I asked them what a Kaiser looked like. They said it looked a lot like a Frazer. I asked them what a Frazer looked like. They said it looked like a Hudson. Before I left, I reminded them about the fire. They asked me when the fire was going to start so they could be sure to call the county commissioners and get them in the courthouse for a meeting. I told them I was going across the hall to the county clerk's office. They said that was a good place to start a fire, that there was enough blue hair over there to burn down the whole damn county.

I walked across the hall and once again put forth the human query of Charlie Nurburn. Wyoming has no income tax, so I asked for anything the ladies there might have concerning Charlie's birth, life, marriage, children, or death, not necessarily in that order. They were nicer than the ladies over in vehicle registration and came back with more. There were three birth certificates for his children, David in '47 and the twins in '48, a death certificate for the sad-eyed young lieutenant, circa 1972, and a marriage certificate dated 1946. Nothing else. No death certificate for Charlie Nurburn, so I copied down his social security number and warned them about the impending fire. They didn't seem to care either way.

I walked down the hall past the stairs that led to the courtroom above but got corralled by Vern Selby. He wanted to talk about the outstanding warrants we had on people who had neglected to show up for jury duty, which told me that we might not have reached our quorum for the afternoon. He leaned an elbow on the newel post like Clifton Webb in repose and twisted the end of his mustache; it was officially winter because the judge had grown his matinee-idol lip warmer. He didn't seem pleased. "We only had seven jurors today."

"Maybe you need to get more entertainment values involved, you know, bang the gavel more?"

He studied me a while longer. "I knew you were the wrong person to talk to about such things."

I shrugged and headed for the assessor's office but stopped after a step. "Vern, do you remember a Charlie Nurburn from the southern part of the county, married to Mari Baroja?" I was saving the lawyers as a final connection.

"Related to Kay Baroja-Lofton over in Sheridan and Carol Baroja-Calloway in Miami?"

I should have known. I noticed he didn't mention Lana; her not being a lawyer probably dropped her down to the level of the rest of us mere mortals. "He was the father, of those two and another one."

"David Nurburn?"

"Yes." So Lana's father had kept his father's name, but she hadn't. Interesting.

"I believe he was about the same age as my William, and you, come to think of it." The judge contemplated the acoustical tiles in the ceiling for a moment. I wondered how he could play with his mustache that much and still leave it intact. "I don't seem to recall the father."

"He wasn't on the scene for long."

"Ah," he smiled. "But I remember her." I was a little taken aback by
the smile. "She used to come to town on Thursday afternoons, park
her car in the exact same spot. I used to watch her from the windows
of my office as she walked up Main Street."

The image of his honor hanging out the second-story window of
the courthouse and watching Mari Baroja sashay down the sidewalk
was almost too much. "Jeez, Vern. You're a pervert."

He looked at me and shook his head. "She was a beautiful woman
and very hard not to look at." He took his elbow from the post and
patted it in thanks for supporting him. Even inanimate objects were
good for votes in Vern's book. "In any case, I'm not the one you should
be talking to. Lucian used to have lunch with her every Thursday, like
clockwork." He stepped down to my level, turned the corner, and
carefully put on his coat and muffler. "At least I assume it was
lunch . . ."

I stood there for a moment, getting my bearings, until I became
aware that the judge had stopped, turned, and was looking at me.
"How is she?"

"Dead."

He continued adjusting his coat. "I suspected as much; too bad, really." He misunderstood my staring at him. "One hates to see that
much beauty go out of the world these days." The next thing I knew,
he was standing next to me with his gloved hand on my arm. "Walter,
are you all right?" I mumbled something, and he nodded. "Let's see
about getting some more jurors, shall we?"

After the stun had worked its way off, I went into the assessor's office and asked Lois Kolinsky if she had anything on Charlie Nurburn.
She looked up with her little Mrs. Santa Claus glasses and asked me
who was asking, and I remembered to tell her about the fire. She snick-
ered and looked for the ledgers as I stood there thinking.

Lucian had lied. Lucian had lied when he said that he hadn't seen
her for all those years. I looked up at the large map of the county that
was illuminated by the flat, winter sun and wondered where in the hell
I was. The place on the wall wasn't where I happened to be as of late;

I was in a strange new place, a place where the people I had safely put on shelves were wandering around getting into messy things.

Lois came back into the room, placed a large ledger on the cast-off library table, and opened it to the exact page held by her index finger. I pulled out a chair. It amused me that the two places that had computers couldn't seem to slap their asses with both hands, but the nice little old lady in the assessor's office could conjure Charlie Nurburn in a matter of moments. Always follow the money; rendering unto Caesar what is his may not be pleasurable, but the records are great. I was having second thoughts about the computer; maybe I didn't need one after all. I could use the extra money for a lie detector.

We have ledgers like these back at the office, three of them to be precise. They are beautiful, handbound leather with golden edging and marbled inner leaves with information that stretched back to the mid-1800s. Now we have floppy discs. The ledger was alphabetically organized, so it didn't take long to find Charlie on the open page; he was the only Nurburn in the county. He had bought a small property in 1946, about 260 acres adjacent to the 50,000-acre Four Brothers Ranch; the brothers had sold it to him. Both Mari and Charlie were on the deed. He had paid the taxes on the property until 1950, whereupon he must have piled his syphilitic, wife-beating ass into his Kaiser, whatever it looked like, and driven off into the sunset. Or not.

Mari had paid the taxes on the property beginning in 1951. The Four Brothers had been split between her and her cousin, the priest, according to the Will of her father, the last of the four brothers to die. I asked for the B book. She said that it had been a popular letter lately. I asked her why, and she said that Kay Baroja-Lofton had been in yesterday to check things out on her mother's behalf and that Carol Baroja-Calloway had requested information to be faxed to Calloway, Moore, and Gardner in Miami; the letters in Mari's room were from that firm. It just kept getting better and better.

Where was Charlie Nurburn? I looked at the nine-numeral scrawl that I had made on the scrap pad. It was time to use my own resources. I left the courthouse, completely forgetting to set fire to it.

I keyed the mic. "Charlie Nurburn." I read her the number from the piece of paper.

Static. "Who is this character?"

"Somebody I'm not so sure I want to find."

It was only forty-five miles south to Swayback Road, then another three miles east toward the Wallows where the Four Brothers Ranch was located, or where I thought it was located. As I drove down the interstate, the tailgate of my truck buffeted by the gusts from the northwest, I started feeling like I was being pushed.

I had stood there in the doorway of Lana's shop. It was one of those moments when you weren't quite sure if what you heard was what you thought you had heard. In the second that it took me to make up my mind, she laughed. It was a wonderfully musical laugh, one that you couldn't help but join. After I did, questions didn't seem appropriate. I told her that if she wanted to see her grandmother, she could probably do it this evening; but, on the lonely stretch of highway between Durant and Powder Junction, with the Big Horn Mountains guarding my right and the Powder River flats racing east, my mind began to wander back to a man who had had the one woman in his life taken away. It's one thing if she'd been gone but, as near as I could tell, she had only been forty-five miles distant.

There's no way I'd have been able to stay away. I flattered myself by thinking that, if faced with such a circumstance, I would respond within the letter of the law; but passion is a strange thing, a thing that warps and twists everything with which it comes in contact. It was like the combination of moisture and sunshine on wood; sometimes it turned out all right, most of the times it didn't, but you couldn't ignore its strength. I had always dealt with passion with an evenhanded balance of attraction and mistrust, but I was talking about Lucian Connally, and he was a mechanism that operated on the caprice of passion as if it were jet fuel. Thursday midmornings would never be the same for me again. Where was Charlie Nurburn, and what was he feeling lately, if anything? Maybe I needed to see what Mari Baroja was about, but if that were the case then I would have to make an extended search in better weather for the place where a small house leaned away from the blows of the wind.

There was an aged wooden sign for the Four Brothers Ranch, which contrasted with the new one that read PRONGHORN DRILLING, RIG # 29, when I cut off the paved road and onto the county gravel. The snow wasn't too deep, and there appeared to have been quite a bit of traffic as late as this morning. I slowed to a stop as I rounded the hill that led to the small valley where the homestead still sat, the snow sweeping around me and dropping into the rolling hills of the high plains. I thought about those hard men on their short horses. I wondered if they were still here and if they were aware that Mari was now with them.

I watched the sage straining at its roots to escape the force of the northwest wind, edged the truck farther out on the road that followed the hills, and descended into the valley of the four brothers and one lost girl. I buttoned my coat, flipped the sheepskin collar up, and twisted my hat down tight. With the sun starting to ebb, the temperature was dropping fast, and I was just starting to hear the little voices that spoke to you when you were out where you shouldn't be when nobody knew where you were and the weather was getting bad.

I stumbled up to the first wheel hub and locked it in, trudging through the midcalf drifts to the other side and locking the mechanism there as well. Over the sound of the big ten-cylinder engine, I listened to the keening of the wind and to the cry of things you didn't hear in town. If I could just separate Mari Baroja's voice from the screaming cacophony, I felt that she would tell me the things I needed to know. There was a small switchback around a juniper tree at the base of the hill where the snow had filled a trough, but other tires had busted their way through and had created a path of sorts. I drove up the slight grade and stopped at the edge. This area was slightly sheltered, and the snow blew over the cab of the truck like a fake ceiling.

I had wondered what it was that could be of so much importance and, now that I was looking at it, I felt like a fool. I could make out at least a dozen methane wellheads, containment tanks, and a compression station. If all the wells I could see, and the ones I suspected I couldn't, were on line and producing, someone was making a lot of money. I followed the most recent set of tracks across the arch of the hill. From this vantage point, I could make out another three dozen wellheads. There was a vague outline of a drilling rig with numerous vehicles parked below it; I shifted into low and headed in that direction.

Methane development in the northern part of Wyoming had become a mixed blessing, and it seemed like every jackleg that could turn a wrench had suddenly become a roughneck. The amount of trucks with plates from Oklahoma and Texas had certainly increased, but the number of people who were actually benefiting financially from the methane boom was few. In Wyoming, there is a practice of carving off a portion of the mineral rights from a property at the point of sale, resulting in ranchers who had very little say over whom the leases were sold to and, consequently, who could drive on your land and pretty much do as they pleased. The methane industry's propaganda poster children were the ones who had retained their mineral rights, could enforce a suitable surface agreement, and got a portion of the money from the gas that was produced.

The impact the industry had made on my life had been relatively negligible. Other than the odd roughneck getting overly self-medicated and needing some downtime in the jail, keeping the ranchers and the drillers from killing each other was about it. I suppose I looked at methane development as a false economy in a boom-and-bust cycle.

When I got to the site, there didn't seem to be anybody outside, and there was no activity on the rig itself. I don't know that much about methane drilling, but just about everything shuts down in my part of the world when the temperature closes in past zero. The printing on the truck doors read NORTHERN ROCKIES ENERGY EXPLORATION, an outfit out of Casper. I waited, but no one in the truck was moving very fast to see what I wanted; finally, the man in the driver's seat tightened the hood of his Carhartt coveralls and climbed out. He walked in front of my truck, opened the door, and climbed in on the passenger side, slamming the door behind him.

He peeled the hood back, pulled the fleece scarf from his face, and revealed a set of pale blue eyes. He was of average height, but was disproportionately large in the shoulders and hands, one of which he had de-gloved and held out to me. Between the glove finger in his mouth and the amount of ferocious red beard he had to talk through, I had to listen carefully to understand him. "Wanna thank you for cumin' down, but I think we got 'er under control."

I looked at him. "No problem." I kept looking at him in hopes that he would say something more on the offhand chance that I might understand it. I took the hand that was almost as large as my own. "Why don't you just tell me all about it?"

We shook, and he nodded and pulled the hood all the way back to reveal a lot more red hair and a yellow Northern Rockies Energy Exploration hat. "He's not a bad ol' boy, he just gets carried away some times." He looked at his lap. "I'm not gonna lie to you, mighta been some drugs. Shit, he's so loopy he couldn't hit the broad side of a barn." He sniffed. "Just a little ol' thirtytu." I looked at Yukon Cornelius and raised an eyebrow. "Ah'm aw right." He nodded. "Just glanced a rib." He assisted the last statement by unzipping his jacket and poking a finger through what I assumed was a bullet hole in both the front and rear of his coat. There was a dark stain at his side where the blue plaid flannel was exposed, but he only shrugged and looked at me. "Just a little ol' thirtytu." He nodded some more. "Told 'em not to call yuh."

As far as I knew, they hadn't. "Well, I like to be informed when people are shooting each other in my county." I pulled the aluminum form folder from the door pocket, placed it on the center console between us, and pulled my pen from my shirtfront. I clicked it. "What's his name?"

He took a deep breath. "Cecil Keller." He looked at me, and I was impressed by the direct and steady quality of his gaze. "Constable, I just don' want him to get in trouble fer this."

"You don't want to lose him?"

He shrugged. "He's just a dumb kid."

After a moment, I clicked the pen closed and placed it on the clipboard. "What's your name?"

He automatically stuck out his hand again. "Jess Aliff, foreman."

We shook again. "Jess, unless you're willing to press charges, seeing as how you're the one that he shot, I can't do too much about this, but I have to file a report on any gunshot wounds in my jurisdiction." He nodded some more and pulled at a wayward blondish-red tuft just below his lower lip. "But I don't suppose you're planning on going to a hospital?"

He blew out a dismissal puff of air and looked at me. "Naw."

"Well, then I guess there's not a lot to do officially." His mood visibly brightened. "But I don't like the idea of drug-crazed individuals running around my county with unregistered weapons shooting people." He nodded and did his best to look serious. "Mister Keller is going to have to come in with the gun and have a little chat with me tomorrow."

We both nodded. I looked out the windshield at the silent rig and the assembled vehicles idling in the frigid air. "Quite an operation you've got going here."

He followed my gaze. "Not today."

"Just out of curiosity, what does an outfit like this produce in a day?"

He thought and pulled at the tuft again; I was starting to see a pattern. "Well, we're on tap with three pods, the biggest on the tail end of the Big George coal seam, 220 heads."

"High production?"

"Oh, yeah."

Millions. I looked back out the windshield and let it sink in. "How long have you fellas been in operation here?"

"A little less than a year."

That was a lot of methane being pulled out of the ground of Four Brothers Ranch. From my quick glance at the mineral rights at the courthouse, I figured the Barojas were making more than a lot of money but, if Mari had died of natural causes, there was no need to search for a motive. I had piqued my own curiosity and was going to have to go back to the courthouse, but it was creeping up on five o'clock. There was always tomorrow. I looked back at the man sitting in my passenger seat. "'Bout time for you guys to pack it in, isn't it?"

He glanced past me to the truck alongside. "They will. I'll stick aroun' to see if the weather changes." Before he climbed out, I reminded him that I wanted to talk to Mr. Keller tomorrow. Mr. Aliff said he'd make sure that the young man would be there first thing, and I had no doubts that he would. Mr. Aliff did not strike me as a trifling individual, bullet holes notwithstanding.

I did some quick figures as I carefully picked my way across the ridge to the county road and back toward the highway. I was tired, but I needed to talk to someone about all of this before I went and talked to Lucian. I figured I'd check in at the office, gas up, stop by the house to check for snowdrifts, and go see Henry Standing Bear.

When I got to the office it was close to six, but I recognized every vehicle, including one that took me a minute. I parked the Bullet and took a deep breath to prepare myself for what was inside.

When I opened the office door, I became instantly aware of a kangaroo court in full session. It was in the air, like the snowflakes. Ruby was seated at her desk, and Vic was leaning against it with her arms folded; Saizarbitoria was standing a little away—he probably didn't want to get blood on the borrowed uniform. I noticed they were all holding plastic wine glasses, except for Sancho, and there was an open bottle of merlot on Ruby's desk.

I closed the door behind me and turned to look at all of them. There were a number of Post-its on the doorjamb of my office, but I figured I'd get to those. I was about to say something witty when I caught a pair of very nice legs out of the corner of my eye belonging to someone sitting in one of my visitors' chairs with a coat and a large dog head on her lap. I leaned forward around the coat rack and met a vivacious set of deep-sea blues, "Hello."

"Hello."

"Slow day at the safe-deposit boxes?" I leaned a little farther and took her all in. Dog didn't move, and I didn't blame him.

Her hand paused on his head, and she looked down; she was also holding one of the plastic wine glasses. "What's your dog's name?"

I felt just a little ashamed. "He doesn't really have one. I've been calling him Dog." I looked back at her. "I've only had him for a couple of weeks now."

She did a slow nod. "I hope you don't mind. I thought I'd stop by and deliver a gift of gratitude for last night." She raised the glass in a slight toast and then used it to gesture toward the pack. "They said it was okay."

I looked at the assembly. "I bet they did." I made a great show of pulling out my pocket watch. "Whose got the watch tonight?" Both Ruby and Vic finally looked at something other than Maggie Watson. I looked over at Saizarbitoria, too. "You pulling double duty?"

He shrugged. "I don't mind. I used to do it in Rawlins all the time."

I turned to Ruby. "You give him the beeper?"

She didn't look at me. "I gave him the beeper."

I needed a quick neutralizer to change the point of interest, so I walked over and poured myself a glass. "Great." I smiled and turned to Vic. "How'd he do?"

She held the synthetic glass at her temple. "He's really polite."

"You say that like it's a bad thing."

She took a sip and glanced over to Ms. Watson. "We all choose where to expend our energies."

I was pretty sure that that arched eyebrow could pierce steel, but Maggie Watson saved herself and me. "I was wondering if you were free for dinner?"

All their eyes swiveled back to her.

"Dinner?"

All their eyes swiveled back to me.

"Yes."

I was feeling a little dizzy with all the attention. "I just have a bit of work to do, and then I'll swing by and pick you up." I looked down at the exposed and very lovely legs. "Dress warm, okay?"

"Okay." It was easier on everybody's eyes since we were now standing beside each other.

I helped her with her coat and opened the door as she turned and looked at the assembly. "Nice meeting everyone. Bye." I closed the door as she stepped into the darkness and onto the stoop, and I turned back to face the afternoon of the long knives.

"Her car was stuck."

"Really?"

I took a sip of my wine. "Really. Look, don't think that you're so big that I can't put you over my knee and spank your little Italian butt."

She looked up at me with a carnivorous smile. "Watch it, big man, it might work with the locals, but I've been to the rodeo." She walked past me toward her office. "Anyway, I'm not into that stuff, and it sounds like you better save it for tonight."

At least she hadn't said fuck fourteen times. Maybe she really was on her best behavior. I turned back to Ruby. "Charlie Nurburn?"

She turned back to her computer, and I noticed there wasn't anything on it except a blank blue screen. I also noticed that her coat was in her lap, even if she still had her half-glass of wine. "Go read your Post-its."

I leaned over and kissed the top of her head, sighed, and trudged off to my office. I glanced back at Saizarbitoria. "You got anything to say?"

"No, sir."

I guess that's when I hired him. He sat in the chair opposite my desk as I tossed the Post-its on the blotter and carefully placed the mostly full goblet on top of them. People always took precedence over Post-its, so I asked him what was on his mind.

"I'm having a good time." The silence hung in the room for a moment.

"Good." I wondered if he'd feel the same way standing in front of the IGA accosting the citizenry. "You can have wine some other time."

He laughed, and I looked at the bright young man sitting in front of

me and felt like Monsieur de Treville with the young Gascon in atten-
dance. It was hard not to with the Vandyke and the mischievous glint.
I wondered if, like D'Artagnan, he was going to be an inordinate pain.
He seemed to be waiting for more, so I reached into my coat pocket
and produced the bookmark I had taken from Mari Baroja's room.
"You've got quite a facility with languages. Maybe you can help me out
with something." I flipped the piece of paper on the desk, careful to
avoid the wine. He leaned over and turned the scrap so that he could
read it. He was smiling. "What?"

"How did you know?"

"Know what?"

"That I'm Basque?"

I kept looking at him and, in a flash, it all fit. "Just a lucky guess."

"I'm French Basque." I contemplated that one as he looked back at
the piece of paper and the scribbled hand. "It says 'We can no longer
say.'" He waited, and it was an old world wait, the kind that doesn't
concern itself with giving you a fast answer. The Cheyenne and Crow
were masters of such things, but the kid was pretty good. "I'm not
sure if it means anything, but it's also a line from a poem by Jean
Diharce about Guernica." It didn't take him long to remember the
translation. "Guernica. This name inflames and saddens my heart;
centuries will know its misfortunes. . . . We can no longer say the
names Numancia and Carthage without saying in a loud voice in
Euskara, lying in its ruins, Guernica." There wasn't a lot of drama in
the presentation; he stated it as if it were history. "Is this from the
woman that died?" I nodded, and he studied it some more. "You think
it's important?"

"Everything's important when you don't know what you're looking for, or if you even should be looking."

"She was Basque?" I nodded some more. "Is there anybody you'd
like me to talk to?"

I sighed, thought about the old priest, Mari's cousin, and looked at
the scrap of paper. "Maybe." I looked back up at him. "You got a place
to stay tonight?"

"I figured I'd just stay here."

"Okay, but you might need a vehicle. If anything happens, take Vic's. There's an extra set of keys on the wall by the door."

I couldn't tell if he was smiling when he left my office, and that probably was a good thing. I picked up the piece of paper. "We can no longer say." It was capitalized at the beginning, which led me to believe that it wasn't the continuation of a stanza or part of a poem. I didn't know Mari Baroja but thought she might have had enough on her plate without political intrigue. She was Basque, though.

I stuffed the paper scrap back in my pocket and picked up my life in Post-it form. Vic appeared in my doorway with her jacket over her shoulder and wine glass in hand. "I can't fucking believe you're gonna get laid before me."

"Maybe you should stop looking at this as a competition?"

"You are such an asshole." She took a sip. "Not that I give a shit, but where have you been all day?"

I took a sip of my wine, its complex bouquet undiminished by the styrene stemware. "Following up on this Baroja thing."

"There's a thing?"

I blew out and thought back on my day. "Spoke with the ME from Billings. His opinion is that she smoked too much, she drank too much, and I'm coming to the conclusion that she might have done other things too much as well."

She shrugged and toasted with her glass. "That's how I wanna go."

I curbed the urge to say something about slow starts. "Talked to the personal physician."

"Who is?"

"Isaac Bloomfield, who concurred. There was something else, though." She held the edge of the plastic against her lip. "She'd been consistently beaten." Her eyes widened. "Massive tissue damage on the back and other areas."

The lip slipped away. "Holy shit."

"It gets better. I went to see the granddaughter."

When I told her what Lana had said, she came and sat in the chair opposite my desk and scooted it in so that she could lay her arms on the flat surface and rest her chin there. The glass dangled over the edge, unseen. Her voice was low, but it cut like only a woman's voice can. "No fucking way. Lucian?"

"It gets better."

"It can't get any better, unless you found the body."

"Trust me, it gets better." I told her about the conversation with the judge.

"Fuck me." She glanced around the room; she had just been given a passport to strangeland where I had spent the day. The big eyes finally came back to rest on me, and they were heavy. "He did it. I'll bet you anything he did it." The cutting voice was back. "The love of your life is taken away and is being slowly beaten to death? Charlie Nurburn is lying in a shallow grave in Absaroka County or eaten by coyotes and shit off a cliff, which is too good for the son of a bitch." She folded her arms on the desk again, having spoken. "What are you gonna do?"

"What do you mean?"

"What are you gonna do?" It was a smile, a wonderfully vicious and lovely smile with no warmth in it. "The sheriff has killed a man, the one-legged bandit, your pal."

I leaned in until our noses were about sixteen inches apart. "I really wish you weren't enjoying this so much."

"I can't help it. This is one of those great fucking moral quandaries, and I can't wait to see what you're gonna do next."

I folded an arm and supported my head with a fist. "I'm going to wait and see what comes back from the NCIC."

"It's going to say that Charlie Nurburn is dead as the proverbial doornail and that somebody hammered him a very long time ago." She trapped her lower lip in thought. "Can I go with you when you go to talk to Lucian?"

"No."

She whined. "C'mon." I didn't say anything and, after a moment, she asked again: "C'mon." We stared at each other for a while, and then she drank the last sip of her wine, placed the empty glass on my desk, and stood. "I don't have to mention that there is no statute of limitations on murder, right?"

I sighed, still holding my head up with my fist. "No, you don't. You also don't have to impress upon me how easy it is to drive a man to the act."

She pulled a wayward lock behind her ear, sparkled her eyes with a quick batting of the lashes, and quarter curtseyed. "Just here to help out." She paused at the door. "By the way . . . ?"

"Yes?"

"I hope you get the clap."

I collapsed my head on my arm and looked at the small amount of wine in my plastic glass, trying to figure out how to drown myself in it. What was I going to do? Hard as I tried, I couldn't see myself marching into Lucian's room and accusing him of something I wasn't sure he had done. I was going to have to feel the outside edges of the thing first. I wanted to know why he had lied to me; it was a start, a chicken-shit start, but a start. As soon as I looked toward the Post-its, Ruby appeared in the doorway.

Her tone was stern. "Have you read those?"

"I'd rather have you tell me."

She came in, and I noticed she had a large mailing envelope under her arm. "You want the good news or the bad news first?"

"There's good news?"

"Charlie Nurburn is alive and well and living in Vista Verde, New Mexico."

My head came off the desk like it was on fire. "What?"

She tapped the Post-its with a bright red nail, which had a little holiday wreath painted on it. "According to the records, Mr. Charlie Nurburn has been paying his taxes in Vista Verde since 1951. Here is his address and phone number."

I yelled out the door. "Vic!"

"She's gone."

I got up and walked around the desk and kissed the top of her head again. "Thank you. You have no idea how much."

She looked up at me. "Does this mean you're ready for the bad news?"

"Not necessarily."

"Mari Baroja is in Billings. The medical examiner said that there were tests he wanted to perform and that he couldn't do them here."

I stared at her for a moment and then rubbed my hands across my face. "When was this?"

"He phoned about an hour ago."

"He already took her?"

"Yes. He said that he left a series of autopsy pictures for you at the hospital. I had the Ferg pick them up before he left." She was watching me, but I was looking out the window and into the darkness of my life. I wasn't in any hurry to see those pictures. She placed the large envelope on my desk.

"Is there any more bad news?"

"Cady called. She said to tell you she was packed and to remind you that she would be here tomorrow."

"Oh, God."

"No, it's not that bad. I've got some ideas. Do you want me to just use the department plastic?"

"Yes, by all means. Just keep the receipts." I nudged the Post-its with my fingertips. "Anything else?"

She shrugged. "The rest of it's all kind of mediocre."

"How's the new kid?"

She brightened immediately and looked directly at me to let me know that she meant business. "We have to keep him."

"I'm working on it." I took the last sip of my wine, my mood having been improved. "He's Basque."

"That's nice."

I laughed. I couldn't help it; it just seemed like such a Ruby thing to say. "I don't suppose Mr. McDermott mentioned what kinds of tests he wanted to run?"

"He did not." She studied me for a while. "This is going to be a problem with the family?"

"Oh, yes."

"The church?"

I snorted. "Worse than that, lawyers."

"What are you going to do?"

"You know, I wish somebody would ask me something besides that today." She waited. "I think I'm going to run away to the Rez."

She smiled and had a little silence of her own. "Maybe you two need to touch index fingers and recharge."

I picked up the Post-it with Charlie's information and the pictures, feeling the weight of the photographs. I followed Ruby out the door and into the snow, scraped off her windshield, and watched her drive slowly away. I loaded Dog into the truck, sat on his snowy footprints, and stuffed the Post-it into my breast pocket. I didn't look at the photos, choosing instead to place the manila envelope carefully in the center console. When the console lid snapped shut, it was very loud.

5

It was a zoo, like it always was. Maggie and the Bear were sorting
through a container full of Mennonite photographs, which were des-
tined for a spring show at the Philadelphia Academy of Fine Art. The
box the photos were in was for a Stetson Open Road model, a hat I had
threatened to switch to about a month ago until Vic had voiced the
opinion that I would look like LBJ. I looked up at the numerous and
sundry pots and pans that glittered copper in the tasteful light of the
small votive candles that were everywhere in the room and in the re-
flections of the bay windows that looked out over a receding hill and
ancient sea. It was a culinary island, an eating oasis at the edge of a
snowy ocean, and it was cozy, even with the other forty-three Indians
eating, drinking, drumming, and roaming around the place.

I tried to concentrate on my appointed task of cutting onions, but
the six conversations and the drumming were making it difficult. There
were about a dozen of us who were seated and standing around the
center island and, as near as I could tell, I was the only one working. I
took a break and looked around to give my eyes a chance to clear.

This house knew my secrets. It knew about the time Henry and I
had gotten so drunk after a junior varsity Sadie Hawkins Day dance
that we had slid from the roof adjoining Henry's room and dropped
twenty feet only to be saved by the deep snow below. Henry's father,
Eldridge, came and got us, sitting us at the kitchen table and forcing us
to drink bootleg hooch for the rest of the night until we both threw up
and passed out. When he made us eat eggs and Tabasco sauce the next
morning, he explained that if we were going to be drunks we should
know what the life was like. The house knew about the night I had

called from Los Angeles to tell Henry about being drafted by the marines only to find that he had received a similar letter in Berkeley from the army. The house remembered when I had introduced Henry to my new wife, Martha. It remembered when Cady was two and established the ritual of barking like a seal for the McKenzie River salmon that always seemed to be on hand. It had been the nerve center for getting out the Indian vote when I had run for sheriff the first time. It knew when Martha had died of cancer, and it had contained the both of us when I had come to tell Henry that four high school boys in Durant had raped his niece. The house knew a million sorrows, a million victories, and Henry and me apiece. It knew when you were hungry, it knew when you were sad, and best of all it knew when you needed comfort.

I looked longingly at the dark beer in the glass to my left through watering eyes, but I had made myself a promise that I wouldn't have another sip until I had finished cutting another onion. I cheated and took a swig.

"Lawman, do you have those onions cut?"

I sat my glass back down. "I need some nourishment."

"Yes, the onions are holding us up." Brandon White Buffalo had pressed me into service when we had arrived, while Henry had absconded with my date. Brandon was the owner/operator of the White Buffalo Sinclair station in Lame Deer.

I looked around the table and knew just about everybody, including Lonnie Little Bird, who sat in his wheelchair, so close to my stool that you couldn't tell his legs were missing. "When is Melissa coming home?"

He smiled so broadly that I thought his head might crack open. "She comes back tomorrow. Um-hmm, yes, it is so." A product of fetal alcohol syndrome, Melissa was finishing her first semester at a community college in South Dakota. I had known the Little Birds for years. They were important in a case that I had solved less than a month ago and so, every once in a while, Lonnie would wheel himself into the office and give me updates on Melissa's progress. "She's liking school?"

"She is liking basketball. Um-hmm, yes, it is so."

I went back to slicing. I yelled to Brandon. "How small do you want these onions?"

He glanced over. "Halves lengthwise into half-inch strips, Lawman."

I shrugged. For me eating was a necessity, but for Henry it was art, and the coda of his art was ease and originality. I was surprised he was allowing Brandon to do the cooking, but it was under close supervision. I glanced at the Bear and Maggie Watson, and it seemed as if they were sitting awfully close to one another. I stuck the knife out to get his attention above the halting tempo of the numerous Cheyenne conversations. "What are we making again?"

He glanced up. "*Ga xao xa ot.*" He looked at my blank face. "Vietnamese."

I thought about it and continued in a loud voice. "I don't remember having anything like this when I was over there."

"That is because everything you ate over there came out of an American can."

"I had a lot of Tiger beer."

"I do not think that could be considered a gourmet item." He reached over and touched Maggie's arm as she smiled and looked back at him. They were drinking white wine; I didn't like the stuff. I remembered a French expatriate at the Boy-Howdy Beau-Coups Good Times Lounge who advised me that the stuff was all right for in the morning when you don't feel well or for the ladies.

I watched her as she talked, the delicate way that her lips moved. They were pretty great lips, really well defined, and they always seemed to have a fresh coat of lipstick even though I had only caught the application a few times. She was positively brilliant now, flushed with the excitement of the exotic, alien surroundings and with the Bear's stories.

"So, the onions are the first part?" He didn't answer, but she stopped listening and smiled. "So, the onions . . ."

The response was a little sharp. "Yes."

I waited a moment to let him know that he'd hurt my feelings.

"I was just asking." He nodded, sighed, and looked back at Maggie. "Well, I just want you to know that you've hurt my feelings." I leaned toward Maggie so that she could feel my pain. "See . . . tears."

She laughed, I sighed and felt a large shadow cast over me from behind; Brandon White Buffalo was a good six inches taller than I. He took the cutting board full of onions with a pair of gigantic hands, and I watched as the plate disappeared. The festivities had started at the Shoulder Blade Elders Center and then had followed Henry Standing Bear home, where the party was always waiting to begin. It was such a wonderful name, Shoulder Blade Elders Center. It sounded like a place where you could go and get a few things straightened out by men and women who had been down the trail you were now traveling, a place where they could lay a leathered hand on your shoulder, look into your eyes through the cataracts, and help make a few things clearer. Things like that happened at the Durant Home for Assisted Living, but they were harder to come by, as there was just no romance in the place's name and therefore in its consideration.

I glanced down at the photograph Henry and Maggie were studying. It was of a uniformed man in riding boots handing an American flag to a small group of what might have been Indian chiefs. The flag draped between them like something to catch the promises. I noticed the uniformed man's end swooped lower, allowing anything that might have been inside to escape. The Indians looked at the flag as if they weren't quite sure what to make of it. The chiefs wore crisp white shirts, woolen vests, beaded moccasins, and a collective countenance of long-standing indifference. I recognized the land behind them, the few trees and the undulating hills that made up the majority of the Northern Cheyenne Reservation's topography. I could even make out the shadow of the photographer on the legs of another white man in a baggy suit who stood to the right. I noticed this shadow did not touch the Indians, as if they were immune. There was another chief in full war bonnet to the right; his lips were pressed together, and he was the only one looking directly at the camera as it attempted to steal his soul.

I looked at the dynamic people surrounding the table, a people who had been cheated, frozen, starved, and hunted almost into extinction, a people who, with the combined nations of the Brules, Sansarcs, Minneconjous, Hunkpapas, Ogllalas, and Blackfeet, fought the United States of America to a standstill. My money was still on them.

I watched as the giant took the assembled ingredients and retreated to the stove. He added a little oil and the onions to a large frying pan set at medium heat. He tossed in a pinch of salt and some garlic and juggled the handle of the cast-iron skillet without the assistance of a pot holder.

Maggie was talking to Henry again, the only conversation that was in English, but Brandon had brought the cutting board back. "More."

I continued to toil in the fields and listened to Henry and Maggie, to the cadence of their talk—not so much the words, but the rhythm. It joined with the wonderful language that encircled us, and I recognized echoes of another time and another woman. Not so long ago, I had sat in a kitchen similar to this one and listened to Vonnie's melodic laughter and, like soundings into a dark, deep, and liquid place, the vibrations were stirring me; they continued to lap like ripples in a strong current. There was a desperate need to make the right choices concerning matters of the heart.

I thought about Maggie Watson. As much as I hated mysteries, she loved them. For me, the cipher was a rosary bead fed through thumb and forefinger, but for her it was catching butterflies. I was an investigator, and she was a fortune hunter. People loved treasure and must have been happy to hear from her; generally, I was not that lucky.

I turned the onions, halved them, and began cutting the half-inch slices, barely avoiding slicing my left index finger as well; Henry's knives were very sharp. After I finished the last quarter, my eyes were drawn back to Maggie. When I looked, she was looking at me with the sea blue at full tide. She smiled just a little and then turned back to Henry. It wasn't fair. It wasn't fair to chase a ghost through someone else's body, to try and capture a part of someone who was lost by taking someone who was found.

"You've cut yourself." It was a small slice just at the last joint. It wasn't bad, so I started to stick it in my mouth, but she reached across the island, took my hand, and turned back to Henry. "Do you have any Band-Aids?"

"Bathroom." He watched us for a moment. "I will get them."

She turned back to me as he left the room, and I noticed the blue of her eyes was deeper around the edges, like the color was falling from her pupils back into the white ocean. She smiled at all the people around us, finally settling on me. "I'll apply pressure."

Boy howdy.

The second bottle was red, so I had a glass. Every so often, Maggie would look over and I would hold up my finger and indicate my wound as an excuse for not joining in the conversation, but she wasn't buying it. She made a living out of poking into forgotten spaces, and I was an intrigue she couldn't solve.

I excused myself to go to the bathroom, took care of business, washed my hands, and leaned my arms on the bathroom sink. I looked at my face. It wasn't a bad face other than needing about eight hours of uninterrupted sleep, a haircut, the loss of about twenty pounds and ten years. My chin was too big, along with my ears, and my eyes were too deep set. I leaned back to my full arms' reach, and I looked a little better. I still wasn't sure about the beard, but it hid a lot.

It was easier when there was a case to distract me, but with Charlie Nurburn alive and Mari Baroja having died of apparently natural causes, there wasn't any corner of my mind in which to take refuge. Just the same, when I got back into town tomorrow morning, I would have to make sure I called Bill McDermott and the courthouse. Something still wasn't squaring up somehow. I suppose my next step would be to go to the Durant Home for Assisted Living again. Common sense told me to just let it go, but I had never regarded that voice as being either common or sensible.

I thought about Maggie and how passion was a difficult thing to sustain, but that friendship had a pace that could go on forever. I guess it was that moment that I firmly decided she and I would just be friends. It was disappointing but a relief. I had made a decision. I stepped out of the bathroom and was greeted by my best friend.

"How is your finger?"

"I think I'll live."

He took a deep breath. "I followed you here to talk you into what you are in here attempting to talk yourself out of." The dark hair, the dark skin, the dark eyes, it was like he was carved out of mahogany. Some golem of the Northern Cheyenne, but I knew the heart that rested there.

"You make it sound like a new car."

He waited as someone slipped by us and went into the bathroom. "Are you sure you are okay?"

I told him about the dream, which had featured Mari Baroja.

He listened quietly and nodded periodically. At the end, he smiled. "It would appear that you now have an advocate in the Camp of the Dead."

My knowledge of the intricacies of Indian religion was spotty, but I knew about the camp, a place where the Cheyenne tribal ancestors gathered in the afterlife. The elders in the Camp of the Dead sought the society of interesting people in this one. There were items that carried their touch, like the old Sharps buffalo rifle that Lonnie had given me a month ago that stood in the corner of my bedroom. I could see that rifle as we stood there, the long, heavy barrel glowing with a ghostly sheen, cold to the touch like a dead body. I could see the beaded dead-man's pattern on the fore grip, the ten distinct notches at the top of the stock, and the way the gray feathers ruffled even when there was no discernible breeze, messages from the dead on the wings of owls.

We waited as the person from the bathroom passed us with a smile. "Any more advice?"

"You should be able to figure the rest out for yourself." He was silent for a moment. "If you cannot, then we are going to need more time than this conversation will allow."

On the way back, I stopped off at the massive refrigerator, took out a beer, and paused to look at a few of the photographs lying on that end of the center island. The top one was of three boys, one standing and the other two seated. They wore what looked like military uniforms, and the relaxed quality of their posture was only belied by the tension in their eyes. I knew why; their hair had been cut by the teachers at the Indian boarding school from which, if they were lucky, they got to go home for a visit every two years. I slid it over and looked at the next.

Willy Fighting Bear and Zack Yellow Fox were standing between a couple of ornery-looking Appaloosas and were wearing two of the most enormous cowboy hats I had ever seen, the kind from an earlier period that must have been meant to protect the wearer from meteor showers. Willy and Zack looked comfortable, even though they had probably been in the saddle a good fourteen hours. My dad knew them and had said they were two of the finest horseman he had ever seen. I slid this one over and looked at the next.

I knew Frank White Shield. He was in full Cheyenne chief's regalia and was standing between his two sons, Jesse and Frank Jr.; they were in their army dress uniforms, circa 1943. Frank Jr. died in Okinawa, while Jesse went to Kwajalein Atoll in the Marshall Islands with the Seventh Infantry Division as a sniper. He became famous for tying himself high in the trees so that if he were shot the Japanese would never know if they had scored a hit. They finally did, but never knew.

I looked at the next few photographs. There was one of a group of men and women standing around with the church in the background, and there was one of a young man with beaded leggings standing on a makeshift baseball field. I looked at the broad smiling face and the delicate way the nimble, dark hands held the ball. I could hear the snap when it hit the pocket and the catch phrase of a man without legs, "Um-hmm, yes, it is so."

The words had escaped my smiling lips before I was aware. I looked at Lonnie Little Bird who was involved in a whimsical conversation at the other end of the kitchen. I tried to imagine him playing professional baseball before losing his legs to diabetes. Lonnie with legs. I took a deep breath along with a swig of beer and made my way to the other side of the kitchen where my romantic fate awaited.

She was leaning on the counter with one elbow, the palm of her hand supporting her chin. " I thought only women went to the bathroom together."

She shifted to the other palm and was suddenly a lot closer. "He's a good friend." I squeezed in and popped an elbow on the table and rested my chin in my own palm only a little ways away from her face. "I'm beginning to think that you are, too." I smiled and looked down at the table. The flame of the candles shifted like the owl feathers on the Cheyenne Rifle of the Dead. There was something bothering me about something I'd just seen, an inkling of sorts, but nothing I could pin down. Was it something in the photographs or something Henry had said? I looked back up to Maggie just as Henry came back in, and I'm sure I looked like I had just broken a vase. Maggie, on the other hand, leaned back in her chair, reset a pixie chin on the palm of her hand, and batted the blue like a signal. "How's dinner coming?"

He smiled and joined Brandon at the stove. I sat there for a moment and stared into her eyes, but it became too much, so I glanced out the window. I watched the flakes fly at the pane and momentarily pause before slipping away. It was as if they were trying to drift through the glass and remind me of something that skipped like a stone on smooth water.

The photographs, it was something in the photographs.

I stood quickly, made my way around the room, and threaded through the crowd until I was standing over the assorted snapshots. They were as I'd left them. I studied the one of Lonnie with the beaded leggings that encased the now missing legs and could see him sweeping through the infield like a red-tailed hawk, the top grain leather sailing toward first like a war lance; but it was the car that was parked to the side along the foul line, a large convertible, fancy for the period in two-tone paint that had pricked my thoughts.

I slid the photo aside and looked at the next. A small group of Indians were gathered around the same car. The automobile was closer in this shot, and I could make out the buffalo hood ornament and the letters running down the chrome.

Maggie had followed me and placed her hand on my arm. "Is there something wrong?"

"There is." I let my heart slow back to normal and looked at the photo again. "Let me ask you." I placed a finger on the picture for clarification. "Does that look like a 1950 Kaiser?"

She leaned in and inspected the car in question. "I'm not so sure about the year, but the front emblem says Kaiser."

There was only one white man in the photograph, and I was pretty sure who he was. Henry had come over to my other side, and I shifted my finger. "Does the name Charlie Nurburn ring a bell?"

His eyes narrowed as he studied the image. "Yes, I have heard that name." He breathed for a moment. "From the southern part of the county, sold bad liquor for a year or so. He blinded and killed some of my people."

I shook my head and studied the tall, thin man in the photo. "That sounds like Charlie, all right."

His head shifted. "This involves a case you are working on?"

"Yep." I thought about it. "No. I mean there really isn't a case, and he's really not a part of it since he's alive and living in Vista Verde, New Mexico." I stopped talking for a moment to allow myself to think.

I turned to look at Henry, but as I did, the lines on his face disappeared, his cheekbones were more pronounced, and water trailed from the crow-wing black hair. His shoulders were narrow, before the high-octane testosterone of adolescence had made an all-state middle linebacker out of him and, when he smiled, the canine baby tooth that had stayed with him through junior high suddenly reappeared.

"You are chicken!"

I looked down at him and the swirling water of the Little Powder near the confluence of Bitter and Dry creeks. A bridge was to our right, with a black framework that loomed against the brilliant blue of a July day. My spine felt as though it was falling through my rib cage, and a cold chill scraped along my arms and shoulders. "I am not!" I yelled back.

"Then jump!"

I looked down and instead of the man-sized boots, I saw a pair of scrawny, sunburned legs that shot from a pair of cut-off jeans to bare feet. I shifted, and the sheet metal I was standing on popped back against my weight.

He cocked his head and laughed, the skinny fists resting on the narrow hips. "You are chicken!"

I stared at the faded yellow paint on the metal, the chrome strip with the letters indented, Powder River sediment lying in the lower edges. I looked at the buffalo standing on the hillock of the hood's crest and the large K insignia . . . and jumped.

I refocused my eyes in the kitchen and met his. "I know where it is." I turned to look at Maggie. "Stuck in the bank of the Little Powder, about a mile from here." I tapped the picture for emphasis. "This very car." I looked again. "Along with seven or eight other cars that are used to hold the bank where it curves under the bridge."

His voice doubted me. "How long has it been there?"

I smiled. "As long as I can remember. It was there when we were kids."

He smiled for a moment, and I watched as he made the journey. "You cracked your head open there." He didn't move for a moment. "This is important?"

"Maybe." I continued to look at the photograph. "This is the car."

He shrugged. "There were not that many two-tone Kaiser convertibles on the Rez."

The blue eyes shifted back to the photograph, and her lips thinned in concentration. "Why would somebody bury a practically new car in the river bank of the reservation?"

I looked closely at the man I assumed to be Charlie Nurburn. He was thin, tall, with the thumbs of his bony hands hitched into the front pockets of his work pants. You could just see two pearl-handled automatics sticking out from the waistband, and there were two more in a crossed, two-rig shoulder holster. Charlie Nurburn was well armed. His jeans looked like shedded snakeskin that rolled at the cuffs to reveal a scuffed pair of lace-up logging boots. An old CPO jacket was draped on his narrow shoulders, and a flannel plaid shirt buttoned up to the turkey throat. He wore one of those old hunting caps, the ones with the earflaps that tie on top, perched at a rakish angle to the left. I looked at the face and could make out what appeared to be a gold tooth, front and right. I tried to see a woman-beater and a murderer behind the lowered eyebrows that hid his eyes, but he looked like everybody else. It's that kind of thing that worries me.

If Charlie had left Absaroka County forever back in 1951, why wouldn't he have taken his almost brand new Kaiser with him? I looked at the two of them. "This is the man who was married to the woman in the nursing home, the Basque woman who just died."

Maggie Watson took a seat on the nearest stool and folded her hands over her lap. "What woman in what nursing home?"

"Mari Baroja, the one that was married to Lucian."

It took a good three seconds for the Bear to respond. "What?"

"Mari Baroja is the woman that died in the nursing home. She and Lucian Connally were married for a couple of hours back in the mid forties before her family annulled it. He said that he didn't see her again till about a year ago when she got planted in the Durant Home for Assisted Living. For some reason, Lucian has suspicions that the cause of her death might be more than natural, so I locked up her room and called in an ME from Billings for a general. He says she probably died of heart failure, but there are millions of dollars being pumped out of the ancestral manse down at Four Brothers."

"And that is the Baroja place?" He raised an eyebrow as I nodded. He looked like he was getting ready to ambush a stagecoach. "Motive, yes, but is there a case here?"

"During the autopsy it was discovered that Mari Baroja was beaten and, during consequent conversations with Lana Baroja, Isaac Bloomfield, and Vern Selby, I discover that Charlie Nurburn was possibly the slimiest thing to ooze across the surface of the earth until his disappearance under ever increasingly mysterious circumstances."

He still looked puzzled, and I was aware that most of the conversation in the room had stopped. "Lana Baroja is?"

I took Henry by the arm and steered him to the far side of the kitchen. I apologized to Maggie as we receded. I pressed Henry into a corner. "Lana Baroja is the granddaughter of the deceased and clearly of the opinion that Lucian Connally had something to do with the death of her grandfather."

"I thought you said that he is alive."

"It's complicated. Also, it appears to be common knowledge that Mari Baroja and Lucian were involved in a Thursday afternoon tryst that lasted for years, but Lucian doesn't admit to the affair." I thought for a moment. "That and a '50 Kaiser imbedded in the bank of the Little Powder for as long as we can remember."

"So, we are talking about two potential murders separated by more than fifty years."

I stood there for a while looking at him. "What do you think?"

"About what?"

"Do you think Lucian did it?"

For the first time that evening, the Cheyenne Nation was silent.

6

"I like your friend Henry."

I had taken route 87 back from the Northern Cheyenne Reservation because, in a fit of optimism, I thought it might have been plowed. Mari Baroja had probably traveled this way in the opposite direction a few hours earlier; I wondered how she had felt about it. She rested uneasily on my mind, so I thought about sharing part of the burden with Maggie as we rode along on the inch or two of compacted snow. I looked over at her; if women knew how good they looked in the dash light of oversized pickup trucks, they'd never get out of them. "Really?"

"Uh, huh."

The snow had slackened a little, but the fat wide flakes still swooped out of the darkness into the headlights and disappeared around the windshield in uncountable little games of chicken. I was munching on ruggelach and was trying to concentrate on the road and not let the thrill of a new association put us in a ditch.

"How long have you known each other?"

"Since grade school." I felt a slight twitch as the rear wheels of the truck slipped a little. "I used to go to his auntie's house, and we would watch the Lone Ranger. We'd play in the yard, and I always got to be Tonto." She laughed, but I thought about the case. I wondered if Saizarbitoria had spoken to Charlie Nurburn. I'd given Sancho the job in hopes that I'd never have to speak to the man.

"You're thinking about the Basque woman again?"

I glanced over. "Just concentrating on the road."

It was pretty obvious she didn't believe me. "What was her name again?"

I took a glance at the center console, where I had stowed the autopsy photographs. "Mari Baroja." She was smiling. "What?"

"It sounds like ambrosia."

I sighed. "Yep, it does." I watched the snow for a little while. Lana's statement still worried me. I guess Lana's statement didn't matter if her grandfather was alive but, if he was, why would he have abandoned a perfectly good Kaiser and moved to Vista Verde, New Mexico, without it?

She was still looking at me. "You're a funny kind of sheriff."

I chewed on the inside of my cheek, something I always did when I was forced to really think. "I don't like mysteries, and I don't like it when things don't add up." I turned and glanced at her. "How about we talk about you?"

"Hey, I'm one of my favorite subjects. Let's talk about me." I laughed. "What do you want to know?"

"Oh, everything." I glanced back at the road but ended up looking at her again. "How does something like you get around without being married?"

She folded down the visor and opened up a small leather purse. "As the queen apparent of Norway, I am only allowed to marry once I've reached the age of consent." She pulled out an even smaller cosmetic bag, glanced at me, and reapplied her lipstick.

I nodded. "That age being thirty-five?"

She closed the vanity mirror and turned back to me with a ravishing smile. "Oh, I do like you." She replaced the lipstick in the tiny bag and then the bag in the hand-tooled leather purse. "It's really not all that interesting. I just found myself in an emotional and geographic place where I wasn't happy."

"And where was that?"

She cocked her head. "Charlottesville, Virginia. Louis taught at UVA, and after a while we began to regard each other as electives."

"You chose Cheyenne, Wyoming, instead of Charlottesville, Virginia?"

"It seemed like a clean slate, and the South is full of ghosts. I had a job similar to this one and a degree in economics, so I came out for an interview at the Wyoming state job fair which, by the way, consisted of three balloons tied to the end of an event table in the conference room of the capitol building."

"We're a frugal state."

She kept studying me, but it took a while for her to get up her nerve. "You don't seem divorced."

"Seem divorced?"

Her eyes squinted, but the blue sparkles were still evident. "Too much unreined compassion still there, not enough baggage."

I waited a moment in respect. "Widower." She nodded but sat there silently with her legs curled beneath her. I didn't want to talk about Vonnie, but that wouldn't have been fair. "There was another woman about a month or so ago." She didn't say anything. "I don't think you could call it a relationship in the sense that it was consummated, but we were close, and it didn't end well."

Her voice seemed small and far away. "Can I be honest with you?"

"I would hope."

"I read about it in the newspapers."

I felt strangely violated, like somebody had burgled my personal life. "Well . . . that's a price you pay for being a public figure." She reached an arm out and rested a hand on my sleeve, somewhere alongside my heart. I could feel the welling in my eyes, and I wasn't sure whether it was for me or for the women whom I had lost. I concentrated on the road and none of the moisture escaped, but I'm pretty sure the blue eyes didn't miss the emotion. I was pretty sure those eyes didn't miss much of anything. "We're talking about me again."

"Sorry." Her head tilted forward. "Well, you're stuck with me for another couple of days at least. I've got nine unclaimed security boxes at three different banks so I'm thinking that my predecessor didn't consider Durant to be high on his list of priorities."

I was relieved at the change of subject. "So, what do you do when you crack one open?"

"First I ascertain whether the owner is alive and the box has been forgotten or if the box is abandoned due to a death. Next I check on-line credit records or cold-call for possible relatives; if there's no contact with an owner and the rent hasn't been paid in five years, it gets turned over to us."

"How does that go?"

"I get hung up on a lot." She laughed and shook her head. "It's really hard to get people to believe that we're legitimate. They always think it's some kind of scam, but we turned over eight million dollars to recipients and generated over fifteen million in unclaimed property just last year."

I whistled. "Fifteen million. I'd say the state is getting its money's worth. Maybe they'll buy more balloons." The visibility was dropping, so I slowed the truck down even more. At this rate, we might as well have gotten out and walked from the Rez. "You're the department?"

She saluted. "Unclaimed property manager. I'm my own branch of the Wyoming State Treasury Department."

"I have to ask. What kind of stuff do you find?"

She looked back out the windshield. "All kinds of things. We found an 1863 ambassadorial appointment signed by Abraham Lincoln, and just last week I found an old collection of Nazi campaign ribbons from World War II. Pocket watches, stocks, bonds . . . There was this one in Gillette that had a complete change of clothes, a ski mask, and a pistol." I turned and looked at her. "Then there are the Polaroids. We've got a stack of nude snapshots that is over a foot tall."

"Must be great decoration for the bulletin board."

"Not really." She rolled her eyes. "Most of the time they're of people you wish hadn't taken their clothes off."

That image was broken by an ice slick where melted snow must have collected on a short overpass and frozen. Past that, there was another, and the truck kicked sideways; I steered into the skid and touched the brakes but, as the snow curtain blew away, the dark bulk of a vehicle loomed in front of me. I stomped the ABS brakes and felt the surge of the master cylinder as it attempted to keep me from locking the wheels and sliding into the ton of steel that lay on its side ahead of us. Even with the system-assisted brakes, I wasn't going to get it stopped. In that split second, I saw the opening between the bridge guardrail and the undercarriage of the disabled car. The adrenalin-induced slow motion allowed me to categorize the median beyond as sloping but not bad enough to tip the Bullet; I just had to make sure I kept the tonnage pointed straight so that we didn't end up like the other vehicle. As we went off the road, I could feel the sudden deceleration as the big tires snagged on the fresh snow. We slid down into the shallow frontage, up the other side, and slowly mired to a stop past the last post and out of harm's way. I took a deep breath and looked down my outstretched arm, which was holding Dog from catapulting through the windshield and was pinning Maggie against her seat. Dog scrambled as I studied Maggie. "Are you all right?" She opened her mouth but didn't say anything.

I flipped on the light bar and hit the automatic program two on my radio, landing me at 155.445, the HP's frequency. I needed a lot of help, and I needed it pretty fast. I handed her the mic. "Tell the highway patrol that you've got a 10–50 at mile marker 12 on route 87, that you need emergency response with an ambulance and a wrecker." I smiled. "Got it?"

Her eyes were very large. "How did you know what mile marker?"

"Habit. Stay here, but look for me? 10–50, mile marker 12 on route 87, emergency ambulance and wrecker."

I crunched through and sank past the powder to the slick surface below. The hard ring of ice at my knees was the only traction I could get, so I used it to bull my way up the slope. The air was burning in my lungs as I got to the shoulder. I looked back in the direction from which we had come; there hadn't been anybody on the road since we had passed Sheridan, so I had a chance.

I looked at the car again and froze. Lying on its side was Isaac Bloomfield's '71 Mercedes.

The doors hadn't sprung and the windows were intact, the motor was running, and the wheels turned like a gut-shot horse. The lights of the metallic-colored sedan pointed off toward the hills of Lodge Grass as the motor sputtered and started to fail. The steam was still rising from the surface of the road so it must have just happened. I slid into the trunk lid. The glazed surface of the road made it difficult to navigate, but I traversed my way around to the back glass; the condensation had fogged the surface from the inside so that I couldn't see. As I scrambled, I heard a groan, and I suddenly had a little trouble breathing. I threw myself around the rear bumper and was relieved as the motor finally died, taking with it the hazard of internal combustion and two wheels driving.

Somewhere along the way I must have put my gloves on, which was good because the bottom of the car was still hot. I climbed up, and the sizzle of the wet leather on the exhaust smelled like a burning steak. I reached and grabbed the bump strip at the middle of the passenger-side door. I pulled at the handle and the damn thing actually gave with a quick bump but then settled back and fastened. I yanked it hard enough to get my fingers under the lip of the door and leveraged it open again. It wasn't going to stay, so I lodged my feet against the opening and hit it with all the weight that had inconvenienced me up to now. The door bent completely back on its hinges and ripped loose, flipping past the hood, and sliding away on the frozen sheen of ice. Piss on Ralph Nader, they never made 'em like they used to.

Isaac wasn't moving. His eyes were closed, and there was blood on the side of his head. An arm was lying across the trunk of his body. It's always the same, if there's even the remotest possibility of neck or back injury, you might do more bad than good. If I went in, I was going to crash down on top of him, so I put a leg over the side to give me a little advantage. He was warm, and there was a familiar rhythm at the inside of his wrist. It was then that one of those little miracles happened. He stirred once, adjusting his weight as if trying to find a more comfortable position. It wasn't much, but it told me that his spine and nervous system were intact. He could be moved. I strained to reach the seatbelt that had saved his life and thanked God that seatbelts were designed to fasten on the inside. As I pulled him from a sitting position, his legs caught below the steering wheel, and I had to hoist him a little to the right to get him free. As I negotiated the controls of the vehicle, I got my other hand on the front of the doctor's coat and lifted him up.

That was when I felt the lights. Nothing I had called would have flashing yellow lights, and nothing I called would be that big. The state of Wyoming uses large five-ton plows equipped with shale spreaders that could disseminate five yards of granulated scoriae; this meant ten tons of bad news arriving in a little more than a minute.

Suddenly rediscovering my strength and glad that Isaac hadn't gained that much weight since prison camp, I pulled him free from the steering wheel and almost had him when his foot caught on the seatbelt. Forcing myself to be calm, I turned him to the side, but the seatbelt clung there. I took a breath and twisted him in the other direction as the belt slipped free and slithered back into the darkness. I raised him up the rest of the way and turned.

It was way too late. The driver must have seen my emergency lights and he had started braking, but it didn't look like he was going to make it. I looked down at the icy reflection of the black road. There was nowhere we could go. Anywhere we went from here would be just as bad as where we were and probably worse, so I did nothing. I watched as ten tons of WYDOT equipment hit the first ice slick and started its sickening slide sideways.

As we sat there on the side of the car like some bizarre modern pieta, I couldn't help but think that this is what I got for thinking I could have a night off to take a beautiful woman to a magical place to meet wonderful people. Retribution was at hand in the form of cold rolling steel and red shale.

The guardrail of the underpass looked like a galvanized funnel, and I glanced at the ice plastered on the northwest surface of the metal. Arching showers of melted snow flew from the tires of the truck. The plow seemed as big as the ones I had seen on the front of Burlington Northern locomotives.

I looked down at Isaac and smiled; this shit didn't happen to Tom Mix when he was saving some nubile young thing who had been tied to the tracks. What happened to me didn't seem to matter, but Isaac was different; how could a life so full of meaning end so meaninglessly? I smoothed the old man's hair on one side; there was blood, but I didn't think he was hurt badly. As the light of the oncoming truck lit the red liquid streaks, I heard a noise in the distance. It might have been the rhythm of the big studded and chained Bandag tires clawing the aggregate surface of the highway or the thump of the Bullet's V–10, but it sounded like drums.

When I looked up again, the back of the truck was sliding toward us, and the taillights were two angry eyes. The spin continued, but the showers of slush didn't seem to be arching quite so high. I watched as the headlights turned back toward us again along with the vaulted metal of the plow. The truck slid to a stop about nine feet from where we sat. It looked like an irate buffalo, blowing steam from its stacked nostrils and dripping sweat from its forehead. The drums had stopped.

Static. "Unit Six, 10–55, over."

I knew Wes Rogers because he was old like me. He was the first highway patrolman on the scene, and I was helping him with his report. The other HPs oozed in under throbbing blue light in their mercury black cruisers, and the EMTs loaded Isaac Bloomfield into the back of the ambulance.

"So you just sat there?" He was smiling as he wrote on the metal clipboard, his Smoky the Bear hat pushed back in a pretty good likeness of Will Rogers, no relation. It was strange being on the passenger side of the cruiser. He shook his head and chuckled. "You got an extra pair of shorts?"

"I don't wear shorts; that's why women are drawn to me."

He stopped writing. "Well, I don't mind telling you, I'da had to go home and change mine." He handed me the clipboard to sign the forms. "How far you away from retiring?"

When I pushed on the pen it lit up the writing surface. "Chronologically or financially?" I handed him back the clipboard and stuck the nifty pen in my pocket. "Why do you ask?"

He tucked the forms back into the center console. "I'm gone next month. Scottsdale, Arizona."

I was surprised; I figured Wes was going to be around forever. "What're you gonna do in Scottsdale?"

He looked out at the frozen landscape, and we might as well have been on the dark side of the moon. "Watch my grandson grow up, and keep the Mexicans outta the golf course ponds at night."

I thought for a moment and came up with Wes's wife's name. "What's Ruth got to say about all this?"

I followed his eyes, and we watched as Pete's Towing pulled the lowered and narrowed Mercedes over and onto its wheels. "I figure she'll take it all right, seein' as how she's been waiting for it for the last twenty-six years."

I stuck my hand out, and he shook it back. He told me I could keep the pen as a token of his affection and a fond farewell.

I trudged through the crusty snow of the roadside toward the Bullet and pulled up short as a chain line dragged Isaac Bloomfield's sole transport up onto the levered platform of the wrecker; a coveralled driver cinched the vehicle down with log dogs. The elderly physician's baby was headed for Sonny George's junkyard, just outside of Durant. They would hold the car there until Isaac could decide what to do with it. It was a shame, really. The doc had owned the car for as long as I'd known him, and he kept it in tip-top condition. Fred Ray, the mechanic at the local Sinclair station, had once told me the car was in immaculate shape due to Isaac's preventive maintenance. I suppose even German engineering failed sometimes; that, or the eighty-five-year-old driver had.

In the brief conversation we had had while the EMTs had loaded Isaac into the van, he told me that he had grown uncomfortable with the idea of someone else performing the autopsy on Mari Baroja and so had decided to hop in his classic two-wheel-drive Mercedes and motor a couple of hours through a high-plains snowstorm at midnight. He thought it was his brakes that had failed.

As I stood there thinking, my eyes drifted past the ghostly silver of the German car to the rolling snow-covered hills to the east. Henry Standing Bear had said it best. He had started me running about a month ago as the first part of a four-part plan of redemption. I had had one of my collapses along Clear Creek and had stalled for rest time by telling him about the improvements I was going to make to my place with the help of friends of his who owned Red Road Contracting. He didn't look at me but rather looked across the small valley at the land where his grandfathers used to hunt and fish. I had seen the downturned corners of that mouth before and asked, "What?"

"You don't own the land." I had slumped against a pole and prepared myself for another tirade about the heathen-devil-white-man's theft of the North American continent, but instead Henry's voice was softened with dismissal. "You do not own your mother, do you? Sounds silly, owning your mother? It is like that with the land, silly to think you own it." He was silent for a moment; when he spoke, his voice had a tiny edge to it. "But this land owns you."

I thought about the drums; they were the same drums I had heard on the mountain, the ones that had kept me going when there wasn't anything else to go on. I wondered if the Old Cheyenne were there, just out of sight. Had they held the big buffalo truck back? Had they ridden alongside it on their war ponies, using their spears to coax it to a sullen stop and had it cost them? Even in the spirit world, I would imagine such actions are not taken without risk. I looked north and west toward the Little Big Horn and the Northern Cheyenne Reservation. It was comforting to think that they were still here, stewards of a mother they did not own. The stinging wind began making my eyes tear, at least I think that's what it was, so I laughed and lifted a hand, tipping my hat just to let them know I knew where they were and to say thanks.

I turned toward my truck. Fatigue was starting to drag at my shoulders, but I made it. I was almost too tired to walk but drove us safely back to Durant and deposited Maggie at the Log Cabin Motel. "Are you sure you wouldn't like to come in?"

I looked past her and into the inviting little cabin, and I was tempted but very tired. "I better take a rain check." I couldn't see her face, backlit as she was and standing in the doorway. "I've got Dog."

She studied me for a moment. "Are you sure you're all right?"

"Tired, that's all." I smiled. "I usually pay more attention to my dates."

I could just make out the glow of her eyes in the shadow. "When I want your attention, I'll get it."

I looked down at my boots that were covering with snow. "I guess it's only fair to tell you . . ."

"Hey, Sheriff?"

I glanced back up, and her face was very close. "Yep?"

"Maybe you think too much." She leaned over and kissed me very softly, and my lungs felt as if they were going to burst through my chest. She didn't close her eyes and neither did I. It was a long kiss, and I leaned in after her as she drew away. A chill fired off from my spine like a coiled snake.

She smiled a slow, languid smile. "How was that, without thinking about it?"

It took me a second to reacquire speech. "Pretty wonderful."

"Maybe you should try it more often." She looked into me for a moment more, taking soundings, and the door closed.

I stood there for a while, maybe hoping that the door would open again, but finally trudged back to the Bullet and drove Dog and myself over to the hospital to check on Isaac.

I didn't know the young man at the desk, but he told me that Isaac had suffered minor scrapes and contusions and that his head had a bump the size of a goose egg, but he was resting comfortably and was in room 111 if I wanted to take a look. I declined, and the kid surmised that as old as Isaac was, he was one tough cookie. I told him he had no idea.

When I got back to the jail, Vic's unit was parked out front, and the office lights were on. Dog followed me as I made my way in and started down the hallway. There was a Post-it on my doorjamb, but the handwriting was strange. I leaned in and read it: SHERIFF LONGMIRE, I CALLED CHARLIE NURBURN'S NUMBER IN VISTA VERDE THREE TIMES AND LEFT MESSAGES. SO FAR, NO CALL BACK. SANCHO. It gave the date, and the times of the three separate phone calls. Jeez, the kid was even polite in his Post-its, and obviously Vic was making an impression in that he had signed with his new nickname.

I walked down the hallway to the holding cells in the back. Santiago Saizarbitoria was asleep on my usual bunk, and evidently he was not completely trusting in that his handcuffs were locked around the bars to hold the cell door open. Once a corrections officer . . . Dog and I stood there in the dark, listening to the soft rhythm of his breath as the beeper rose and fell on his chest.

I looked down at Dog. "No room at the inn." He stayed close as I turned the corner to the other holding cell, and we crawled onto our individual bunks. I pulled my jacket over me, carefully placing my hat over my face. Maybe it was the emotional drain of the evening or just the length of a very physical day, but I forced my eyes closed in a furtive and uncomfortable sleep. I held my eyelids together, and what I saw was like the credits on a movie whose format had not been changed for television.

〰

I watched the rainbow threads of grass shimmer in a gentle summer gust that traveled across the middle fork of the Powder River with the swell of something beneath. It rolled like the ocean, moving with a quality that was sensual and female. There was a moist, weighty warmth, not in the scorching of the summer sun, but in the laden air the grass trades for carbon dioxide. Heavy riches.

I was floating now, even though I was lying deep in the swaying stalks. The sky was without a cloud. It was late, though, because the light was parallel to the earth and flat.

I could feel the heat burning through my limbs, easing the ache of my throbbing joints and loosening the tightness in my muscles. As the tendons in my neck relaxed, I felt my head slip to the right, and I could see someone lying beside me. I knew who it was before I could really see her; the scarf that I had seen before trailed across the seed heads of the buffalo grass and back to her hand. I was so close I could make out the texture of the material and the quality of the work.

She knew I was watching her. Her profile was sharp against the light of the sky, and the angles of her face planed the colors of the late afternoon like a prism. I felt the breath catch in my throat at the wonder of her and knew that everything I had heard was true. After a moment, she rolled over and looked at me with those dark eyes, a plucked piece of grass between her teeth. She smiled and reached a hand across to touch my shoulder. Her fingers were light, and a shiver went through me; the coolness of her spread like a welcome cloud on an overly sunny day.

She looked toward the mountains, as if she were trying to think of how to say what she wanted to say. After a moment, she looked back, pulled the thick sweep of hair from her face, and withdrew her hand as she rolled over and supported herself. She was still wearing the blue-and-white spotted dress, the one Lucian had described. She had trouble steadying herself, and it was only then that I noticed she was very pregnant. Her hand came out again, slowly, as if she didn't want to frighten me. The slim fingers wrapped around mine and lifted my hand toward her. A few clouds appeared like solemn voices and broken hearts.

I started, caught my hat against my chest, and sat up with my weight on my arms. I stared into the small amount of light from the hallway, pulled my pocket watch out to read the time, and took a deep breath; I'd only been asleep for an hour or so. I could feel a cooling sweat at my throat and decided I wasn't going to be able to go back to sleep so I reached down slowly to pick up my coat where it had fallen and placed my hat on my head. I was a little unsteady at first but walked out to the main part of the room and turned the corner to check on Saizarbitoria. He was still sleeping, and I had a brief twinge of jealousy; oh, to be twenty-eight, clear of conscience and young of body. "In the May-morn of his youth, ripe for exploits and mighty enterprises." I wondered how the kid was with Shakespeare.

Dog followed as I made my way to my office and then curled up beside my desk and fell fast asleep; he didn't have a care. Something was bothering me though, in the recent scheme of things, and the first thing I could think of was Isaac's car. The old Mercedes was in miraculous condition; why had the brakes failed? In the few words that had passed between us, he had said that they hadn't worked. It was crazy, but a lot of things were as of late. I got an empty Post-it from Ruby's desk and wrote a note to Saizarbitoria to go over to Sonny George's tomorrow and check the Mercedes's brakes for tampering. I stuck the note on his handcuffs, still locked to the door.

I absentmindedly plucked Sancho's Post-it from the doorway of my office, walked around Dog, and sat at my desk. It was the middle of the night, and I was too awake to sleep. I looked at the Post-it in my hands, noting that the last time Sancho had called the notorious Charlie Nurburn was at 9:32 P.M. The kid was courteous to a fault.

I looked at the phone and figured what the hell, he'd be home. As I dialed the number, I entertained the thought that there wasn't anybody who better deserved to be woken up in the middle of the night. It rang four times and then picked up. I started to say, "Absaroka County Sheriff's Department, I'm sorry if . . ." but stopped speaking when I realized it was the answering machine. Charlie Nurburn introduced himself, apologized for being unable to answer the phone, and then invited me to leave a message after the tone. All was as it should be, just another voice on another answering machine.

The only thing was that it was the voice of Lucian Connally.

7

The stamped plate made a god-awful noise as it clattered across the counter and came to rest beside the little chrome cradle that held the menus, ketchup, mustard, and salt and pepper shakers. "You know what that is?"

He looked at the rusted metal and the small amount of dirt that had shaken loose from its surface, took a sip from his cup, and then placed it back on the half ring of spilled coffee on the counter. "That is a license plate, an old one." It was early in the morning, and it had taken me awhile to find him. There was nobody in the place, but I took the seat diagonal to him across from the cash register. I was very angry, and I thought that if I sat a little away, it might keep me from grabbing him by the throat. "You know where I got it?"

He took another sip of coffee as though he hadn't a care in the world. "Off a car, I suspect."

I got up, moved around to his side, and sat on the stool next to him; it would be hard to grab him by the throat from where I had been before. "You got a story to tell me?" I unbuttoned my sheepskin jacket and pushed my hat farther up on my head.

My own cup of coffee appeared to my right. "The usual?"

"The usual." She disappeared, and I turned back to the old sheriff. He kept sipping his coffee and staring at the bee collection above the grill. "I wanna hear the one about an answering machine and a vacant room in Vista Verde, New Mexico. I wanna hear the one about your buddy Sheriff Marcos DeLeon down in Rio County, who's been taking care of the W-2s and social security. I wanna hear the one about an abandoned Kaiser lodged in the embankment of the Little Powder since 1951."

"52."

I leaned back and breathed for the first time since entering the little café. "Keep talking, I'm all ears." It got very quiet, and you could almost hear the water running below the frozen surface of Clear Creek, which flowed alongside the Busy Bee.

"Yer all nose not ears." He sat the coffee cup down and swiveled his head around to look in my general direction. "What's the ME say?"

"Not a thing until you tell me about Charlie Nurburn." I pulled my pocket watch out of my jeans: 6:37 A.M. "I've got all day but, this being a Thursday, you've probably got an appointment."

It took him quite a while to come out of the stillness that overtook him, get his coat on, and position his prosthetic leg. I waited as he zipped up an old Carhartt, far too light for the weather, and placed his hat on his head. "You . . . can go to hell." The heavy glass door swept shut, allowing a gust of snowflakes to skitter across at my boots. I watched as they melted.

"I hear hell's nice this time of year." She reached down and studied the license plate as I stared at the floor. "Want some advice?" She continued on course and ignored my warning look as she always did when I needed ignoring. "Go easy."

I took a deep breath. "I'm trying." She had held off on the usual and watched me as I rebuttoned my coat. I took the time to sip my coffee; I figured I could catch a one-legged old man in a snowstorm.

When I got outside, he was gone. "Damn." I watched the vapor of my breath whip past me as I looked up and then down. Nobody. The streetlights were still on, and there was only one set of tire tracks on Main Street. It was about then that I fell back on one of my old Indian tricks and followed the only set of footprints on the snow-covered sidewalk other than mine. I opened the door of my truck, which was parked outside the Busy Bee, and let Dog out. I figured I needed backup.

The tracks stopped in front of the Euskadi Hotel, and the snow was pushed back from the door like the broken wing of a fallen snow angel. I pulled the handle and saw him sitting there, filling his pipe from the beaded tobacco bag. The jukebox was crooning Frank's "Ave Maria," and he was at the table in the center of the room, looking very fragile and alone. "Get the hell outta here."

I stood and looked at his silver belly hat that rested crown up on the white tablecloth; it was still in good shape and was probably the last one the old sheriff would buy. Dog didn't move. We looked at each other and then back to him. "Dog is cold."

He shifted his weight and turned away from the door as he zipped up the bag and laid it on the table along with the keys to the building. "The dog can come in, but you better damn well go." He patted his leg, and Dog was there in an instant. The gnarled old hand gently smoothed the fur behind his ears. "You don't care who you hang around with, do you?"

The door swung shut behind me as I walked over and sat at the other side of his table and adjusted the plastic flowers so that we would have an unobstructed view of each other. I unbuttoned my coat and waited for a good long time, breathing the warm air. I wanted to start asking questions again, but it was too close and raw. I sat the license plate on the seat beside me, looked at the keys on the table, and settled on another subject. "So, you're the one who owns the Euskadi?"

It took awhile but, after lighting his pipe and taking a few puffs, he answered. "Hahhm." After smoking for a while longer, he spoke. "Came up fer sale back in the sixties and bought it for a song. Brought Jerry Aranzadi in as the vocal partner and to run the place; only way to keep it on the up and up, and he doesn't steal too much." He took a deep breath. "Still the only place in town where you don't get offered a blueberry beer."

"Jerry's Basque?"

"Yeah, he's one of them high-altitude Mexicans."

I smiled; it was a common phrase in these parts. "It's always been a nice place."

He looked down at the dog's head, which he continued to pet. "They used to bring 'em through here, the Basquos. Kind of a halfway house for sheepherders." He leaned forward and rested his elbows on the table. "They'd sponsor a Basquo to come over by contacting the Wyoming Range Association, put the herder's name in, and pay five hundred bucks to cover the immigrant's travel expenses. The Range would check the fellow out, and if he hadn't pitched any bombs into any cafés they'd run 'im through a quota system. Usually it was a relative, somebody they could count on. They'd deduct the money out of their pay once they got here. Poor bastards only made about thirty a week; took a while."

I waited a moment and glanced over at the bar back, which continued to insist on older and gentler times. "You met here on Thursdays?"

"After Charlie was dead." It took a moment, but he smiled. "We never got remarried. The Basquos are pretty hung up in that religious stuff, but I think I got her to understand that she was missing something. I'm just not sure if I got her to understand that it was me."

I waited a respectful moment before asking. "Lucian, what happened?"

He stared at his arm on the table, his fingers brushing the brim of his hat. "Do you think I killed Charlie Nurburn?"

I continued to look at him and thought about what the old outlaw was capable of, the stories I'd heard, the stories I knew. "Right now, yes, I do." I sighed and thought about Dorothy's advice. "Lucian, I don't particularly want to get into a pissing contest. You had to know I was going to discover all of this, you trained me too well." I thought about Mari Baroja, Isaac Bloomfield, about Lana and the pack of lawyers soon to be snapping at my heels. I placed my elbows on the table and rested my chin on my fists. "Do you know she has a granddaughter here in town?"

"Yes, I do." His look continued to darken. "You'd be amazed at the things I know."

"No, I wouldn't, Lucian. I wouldn't be amazed at all. I'll tell you what I would be amazed by, you telling me what the hell happened fifty years ago." I didn't move, just leaned on my fists and stared at him. I took a deep breath and went easy. "For me to know what's happening now, I need to know what happened then."

He nodded almost imperceptibly as something old and brittle broke loose. I watched as it fell into the river of memory and slapped against the rocky cliffs of Lucian's mind. "What good would it have done?" His eyes took on a long dead look. "What good would it have done for a woman like that to go to prison for the rest of her life?"

I listened as Lucian's voice carried us back to a summer night in the middle of the last century. I can still play it back in my mind, like a home movie that is grainy and overexposed. The film slips with the clattering of spanners in the works as a thin man comes home late one cloudy night, a mason jar half full of clear liquid still dangling from his fingers as he fumbles with the knob on the door. The jar slips and busts on the uneven steps with a loud pop, shards of glass and homemade liquor falling through the cracks of the warped and cupped wood. Cursing, he continues to fumble with a latch that has been locked since early in the evening.

There are three children in a bed at the backside of the little house, illuminated by the flashes of lightning along the Big Horns; two are three-year-old girls, twins, with their arms wrapped around their bony knees. They are clutching a threadbare star quilt between them; its floral pattern fades like distance. There is a boy who is a little older. He sits at the foot of their bed, unmoving, but holding a large hammer as best he can in his shaking small hands.

There is a slam against the door as the man throws himself against it in an all too familiar rage. This is the pattern, the framework to which these children have accustomed themselves. They shudder in fear and try to remain silent. A promise made and a promise kept in an attempt to keep the bad from being so bad.

There is a woman standing against an old Republic steel sink, her palms pressed against the coolness of the counter's lip. The cool feels good on her hands, calloused and raw from a short lifetime of hard struggle. Her long dark hair hides the face that is bowed to a god that no longer hears the trembling split lips pray for just a small salvation.

The slamming on the door continues. It is softer this time, and shortly thereafter there are soft words, words that she has responded to before but cannot anymore. He slams the door again, loud, and her head rises, revealing a dark and seeping bruise. The damage has been inflicted at her cheek but has drained to the jawline and is yellowing like something gone bad.

Words again, and then silence, an active silence that ends with the crash of a kitchen window and a piece of firewood that slides to a stop on the linoleum floor with the broken glass. She screams and rushes to the window, heedless of her bare feet and the triangular shards of heavy lead glass, in an attempt to push him away from her and from her children. His hands reach out for any part of her that he can grasp, finally tangling in her hair, and he yanks her head forward as he brings his other fist upward, propelling her backward in a lazy arch to the wood-burning stove at the other side of the small kitchen, where she lies, crumpled on the floor, still.

He scrambles in a drunken attempt to achieve purchase on the slick clapboard of the house, finally getting enough leverage to balance his weight on the sill, but slips on the edge, the glass slicing his hands as the house itself defends against his intrusion. He falls when he gets inside, rolls over onto his stiffened arm, and looks at his hand, at the glass splinters that continue to make him bleed. He attempts to pull them out but gives up in a thundering slam against the kitchen wall. He cries like a wounded beast before his attention is drawn to the opposite side of the room where a shapely calf and a well-formed foot stretch toward him in an unconscious but provocative manner.

Her father and uncles had said that she was a virgin, but they lied. Slut. She did it too well and enjoyed it too much. Bitch.

It is time for a lesson, time to teach her how to take what a man could give her. A flood of heat accompanies the anger and drunkenness giving it direction and focus. He pushes off with the good hand, tries to straighten his head, and considers the curves and softness barely concealed by the cotton dress. Even unaware, she begs for it.

She is small and easy to lift by the bodice of the dress. Her head slumps to one side, allowing the damage to her face to show. Ruined. So he turns her around and forces her over the sink. He thought of the stove, but the sink is higher and will afford a better angle for his purpose. He raises the dress over her hips and pulls at the cotton panties so that they slide down one leg and dangle from her foot, which is a good six inches from the floor.

There is blood on her undergarment; it is her time. He smells it, a different smell than that on his hands. He grabs the thick mane of her hair, pulling her head back and placing his face beside hers, telling her that he will not soil himself with her blood, that any hole is a hole. He fumbles, one-handed, with his belt and the thick buttons on his pants, shrugging the straps of his suspenders off his narrow shoulders and extracting himself for the work at hand.

She is partially awake now. The coolness of the porcelain has given her the slightest release, has allowed her the ability to center enough to bend her knees and kick. Her arms swing back and claw at him. Dishes fall from the counter, utensils crash to the floor with the melody of broken wind chimes, and the point of a large butcher's knife sticks in the green linoleum. He slams her head forward again, still holding the fist full of hair. The only sound she makes now is an involuntary grunt as he drives himself into her, forcing the air from her, over and over again.

He has not seen the door at the end of the short hallway open and is not aware that the boy has crossed the room at a desperate but determined pace. The boy is troubled by the burden he carries and surveys the scene before him in a despondent and inevitable fashion, raising the weight as high as he can, not sure if the leverage of the thing will allow it to be brought down on the appointed spot. He does not understand exactly what is happening here, other than the same one is hurting the same one again, and it has to stop.

The three smallest toes on the man's left foot are broken on impact. He slips and falls sideways, back toward the busted window, where he curses and howls like the animal he has become. The woman still lies facedown on the counter, her feet still dangling above the floor.

The boy moves forward again, raising the pointed edge of the shoeing hammer in an attempt to strike once more before retribution. It is too late. The man reaches forward and grabs him by the shirt and most of his undersized chest. The hand sledge falls from his small hands. The man feels a surge of pain from his foot and pulls himself up and onto his knees; he shakes the little body, draws it close, and slaps the boy backward with his open hand. His free one scrambles across the floor in search of the hammer and pounces on it like a five-legged spider. He smiles through his teeth as he raises the heavy metal head and takes aim on another man's child.

There is a sudden tugging at his collar.

He feels strange, almost peaceful, as he looks down at the unconscious boy. He stares at the geometric pattern of the floor, having never noticed it before. The hammer drops to the side, forgotten, as he reaches up to his throat. It feels strange and wet, and he coughs as thick, dark liquid passes from his mouth onto the child. The weight of his head pulls it forward, and there is more blood flowing onto his shirt and arms and hands. He opens his mouth to scream, but the liquid blocks his voice and spills onto the floor with the force of an open spigot. It fills the room with its smell and slippery texture, and it is everywhere.

The man tries to raise his head, but the muscles refuse to work, and his face will not rise to follow the boy who is being pulled from him. He slips sideways and falls back against the cabinets below the sink. He lies there, blinking at the tableau before him, as the mother holds her eldest in her lap close to her, her legs tucked as she crouches against the stove like a panther.

He feels cold. He blinks again and remembers how one of the uncles had told him how they always allowed her to butcher the hogs in the autumn, how she had the blood touch. He looks into those baleful eyes, which are willing him to die. Slut. And she is the most beautiful thing he has ever seen. Bitch.

He takes forever to die, but she waits, unmoving, and watches him for the better part of an hour to make sure, finally kicking his leg to see if there is any reaction. She gathers the still unconscious child and feels his breathing on her neck, and this is when she cries, smearing the tears away with the back of her hand. She carries him to the bedroom where the twin daughters wait, eyes wide, as she gently places their brother between them. She tells them that she must go to the Aranzadi's, eight miles distant. It will be late when she returns, but they must remain in the bed. They must not move, and they must not make noise, but most of all they cannot go into the kitchen. The smallest cries that she is thirsty but is silenced by her mother's look.

She reins in the large bay and wheels him around the motorized carriage. The automobile is his, and she does not trust it. The bay is spooked by the lightning that pounds the black edges of the Big Horns. The wind is up, and it might rain; the buffalo grass sways like an undulating ocean of flax and seed. Tired as she is, she hopes for rain. She drives her naked heels into the horse's flanks and gathers herself low behind his neck. There is only one two-track back to the main road and the nearest phone.

The rhythm of the horse's hooves on the hard ground lulls her; she tries to stay on, gripping the hair of the horse's withers. The first drops of rain hit like mercury dimes as she makes the rise overlooking the neighboring ranch house. There are no lights, but they will understand.

The hard flat drops of the high-altitude rain continue to strike at her as she urges the horse faster down the slippery track. Lightning flashes again, and the horse sidesteps in the yard, his stocking feet glowing like spats. She has started off, but the horse has taken her by surprise, and she tumbles forward. He backs away, dragging her as he goes. She holds to the single rein as the horse shakes his head up and down in an attempt to be free. He stops when she speaks to him in the language her husband had never tried to know. *"Ialgi hadi kampora . . ."*

She drags herself up toward the door and stumbles at the steps, is pounded by the rain, and shakes with the chill of the cold water as it streams from her hair and onto her skin. Her muscles contract, and it is all she can do to drop a clenched hand against the screen door. She cries and tries to strike the door again but can't. Her head sinks to the step, and she rests there; it cannot end like this, it must not. She stirs, but her hair clings to her broken face, and her joints ache with the strain. Whatever was there, whatever had pushed her to this point, is washing away with the cold wind and rain. She pulls her legs and arms in to protect them, to allow them rest.

There is a sound from within the house, and the door swings wide. A kerosene lantern shines on her with the pointillist pattern of the reinforced screen. Someone is kneeling now, lowering himself to her view and reaching out a thin and gentle hand. As his fingers close around her shoulder, she raises her head and, shivering with the last strains of energy she can afford, she speaks. *"Polizia constabule . . . Lucian."*

He smoked his pipe for a while and then got up quietly, positioning his leg, and moved around to the bar. He pulled a paper filter from a stack on the shelves, placed it in the maker at the bar back, pulled the urn from the burner, and filled it with water from the small bar sink. "You ever seen a man cut like that? Ear to ear?"

"No, not like that."

He nodded, poured the water into the machine, and placed it back on the heating element. "If you cut an artery completely through, it tries to heal itself by pinching off but, if you've got the touch, you only cut the blood vessel halfway so it keeps bleeding until there's nothing left to bleed."

"Lucian, this was a clear case of domestic abuse and self-defense."

He shook his head as the coffee began to percolate. "Not in 1951."

I waited. "I thought you said it was '52."

"That's when the goddamned Indians stole the car out of the irrigation pond Isaac and I stuck it in down on Four Brothers." He crossed his arms and leaned against the bar. "How's I supposed to know it was gonna be a drought summer?"

"Why the elaborate charade with Marcos down in Vista Verde?"

"She wanted him alive."

"Why didn't she just file for abandonment?"

He shrugged. "Religion."

I waited. "Bloomfield was in on this?" He looked away for a moment and didn't speak. "He's in a room over at Durant Memorial." I got Lucian's undivided attention. "He tried to drive to Billings last night to assist in Mari's autopsy and wrecked his car near Sheridan."

Lucian nodded. "She needed medical attention, and I knew he would understand." He looked at me. "He all right?"

"Yep." I sat on the stool opposite him. "Lucian, her heart gave out."

"I don't believe that."

I thought about the things I had believed when my wife died, complicated, hurtful things, and how the only thing that seemed to help was to have somebody listen. I glanced back over at him as he waited for me. "Did you see anything that night?"

"No."

"Would you tell me if you had?"

"Yes, goddamn it. I ain't got nothin' to hide."

"You have up to now."

He shook his head and turned around, pulled two cups from the cluster below the coffeemaker, and poured us a fresh pair. He pushed one of the cups toward me with his fingertips. "That's my personal life."

"Your personal life is this case." The stillness was back, and I was sure he was thinking about the heart that had failed. I thought about bringing up Isaac Bloomfield's theories on substance abuse, advanced venereal disease, and hereditary predisposition but, if Mari was resting easier in Lucian's mind, now was no time to trouble the waters.

When I looked back up, he was studying me. "So, you gonna call in the F B of I on me or what?"

I took a sip of my coffee. "I'm thinking."

He nodded. "Well, you think about this while you're thinkin'. You know what a jury can do. You remember what they did for Melissa Little Bird."

The coffee was hot, or maybe I'd lost my taste for it. I sat the mug back on the surface of the bar and shook my head. "Not the same." I waited a moment then stood up and buttoned my coat. "I have to go to work."

He looked at me as I crossed to the door with Dog in tow. "Big murder investigation?"

"Something like that."

He sat the mug back on the bar. "Which one?"

I looked at the floor and pushed the door open to let Dog out. "I'll let you know."

It was getting colder, so I flipped the collar up on my jacket and scrunched my neck down for cover. So, he didn't do it, at least not technically. He just covered it up or, in the parlance of the law, he was an accessory after the fact, which could get you from twelve to seventeen. I tried to think about how things had changed in our little corner of the world in fifty years. I thought of Lucian rumbling around the county in the old, upside-down bathtub of a Nash, meting out justice with a tin badge, a long-barreled .38-caliber revolver, and a shovel. I had developed my own ideas about murder from a Vietnamese Colonel COSVN who labeled it as the worst of crimes because once you had taken a life it could not be replaced. He had also stated that Ngo Dinh Diem was an idiot, but he was our idiot, one of the statements I had chosen not to take to heart. All in all, murder was a complicated and dirty business that took up a lot of emotional space in your soul; I don't think Lucian could have tolerated that kind of occupancy.

I shifted my thoughts to Mari Baroja. I wondered if she would have preferred to die in one of the small rooms in the Euskadi Hotel rather than in Room 42 of the Durant Home for Assisted Living. Some of their lunches must have been longer than their three-hour marriage. I thought about the effect she might have made on the old sheriff's life had she been able to remain nestled there, the good she would have probably done, the holes in his tattered sails that could have been filled. Why hadn't they remarried? Religion, maybe, but perhaps the clandestine weight of Charlie Nurburn had been too much. Things like that have a way of gathering momentum until there simply isn't a way of dealing with them in one lifetime. Maybe they were two different people by then. Maybe it was that those three hours weren't to be tampered with, that those three hours for those two people had been enough. Some fires can't bear to dampen and can provide heat even from the distance of time.

As soon as I closed the door of the truck and fired her up, I spotted a well-worn unit of the Absaroka County Sheriff's Department sliding down Main Street. She was driving too fast, like she always did, but didn't stop beside me; rather, she pulled around and parked. She got out, ducked her head against her collar, and trudged through the snow with a silent determination. She stood beside the window, and I noticed a piece of folded paper in her gloved hands. I hit the button, but the window only made a brief herniated sound; it was apparently frozen shut. She raised an eyebrow, then calmly unfolded the paper in her hands and slammed the face of it against the glass. It was a fax from the medical examiner's office in Billings, and it said that Mari Baroja had died of complications due to naphthalene poisoning.

"Mothballs?"

We both stared at the speakerphone on my desk. "It's where the smell comes from but, for it to be toxic, it has to be ingested. It forces the hemoglobin out, causing kidney damage and other assorted niceties." We continued to stare at the little plastic speaker cover. "Some people have a hereditary deficiency of glucose-6-phosphate dehydrogenate that makes them particularly susceptible to naphthalene poisoning. Mari Baroja was in that group. It's usually in people of Mediterranean descent, and Basques are on the list."

I shook my head and looked at Vic who seemed lost also. "How would someone know that?"

"The same deficiency makes them sensitive to aspirin. If somebody knew that, it would give them a pretty good indication."

I thought about the stuffed and golden brown crow I was preparing to ingest. "There's no chance that this could be something else?"

"None." The little speaker was silent for a moment. "The amount in her kidneys was miniscule, but her medical records showed that the deficiency was diagnosed back in the forties."

"What medical records?"

"The ones I had faxed up from your hospital."

"Who was the attending physician?"

There was a brief pause as he shuffled some papers. "You know, doctors really do have the worst handwriting." I waited. "I. Brumfield ring a bell?"

"Isaac Bloomfield." I looked up at Vic; I had already filled her in on the Bloomfield front. "Yep, that's the personal physician of the decedent."

"I guess you need to go talk to him." I thanked Bill McDermott, punched the button, and looked back up at my smiling deputy.

"I'm glad I'm not you right now." She started to get up and head for her own office as somebody opened the front door. I assumed it was Ruby. "Sancho is out at Sonny George's checking the Mercedes. Do you really think somebody tried to kill the Doc?"

I took a breath. "I don't know, but the accident sure seems fishy."

She was grinning, enjoying my quandary. "You want me to head over to that hotbed of illegal activity, the Durant Home for . . . ?"

"Do me a favor first?" I couldn't resist, she was looking so satisfied with herself. I stood and pulled the Post-it from my shirt pocket and handed it to her. "Call Charlie Nurburn down in Vista Verde and ask him when he's going to be up here next?"

She took the slip of paper and frowned at me. "You don't think we have more important things to do?"

I smiled back. "It'll just take you a second." She gave me the finger as I passed her on the way to Ruby's desk. Dog was already there. "Isn't Cady supposed to arrive sometime this afternoon?"

"All the flights from Denver have been canceled."

I looked down at her, hoping what I had heard was wrong. "What?"

"All the flights from Denver have been canceled, and I'm not even sure if she made it there yet."

"I better call."

She held the receiver up to show me. "What do you think I'm doing?" I glanced at my pocket watch as Ruby watched me. "Got an important meeting?"

I continued to watch my sweep second hand. "No, but I'm expecting an explosion any time now."

"*Fuck me!*" It resonated down the hallway from her office and, a moment later, my highly agitated deputy was standing beside me and requesting a private audience in chambers. I looked back at Ruby. "Let me know what's happening with Cady."

She smiled. "You bet."

"He's dead."

"No shit."

"But Lucian didn't kill him."

She rolled her eyes. "Sure he didn't, he's too busy providing his answering service."

"She did it."

Her eyes widened. "She did it?" I told her the story just as Lucian had told me and watched as she sat there. "Ugh." She looked at the fax on my desk. "I guess that puts a whole new profile on our victim, huh?"

"That and, from what the foreman told me, she was worth millions."

"Methane?"

"Yep."

She pursed her lips. "By the way, your buddy stopped by this morning."

"Which buddy?"

"Cecil Keller, the roustabout that shot his foreman? Big fucker with bad teeth? Nice of you to give me the heads-up on that one. He said you wanted him to come in and have a little chat." I smiled. "Go ahead and smirk. No current wants or warrants, but I confiscated the weapon and had a little talk with him about resolving his conflicts."

I felt the muscles pull at the corner of my mouth. "I forgot about him."

She shook her head. "You know, I'm glad I'm around, considering the laissez-faire attitude the two previous administrations seem to have taken toward capital crimes."

I looked at the fax. "Yep, well, I guess the salad days are over."

She grew quiet. "I'll go over to the home. Where are you headed?"

"I figured I'd go over to the hospital and talk to Isaac, then I guess I'll start with the family by telling Lana that somebody poisoned her grandmother." She started out. "Hey?" She turned back. "There were some cookies on the floor beside her bed. I know it all sounds very Dorothy Sayers, but I thought I'd mention it."

"And I'll check the drawers for mothballs. Maybe Mari was schnockered and thought they were breath mints."

Isaac Bloomfield wasn't in his room, but he wasn't hard to find; he was snoring in the staff lounge with a large bandage running from his temple and around his ear. I sat in the chair opposite his sofa, unbuttoned my coat, and placed my hat on my knee. The old guy snored like a Husquavarna chainsaw. "Isaac?" I said it three times before he heard me.

"Walter?"

"How come you're not in your room?"

"I'm more comfortable here." He leaned in and took my hands. "I understand I owe you my life?"

I shrugged. "I almost got both of us killed, if that's what you mean."

He shook his head at my inability to accept thanks. "How is my car?"

"Totaled." I leaned back and watched him. "Isaac, last night you said the brakes failed."

"Yes?"

"You're sure of that?"

"Yes."

I took a deep breath and went on, before he could interrupt. "Isaac, did Mari have a deficiency of glucose-6-phosphate dehydrogenate?"

He sat up slowly and looked at me, after rubbing his eyes and putting on his glasses. There was a very long pause. "Naphthalene poisoning?" I nodded. "Clever."

"Why is that?"

"She was a lifetime smoker, it would have made the trace elements difficult to discover, along with the miniscule amount to be effective due to the deficiency."

I leaned back in the chair. "You learn something every day."

"But it must be ingested to be poison. That would create a difficulty under most situations, but Mari's sense of smell had long been deadened." He thought for a moment. "We discovered her reaction to aspirin during one of her clinic visits, and it was a textbook response. I induced vomiting with a syrup of ipecac, since her respiration was not depressed, and then insisted on further testing." He smiled and continued to look at me. "This makes things difficult for you, doesn't it?"

"How do you mean?"

"You are looking for someone who knew her medical history." He continued to smile. "If I were you, I would suspect me but, in that I am innocent, I have nothing to fear from your suspicions. So, I give them and you my blessing." He leaned forward and again took my hands in his. "Find who murdered her, Walter. She suffered enough in life; there is no reason she should have to bear this final indignity."

I took Isaac off the unofficial suspect list on my way out to the truck. Dog was waiting, so I let him out to pee and stretch his legs. I leaned against the Bullet and thought about all the Barojas I was going to have to contact in the next few hours. I loaded Dog up and headed out to buy some overdue baked goods.

Someone hadn't been content to wait for the old woman to die, and all the suspects smacked of being too obvious. That's how it worked, though. Motive and opportunity rode along like two out of four apocalyptic equestrians, grinning with their bony death heads at us lesser humans as we fumbled along, refusing to believe the obvious.

I had eaten the ruggelach, and I didn't die.

I parked the truck and noticed a single set of footprints going in but none leaving. Lana must have walked. I opened the door and carefully shut it against the compacted snow at the sill. She needed to shovel. The bell at the top of the door tinkled, but no one appeared. I took a step in as I followed the dog but stopped to knock some of the accumulated snow from my hat and shoulders and to breathe in the fragrance of rising yeast and baking bread. The only sound was the quiet hum of the coolers and the winds of forced-air heating.

Dog had advanced down the long counter but had stopped at the end. His head dropped, and he stared at the small seating area in the back. I was surprised when he retreated a step or two, froze and growled, and looked at something around the corner. "Dog?"

It took about two strides to get to Lana Baroja who was lying at the top of the steps to the basement in a considerable amount of blood. Spikes of black hair were matted at the back of her head where there was a deep wound. One arm was turned while the other shot off to the side in an unnatural position.

I checked her pulse; the rhythm was fast. Tachycardia—no way to know the pressure. She was pale, bluish, and clammy, with a light sweat, classic symptoms of shock.

The numbers started up like an adding machine in my head; large bold numbers that stated simply that one third of the victims of head injury are unconscious and that more than 80 percent of the total deaths came from this group; that a full 50 percent of the individuals who could speak at some point after their injury and later died could have been saved with immediate treatment. I thought back to Isaac Bloomfield on the highway, my recently accumulated experience, and momentarily considered another line of work.

I checked her neck, but nothing seemed broken. I made the decision I had been making a lot of lately and scooped her up, yanking a tablecloth from the nearest table and wrapping it around her, being careful to support her head. As I made my way toward the door, Dog followed.

I had her at Durant Memorial in four minutes.

A doctor I didn't recognize pushed me away from the gurney as he felt the region at the back of her head, palpating the lacerations and bruising, checking for signs of hemorrhage behind the eardrums, and shining a light into her eyes to see if the pupils were equal and reactive. I wasn't surprised when the damaged Isaac Bloomfield appeared and called for a CT scan to examine her brain and the inner lining of her skull for evidence of the subdural hematoma he knew was there. I wasn't surprised when he called for two units of blood as they rushed her into the operating room, nor was I surprised that A-negative was what he asked for, without consulting any files or records. I wasn't surprised as I watched the snow from the waiting-room windows and felt the cold creep in from a winter that showed no signs of ending.

I was surprised when Isaac Bloomfield reappeared after twenty minutes and told me that Lana Baroja would live.

I reached out and pulled her hand down; it seemed that she was probing the wound a little too aggressively. "No idea, huh?"

She smiled, but I think it hurt. "No."

I looked into her eyes again, but the pupils seemed normal; they must not have given her any drugs because of the head trauma. Even in the gauze turban, she was looking pretty good; amazing what youth can do. "How do you think they got in then?"

She was studying me now. "I don't know. Maybe I didn't get the door relocked." I guess I made a face. "What?"

"No footprints and, odds are, they wouldn't rely on you accidentally leaving the door ajar. Anybody besides you have keys to the place?"

She looked at me for a second longer than necessary but then answered. "Nobody."

"Who rented you the space?"

"Elizabeth Banks at Clear Creek Realty."

I made a mental note to call Beebee. "Have you heard from your aunts in the last few days?"

"Kay called and said that Carol was flying in from Miami and that we have to have a family meeting on Thursday; something about the Will."

"Today?"

She looked sheepish, and it was a look that agreed with her. "Is it Thursday?"

"Yep, I think they knocked Wednesday out of you." I was silent for a moment too long, and she blinked and looked at me. They were fine dark eyes giving a clear view into a very fine mind that continued to operate despite recent abuse. "I've got something to tell you, Lana." It hung there between us as the baseboard heaters ticked in the private room.

"It's about my grandmother?"

"Yep, it is." She didn't move as I told her about the evidence we had assembled; instead, her attention shifted to the knees that were pulled up to provide a resting place for her crossed arms. As I talked, it seemed as though she was drawing in, growing smaller as the world grew colder. I calculated the risk and decided to go ahead. "Lana, do you know about the methane development that's going on down on your grandmother's place?"

Thought clouded her eyes for a moment. "Kay is in charge of the estate, but I'm not sure. Carol might be in charge of the ranch. There's a manager who lives in the old house on Four Brothers." She shrugged. "I really don't know." She was still looking at me when I glanced back up. "You think the same person that killed my grandmother tried to kill me?"

I rubbed my face and looked through my fingers. "I'd rather be chasing one killer than two; it gives me better odds."

I got all the way to the front desk before Vic accosted me. She was eating an almond cookie. "So did you have to step on every one of the fucking footprints at the bakery?"

"I didn't want it to be too easy for you." I leaned against the receptionist's desk. "I'm assuming you checked those?"

She winked and pulled two more out of a ziplock bag and held them out to me. "That's what I'm doing now. Want one?"

I shook my head. "I'll wait till the report's in."

She shrugged and ate another cookie. "Naphthalene's easy to trace in food. The smell is hard to hide."

"Where's the high-altitude Mexican?"

"I left him at the office. He went there from Sonny George's."

"Anything at the junkyard?"

I noticed she wasn't smiling. "The bleeders on both the front and rear brakes had been loosened just enough for the fluid to escape. I called Fred Ray over at the Sinclair station, and he said he did a full brake job on the Mercedes about two months ago, and there is no way the car could have lasted that long with them loose."

I took a deep breath. "I'll need to talk to Sancho."

"He's going through the boxes and cataloging the crap from Mari Baroja's room which, I might add, is a lot of crap cataloging." She looked off toward the windows and casually walked over to the waiting room to watch the snowfall. "Letters, boxes, and boxes of letters, notes, and telegrams. You name it. If it was written, she kept it."

"That may be handy."

"Yeah, we got her whole life in boxes." She turned, and her eyes locked onto mine. "Note the phrase whole life in boxes and note that Sancho is at the office. When we got there this morning, there were the cartons. We found out that the staff at the Durant Home for Assisted Living had taken it upon themselves to box up Mari Baroja's life, send it to us, and clean the fucking room."

I could feel my jaw muscles tightening. "I guess they didn't notice the bright yellow tape across the door that says SHERIFF'S BARRICADE DO NOT CROSS?"

"Maybe they can't read." She cocked her head and continued to look at me. "Are you going to get really mad? 'Cause I like it when you get really mad."

I ignored her. "Anything in the letter boxes?"

"Well, we're just getting started, and a lot of it's in Basque, so Sancho's the only man for the job. A couple of letters from Northern Rockies Energy Exploration, pretty straight forward stuff, and all of it from Baroja-Calloway down in Miami."

She waited, the tarnished gold of her eyes lying heavily upon me. Then she pulled what looked like a stack of assorted letters from her other jacket pocket. They were old and tied together with a faded piece of red fringe that had been pulled from the edge of a scarf. It looked like the one that had blown across the Powder River and had snagged on the European blue sage that I had seen in my dream. I carefully took the stack of thin paper and looked down at the address: Room 201, The Euskadi Hotel, Durant. In a swirling hand, the letters were addressed from Lucian.

"I thought you might want these."

I nodded and looked at the fragile letters with the faded words and the worn fuzzy edges. Words like accessory to commit fraud, conspiracy, tampering, and a myriad of others hung there in the small space between us. I glanced up at her, but she was watching the snow, and I stood there for a moment, looking at the reflection in her eyes before quietly shoving the letters in my own jacket pocket.

She remained silent for a moment, then reached out to place the tip of her forefinger against the glass, and I saw her as a child, the kind of child who had to touch everything, the kind of child you couldn't say no to. I had a child like that and reminded myself to ask Ruby if I could expect Cady by Christmas. "So, are you going to go over to the Home for Assisted Living and assist the staff in an ass-chewing or what?"

I ignored her some more. "No moth balls?"

She licked her cookie-crumb lips. "No moth balls." She held the bag out to me again. "Last one." She smiled. "So . . . you think we should have a look at Mari Baroja's last Will and Testament?"

I looked through the glass doors of the hospital at the gentle but ever-falling precipitation. "We should be thankful for the snow, it's probably the only thing that's holding Baroja-Lofton-Baroja-Calloway at bay."

"Oh, the hyphen-harpies called."

I sighed. "When?"

She finished off the last almond cookie and stuffed the bag in the inside pocket of her coat. "This morning. I'm assuming they are assembling for the charge."

"Well, that's my problem. If there's nothing over at the bakery, then I guess you should go back to the home. Get the names of everybody who went into that room. Start fingerprinting with the easy stuff, get what you can from contrasting powder and silicon lifts, superglue fuming, and simple photography. Hit the AFIS. It's a long shot, but you never know." She was already nodding and smiling. "What?"

"I love it when you talk dirty."

I nodded and self-consciously adjusted the brim of my hat. "I want the names of everybody who was in that room, and I want all of them in my office at exactly 3:45 or I come and get them. Remind them that if I have to come and get them that I will not be happy. We will impress upon them the seriousness of our line of work by fingerprinting all of them in the jail."

She looked at her watch. "What're you going to do between now and 3:45?"

"Find the Will."

She continued to smile. "The will to what?"

"That would be Jarrard and Straub."

"That was your old firm. Do you remember any of the details?"

He reshaped the corner of his mustache and smiled. "It was not a close relationship. I think the law made her uneasy."

Amen.

"When was her Will attested?"

"Which one?"

I studied him for a moment. "Oh, now why do I not like the sound of that?"

Vern leaned back in his chair and laced his fingers behind his head. "She was of a mercurial disposition and, according to her mood toward her children and grandchild . . ." He paused. "This is all completely off the cuff and an old cuff at that. You understand that I had already left the firm?" I nodded for official purposes while he captured the front of his mustache in his lower lip and thought. "The last one that I saw was a three-way split, straight up the middle."

I wondered about the judge's ideas on percentages. "Which three?"

"Carol, Kay, and Lana. I assume she didn't care for David's wife."

"Executor of the estate?"

"Carol, I think."

I thought for a moment and went on. "You know about the methane development down on Four Brothers?" I waited, but he didn't respond. "About a million a week. It's going to complicate matters, especially since Mari Baroja died of naphthalene poisoning." He didn't say anything, so I told him what I wanted. "Vern, I'm about to be ass-deep in lawyers, but I need room to work. Are you going to help me out with this?"

His eyes drifted to the window that overlooked Main Street where I'm sure the vision of Mari Baroja sauntered down the snow-covered sidewalk in a blue polka-dot sundress and clunky heels. I wasn't sure if the judge's daydreams allowed for current weather conditions. "What can I do to help you?"

"I need a peek at that Will."

Vern nodded out the window. "I'll call Kyle Straub." He looked at me. "You need this now?"

"Yes." I waited as the judge made a telephone call. "Well, I have some good news and some bad news." It didn't sound like the first time the judge had expressed this particular sentiment. "He says the reading of the Will is in his office today at 5:00 and that you are more than welcome to attend."

"Did I mention that Lana Baroja is over at Durant Memorial with a blunt trauma wound to the head, a probable victim of attempted homicide, and that somebody may have attempted to kill Isaac Bloomfield as well?"

The judge stalled out there for a second but got going again pretty quickly. "No, you did not."

"I don't suppose Kyle would like to exchange venue for the hospital?"

"He's under no obligation."

I sighed; dealing with lawyers always made me tired. "What's the good news?"

"That was the good news."

I sighed again. "What's the bad news?"

"As suspected, Mari Baroja viewed revising her will as something of an avocation."

I couldn't risk sighing again; I was losing too much air. "Two quick questions: how many and when was the last?"

"Fourteen, and the latest revision was last Friday afternoon."

I went ahead and sighed again; maybe my lungs would collapse, and Vic and Sancho could handle the whole thing. "Any idea who attested it?"

He glanced up at the aged Seth Thomas on the wall, which was not unlike the one in my office. I figured a clock salesman at the turn of the last century must have made out like a bandit in this county. "I imagine you will find out at 5:00."

I got up and shook my head. "If you talk to Kyle Straub again, remind him that I'm going to start taking a personal interest in his miseries." As I went down the steps, I turned and looked at him through the doorway. "And I'm considering yours."

He closed his eyes and nodded slowly. "Always comforting to know one is in your thoughts, Walter."

I'd have never made it as a lawyer.

It was just past 3:15, and I was hungry, but I knew there was supposed to be a small crowd waiting for me at the jail in half an hour. There was no time to eat, but I had an extra twenty minutes, so I rolled past Clear Creek Realty. Beth Banks, or Beebee as the locals had called her as long as I'd been aware, was attempting to lodge her considerable girth into a spanking new Cadillac. I smiled at her as I pushed the button on the passenger window and watched as about a cubic foot of snow fell inside my truck; I really had to get some seat covers. "Hey, Beebee."

She giggled. "Uh-oh, what have I done now?" She was wearing a flaming red wool coat, and the flakes were beginning to accumulate in her platinum blond hair.

I left the motor running, so she wouldn't think I was going to hold her for long. "Beebee, did you lease that building next to Evans's to Lana Baroja?"

She thought. "Yes, about three months ago." The smile faded a little. "Is there a problem?"

I thought it best to keep things simple. "Somebody broke into the place, and I'm thinking that they might have had keys. I was wondering if you knew of any other sets?"

"No, but I'll check." She thought for a moment. "I don't know if there were any other keys to that building, but it's always a good idea to change the locks in a new business." The smile returned. "Like I have to tell you that."

There was a substantial group of vehicles in the office parking lot; I guess Vic had been able to corral all the usual administrators for the mass imprinting. I put on my serious face which, I'm told by some, makes me look like I am mildly constipated and walked in, ignoring them and standing at Ruby's desk. She was the first to speak, Dog by her side. "Walt . . ."

I whipped my hat off and spoke in what my father used to refer to as a full field voice. "Damn it." Dog rolled his eyes up in a worried look at my tone of voice. I winked at Ruby, and she almost smiled. "Get me Vern Selby on line one, and tell him that I want to know the sentencing guidelines on obstruction of justice."

She nodded. "First degree?"

I almost broke, but bit my lip and nodded back. She didn't mention the chair or the big house, so I made a safe escape into my office and slammed the door behind me with a thunderous clap. The knob came off in my hand. I bent down and looked at the mechanism still imbedded in the core of the wood and hoped somebody would come in before too long. I tossed the knob on my desk and sat down to wait.

After a few moments, the intercom buzzed on my phone. I punched the button, "What?" I made sure it was loud enough for them to hear in the reception area.

"Walt, Louis Gilbert and the people from the Home for Assisted Living are here."

"Tell them I want them in my office, right now." I scrambled around and picked up Saizarbitoria's folder, attempted to look like a captain of destiny, and waited a few more moments. Somebody quietly knocked against the door, and I was relieved that it pushed open a little with the knock. "Come in."

Louis was talking as he opened it and looked at the hole where my doorknob used to be. "Walt, this is all just a big mistake."

"I hope so." I didn't sound as angry; it was a hard emotion for me to sustain.

There was a small crowd behind him, and I recognized Jennifer Felson and Joe Lesky for starters. "There was a memo we put out saying that unoccupied rooms should be cleared in twenty-four hours." Louis introduced a small, frightened old woman in the back of the group, Indian and probably Crow. "Anna Walks Over Ice thought she heard Joe tell Jennifer that that meant all rooms, including Room 42, but Joe doesn't remember having that conversation with Jennifer." Louis nodded toward the elderly woman. "She doesn't understand English very well."

I stared at the blotter on my desk. "Who cleaned the room?"

Louis was quick to speak. "Anna." It is a long-standing western tradition—when in doubt, blame the Indian.

I looked at the group as they looked at each other. "Jennifer, you were on duty?"

She looked up and slightly raised her hand. "Yes."

"Joe?" He raised his hand, too, and I started feeling like I was teaching class. I sighed. "Okay, you don't have to raise your hands. Both of you were on duty?"

Joe was eager to clear things up. "It was near the shift change. I come in at ten o'clock, but I had some extra work to do, so I came in early."

"And you found her, Jennifer?"

She started to raise her hand but stopped herself. "Yes, I was doing the eight P.M. rounds."

"Did you have any contact with her earlier in the evening?" She nodded. "What was she doing?"

"Reading. She liked to read."

"Was she eating or drinking anything?"

"She had some cookies."

I wondered if Vic had eaten all the evidence. "Anything else?"

Joe piped up, "She always had a glass of Metamucil in the evenings as a fiber supplement."

"Who mixed that up for her?"

Joe shrugged. "I did."

"Did she eat or drink anything else that evening?"

They all looked at each other, and Louis was the first to speak. "She probably had her dinner at six with the rest of the clients." He looked puzzled. "Do you think something disagreed with her?"

I looked at all their faces. "Mari Baroja was poisoned."

Jennifer crossed herself, Louis stared at me in shock, and Joe paused and then translated to Walks Over Ice. They all looked sad, but they didn't look like killers; they looked like people that cared a lot and got paid very little for their concern. The Indian woman said something to Joe, who looked at me, shrugged, and translated. "She says she will pray for Mrs. Baroja."

We all sat there in silence for a moment.

The shock was still in Louis's voice when he spoke. "Walt, this is horrible."

"Yep, that's the official view as well." I studied them a while longer. "You can see how important this is?" They all nodded again. "Joe, do you have the Metamucil container?"

They all joined me in looking at Joe as his eyes widened. "Yes. Do you . . . ? I mean, do you think . . . ?" They all looked worried, images of other patients flopping around on the floor crowded in on them.

"I don't think there's anything to worry about. The amount of this particular poison wouldn't have an effect on most people." I leaned back in my chair. "I'm going to need the can of stuff that was used to mix up her dose for that night. I'm also assuming that her meds would be with her personal effects?" Louis nodded. "Were there any glasses or plates left in her room?" After a brief conference, it was ascertained that there had been but that they had all been run through the dishwasher and were now perfectly safe.

There didn't seem to be any more questions to ask, so I invited them to go down to the jail to be fingerprinted and called Vic to ask her to accompany them back to the home after she finished to collect the rest of the evidence.

It was 4:15, and I had three-quarters of an hour before they read the Will, so I punched the intercom. Ruby answered, "Are you through terrifying the people from the old folks home?"

"Laugh it up, I'm sending you there next. Do we have anything to eat?"

"Potpies in the jail refrigerator."

It didn't sound like it would hit the spot. "Vic didn't bring any bread back from the bakery?"

There was a pause. "No, that would constitute stealing, and we try and refrain from that type of activity within our sheriff's department." There was a murmuring on the other end. "But somebody just came in, and he says he's willing to buy you a late lunch-early dinner as long as it doesn't come in a bag.

I put my hat back on and hurried out before the Cheyenne Nation changed his mind. As a precautionary measure, I left my office door open.

He was staring at his chicken-fried steak sandwich; the long dark hair hid his face and muffled his voice. "How many murders have we had in this county since you became sheriff?"

I counted up quickly, then recounted. "Five."

"Three in the last month?"

"Yep."

He picked up the sandwich and looked at it. "You should retire . . . quickly."

I chewed on my usual as Dorothy came over and poured us more iced tea. "It's very tempting to go with the lawyers."

"They have the most to gain." He growled it, the way he always did when talking about violence. "Assuming Lana did not beat her own brains out with a tire iron . . ." The chief cook and bottle washer looked over at the brave, and they both nodded.

I looked at them and wondered if people in other parts of the country were as smart-ass as the ones that I had to put up with. "You two are a lot of help." Dorothy shrugged and went back to work. I took a sip of my iced tea and looked at the Bear.

He chewed. "Tell me about the timing on naphthalene poisoning."

"Five to twenty minutes, so it had to be introduced to the victim less than a half an hour before her death."

"Then it had to be someone who saw her at the home that night."

"Possibly, but it could have been left for her in some form of consumable; of course, they washed all the glasses and dishes that were in her room." I turned and caught Dorothy's eye. "I need your phone." She brought it over and sat it in front of me. I looked at Henry. "Why are you in town during a blizzard?"

He looked out the window behind us. "In case you have not noticed, it has stopped."

I turned, and it had. "I've been kind of busy."

He sat the glass down and continued. "I needed filing supplies and discs for the photo collection I am working on."

I went ahead and dialed the number of the jail. "How's that going?"

The lines at the corner of his lips pulled south, pinning his mouth like a pup tent. "The problem with leading Indians is you are never quite sure if they are following or chasing you."

The telephone began ringing. "Absaroka County Sheriff's Department, Officer Saizarbitoria speaking. How may I help you?"

I stared at the phone. "Wow." I jumped in before he could deliver another schpiel. "Sancho, it's me. Is Vic around?"

"No, she's done fingerprinting and went with the staff over to the Home for Assisted Living."

I had seen her fingerprint before; with her Philadelphia technique, I was pretty sure she was the fastest fingerprinter in the West. "How long do you think it will take you to go through the boxes?"

"I'll be done tonight."

That's when his trial period would be over, and I suspected he would hightail it back to Rawlins after that. I waited for a moment and then spoke again. "Hey, Troop? I want you to know that what you're doing is important, and I really appreciate it." He didn't say anything. "About Isaac's car, what makes you think somebody fooled with it?"

"There was brake fluid all over the place, and two of the bleeder valves were left just loose enough to leak over a short period of time." He paused for a moment. "It was a front wheel and a back one. The car has a two-reservoir master cylinder, so it could only fail if both systems lost pressure. It just seems like too much of a coincidence."

"You sound pretty sure."

"My father was a shade-tree mechanic his whole life. It's something I'd know."

I hung up the phone and looked at the Bear. He had put his sandwich down but continued to chew. "Was that Anna Walks Over Ice in your office?"

I nodded and started to take another bite of mine but sat it back down. "She works at the home." I drank the last of my iced tea and glanced over at Dorothy. "She doesn't speak English?"

"No. Some of the elders believed it diluted your power." He drew a deep breath. "She did not speak when she saw me."

I continued to look at the 220-pound man who looked like he could have stepped from a Curtis photograph or a Remington oil. "You're kind of hard to miss."

"Perhaps."

"If you get a chance, would you talk to her?" It seemed like I was always asking the Bear to help me out in an unofficial capacity. I smiled. "You speak Crow well enough not to embarrass yourself?"

He nodded. *"Chiwaxxo diataale, baalaax bishee."* He stood and reached for his long leather coat hanging on the hook behind him, then turned and looked at me as he pulled it over his shoulders. "Anything else?" I was disappointed that he was leaving; I was just remembering the pleasure of his company. I suppose he read my disappointment. "Where are they reading the Will?"

"Jarrard and Straub, on the corner of Main and Gatchell."

He nodded. "Maybe I will stop by."

"Bring a lawyer, everybody else is."

His mouth stiffened before he flipped on his Wayfarers. "Perhaps I will."

He thumped me on the back and made me spill a little iced tea on my pants. One of the big bronze hands reached out to touch fingertips with Dorothy as she passed him. They did it with the casual assurance of professional basketball players. "Ha-ho, Queen Bee."

She nodded to him, and he swung the door open. She refilled my glass. "You paying for the Noble Savage?"

"Yep, he's working undercover."

He stood on the snow-laden sidewalk and raised his arms to the brief strands of sunshine cascading down on Main. His arms stayed stretched out, the duster splayed like wings, and the dark hair dropped across the black leather to the small of his back. He looked like a six-and-a-half-foot raven, gleaning what warmth he could from the available light in a full Technicolor moment.

"He looks it."

The war cry rattled the glass in the closed door.

Jarrard and Straub was the premier law office in the county, having been started by Jim Jarrard and Larry Straub back before Lexis-Nexis and an hourly rate above two hundred dollars. I was more comfortable in the old place with its partners' desks and tortoise shell lamps and quiet-voiced men. There used to be a remarkable mount of a bugling

elk that Larry had taken up near Rock Creek before it became un-
fashionable to sport such things on the wall of a law office. The elk,
of course, was gone, and all I saw were walnut-paneled walls with
tasteful watercolors of the area carefully illuminated by recessed
lighting.

"Good to see you, Walt."

"Hello, Kyle. Thanks for letting me sit in."

"No problem."

Sarcasm was lost on the man. "Where is everybody?"

"They're in the conference room upstairs. I just wanted to check a
few things with you before we went in." He stood there for a moment,
nodded and looked at the wall-to-wall carpeting. "If I were to give you
a copy of the Will now, would you still feel compelled to participate in
the reading?"

This was an unexpected turn. "Why would you do that?"

He crossed his arms and sat on the corner of his desk. "I have been
in communication with both Kay and Carol." He hugged himself a little tighter and continued, "With the Will being what it is, I think it
might be best for all concerned if you were not present at the time of
the reading."

I gave Kyle my undivided attention. "And why is that?"

"I think they may become agitated." He handed me a closed manila
envelope with the firm's address neatly affixed in the upper left-hand
corner. His eyes came up to mine. "You might tell Lana that I'll be by
later with a copy for her."

I nodded but, as I opened the door leading from Kyle's office to the
hallway from the reception area, what looked to be the entire Baroja-
Lofton-Calloway clan was headed our way. Since Kyle had not appeared on time, they had decided to go looking for him en masse. Kay
was in the lead, sweeping and clattering jewelry as she came, husband
in tow. A blowzier version of Kay, with a few more pounds of bosom,
was bringing up the rear in a full-length mink coat and what looked
like a full-body tan.

I rolled up the envelope and stuffed it in my coat pocket. "Hello."

Kay pulled up a stride away and looked past me. "Is this the reason we've been cooling our heels in your conference room?"

I leaned over and blocked her view. "I had some official business with Mr. Straub. I'm sorry for any inconvenience."

She stared directly at the manila tube sticking from my coat pocket. "Is that the Will?"

I turned to look at Kyle, figuring it was his play, but Kay actually started to snag the envelope from my pocket. I suppose if I'd had time to think about it, I wouldn't have grabbed her hand with so much force. She yanked back, and about twelve hundred dollars worth of silver, coral, and turquoise came off in my hand.

"You son of a bitch!"

I tried to give her her jewelry back, but she stepped away. I tried to hand it to her husband, but he backed away, too. I was getting ready to hang the Baroja-Lofton Collection on the doorknob when Carol, at least I assumed she was Carol, extended her hand, so I deposited the bracelets with her. "I'm sorry, I . . ."

"You son of a bitch!"

Tears were welling in Kay's eyes, and she clutched her hand as if she had just pulled it from a #16 bear trap; I had to admit it was a pretty good performance. I looked up and became aware of Henry standing with a young woman behind the Barojas in the overcrowded hallway. The young woman pushed her way through the lawyers and held up a piece of paper in a freshly manicured hand. "Division of criminal investigation. I'm looking for Sheriff Walter Longmire?" She was a tall redhead, long-legged, with an athletic figure and frighteningly direct gray eyes.

"Uh, that would be me."

She turned to regard me as the very red, full lips kicked to one side in painful annoyance. "I just flew through a blizzard to get up here at your request, Mr. Longmire. The least you could have done was to meet me at the airport." I looked up at the stone-faced Indian behind her as she stared at the ceiling and expulsed a strong gust of dissatisfaction. "Do you mind if we head back to your office to get me up to speed on things?"

If the Barojas had looked a little closer, they might have seen that the paper she was holding was an airline itinerary. When we got to the steps leading to the parking lot, she paused and cut loose with a toothsome grin. "Hello, Daddy."

9

"You identified yourself as division of criminal investigation."

She sat in the chair opposite my desk with her expensive Italian boots curled around its front legs, something she had done with her feet since first grade. "No, I didn't. I simply stated division of criminal investigation, period, and then said I was looking for you." She smiled and sipped the coffee Ruby had given her as she studied the Will.

I looked over at Henry who was sitting in the other chair and at Ruby, hovering in the doorway; neither of them was going to be of any help.

She glanced up but not at me. "Ruby, can you believe he hasn't said a word to me about how good I look?"

Ruby shook her head. "Shameful. Honey, you look great."

"Thank you." She flicked her eyes at me before returning to the document.

The phone rang, and Ruby disappeared after giving me a warning look. I glanced back at my daughter. "You can get into a lot of trouble . . ."

"You can get into a lot of trouble manhandling lawyers, but you don't see me dressing you down, do you?" She took another sip of her coffee, careful not to muss her lipstick. "Can you believe that woman was actually going to grab the Will out of Dad's pocket?" She turned. "For a professional, that seems like suspicious behavior, if you ask me."

I sighed and looked at my nameplate on the door, desperately trying to convince myself that I was there, even though no one seemed to be hearing me. "Does that Will say what I think it does?"

She cocked her head to one side and placed the Denver Broncos coffee cup on my desk. "The Testatrix, Mari Baroja, has bequeathed specifically a very large portion of tangible personal wealth and property to the beneficiary hereafter known as Lana Baroja." The lips pursed again. "Your little baker with the broken head is now a multimillionaire."

"What about the twins?"

Her mouth kicked to the side again. "Well, they didn't get chicken feed, but in comparison . . ." She looked up. "They got chicken feed."

"They'll contest it."

"They can try. It's not my field of expertise, but it looks like a good Will, a Revocable Living Trust with Mari as the Trustee and all properties placed in the Trust. Lana is the appointed Successor Trustee with very specific duties in how the inheritance should be divided. I guess with this amount of money, Ms. Baroja was trying to avoid probate." She flipped through the pages. "It's been transposed from the handwritten original, but that's included." She turned the pages around and showed me. "Mari Baroja had beautiful handwriting."

"Who attested it?"

"Two people, which is pretty much standard." She searched through the signing portions of the document. "Kyle . . . I can't make this out."

"Straub?"

"That's it."

"Her lawyer. Who's the other one?"

She smiled. "Uncle Lucian."

I was getting ready to take my hat off but froze as Henry and I looked at each other. "Does it make any difference if she was married and then divorced from one of the witnesses?"

She continued to scan the papers in her lap. "The Baroja woman was married to this Straub character?" Neither Henry nor I said anything and, after a moment, she looked up, her eyes wide. "No way. Uncle Lucian?"

I went ahead and tossed my hat on my desk. "I'll give you the details later. If it was annulled, does it make any difference?"

She shrugged. "Not if the annulment was legal; if it wasn't, it would still be an abandoned marriage and any subsequent marriage would undercut any previous claim." She looked back at the figures on the papers. "He should have stayed married to her."

"I don't believe he had much choice in the matter." I stayed quiet for a moment.

"It all keeps pointing back to the daughters, doesn't it?" I listened to the phone ring in the other room and hoped it was Vic. Cady watched me and anticipated my next question. "Are you wondering who gets the money if the little baker should meet with unforeseen circumstance?"

"It was on my mind."

She looked back at the Will. "The sisters."

Henry shifted his weight in the chair and looked at me. "Are there other family members?"

"Well, there's the priest who is Mari Baroja's cousin."

"Mari Baroja's father had three brothers, and they only had one other child among them?" He studied me. "For a very Catholic family that strikes me as unusual." He waited for a moment. "How about Charlie Nurburn?"

"Who is Charlie Nurburn?" She had been watching us like a tennis match.

"It's a long story."

"I believe he is just the sort that might have angry little bastards strung all up and down the Powder River."

I looked back at my daughter. "Stepchildren?"

"Nope, not unless adopted and stated in the Will."

Ruby appeared in the doorway. "Vic, line two." She disappeared.

I punched the conference button. "Absaroka County Sheriff's Department, Sheriff Walt Longmire speaking. How can I help you?" I thought I'd give Sancho's methods a try.

"What the fuck?"

I guess it lost something in the translation. "What've you got for me?"

"We have a problem."

I stared at the phone. "You mean besides the murder and the two attempted murders?"

"The can of Metamucil is missing."

I continued to stare at the little red light on the phone. "You've got to be kidding."

"No, I'm not kidding, and they're having a shit hemorrhage over here. You'd think that somebody stole one of the Dead Sea Scrolls or something."

"What the hell happened to it?"

"Jennifer Felson saw it yesterday. Jesus, Walt, it's a can of Metamucil. I can't believe our case is hinging on this."

I started wondering what, exactly, our case was hinging on. "I guess I need to come over to the old folks home?"

The line went dead, so I punched the button and looked at my daughter. Just shy of six feet, most of it leg, she ate like a tiger shark but never broke over 135 pounds. "I bet you're hungry?"

"Famished." She smiled, but it faded quickly. "I'd rather not eat at the home."

I looked over at Henry. "Do you mind?"

He glanced at her and then back to me. "Dinner with beautiful learned counsel?" He sighed. "I suppose not."

I helped her with her coat and looked down at her. "You've only been here for a few hours, and I'm already pawning you off." She put her arms around me and rested her head on my chest as I breathed in the scent of her hair.

"Daddy, I know what I'm going to get you for Christmas."

"What?"

She looked up at me through mascaraed lashes. "A razor."

I remembered all the hours we'd spent napping when she was a baby, her tiny body only covering a quarter of my chest; how she didn't speak for the first year and a half of her life, and how it seemed that she had been trying to catch up ever since.

She pulled back and smiled as I lowered a fuzzy cheek for a soft kiss. "I love you."

"I love you, too. It's wonderful to have you home." I let her go and watched as she swirled around the corner toward Ruby. Henry turned back after she was gone, and I reached for my hat. "How in the world did you get Cady a flight up from Denver?"

"Omar's Lear. He says the labor is gratis but that you owe him for the fuel. Merry Christmas." He took a deep breath. "I suppose the Bee is the only place open?"

"Lucky Dorothy, getting to see you twice in one day. What an embarrassment of riches."

It took me a little more than five minutes to get over to the den of iniquity. I had stopped off and bought a six-pack as a peace offering for Lucian; I figured I was going to run into him before too long, and it was better to be wrong with beer than just wrong.

I sat there in the parking lot of the home watching the ever-present Wyoming wind kick at the ridges of the drifts like a gale cutting the tops off waves. I sat there on my heated seat with the defrosters on high and stared at my mountains. I had liked California; it was a beautiful place, but my spirit developed a restlessness there that I couldn't seem to shake. I had liked Vietnam, except that native peoples were shooting at you all the time, kind of like Wyoming in the 1870s.

I gazed at the mountains and allowed my eyes to relax into the monochromatic landscape where the earth blended with the sky. There was a faint glow separating the two firmaments near Black Tooth, and it was almost like the moon had gotten hung up on the crumbling granite incisor.

I sighed, switched off the ignition, stuffed the keys in my coat pocket, and began the trudge into the home. When I got inside, the place was in turmoil with the soothing strains of Dean Martin's "Silver Bells" in the background. Vic was talking with Jennifer Felson, who always seemed on the verge of tears. I figured it was time to do a little social damage control.

I collapsed in a seat after I sat the brown paper bag of beer under the chair closest to me. "I didn't bring the rubber hoses, do you think we can find some here?" Jennifer smiled but still clutched a tattered Kleenex in her lap with shaking hands as her eyes continued to fill. "You know, they got Capone with a can of Metamucil." I studied the wall, trying to give Jennifer a little room. "You saw the container yesterday?" She nodded. "Who's been in contact with it since then?"

She slumped into her chair and sobbed. "The entire staff, anybody."

I looked over at Vic, who seemed to be on her very last nerve. "You can check with the others?" She nodded but didn't say anything, which was probably for the best, and went back to her reports.

I watched Jennifer for a moment, letting her purge the ducts. "Now, Joe Lesky would have worked last night. Who worked today?"

"Shelly Gatton."

"Is she already gone?"

Vic interrupted. "Louis called her, and she's on her way in. Joe Lesky didn't answer his phone, but Louis said that that's not unusual since he sleeps through the afternoon and might not get the message until he gets up to come here."

After Jennifer had gone, I leaned against the back of my chair and perused the AARP posters. I figured I'd let Vic start, just to see if her line of thought was the same as mine.

"This makes no fucking sense."

I threw my arm over the back of the chair Jennifer had occupied. "Why would anybody go to the trouble of taking the can?" I didn't really feel like getting up from my chair. "I guess I better go by Lucian's and take my beating. I haven't even told him that Mari was poisoned." I stood up and tried to think of the last time I'd taken my coat off.

"You look like shit."

I adjusted my hat, just this side of jaunty. "'At's when I do my best work, when people are underestimating me. Check the supply closet, if you haven't already; maybe the Metamucil is there. You can take a statement from Shelly Gatton and from Joe Lesky when they get here?"

"Yeah." She changed the subject. "Cady make it in?"

I nodded. "So you were in on it?"

She was already back to her reports. "Everybody was in on it."

I picked up my beer and left. Some detective.

The door was closed to Room 32 when I got there, and no light was showing from under the sill. I checked my pocket watch, but it was too early for bed. I went ahead and knocked.

Nothing, so I knocked again.

Somebody moved in the room. "I got a gun."

"Me too." I tried the knob, but the door was locked. In fifteen years of visiting him, he had never locked the door. "Lucian, what are you doing in there?"

No answer. I leaned against the wall and gauged how much energy it would take to kick the door in. I was tired and didn't feel like kicking in doors, so I went down to the end of the hall and got a passkey. Dean had moved on to "Winter Wonderland," his voice gliding like a sleigh on cream cheese. Jennifer wanted to accompany me, but I wanted Lucian alone.

"Lucian, I'm unlocking the door and coming in."

It took a moment for him to respond. "Go to hell."

He said he had a gun, and I believed him. I unlocked and stood just to the side in case he was drunk enough to shoot. I brushed my fingertips across the door as the slab of light from the hallway bolted across the sand-colored carpet. The first thing to hit me was the smell. At some time during his vigilance, he must have soiled himself, and that smell overrode the tang of his unwashed body, the high heat of the room, and the bourbon. He was seated in a cowhide high-back chair with a 10-gauge sawed-off coach gun across his lap. Both hammers were pulled. "Lucian?"

"Go away."

The empty bottle of Pappy Van Winkle's Family Reserve was on the floor next to his artificial leg. He was wearing his tattered, checked bathrobe, his Stetson, and one cowboy boot. There were no lights on, and the chair had been pulled against the wall. "What're you up to, Lucian?" I put the beer down by the door, which I closed, and crossed to stand in front of the brindle sofa against the other wall. I took my jacket off and tossed it behind me. "It's hot in here."

"Wha . . . ?"

"It's hot. You mind if I open the outside door?" He watched me, then took his fingers from the shotgun long enough to gesture toward the sliding glass. I slid the heavy, double-paned glass back about a foot and took a deep breath. The miniature multicolored lights blinked around Lucian's patio, flashing blue, green, red, and yellow across the icicles on the canopy and across the dimpled surface of snow that had dumped into the small bowl at the back of the building. There was a claptrap Datsun pickup parked in the closest spot of the elevated parking area. The motor was running, but there wasn't anybody in it. Probably somebody warming his truck up for the cold ride home. I went back and sat on the sofa opposite Lucian and picked up the empty bourbon bottle. "You been drinking?"

He snorted. "Drinkin' hell, 'm drunk."

I nodded and watched his fingers still on both triggers. "Scattergun out for a reason?" The smell was getting to me, so I breathed through my mouth.

He wobbled a little, attempting to think and sit still at the same time. He stared at a space to my left, but I was pretty sure he was still talking to me, "'M waitin' . . . ." The glittering mahogany of his dark eyes was still visible in the gloom of the unlit room. "You wait with me."

"You bet." I sat back in the sofa and wished I had one of the beers in the paper bag, but one drunk and armed sheriff in the room was enough. I scratched my face, felt the hair, and tried to remember the last time I'd trimmed my beard. I reached out with my foot and nudged the prosthetic leg. "Maybe while we're waiting, we should get you cleaned up and put your leg on?"

He was quiet for a while, staring at the floor between us. "You can't keep 'em safe, y'know?" His eyes strayed up to mine where they wobbled. "Not always."

I thought about the woman who had died in Room 42, how she had haunted Lucian long before her death, and how she was now galvanized to his soul forever. "I know." He started to fall forward, but I caught him before the shotgun fell to the floor. He leaned against my shoulder; he weighed about as much as Cady. "Spent most of my life tryin' to decide whether ta shit or go blind. Guess I made up my mind to do both."

I laughed until there was a warm soft lump in my throat and a heat behind my eyes. I palmed the Damascus-barreled coach gun from him and gently lowered the two hammers. "Don't worry, we'll get you cleaned up."

It didn't take as long as I thought. After I got him in the bath, Lucian was able to seat himself on the specially constructed seat. I was stunned at how old he looked: small, naked, and drunk. I watched him as he clung to the stainless steel help bar and allowed the water to cascade over his scalp and carry the bad things away. The dent where Mari Baroja's uncle had finally settled the matter of Lucian's one and only marriage was evident. The water pooled there like some little eddy in his life and collected memories that refused to be erased.

I patted the old man on the shoulder, closed the curtain, and sat on the seat cover. There was a fresh copy of the *Durant Courant* on the floor next to the toilet brush. When I picked it up, I noticed that it had been carefully folded back to the obituary page. I sighed and looked into the black and white of Mari Baroja's obit. She had died on her birthday; that explained the drunken jag. I dropped the paper on the floor and went back to the main room to give the poor man a little privacy.

I took the soiled chair and put it out on the patio for future cleaning. The Datsun truck was still warming up and, as I slid the door closed, I could see the ghost of myself in the reflection of the glass, or maybe it was the real me trying to whisper in my ear and tell me what it was that was specifically rotten in Denmark. There were other eyes out there, other shapes that shifted and fell away only to drift back up from the falling snow to watch me and see if I was going to get it right. These shapes moved softly in the deep snow and between the trees; they provided no insight, just audience.

I thought about Vic who was doing my investigative work. I should let her go home. There wasn't any reason I couldn't stick around and gather what little information needed to be gleaned here, my daughter notwithstanding. I went back to the partially closed bathroom door. "Hey, Lucian?" I heard some shuffling noises. "You're not going to drown if I go tell Vic to go home, are you?"

"I don't give a damn what you do."

I took the beer with me.

On the way back to Louis's office, I discovered Joe had replaced Jennifer at the front desk. He looked much as he had two nights earlier when I had fought the Christmas tree. He wheeled his chair back and stuck his arms out, blocking my passage to the bottlebrush conifer. "Very funny."

"I just didn't want you to risk electrocution again."

I leaned against the counter and listened for a second. "How come there isn't any music?"

"Oh, shit." He fumbled under the counter with the stereo system, and pretty soon Gene Autrey was crooning "Rudolph the Red-Nosed Reindeer."

"Joe, do you have any idea what could've happened to that container of Metamucil?"

"I'm sorry, Sheriff, but it was just on a shelf in the main supply closet. I showed your deputy where it was supposed to be, but a lot of the clients get in there. None of the stuff is prescription, but we try and keep everyone's name labeled on them."

Vic said Shelly Gatton didn't know anything about the missing container. She had seen Lana the morning I had seen her, after her grandmother had died, and the day earlier when she had brought Mari lunch, along with the cookies. She said Joe Lesky was less helpful in that he hadn't seen anyone with or without cookies, and that, when he showed her the supply closet, there were four containers of the Metamucil, but none with the name of Mari Baroja. "You gonna test them all?"

She absently pointed to the cans that were on top of her jacket in a brown paper bag. She had been kind of surly about where I had been for the last hour but got over it when I handed her a beer. I watched as she ate the rather bland meat loaf, limp green beans, and pasty mashed potatoes she must have been served quite a while ago.

"You didn't get me any dinner?"

"You want mine?" She took a sip of her Rainier. "This beer's not very cold." I watched her play with the meat loaf, trying to give it a palatable posture on the turquoise plastic tray. "What are we going to do next?"

"The cookies were clean?"

"Will you give up on the fucking cookies?"

"I wish we had them now." An elderly woman on a walker paused at the doorway of Louis's office long enough to register a dirty look; maybe it was the language, maybe it was the beer, or maybe that was the way she looked at everything. I noticed that the cans of Metamucil had been opened. "You already start testing these?"

She nodded. "It doesn't smell like they've got anything in them, which means they probably don't have anything in them."

"Well, so far that is pretty much representative of the case: where there's smoke, there's smoke." I thought about all the things that needed to be done. "Could you throw a check on the terrible twins and see if anything turns up? I realize it's a long shot."

"I already did; Kay's clean as a whistle, and Carol's been involved in some questionable deals down in Miami, but nothing that leads me to believe that she'd be capable of something like this." She continued to study me. "Walt, trust me, I'd like to like them for this, but there's just nothing there."

I stared at the window until she spoke again. "Now what's the matter?"

"I'm resigning myself to the wonderful homecoming I'm giving Cady."

She crossed her arms and considered me. "Yeah? Tell her to come out to the Morretti mobile manse by the motorway and listen to the wind and the 18-wheelers jake-breaking, then she'll appreciate what she's got."

I looked at my recently divorced deputy, a beautiful, intelligent woman with a body like Salome and a mouth like a saltwater crocodile. I had been to her house trailer when I had hired her, but that was the last time I'd been there. I started to wonder why she hadn't ever invited me over for dinner when it came to me that I had never invited her out to my place either. I guess it had never really occurred to me, even though I continually swam against the undertow of my attraction toward her. The thought of myself involved with a woman who was about the same age as Cady was an image so pathetic that I erased it in wide sweeps on a regular basis. "You going home for Christmas?"

"No. Mom says Nona should be dead by then, or so she's promising. Vic Junior got this new girlfriend/fiancée who's a hairdresser and pregnant, and Alphonse is running off upstate with some friends. Tony's working at the restaurant with Uncle Al, and Michael said fuck the bunch of us."

We talked about her extended Philadelphia family on an infrequent basis. As far as they knew, the world stopped at the Main Line in Paoli. I had the most contact with her mother, had spoken to her on the phone a couple of times and seen a picture of her once. Lena was languorously gorgeous with the same olive-skinned, exotic beauty as her daughter but with a few more years on the vine to ripen. She had an equally handsome husband who Vic said pretty much ignored her mother. He was severe and driven and occupied himself with being the Chief of Detectives North, Sixth District, and liaison officer with the Mayor's Task Force on Organized Crime. "How's your Mom?"

She crushed the Rainier after the final swallow. "She says I need a good fuck."

I nodded, sage-like, and looked at the crumpled can still in her hand. "Maybe she's right."

"She says you need one, too." She tossed the wad of aluminum in the trash can under the desk. "Don't take it personally. It's been her advice on the human condition since Khrushchev pounded his shoe on the table at the UN, and Dad says it's always been the case."

"Something tells me your mother doesn't use the term good fuck."

"No, she uses the term roll in the hay, but it just doesn't have the same poetic ring."

I found myself becoming slightly aroused as it dawned on me that Vic probably talked dirty during sex, which shouldn't have come as such a surprise since she did it in accompaniment with everything else. "So, you think your mother needs a roll in the hay?"

"Since Khrushchev."

"That's a lot of rolling."

Her attention went back to the reports. "Yeah. Well, she's married to supercop."

She didn't talk about her father all that much, but his influence was plainly felt. It would have been easy to dismiss Vic's relationship with him as the difficulties a man with four sons had when confronted with a daughter, but his dealings with the four boys didn't seem any less rocky. She yawned.

"Go home."

I helped her put her coat on, and she turned and stood there studying me, looking nothing like a deputy is supposed to look. She grabbed the lapels of my sheepskin jacket and then smoothed them with the palms of her hands. "I still can't believe you're getting laid before I am."

I exhausted a short breath, a reasonable excuse for a laugh. "If it makes you feel any better, I'm not."

She picked up the containers of Metamucil and waited till she was around the corner and a couple of steps down the hall before calling out. "It does."

～～～

When I got back to Lucian's room, it was quiet. The door was closed and locked again. I knocked. "Lucian?" There was no answer, but I could hear muffled sounds along with some splashing noises. "Hey, you getting bashful in your old age?" I listened and could swear I could hear more than one person in there. I glanced back down the hall, where I had returned the passkey, but there was another sharp noise, and I was committed.

I couldn't hear anything anymore, and a surge of panic raised my head by contracting the muscles along my shoulders. "Lucian!" I pulled my .45 out and crossed the hall; I knew from past experience that if I used my foot to break down the door, my foot would be the only thing that went into the room. I could hear more noises now, so I charged across and planted my entire side, shoulder first, into the door. It exploded and blew me against the wall beside the bathroom. I saw a leg move in the bathtub and brought my head around to see someone running up the hillside outside Lucian's patio, someone big.

"Sheriff, freeze!" He was gone. I rushed into the bathroom, my lungs settling as I holstered my sidearm and bounced off the edge of the tub as I hit the slippery floor.

The shower curtain was wrapped around the old sheriff's body, and the water was still running. I pulled the curtain from around him and cut the tap. His leg was still up on the seat, but the rest of him was lying on his side with a fist clenched at his chest. I reached under his neck and pulled him up from the accumulated water that, having been freed from the curtain, was now swirling down the drain. He coughed, and I turned his face so that when he threw up, it would follow the water. It smelled like bourbon, and I held the one-legged man against my chest as he retched to a stop. He blinked his eyes and looked up at me. "What're you doin' here? Go get that son of a bitch!"

I grabbed a towel from the rack, placed it under his head, put him back down, and raced from the bathroom, through the main room, and out the patio doors. I pulled my sidearm, slid to a stop, and looked at the boot prints. They trailed up the hillside. It looked as though someone had brushed against one of the pine trees about halfway up the hill. He must have slipped but had regained his footing and had continued on. The Datsun pickup was gone.

I paused at the edge of the parking lot, having been careful to make my own path up the hill. The tire tracks and the exhaust melt of the Datsun were still compressed in the snow, and I knelt to look at the boot print where he had gotten in the truck. All the prints were marred enough so that we'd never get a decent imprint, but I placed my boot alongside: big, bigger than mine.

Lucian had struggled up to a sitting position by the time I got back to the bathroom, and I was glad I'd shut the sliding glass doors. He was shivering and clutched his remaining extremities, so I propped him back up on his seat and wrapped another towel around him. I pulled a thick Royal Stewart bathrobe that Cady had given him last year from his closet and picked up one moccasin. I caught myself looking for the other one before remembering that he didn't need it. His prosthetic leg was leaning against the door and on it was the other slipper. I snatched up the leg and continued back into the bathroom, where he looked up at me, still clutching himself. I sat on the toilet and wrapped the bathrobe around him, placing the leg against the tub, secure in the thought that this should be the order of things.

There was a little blood in his smile; he must have bitten his tongue in the struggle. I pulled the old man in and tried to warm him up before looking for a phone. He was struggling with something and, after a moment, his clenched fist came out from the folds of the robe, and he opened his hand. In his palm was an almost foot-long hank of jet-black hair.

The bloody smile held. "Got a piece of 'im."

10

No one at the home drove a Datsun pickup, and the only one in our tax records was a rusted hulk out on the Miller Ranch down near Powder Junction. It hadn't run since Steve and Janet's daughter Jessie had planted it in an irrigation ditch back in '89. Steve told Ruby I could have it for the annual sheriff's auction if I came and got it; I gratefully declined.

I sank my head back onto my folded coat and draped my arm down to pet Dog. I was having a hard time getting Ruby to concentrate on the Datsun pickup rather than Lucian.

"How about the DMV?" Except for the sound of the plastic keys, it was quiet in the office. Cady had left a message last night that she had gotten a ride from Henry and that she had arrived at the cabin safely. She also said that she and the Bear had stopped at the grocery on the way out. She also thanked God that they had. She also reported that it had only taken ten minutes to shovel out the living room and that Henry had used more duct tape to seal up the roof. She was asleep when I got there and, when I risked a kiss on the top of her head this morning, she hadn't stirred.

The tapping stopped. "Three."

"Locations?" From my perspective on the wooden bench of the reception area, I could see the serrated clouds on the ridges east of town. The sky was a striped fiery orange, and the snow between was pink.

The thin, nimble fingernails coated in lacquer continued typing. "Lusk, Laramie, and Lander."

I gave out with my best Basil Rathbone and wondered about the location of Watson. "Hmmm, I'm beginning to see a pattern."

"They all start with L?"

I held up an index finger. "Perchance a clue. Let's start with the closest."

Tapping. "Ivar Klinkenborg."

"You're kidding."

"Nope."

"Wants or warrants?"

More tapping. "None."

"Age?"

"Sixty-eight."

"Next."

There was silence for a moment. "Which is closer, Lander or Laramie?"

I didn't answer, because I wasn't sure. Vic and Saizarbitoria had gone out to a vehicular altercation on 196 just south of town, and it was the Ferg's day off. The Bear was MIA and was probably back on the Rez. I was idly thinking that at least I had Dog, when he got up and moved back over to Ruby. "Let's do reverse alphabetical order."

I got a look on that one. "Jason Wade."

"Wants or warrants?"

Tapping. "One DUI, two moving violations, both HPs. Recent registration from Nebraska."

This time I stuck a fist in the air. "Go Huskers. The big red *N* stands for knowledge."

Another pause. "Is that a no?"

I threw my arm back over my eyes. "Height?"

"Five-eight."

"Next."

More tapping. "Leo Gaskell, thirty-six, three moving violations and a domestic violence charge from two months ago." Even more tapping. "Involuntary manslaughter, did a five spot in Rawlins, weapons possession, processing, drug abuse violations, clandestine lab operation five years ago, did a year in Fremont County, more drug abuse violations. There's an assault on a law enforcement officer with no charges pending."

I was already up and watching her. "Height?"

"Six-five."

"Hello." She looked over at me as I thought about it for a moment. "Call up Bill Wiltse in Fremont County and ask him what he knows." It was quiet for far too long. "What?"

"Had it occurred to you, as a trained and veteran officer, to get the license plate number?"

I let out a large sigh in hopes that she would feel sorry for me. "Maybe I'm slipping." I slumped back on my folded coat. She took a sip of her green tea that I knew, from one small sample, tasted like lawn clippings. I rearranged my arm and pulled my hat down, knowing full well the silence was about Lucian. "He's fine, Ruby."

She exhaled a response, and I waited in the silent darkness of my hat. "You're sure?"

"You couldn't kill him with a ball bat." I thought about how Lucian had looked when I'd run him over to Durant Memorial, flushed with excitement. "He looks better than he has in years. If I'd known what an effect it was going to have on him, I would've tried to kill him years ago." I waited, but she seemed satisfied. "Can I ask you a question?"

"Yes."

"Why did you lie about not knowing Mari Baroja?" It was quiet again.

"At that point in time, I thought it concerned Lucian's personal life."

I lifted my hat. "Fair enough." I stood up and started down the steps to the little kitchenette in the basement. "I'm going to go make coffee."

"I'm sorry I lied."

I stopped on the landing and looked up at the painting of Andrew Carnegie, a leftover from the library years. All the time I'd worked with Lucian, he would salute Andy every time he went by. I smiled back up at her. "It's all right, you weren't that convincing."

I paused there on the landing and looked at the photographs, the six black and whites and the one color photo, all in cheap frames. I was the color photo, the one with the silly mustache and the too long sideburns. I scratched my beard and thought about my professional lineage.

Red had retired to ranch in the southern part of the county, had listened to the wind until he had grown loopy as a barn swallow in late elderberry season, and had finally shot himself in the heart. A drunk fourteen-year-old cowboy had knifed Del; Otto was crushed under a team of horses; and, as near as we could tell, Charley and Conrad had just disappeared. I knew why Lucian had called it quits. Things had changed in the seventies, and the world could no longer leave his peculiar brand of law enforcement well enough alone. He had ridden the trail for more than a quarter of a century and that was enough. It wasn't a happy collection of fortunes, but it did help to put Room 32 at the Durant Home for Assisted Living in perspective.

The old sheriff was a little roughed up, but he was going to be fine. I had saved a small strand of the hair, but the rest was already on its way to Cheyenne and DCI.

I scared up the coffee, folded a paper towel in lieu of a filter, and stepped back to the satisfying gurgle of impending caffeine and thought about another nine months in office. Somehow, it seemed longer than the past twenty-three years and three months altogether.

I noticed the blinking red light on the wall phone in the hallway, picked up the receiver, and tried to think of what Saizarbitoria would say, finally settling on. "Jail."

"It's Bill Wiltse. He says he wants to talk to you about this Gaskell character."

I punched line one. "Hello?"

"Have you got Leo Gaskell?"

I raised my eyebrows and looked at the phone for my own entertainment. "Hi Bill, how are you?"

He was quiet for a minute; I think for emphasis. "Do you have him?"

"No, actually I don't." I looked in at the coffee pot, but it wasn't quite full. "You wanna tell me what this is all about? He doesn't seem to have any outstanding . . ."

"He assaulted one of my off-duty officers at the Lander Saloon about two weeks ago and broke the orbit around his left eye and dislocated his jaw."

The coffee was ready, so I turned over one of our rare official mugs with the sheriff's star, poured, and watched as a few drops sizzled on the warming pad.

"What's this all about, Walt?"

I took a sip of the coffee, a little strong but it would do. "Oh, I ID'ed a Datsun pickup last night, and we've had someone over here attempting to do that thing that ends all other deeds."

"What?"

That's what I got when I quoted Shakespeare to other sheriffs. "You wanna fax over a copy of your files and a photograph of Gaskell?"

"You bet. Hey, Walt?"

"Yep?"

"Be careful with this jaybird, he's bad news."

Leo Gaskell fit the bill, but what connection could he have with the Barojas or Lucian? I would have to deal Leo around like a bad card and see what came up. Just for the luck of the draw, I had put out an all points bulletin last night.

I started up the stairs with my cup of coffee. "Anything on that APB with the HPs?" Ruby shook her head. "Add the plate number." I called back to her as I made for my office. "You find anything on the priest?"

"He lives at the rectory over at St. Mathias. Father Thallon looks after him."

I could go find the old priest but, without Saizarbitoria, I couldn't do much. I could check on Lana, Isaac, or Lucian at the hospital, head over to the home and ask around, or maybe even call in the Baroja twins and have a little chat. The opportunities were endless.

I swiveled my chair around and looked at the orange mountains that paled to lighter shades in the morning light. The sun was out, but it was doubtful we'd get much higher than the teens during the course of the day. The foothills were covered with a deep drift of snow that had piled on from the northwest so that the whole county looked as if it were leaning to the southeast.

I knew better than to call the greatest legal mind of our time before noon on a day she wasn't billing on an hourly basis. It was still relatively early, and I needed company for breakfast. I figured the Log Cabin Motel was a good place to look.

"What if I want the special rather than the usual?"

Dorothy crossed her arms and smiled at me like a magician forcing a card. "The special is the usual."

I nodded, looked at Maggie Watson, and raised an eyebrow. "I'll have the usual special."

She looked to Maggie. "Me, too."

Dorothy opened the waffle iron, set up for Belgian. It wasn't the usual usual. I looked at the menu absentmindedly and wondered, if I were a breakfast, which one I'd be? Probably the usual. "So, how are our abandoned safe-deposit boxes measuring up?"

She sipped her coffee. "Pretty boring, actually."

"How much longer do you think you'll be?"

"Maybe two days." It was quiet in the little café. "How's your case going?"

"Don't ask." A thought occurred to me, and I looked at the chief cook and bottle washer. "Hey Dorothy, who in this county is bigger than me?"

She was still but didn't turn. "Bigger in what way?"

"Taller."

"Brandon White Buffalo."

I took a sip of my coffee, glanced toward Maggie, and dismissed that suggestion. "Anybody else?"

She sat the bowl against her hip and tilted her head. "There was a guy in here about a week ago, construction worker, really big."

"Not a local?"

"No."

"Working around here?"

"Maybe. Outside work; wearing those big arctic Carhartts." She motioned to the farthest stool at the end of the serving counter. "Sat down there, kept to himself."

Maggie was watching me prime the pump. "Did he say anything that might've given you an indication as to who he was or where he was working?"

She shook her head. "No, he hardly said a word, and it was busy."

I decided to go with the big indicator. "What'd his hat say?"

"I don't read every ball cap that comes into this place, life's too short." She poured the batter into the waffle iron, closed it, and then turned back to look at Maggie. "Asks a lot of questions, doesn't he?"

When they had stopped steaming, she flipped the Belgian waffles from the iron, drenched them in maple syrup, and dressed them with confectionary sugar and a few strawberries for good measure. She slid the hot plates in front of us, reaching back for the pot after noticing our cups were about empty.

I started eating as she watched. Dorothy liked to watch me eat, and I'd gotten over it. Maggie seemed to be enjoying her usual usual. "You ever hear of Jolie Baroja, the cousin?"

She poured herself a cup. "Some talk about the ETA. He was over there for a few years during and after the war."

"That's a nasty little terrorist group for a priest to be tied up with."

"Like I said, just talk." She took another sip of her coffee. "He must be older than dirt. He did the mass at the Basque festival a few years ago in Euskara. As a matter of fact, I don't think he speaks English, at least not anymore." She glanced at Maggie, who was doing her best to ignore us. "You know what they say about the Basques; like a good woman, they have no past."

I dropped Maggie off at the Durant State Bank and picked up Sancho at the office.

St. Mathias is near the creek where the giant cottonwoods tower over the aged stone buildings that make up the abandoned portion of the Pope's compound. They built a new church back in the sixties, a really ugly one, the one I always associated with Pancake Day, but the old rectory and chapel still stood by the creek where they always had.

I froze as Saizarbitoria dipped his fingers in the water, knelt, and crossed himself. I stroked my beard and felt like a Viking, there to raid the place. I followed him down the aisle and passed through the sunlight that skipped onto the hardwood floor. The stone pillars stretched to a small gallery where there were ornate stained-glass windows. They were not the usual Jesus lineup but were odd, with strange depictions of biblical passages foreign to me; at least I couldn't remember any parts of the Bible where Goliath stacked rocks or tiny angels flew around people's heads.

We shook hands with the amiable blond-bearded priest and followed as he led us to the kitchen where Father Baroja was seated at a table with some hot cocoa. He paid us little attention as Father Thallon put the kettle on and pulled out a few more mugs. "Jolie, you know you're not supposed to operate the stove without Mrs. Krauss." The old priest gave no response. "We had a little accident about a month ago."

I sat at the end of the table and studied the old man. He continued to look at his hot chocolate and pulled it a little closer as if we might take it away from him. He had a long face with a bulbous nose, dangling earlobes, and wrinkles that all congregated at his mouth. He looked like some ancient monk with a heavy wool cardigan that buttoned up around his neck. He could have been any of the hard men I'd seen on horseback in Mari Baroja's photographs.

Gene Thallon had warned us that Basque was not his second language, or his fifty-seventh for that matter, but that he knew that the language had four distinct dialects, and that the vast number of grammatical tenses included a subjective, two different potentials, an eventual, and a hypothetical. I looked over at my secret weapon and hoped we could get out of there before Father Thallon had us diagramming sentences.

He brought over some cups for us and, with this ecumenical distribution of cocoa, the old priest loosened the guard on his own. It seemed rude to not say anything to the old guy, so I said hello.

He studied me for a moment but dismissed me for the cocoa. I looked at Father Thallon. The young priest smiled. "He can be a little incommunicative at times."

"*Kaixo, zer moduz?*" Saizarbitoria casually sipped his own hot chocolate and glanced sideways at Jolie Baroja after speaking.

"*Zer da hau?*" The gravel in the old priest's voice could have filled a driveway.

Sancho set his mug back down with a tight-lipped smile. "*Bai?*"

Jolie Baroja's head slipped to one side, and then he leaned in close to Santiago, placing a hand lightly on the young deputy's arm. "*Ongi-etorri . . .*"

They talked at an impressive rate for a solid five minutes before my translator turned back to me. "Was there anything specific you wanted to know?"

"What was all that about?"

"Cordialities. He thinks I'm a local, and I didn't dissuade him."

"Good." I had watched Sancho carefully, the way he actively listened to what the old man had to say, didn't interrupt, and maintained eye contact. It was all textbook and well done. It looked as though he had adopted the role of friend and ally with the old priest, a posture that would enable Jolie to speak freely within the coded language they shared.

I looked at Father Thallon, who had been watching the proceedings with great interest, and then back to Saizarbitoria. "Can you gently ask him about his cousin, any family contact he might have had?"

The kid looked at me for an extra moment, then turned and renewed the conversation.

"I had no idea you had deputies that could speak Basque."

I nodded. "We try and stay close to the constituency."

The old priest glanced back at me, and Sancho weighed his next words carefully. "He doesn't like you."

I glanced at him and then back to Santiago. "He doesn't even know me."

"He thinks he does."

I stood and gestured for the younger priest to lead on. "Well, we know when we're not wanted." He paused for only a moment and then led me back into the cathedral. It was small by modern standards, but exquisite. It had been pieced together by the sturdy and articulate hands of not only the Basque but also the Scottish, Polish, Czech, and German faithful. They had been tough men who had brought the old ways with them along with the skills to build beauty such as this. I followed the king's-bridge truss system of hand-adzed beams that held the roof and admired the wide-plank floors with no board less than a foot wide; the altar and the adjoining walls were local moss stone with the lichens flourishing in the cool of the open stillness.

I took a sip of my cocoa. "Must be tough with all these Basquos around."

"It's difficult, especially with the older parishioners; they're still not sure if I'm going to last." He smiled. "They have a saying, the Basque. That just because the cat has kittens in the oven, it doesn't make them biscuits."

I laughed and looked at him. "You're probably wondering why we're here. We're interested in his relationship with his cousin, Mari. Did you know her?"

Thallon nodded. "Mari? Yes, I did know her. I visited with her last Friday. A terrible shame."

I nodded. "Do you know any of the rest of the family?"

"I've met the granddaughter, the one that owns the bakery. Lana?"

"Seems like a good kid." The priest remained silent. "Have you met either of the twins?"

"I've met Carol; she's come over to meet with Father Baroja a number of times."

"How many times?"

He thought. "A half a dozen or so, over a lengthy period. I would imagine that it's very difficult to visit more often from Florida."

"Can you remember when she was here last?"

He thought some more and exhaled very slowly. "About two years ago, I think."

I thought about it. "Was Father Baroja very close with Mari?"

"No."

"That was a pretty definitive answer."

"I think there was some tension there." He glanced back toward the chapel as Saizarbitoria entered from the doorway.

Sancho asked about the church, the congregation, and the community. As they talked, my attention was drawn back to the stained-glass windows. The stone church wouldn't get long beams of sunshine today; only short blasts of golden light that illuminated first one window, then another. I watched the seemingly random pattern and wondered if I concentrated would I get the message. Probably not.

When I looked back, Father Thallon was looking at me. "They have a name for you, you know."

"I beg your pardon?"

"The Basques around these parts, they have a name for you."

Saizarbitoria was all ears. "They do?"

We waited a moment, before the priest said it very carefully. "Jentil-lak." They both laughed.

〰

I adjusted the heat in the truck and looked at the Basquo. "Well?"

"What do you want to know first? There's a lot of ground to cover."

"When is the last time he spoke with his cousin?"

"Nineteen seventy-nine."

I stared at the fog on the inside of my windshield. "That takes care of a lot of the other questions."

"That was the last time he saw her alive."

I turned up the defroster. "And what does that mean?"

"She comes to him in his dreams." He misinterpreted my stare. "He said that she visits him when he sleeps, that she asks for forgiveness. The dreams he described were very vivid, very detailed." He turned and smiled at me; he was a handsome kid. "I think the old man may have some demons."

I thought about my own dreams, about the house and the scarf. "Don't we all."

He adjusted his jacket and mindlessly fingered the knob of the glove box. "He said she was immoral. That he had tried to save her his whole life, that the family considered her their greatest failure."

I drove across the unplowed snowpack of Durant's side streets. Santiago studied the road ahead. "The old priest doesn't like you because he thinks you're Lucian."

Of course. I nodded and thought about it. "Well, he and Lucian probably didn't get along." I thought about filling the kid in, but it still seemed early, so I changed tack. "The old guy seems pretty sharp?"

He paused, the way I was learning that he did whenever you did something to him and he wanted you to know that he knew it. "Well, yeah, kind of." Santiago sniffed and glanced back at the dash as the windshield began to clear. "He told me to be careful, that there were *laminak* in the room."

I turned to look at him. "*Laminak*?"

He chewed his lip. "Fairies."

I sighed and made a turn. I had the Old Cheyenne, he had the fairies, and it was all in how you looked at it. "Anything else?"

"I think that about covers it."

I pulled out onto the main drag and started for the office, barely being missed by an inattentive truck driver. He slowed after he saw the lights and the stars. "All right, what the hell does *Jentillak* mean?"

He smiled to himself, happy to know something I didn't. "There are these dolmens, like Neolithic monuments, all over the mountains back in the Basque lands." He continued to smile. "The *Jentillak* are a people that once lived alongside the Basque. One day a strange storm cloud was seen in the east and the wisest of the Jentillak recognized it as an omen that their time had ended. They marched off into the earth, under a dolmen still there in the Arratzaran valley in Navarra." I glanced at him, and he savored the moment. "Jentillak means giant."

I drove along silently and thought about it. "Giant, huh?"

"Yeah." He looked back out. "There was a Jentillak who was left behind whose name was Olentzero, and he explained that they had all left because *Kixmi* had been born."

I nodded. "Who was this *Kixmi* character?"

Santiago looked out into the slight sifting of snow and Christmas lights. "Jesus."

I dropped Sancho off at the office just as Vic was heading out to a chimney fire on the south side of town. I waved as Saizarbitoria jumped in her unit, and she flipped me off.

It was a quiet day at Durant Memorial, with only a few cars in the lot. " Janine, is Isaac Bloomfield still wandering around in here?"

She traced a finger down the register and smiled. "You're in luck, he's making his late morning rounds."

I thought about the eight-five-year-old man who had been knocked unconscious only two days ago. "His rounds?"

She nodded. "He has been stalling out in the B Ward dayroom about this time."

I leaned against her counter and rested my chin in the palm of my hand, happy to discover the Doc was human. "Well, we're none of us getting any younger."

She smiled. "That's not why he stalls out."

Lana still looked like a Hindu, but she had obviously gotten supplies from home since she now wore flaming red silk pajamas, a white terry-cloth bathrobe, and pink bunny slippers. The most recent copy of *Saveur* magazine lay open in her lap. "Looks like you're settling in." It was a kooky smile, but a warm one nonetheless.

"I've decided to treat this like a spa vacation."

Isaac was seated on the ottoman next to the bunny slippers, the picture of the attending physician. "Well, Doc, what's the prognosis?"

He continued to smile at her and, if I were a betting man, I would have labeled him as smitten. "If we can get the patient to stop playing with her head, we can probably save it."

I stood by the plastic chair. "Stop playing with your head, or it'll end up looking like my ear." I glanced over at the Doc. "Or his head."

"I like your ear and his head."

Okay, I was kind of smitten, too. "Lana, I need to talk to the Doc. Will you excuse us?"

Isaac and I codgered our way out to the hallway, where I stopped. I didn't see any reason to drag the Doc any farther than I had to. "How's Lucian?"

"Asleep in the lounge; it's where we've both been staying."

I nodded. "Isaac, I need to ask you a question, and the situation being what it is, I don't have a lot of time for niceties."

He leaned against the smooth wall of the hallway and crossed his arms. "Yes, Walter?"

I hitched my thumbs in my gun belt and then shifted them to my jacket. It was enough that I wore a gun around Isaac; there wasn't any need to broadcast the fact. "This human suppository, Charlie Nurburn, did he leave any illegitimate children that you know of?"

He sighed deeply. "This concerns the case at hand?"

"You know, a lot of people have been asking me that lately." I waited to see if police prerogative would override medical confidentiality. I hated leaning on the old guy, but I needed some answers and, after all, we were talking about ancient history.

"There were a number of women."

"I'm listening."

"Perhaps an Indian woman."

"I'm still listening."

He took off his glasses and cleaned them with the corner of his smock. "I don't know her name, or if I did, it has been too long, Walter."

"When?"

"Early fifties. I could check my private journals and give you an exact date, perhaps a name." I studied the small indentations at the Doc's nose, where the same glasses had sat for a half a century. "I have those journals here."

I straightened a little. "Here at the hospital?"

"In my office here."

I laughed because it was all I could think to do. "Why would you have those specific journals on hand?" He looked ashamed but not particularly guilty.

"I was transcribing some historic familial selections for the young lady."

"Lana?"

He smiled and shook his head at himself. "Foolish, yes?"

I smiled back at the charming old man and gently put my arm around his narrow shoulders. "Isaac, everything to do with women is foolish and, therefore, absolutely essential."

11

"I need to do a little cleaning up."

His diaries were piled on the desk and looked like old ledger books, the kind that businesses used to use for accounts and which the Lakota used for painting. He sat in the only chair, and I propped myself against an unoccupied corner of the desk.

I watched as Isaac deftly slipped a journal from the stack. It was the oldest of the tomes, and I was beginning to feel like some cleric in training. "My notes are not as complete as I hoped but perhaps something is relevant." The thin finger with the yellowed nail traveled along the lines like the carriage on a typewriter, pausing here and then there; finally, it stopped.

"Something?"

"It was when I first started the clinic north of here near the reservation." He looked up at me, his fingertip still on the spot. "December eighth, 1950, a boy, six pounds, two ounces." He looked back at the ledger. "No name was given to the child at that time."

"You think this baby was Charlie Nurburn's?"

He carefully placed the book on the surface of the desk as if the years were in danger of tumbling out, and I thought about all the time that had been collected between the lines. "Acme was a hamlet up near Tongue River, small, even then. Once they stopped producing coal, it became even smaller." He looked up at me with a thin smile. "It is difficult to hide things in small places."

"What was the mother's name?"

He watched me through his overlapped eyelids, which were magnified through the bifocals. He checked the ledger. "Ellen Walks Over Ice."

I hadn't moved since he had spoken. "Ellen Walks Over Ice . . . not Anna Walks Over Ice?"

He looked at the ledger again. "Ellen." His eyes locked with mine. "Anna Walks Over Ice is the woman that works at the Durant Home."

I looked back at him for only a moment. "Can I borrow your phone, Doc?" He looked around, finally giving up on the landline and handing me the cell phone from his smock pocket. Isaac didn't have any staff, so he could have anything he wanted. "Isaac, what's the number for the home?" The phone made a loud beeping noise. "I think you have messages."

"I'll check them after you make your call. The phone was in my car, and your new deputy, the young man, was kind enough to return it to me. I get most of my messages through my answering service, but sometimes people don't want to talk to anyone but me." He took the mobile, dialed the number for me, and handed it back.

Jennifer Felson answered. "Jennifer, is Anna Walks Over Ice working today?"

"Let me check." I waited as she dropped the phone, picked it up, rustled some papers, and declared Anna Walks Over Ice missing for the day.

"She's sick?"

"She's an Indian. Sometimes they don't show up, and mostly they don't call." Racial slurs aside, most Indians did have their own sense of time; these priorities had worked fine for centuries, so I guess they saw little reason to change. "She doesn't speak much English anyway."

I dialed the number for the Red Pony and asked Isaac which button to push. "Ha-ho, it is another wonderful day at the Red Pony bar and continual soiree."

"Hey, do you know where Anna Walks Over Ice lives?"

"No, but I can find out."

"Can you check on her for me?" He said he would, and then I asked him if he'd ever heard of Ellen Walks Over Ice. He said no, but that they were a large Crow family. He would ask Lonnie and then get back to me.

"Call me at the office."

I handed the tiny phone back to Isaac and watched as he hit a few buttons and held it to his ear. He looked at the journal as he listened. "I have her age listed as late teens, possibly early twenties."

"So she'd be in her seventies?"

He smiled. "You don't have to make it sound so old."

I glanced for the ghostly numbers on the inside of Isaac's arm but the sleeve of his smock hid his dreadful distant past. "She probably hasn't had as easy a life as you, Doc."

He continued to smile and nodded. "You're probably right." He made a face as he listened to the cell phone. "That's strange. The messages are from Anna." He waited for a moment, listening. "She sounds very agitated."

Evidently, the Doc spoke Crow.

When I got back to the reception desk, the more tanned and less anxious version of Kay Baroja was standing at the counter talking with Janine about how easy it was to get certified as a scuba diver in a three-day crash course in the Keys. I thought about slipping out the side door, but I needed to talk to her and this was the first time I'd seen the twins apart since she'd arrived. "Carol Baroja-Calloway?"

She turned with a smile like a barracuda. "Carol Baroja, period!" There had been some work done, the face a little tighter, the lips a little fuller, and the hair with bleached sun streaks. She smiled a perfect smile, the teeth a little too white, and extended a hand with no trailing bracelets or wedding ring. "Sheriff Longmire, I am so pleased to meet you!"

Yikes. I smiled. "We've met."

She leaned in and exposed a formidable cleavage, which also looked engineered. "I was hoping you would forget." She scooped up my arm and steered me toward the chairs at the other end of the waiting room. "I just wanted to apologize for my sister's behavior. Kay can be rather trying."

"That's all right. I didn't take any of it personally."

"Even the part about being a son of a bitch?" She sat us on one of the sofas; if she had been any closer she would have been lap dancing. She was still holding onto my arm. "I was on my way in to check on Lana, but this is just too good of an opportunity to let pass. I just want to thank you for taking such a personal interest in my mother's death and Lana's welfare."

"It's nothing, I . . ."

"No, you have no idea how reassuring it is to know that we can depend on you in these difficult times. Is that horrible young woman from the division of criminal investigation still bothering you?"

I thought about it, finally remembering that she was talking about Cady. "Continually."

"I'm so sorry." She blinked, the steady way that contact lens wearers do. "Are there any leads as to who might have done this to poor Lana? The word is leads, isn't it?"

I nodded and readjusted, but she still clung to my arm. "We're following up on it, but there isn't anything strong enough to discuss just yet." She continued to look at me, and it was the first pause since the conversation had begun. "Would you mind if I asked you a few questions?"

Another pause, and the grip on my arm lessened. "I'm not a suspect, am I?"

I cleared my throat. "When was the last time you visited your mother?"

She thought. "About two years ago."

"And what was your relationship like?"

The animation in her face subsided for a moment, and I think I was getting the first unrehearsed performance of the day. "Did you know my mother, Walter? Do you mind if I call you Walter?" She measured her next discourse. "In a word, she was a pickle. Don't get me wrong, I don't think my mother had a very easy life." That was the understatement of the century. "And I think that that had an effect on her financial views."

"I see." I was wondering how long it was going to take for the money to come up.

"She had a simplistic view of our financial situation, all our financial situations."

"Meaning yours, Kay's, and Lana's?"

"Yes. I don't know if you're aware of the arrangements my mother made concerning her estate?"

"As you know, I have a copy of the Will to aid in the investigation of your mother's murder."

The word murder didn't stop her. "Lana is not really capable of understanding the magnitude of our financial situation, especially concerning Four Brothers."

"You mean the meek shall inherit the earth, but not the mineral rights?" She leaned back and studied me as though I were suddenly a stain on the bathmat. In for a penny in for a pound, I continued. "What about your father, Charlie Nurburn?"

The look held. "He abandoned my mother fifty years ago, so he's no longer an issue."

She looked as though she was ready for the interview to be over. "Just a few more questions. Where does Father Baroja fit into all of this financially? He wasn't mentioned in the Will."

She ran a tongue across her teeth and pivoted at the waist, allowing her blouse to open—no tan lines. "Mother and Jolie were the only children of my grandfather and his three brothers. There was another child, Arturo, but he died of pneumonia. When the last of the brothers passed away a number of years ago, the estate was divided between Jolie and my mother, at which point Uncle Jolie sold his half of the ranch back to Mother along with half of his half of the mineral rights and began giving his money away to charity." She paused, but I didn't say anything. I was used to quiet, but she wasn't. "He did not get along with my mother, so I took it upon myself to counsel him on a certain amount of financial responsibility, but I fear that his faculties are beginning to fail him."

"In what way?" I wanted to hear her talk about the fairies.

"His grasp on reality is a little fractured."

"So Father Baroja was found psychologically incompetent?" She wasn't going to talk about the fairies.

"Oh, no. He voluntarily put his part of the estate in a Trust, controlled by a money manager."

"And who is that?"

She smiled. "I really couldn't say." It was probably the fairies.

I cleared my throat and took her hand from my arm as I turned. "Do you have any idea who might have murdered your mother and would wish your niece harm?"

"I wasn't that good a daughter, and I haven't been that good of an aunt. I should have kept closer track of Lana, but I'm afraid she's a little headstrong. The whole Basque thing . . ."

"Basque thing?"

She placed a synthetic fingernail across a mouth I was sure wasn't finished speaking. "I think she may have been involved with some political activities when she was over there at culinary school." She said over there as though it were a venereal disease.

I tried hard to not roll my eyes. "Hmm . . . ETA?"

"Yes." She clutched my hand with both of hers, and it was starting to seem more like a wrestling match than an interview. "I'm afraid that she might have gotten involved with some sordid characters while she was in Europe. It could be that they are interested in Mother's money."

"I see." I let the dust settle on that one and tried to reconcile Lana as the naïve innocent with Lana the intriguing terrorist and couldn't.

I went back to the office to see if Bill Wiltse had faxed the picture of Leo Gaskell, but Leo didn't fit as Charlie Nurburn's illegitimate mystery child. That child had been born in 1950, which meant he'd be in his midfifties. Leo Gaskell was in his thirties. But someone poisoned Mari Baroja, someone tried to kill Isaac, someone tried to bludgeon Lana Baroja to death, and someone had tried to kill Lucian.

Someone was killing everybody who knew or thought that Charlie Nurburn was dead. Maybe they thought that they could get money from Mari's estate if Charlie could be shown to be alive. Illegitimate children could not inherit, but Cady had mentioned that in Wyoming a husband could claim half of an estate, even if he was not in a Will or Trust, as an elective share. Maybe they wanted him alive for that purpose and then they could kill him off and inherit?

The sky was the color of liberty ships left in the sun too long with faint tinges of a deeper gray at the horizon. It wasn't snowing, but what had fallen looked like albino BBs rolling around the parking lot. Vic and Sancho pulled up beside me and disturbed my reverie. I shut the Bullet down and climbed out. Saizarbitoria trailed along after Vic, and I could see that he was covered from head to tactical boot with a thick coating of ice and black soot; even his face was only marginally visible. "The chimney fire?"

He shifted from boot to boot. "You two don't mind if I go in before I completely harden?"

I stepped aside and allowed him to continue up the handicapped ramp and into the heat and relative comfort of the office. I turned and looked at Vic. "I see your uniform is clean."

She smiled. "He's the mountain climber."

When we got inside, Dog came to greet me and sat with his haunches on my foot. He had carefully avoided Vic. Saizarbitoria was on his way to the jail shower with a fresh towel held between forefinger and thumb. Ruby had obviously fussed over him, and he now had a cup of coffee. "We don't have much here in Absaroka County, but we do have a fire department."

"Their ladder truck froze."

We all watched him go. Vic was still on her best behavior. "He's fearless. We have to keep him."

I nodded, and it was unanimous.

Ruby handed me a folder. "Leo Gaskell."

I flipped it open. There was a regular arrest dossier on Leo Cecil Gaskell, a four-pager to be exact, and a quarter page photo of Leo at his last retreat in Rawlins. He was big, with long dark hair that hung just past the shoulders. Bingo. He had lousy teeth and a broken nose that completed the package, but it was his eyes that were scary. Devoid of any feeling, Leo looked like one of those guys who could strangle a kindergarten and then go home and water the plants.

"Not that fucker again."

I turned to look at Vic, who was peering over my shoulder. "What?"

She looked at me as if I were the only village idiot left in town. "This is the guy who shot the foreman down on the methane field; Cecil Keller, the one you made come in and write on the blackboard."

"Cecil Keller?"

"Yeah, this is the guy. He's got a mustache now, but it's the teeth. I swear it's him." She looked at me. "I've still got the gun."

"Get it." She disappeared.

I thought about the photograph of Charlie on the Rez with the pistols. I snatched the photo of Leo from the folder and held it up for Ruby to see. Her face reddened. "It's not the name he gave us before, but that's him. I'm sorry, Walt, but I didn't bother to look at the fax when it came in. I know it's no excuse, but the phone was ringing, and I just shoved it into a folder."

"Tell Saizarbitoria that he's earned an inside day and keep him off the roof." I handed Vic the file as she handed me a chrome-plated, pearl-handled .32 automatic, identical to the four that Charlie Nurburn had worn in the photo. As Vic read the file, she whistled softly at the details. I turned to my second in command. "Looks like we're going to Four Brothers."

"I have to pee first."

I took the file back and sighed. "Go pee." I sat on the edge of Ruby's desk and thought about whether Cecil Keller/Leo Gaskell was at work today and about his possible connection to the illusive Charlie Nurburn. The phone rang, and Ruby picked up her receiver and held it out to me. "Henry."

"I am at Anna's house, and someone has broken in."

I looked at the phone. "What?"

"Someone has pried the backdoor open, and it looks as if they were searching for something."

"I take it she's not there?"

"No."

Anna wasn't at work and wasn't at home. "Any word on Ellen Walks Over Ice?"

"Her married name is Ellen Runs Horse, and she lives in town at the trailer park by the highway; sometimes Anna stays with her when the weather is bad."

I closed my eyes and then opened them to glance over at Ruby. "Can you get me an address for Ellen Runs Horse, here in town?" Her fingers began working the keys of her computer.

The Cheyenne Nation cleared his throat. "She is related to Anna. Lonnie says that they are half sisters."

The wagons were beginning to circle, and all the Indians were related. "Do me another favor?"

"We also serve who drive all over the Rez."

I ignored the sarcasm. "Could you and Cady go over to Durant Memorial at 2:30? Lana Baroja's got a meeting with the terrible twins, one of whom just tried to rape me, and I was thinking it might be nice if she had a little representation."

"At this meeting, what are we supposed to represent?"

"Brains and brawn."

"Which of us is which?"

I hung up the phone and watched as Ruby scribbled the address down on a Post-it for me, 23 EVERGREEN CIRCLE.

Vic returned from the powder room. "More good news?"

"Unless I am mistaken, Ellen Runs Horse is Ellen Walks Over Ice."

Ruby and Vic looked at each other and then back to me, Vic the first to speak. "The woman from the home?"

I rubbed my eyes in an attempt to stave off the headache that seemed to be coming on with the velocity of a Burlington Northern/ Santa Fe. "The mother of Charlie Nurburn's illegitimate child from back in 1950 and the half sister of Anna Walks Over Ice, who works at the home. The same Anna Walks Over Ice who I believe has left messages on Isaac Bloomfield's cell phone and appears to have just had her house burgled."

Vic nodded and looked at the Post-it in my hands. "You'll be wanting to go over to the trailer court first."

On the drive over, I stuffed the small chrome automatic into the center console on top of the autopsy photographs. "That's the pistol he shot the foreman with, which looks remarkably like one of the four pistols I saw in a picture of Charlie Nurburn."

"Where did you see a picture of Charlie Nurburn?"

"At Henry's. He's collating a couple of hatboxes full of old photographs for the tribe."

"Charlie was on the Rez?"

"Yep."

She looked through the windshield at the snow darting past us. "The guy got around."

I looked past her shoulder at the space where a trailer house had been, at a pole with the number 23, and at power hookups dangling to the ground. There was only an inch or two of snow, so it hadn't been gone long. She turned and looked at me with her hands on her hips. "You know, that's the problem with using these things for a permanent address."

I didn't say anything.

"I'll go check with the manager." She marched off down the row of trailers to the one that sat by the road as I knelt and looked at the snow-covered tandem tracks of a very large truck. This was going to make things difficult. What was this world coming to when you could back up to a residence of reasonable suspicion and haul it away?

There were some trash cans, the large metal ones, chained to the low fence that divided the little yards from each other. I walked over and started going through them. The first contained the usual detritus that assembles in any household, apple cores, newspapers, and a chicken carcass. I closed the lid and moved to the next can but stopped when I saw a tiny nose and a set of eyes looking out at me from a small window in the next trailer house about four feet away.

The glass of the vent was open, and it looked like a bathroom window. "Hi."

I smiled. "Hi." It was a boy, maybe five, Indian and, from the features, probably Crow. It looked like he was having trouble standing on the toilet and talking through the window.

"You the sheriff?"

"You bet."

He continued to study me. "You looking for bad guys?"

"Yep, you seen any?" His face became grave, and he slowly nodded. "Tall guy, like me? Long dark hair with a mustache?" He stopped for a second and then nodded some more. I put my hands in my pockets and got out my gloves and put them on. "You see him lately?" The little face continued to nod. "Last night?" More nodding.

"He has a big truck."

"Did he take this lady's home away?"

He thought about that one for a minute. "She's mean."

"Was she with him?"

"I don't know."

I casually opened the second lid and found some mail on the top. "Did they leave last night?" He nodded again as I picked up an offer for long-term insurance from some fly-by-night firm in California; the addressee was Ellen Runs Horse. "Was it late last night?"

"Uh huh."

"Did they wake you up with the truck?"

"Uh huh." I nodded along with him and casually lifted the top on the last can.

I quickly closed it. My lungs didn't want to work, but I took a deep breath and stood there for a minute. "You see anything else?"

"No."

"Where's your mother?"

"She's at work."

"Who's taking care of you?"

"My sister."

I took another breath. "Where is she?"

"Taking a nap."

"Would you go wake her up and see if she would mind talking to me?"

"Now?"

"Yep."

"Okay." The little face disappeared.

I stood there for a moment longer and then opened the third trash can again. I forced myself to look, just making sure that what I was seeing was real.

I closed it and walked back over to my truck and leaned against the side mirror, getting as much air in my lungs as I could force. I looked over the fences, past the snow-covered hills leading to the highway where the 18-wheelers jake-braked to exit Durant. I had to open the door and make some radio calls, but it seemed like all I could do was look off to the horizon and feel the wind that was picking up from the west.

I didn't think I could trust myself to operate the minute mechanisms of my truck door or the radio, so I waited. I took my hat off and ran a gloved hand through my hair. Still holding my hat, I threw my arm over the mirror and let the truck carry some of my weight. After a moment, I heard Vic coming back from the manager's office.

"I talked to his wife, and she called him. He works at the welding shop up by the high school, but he'll be here in about five minutes." I nodded. "Hey, you don't look so good."

I took another breath to quell not so much the nausea but the anger and watched as my hands shook. "I found Anna Walks Over Ice."

12

Vic was looking at me like I was a crazy person. I hadn't liked Jess Aliff's answers. We were standing by one of the compression stations about four miles from everything with the propane engines running in the wind at full blast. It was loud, but I had been louder.

The snow was the stinging stuff that was whisking across the high plains at thirty miles an hour. It was as if the weather had decided to change from bad to worse after I had found Anna Walks Over Ice in the trash can. The anger I felt was like the wind; rage has no place in law enforcement, and I stand fast against it the majority of the time, but it is there, waiting for fissures of passion, waiting for me to slip, and I just had.

The gist of my outburst had been that I wasn't particularly concerned if Leo Cecil Gaskell/Keller was chairman of the Wyoming Oil and Gas Commission, I wanted his ass and now. According to the foreman, Leo was in a crew that was working in the fields farther south, but he wasn't sure exactly where. I had asked him if they had radios. He said they did, but that they only worked about half the time. I informed him that this time better be the half that worked.

It was a stubby trailer, the kind that was usually used for hunting. I was the last one in; Vic stood in the little kitchenette, and Aliff sat at the fold-down table where he pulled a radio from a holder on the wall. He looked much as he had the day he had told me about being shot. The condensation from his breath had hardened in his beard and was now dripping onto the Formica-covered table and the assortment of papers that lay there. I stroked my own beard and wiped my hand on my jeans. I started feeling bad about yelling at the man; he likely held no great love for Leo Gaskell either.

"I'm going to need an address for Mr. Gaskell, if you've got one."
He tore down a sheet that was taped to the wall and handed it to me.
"When was the last time you saw Leo?"

He stared at the table. "'Bout two days ago. We had a meetin'."

"Did he act suspiciously in any way?"

The foreman looked at me. "Nope, I mean, he was like he always is."

Vic interrupted. "And how is that?"

"Swings back an' forth. Sometimes he's so quiet you don't even know he's there, 'n' other times he's jus' crazy."

"I guess one of the crazy times is when he shot you?"

"Yeah." He slumped against the bench seat of the trailer. "He wanted to borrow some equipment from the company, an' that's against the rules."

"What kind of equipment?"

He shook his head, as if to dislodge the information. I was actually starting to like the guy. "A truck."

Vic and I looked at each other as he picked up the mic from the clip on the side of the radio. "Station BR75115 this is 75033, do you copy?" We listened as the waves of noise lapped against the antenna. "If they ain't in the trailer or in a vehicle, we ain't gonna get 'em."

There was a burst of static; the foreman caught it and began dialing the squelch up to where it was just below constant. "Come in BR75115, this is 75033. Johnny, it's the boss. Y'all there?"

"BR75033 this is 75115, over?"

The foreman keyed the mic. "Johnny, is Cecil down there?"

Static. "He said he was supposed to go to field storage yesterday and then work with you guys."

Aliff turned to look at me. "Well, shit. Field storage is where we keep all the heavy equipment when it ain't in use."

It was the second time that day that I had stood looking at a space where a large thing wasn't where it was supposed to be. "Where would he get the keys?" He nodded toward yet another stubby trailer that was parked by the opening of the chain-link fence next to the highway. I could see that the door of the camper was hanging slightly open. The door had been jimmied; it appeared that Leo Gaskell had a signature tool for all occasions. When we got inside, we discovered that he had also forced open the door of the lockbox. The foreman leaned in and examined the labeled hook where the missing key had hung. "Mack, CVH613."

Vic was trying to close the door behind us, and I watched as her breath billowed from the doorway. "Is that big enough to pull a house trailer?"

He nodded. "Oh yeah. It's a tandem. Haul damn near anythin'." He looked back to me. "I guess whatever Cecil or Leo's done, you can add grand theft auto to it."

Vic half laughed. I turned back from her to the foreman. "Mr. Gaskell is a prime suspect in a number of recent homicides." I always felt like a used car salesman when I did it, but I pulled out a card and handed it to him, watching carefully to see if he understood the gravity of the situation. "If you see or have any contact with him, I'll need you to contact me immediately." He nodded and stared at the floor; the wind continued to beat a tattoo with the loose door. "Is there something else you'd like to tell me?"

He licked his lips and caught part of his mustache with his lower teeth. "Yeah, I reckon there is." We waited as he gathered a thought and muttered under his breath, "Man, our ass is gonna be in trouble no matter which way you cut it. We dug somethin' up, jus' out of the canyon, near that little homestead." He looked back up at me. "A body, an old one."

I straightened. "How old?"

"I don't know exactly, but there wasn't much left of it." He looked from Vic to me. "You know how this stuff works, you find ol' Chief Whosiewatchee and pretty soon yer up to yer ass in archeologists and every tree-huggin' son of a bitch in three states." It didn't sound good, even to him, so he kept talking. "I'm six weeks behind schedule, I can't keep good people no matter what I pay 'em, the weather is bound and determined to kick my ass, and all of a sudden I've got a sack of bones on my hands?"

I tried not to move or do anything that might keep him from talking. "What leads you to believe the bones are Indian?"

"Well, they all are around here."

Vic was now standing beside me when she spoke. "What happened to them?"

He didn't speak, so I did. "Let me guess, Leo Gaskell?" He nodded. "How long ago was this?"

" 'Bout a week ago. Cecil . . . I mean Leo's got the remains. I think he's plannin' on blackmail'n the company." He looked at the dull surface of the table in front of him. "I guess I'm in a lotta trouble, huh?"

"Probably, but not as much as Leo." We all nodded.

Aliff said he didn't need a ride back. We pulled out onto the access road leading to the highway. Vic called in the APB on the truck, and we drove along in silence before she spoke again. "It's him."

"It's not him."

She leaned a little forward to try and catch my eye. "You just don't want it to be him." She pulled a leg up and half-turned toward me, signifying that this conversation was far from over. "Why do you not want it to be him?"

I was getting angry again. "Because Charlie Nurburn never made anything better when he was alive, and I don't think he's going to turn into an asset now that his bones might have been unearthed."

She leaned back onto the passenger door and, after a moment, she crossed her arms. "Jesus, don't get mad at me, I didn't dig him up." She turned and looked out the windshield, and it was very quiet in the cab. She looked like an unfinished oil painting with her profile against the whiteout window, where the artist hadn't bothered with the background just yet. It was symbolic; there was no periphery with Vic.

Here I was again, taking it out on the wrong person. The person I wanted to take it all out on was out there somewhere with a hundred-thousand-dollar Mack truck, a mobile home, a grandmother and, most likely, the bones of his grandfather. I considered how weird life had gotten in the last week.

"Charlie Nurburn . . . Charlie fucking Nurburn." She continued to look through the glass as the frozen landscape slid by. "What are the chances? What are the chances that after fifty years . . ."

I sighed. "Charlie Nurburn's sense of timing, even in the afterlife, is impeccable." I stared at the ice-covered highway and felt the surge of impending deliberation loosening the traction of my mind. "Let's go through this carefully, all right?"

I could hear the smile. "Someone finds out that they are the possible heir to millions and counting."

I swung the Bullet onto the approach ramp and headed back north. "No, they're not. Illegitimate children don't get anything. To get anything, you would need a living Charlie Nurburn, so that he could claim his elective share."

"So, you kill Mari?"

I set my jaw. "And then you try and get rid of every person who knows Charlie Nurburn is dead."

She propped her snowy boots up on my dash and gave me a long look. "Finding the mortal remains would certainly queer the deal." She shook her head. "Jesus." She made a face. "By the way, I don't see the finesse of poisoning being one of Leo Gaskell's definitive skills."

"There is someone else." I stared out the windshield for a while, and she let me. "Mari and Lana could be the money, but why kill Anna Walks Over Ice?"

"What did Anna say in all those messages to Isaac Bloomfield?"

I passed a ranch truck hauling hay as Vic continued looking at me. "Isaac's Crow is a little rusty, so I had Henry listen to them and he said that she was upset, wanted to speak to Isaac, but there were no details. There has to be something, though. Her house was broken into."

She studied me. "So Anna heard or saw Leo do something." I nodded. "Why move the trailer?"

"Evidently, grandmother Ellen Runs Horse nee Walks Over Ice is a
sentimental favorite, and he must have found out that we were looking for him." My thoughts darkened past black as I thought of the
trailer park. "Why leave Anna in a trash can where you know I'm going to find her?"

It was quiet in the cab of the truck. "He doesn't care, Walt. He's
jacked up on meth and bat-shit crazy. He did it before and got away
with it. Hell, Mari Baroja killed somebody and got away with it. It's in
the blood."

I took a deep breath. "Those two aren't related."

She continued to watch the snow through the windshield. "Blood's
in everybody."

When we got to the hospital, there was a dark green Excursion with
Montana plates parked in one of the official spots, and the small blessing
of my day was that Bill McDermott had arrived with the body of Mari
Baroja right when I needed him for the body of Anna Walks Over Ice.

I parked the truck and looked at Vic. "You want to go over to the
other wing and bring Cady and Henry over here? The meeting must
be over by now."

"Sure. Are we going to check out Gaskell's address, or what?" I
handed her the folded sheet from my shirt pocket that gave Leo's address as 23 Evergreen Circle. She unfolded the paper and stared at it. "I
guess from here it gets serious."

I studied the steering wheel. "It was already serious."

Ferg was waiting for me outside the door of the autopsy room. "Hey."

"Hey."

I tried to smile. "McDermott inside?"

"With Bloomfield and the new kid." The Ferg nodded. "He Mexican?"

I was glad I wasn't the only one. "Of sorts. Isaac's assisting at Anna's autopsy?"

"Yeah." The Ferg tugged on the bill of his cap. "Walt, I was there. At the Runs Horse place."

I took a second. "Twenty-three Evergreen Circle? Why?"

"That big ol' boy was the one that dumped that refrigerator and all that trash over at Healy Reservoir."

I waited a second before I asked, "Did he answer the door when you went over?"

"Yeah." It took him a minute to come up with a description but, like all Ferg's assessments, it carried resonance. "He was unconcerned." I nodded, but it seemed like he wanted to say more so I made my final attempt at a smile and waited. "Walt, you don't suppose that woman was in that trash can when I went and knocked on that door, do you?"

I shook my head. "No, she was in my office on Thursday."

He stuffed his hands into his jacket pockets and dropped his head. "Thank God. I don't think I could have lived with that."

We both finally smiled grim tight smiles aimed at our boots and stood there for a moment, letting the trains of silence pass between us, two grown men trying to figure out which way to turn next. "Lord, Walt, this is a nightmare."

After he left, I sat in one of the chairs and thought about Leo Gaskell. I had to get somebody over to the courthouse to look up any records there might have been on Ellen Runs Horse, on the mystery son, and on Anna Walks Over Ice. I figured Saizarbitoria was good for that. I could get Henry to check the tribal rolls and get Vic to light a fire under the HPs. I could let the Ferg take care of the county while I went over and had another talk with Lucian about current events. What I really wanted to do was strangle Leo Gaskell with my bare hands.

I scrunched down in the chair, my collar came up even with my nose, and I fought the urge to go to sleep; I didn't last very long, and soon I had that feeling, not so much that I was falling, but that the world was receding.

The snow was blowing in my dream as well; it seemed that no matter where I went, snow followed. It was dark, with the only light diffused and from a distance, as if the illumination was split and redivided by the air alone. There was the laden feel of fog, which carried a weight in my lungs. I concentrated on the snowflakes as they flew in the light, but it was as if I'd left my peripheral vision behind. There was something out there, a bird maybe, but it was larger than any I'd ever seen, its wings pulling at the air that rushed around us. It was as if it had risen from the snow and was growing as it came closer. I kept looking, but it just wouldn't focus. Something was wrong, and my neck muscles drained as my head lolled forward. There was a weight in my face that was heavier than it should have been, so I freed a hand and brought it up. It was cold, but I didn't have any gloves. My hand was almost to my mouth when another reached out from the darkness at my left. It was small, but I could feel the fingers as they tightened around my wrist. It wasn't aggression but desperation that fed her touch. Dark hair fell into my sight, and she tightened her grip. My head fell forward and my chin struck my chest and there was a flash as my one eye tried to focus. My voice sounded strange to me. "I'm sorry, I don't . . ."

It was impossible to see her face, backlit by the light, but even in urgency her voice was sultry, and I could feel my blood thicken as she started to speak.

"I can't . . ."

She looked up and back toward the light; the large bird-like creature continued to draw closer. Her hand deftly released mine, caught my chin, and threaded its way into my beard. Her eyes locked on mine. I could see the lips moving, but the voice seemed to come from very far away. *"Gero arte."*

〰

"Are you all right, Daddy?" I looked up with both eyes at my daughter, who was standing in front of me in the same, full-length coat she'd arrived in. I watched the width of the coat fall open as she placed her hands on my shoulders, the length of it spreading like wings.

I yawned and glanced around at the assembled group. "Just a little tired." I took one of Cady's hands and turned to look at Lana. "How did the meeting go?" It was a modified turban now, and the absence of the silk robe and bunny slippers made me long for resort wear. She didn't say anything, just folded her hands in her lap. "Well, at least you had good representation." I looked up at Vic and got the ball rolling. "Fax that photograph of Leo Gaskell out to DCI, the HPs, and everybody else on the high plains. Get Bill Wiltse over in Fremont County; tell him I need everything they've got on Gaskell. I want to know where he came from, where he's been, and why. Have Ruby run a check through the NCIC and then get over to the home and get some background on Anna Walks Over Ice. I want to know everything they have on her."

She smiled, and I caught a glimpse of that slightly overgrown canine tooth. "You bet." I watched as she man-walked out the double swinging doors.

"Santiago?"

He left McDermott and came over. "Sir?"

You had to love it. "I need you to go to registration and records over at the courthouse. Hurry because they will close right at 5:00." He nodded. "And find whatever you can on Ellen Runs Horse and Anna Walks Over Ice."

"Yes, sir."

"Hey, Sancho?"

"Yes, sir?" He stopped, but only his head turned.

"What does *gero arte* mean?"

His eyes narrowed. "It's Basque for see you later." He stood there for a second longer and, when he was sure I wasn't going to stop him again, he disappeared, too.

I turned back and met Cady's gray eyes, the ones that had been certain of every situation and had realized how all things were since she was nine. "Would you escort Ms. Baroja back to her room while I have a brief technical conversation with Sweeny Todd and the boys?"

She gathered her purse and pulled her coat around her. "Yes, sir."

Smartass. I turned and looked at Henry. His look told me he was in for the long haul. With the addition of the murder of Anna and with the disappearance of Ellen, the situation had also gotten personal for him.

I turned to Isaac Bloomfield and Bill McDermott, who were continuing their discussion at the nurse's desk across the hall. "Gentlemen?" They both turned and looked at me. "I need your help."

Things had gotten complicated since we had decided to bring Anna Walks Over Ice back from the dead. Henry had been cast in the lead role as he was the only Indian. The Bear had wanted the room directly below us, but I figured we had a better chance of isolating Leo on the second floor.

"Were they able to get it out this afternoon?"

"The paper came out late, kind of like a special edition." I handed him the paper I was holding with Anna Walk Over Ice's photograph on the front page. In bold type it read, LOCAL WOMAN STILL ALIVE AFTER TERRIFYING ORDEAL. "If this works, I owe Ernie Brown, Man About Town, a beer."

Vic came in from the hallway and stood at the foot of the bed as the Bear read about his pseudo-self in the *Courant*. She looked strange in the scrubs, her disguise complete with a mask, matching cap, and stethoscope. "How's the patient?"

He didn't look up. "Resting comfortably."

I glanced back at the Bear. "You want to keep the paper?"

"Yes, it might be a long night." He pulled his Vietnam tomahawk from behind his pillow and placed it in the fold of his sheets, just under his right hand. It was a wicked little beast with an adze end in one direction and a hatchet blade in the other, and Henry could throw the thing with a frightening accuracy.

"You do know we want him alive, right?"

I met with the rest of our little troop out by the second floor nurse's station. We were a motley bunch with Dr. Moretti, Saizarbitoria in his North Face cap with a blanket in a wheelchair, and the Ferg in street clothes with a shopping bag. I looked around at our assortment of hidden firepower and almost wished Leo Gaskell wouldn't come; somebody was sure to get killed.

"There are only two ways he can get to the room, either past the nurse's station here or the end of the hallway. "Ferg, I want you seated in the waiting area with a clear view down the hall. Santiago, I want you at the doorway near the stairwell as if you're getting ready to go into or have just come out of your room and get rid of those tactical boots. You look like a cop from a mile off." I turned to Dr. Moretti. "Vic, you can wander. Everybody ready?"

They all nodded.

"This character doesn't show a lot of patience, and he's desperate, so I'm expecting him tonight. It's still relatively early but that doesn't mean he won't come waltzing in here in the next five minutes, so stay sharp. He's big, he's mean, and he's probably self-medicated, so don't be a hero. If you spot him, sing out."

They all nodded again.

I checked all the hallways on my way to the elevator and ran into Leonard Goes Far, the Crow gentleman that made sure the floors of the hospital glowed like thin ice. He nodded, which was all you usually got out of Leonard, so I continued into the elevator and felt the drop of my internal organs match my descent.

There was no third floor on Durant Memorial and there were no patients on two that weren't in on our deception, so there was only one floor and one direction we'd have to worry about. When I got to the front desk, Ruby was waiting, straightening her wig, her eyes a little wider than usual. "You sure he's not going to recognize you?"

"I am." Ruby relaxed just a little. "Vic caught him at the door and ushered him back to her office. I doubt he even remembers I was there."

I nodded. "All the other doors are locked, so the only way he can get in is through here. If he comes in and asks, you just tell him that she's on the second floor and then get busy with something else. "When you're sure he's gone . . ." I waited a moment until she looked back up at me. "When you're sure he's gone, use this." I pointed to the two-way that was under the counter. "Just hit the red button once, that's all it'll take. Nobody else is going to use that red button, so I'll know it's you, and then I'll know he's in." We were all wearing the walkie-talkies set on vibrate.

I had moved Lana to Room 132, one of the inside corridor rooms where there was a thick, metal-core door that could be locked from the inside. She was in there with Cady. I could have taken them both back to the jail, but I figured it was more prudent and safer to keep all the eggs in one basket. I knocked three times, then once. Cady asked who it was, then opened the door enough to look up at me. "C'mere." She followed me just outside the doorway where I tried to hand her a snub-nosed detective's special. "Still remember how to use this?"

She looked at the gun in my hand. "Yes."

I extended it a little toward her. "Just in case everything goes wrong. Whether it was an accident or not, it looks like he tried to kill her before, he may try again." I placed the revolver in her hand. "There's no safety. It's resting on an empty chamber, double-action, all you have to do is pull the trigger."

"I remember." She glanced up at me. "Anyway, I belong to a gun club back in Philadelphia."

"What?"

Her gaze intensified. "A bunch of the attorneys go out every week and shoot at a local gun club up on Spring Garden. One day they asked me if the cowgirl knew how to shoot, so I went with them." She leaned against the wall. "I had a really good teacher."

I waited a moment, but she didn't say anything, so I pulled her in and hugged her. I held her there and squeezed her close. "If you pull it, use it, if you use it, use it to kill."

It was a large closet as supply closets go. There was a built-in drain in the floor with a set of faucets and shelves full of cleaning supplies, mops, brooms, and buckets. I had been smart enough to place one of the waiting-room chairs in there earlier. With the door slightly ajar, I could see the one leading into our Special Forces Anna Walks Over Ice. I hadn't checked on the Bear; I figured he had his tomahawk.

I settled in and tried to think of something to do while I waited, something other than waiting. I read a couple of labels on some bottles, flipped a mop handle between my hands, and thought. I thought about whether Leo Gaskell would win, place, or show.

I heard someone at the end of the hall. It was a familiar voice. I picked up my hat and opened the door as he continued, "And undercover means you don't leave the handle of that goddamned Remington, sawed-off scattergun hangin' outta the shopping bag for every Tom's Dick and Convict to see."

Vic was already there when I got to them. "Lucian, what are you doing here?"

"This the way you run a stakeout, with peckerhead here advertising the whole show?"

Peckerhead was the descriptive term Lucian used equally for plants, animals, and inanimate objects. "Lucian . . ."

"I come up here to see how this pissant operation was goin', and from what I can see, it ain't."

I pushed my hat back and sighed. "You were supposed to stay with Isaac."

"Christ, he snores loud enough to wake the dead. I locked the door when I left."

I looked back at Vic, who was smiling and folding her arms over her breasts the way she always did when Lucian was around. The Ferg continued to look at the floor. The old sheriff wasn't going to go back willingly, and I couldn't leave him out in the open to abuse the staff and draw attention to himself.

"Dark as the inside of a cow in here." He sniffed. "Smells funny."

"It's a supply closet." I heard him rustling around and smelled the tobacco pouch he had just unzipped. "Don't even think about loading up that pipe and smoking it."

He continued, "Tryin' to improve the environment."

"And Leo Gaskell will smell it from halfway down the hallway."

He zipped up the beaded pouch, for now. "Who the hell is this Gaskell person, anyway?"

"Please keep your voice down?" I leaned my shoulder against the doorjamb and tried to find a comfortable position. "We're pretty sure he's the one that tried to drown you in your bathtub." I let that one settle in for a while. He didn't say anything. "Leo Gaskell may be related to Ellen Runs Horse. That name mean anything to you?" He still didn't say anything, so I turned around and looked at him. "Maybe Ellen Walks Over Ice?"

He was sitting with his real leg propped up over the fake one, staring at the tobacco pouch and pipe sitting in his lap. "Yep, Anna's sister."

"Did you know she had a kid with Charlie Nurburn?"

"Yep. I was a deputy, for Christ sake."

"Is there anything else you'd like to tell me, while we're on the subject?"

He exhaled deeply. "Kid's dead."

I continued watching him in the thin strip of light from the partially open door. "Charlie Nurburn's illegitimate son died?"

"Yep."

"How do you know that?"

"She told me."

"Ellen Runs Horse?" He nodded but didn't look up. "Saizarbitoria couldn't find any reference to Ellen Walks Over Ice or any children at the courthouse."

"It was an illegitimate, half-breed kid born and died of cholera in Acme in 1950, and you think there were gonna be certificates?" He snorted and stuffed his pipe full.

I decided to let him smoke; maybe it might occupy his mouth. "I'm working on a motive, and I was trying to put together a connection between Leo Gaskell and the Barojas, but if Charlie and Ellen's kid died, then there isn't any way to connect the two. I was working under the assumption that Leo might be the grandson, since he had one of Charlie Nurburn's pistols." He lit the pipe, and I had to admit that it smelled better. I watched him in the half-light, the smoldering embers of the pipe glowing red in the dark closet. "Lucian, where did you bury Charlie Nurburn?"

A second passed. "Yer just not gonna let that go, huh?"

"I think Leo Gaskell may have found him."

He was silent for a moment. "Yer shittin' me." He chewed on that one for quite a while. His dark eyes blinked, he took the pipe from his mouth, and pointed with the stem across the hall. "Who you got in the room?"

"Henry Standing Bear."

"Well hell . . . if he gets in there ol' Ladies Wear'll cut him from cock to crown with a dull deer antler and save the taxpayers some money."

Lucian had a way with Indian names that was nothing short of creative. I started to respond, but the air caught in my throat for a second, and we both remained absolutely still. There were voices at the end of the hall, this time they came from Saizarbitoria's direction, and they were growing louder. I had forgotten that the door opened to the inside of the closet, and two sheriffs with a collective three legs trying to get out offered a variety of excitement.

Once we finally made it, I could see Vic talking to a man whom they had against the wall beside the stairwell door. Santiago had the man's arm in a reverse wristlock high at the middle of his back with his feet pulled out and spread so that his weight was against the partition. Vic had holstered her Glock, and it looked as if she was trying to keep from smiling.

As Lucian followed me down the hallway, I noticed a potted poinsettia and a card lying on the floor and scooped them up. I stopped a couple of yards away and called off the armada. "Let him go." Sancho did, and Vic stepped behind Saizarbitoria so that he couldn't see that she was trying not to laugh out loud. "Joe, what the hell are you doing here?"

He cleared his throat and gestured to the card and plastic-wrapped flowers I held. "We were just glad that Anna was all right, and we all chipped in." He glanced around again and then over to Saizarbitoria's empty wheelchair. "Do you mind if I sit down, I think I might be having a little trouble . . ."

Santiago holstered his weapon and held the chair as Joe sat. I thought he might be having a heart attack but then noticed the dark spot on Joe's pants. I glanced over to Vic and she nodded, knowing I would want to speak with Santiago. I looked back down to Joe. "How about we get you to the bathroom, then we can talk?"

He folded his hands across his lap and nodded, his face pale and his hands trembling. "That would be good."

I watched as Vic wheeled the poor man down the hall toward the bathrooms near the nurse's station and turned to the Ferg, Lucian, and Saizarbitoria. "What happened?"

"He came out of the stairwell, and I spoke to him, but he didn't stop, so I bumped him, and he started yelling like a mad man."

Great. I glanced to the elder statesman. "What are you smiling about?"

Lucian responded, of course. "Well, as incapable as this outfit may look, we're still able to scare the piss outta the local gentry."

I shook my head, turned, and made my way back down the hallway to Henry's room. He was at the door when I got there with the handle of the tomahawk palmed against his forearm as he leaned against the opening. I noticed that the surface of the thing absorbed light. He seemed perfectly relaxed. "False alarm?"

I was about to speak when the walkie-talkie at my belt began to vibrate.

13

I jerked my head up and looked down the hall at Ferg and Saizarbitoria as they stared from their belts to me. I searched in the other direction, but Vic had disappeared around the corner; when I got back to Henry all he said before shutting the door in my face was "Go."

"Santiago, throw the blanket over your shoulders and stay there till Vic gets back with the wheelchair. Lucian, get in the closet, and Ferg come with me." I charged down the hall and almost collided with Vic and the wheelchair as I turned the corner at the nurse's station. "You vibrate?"

"Yeah, and it was very exciting."

"Where's Joe Lesky?"

She was already past me and had forced Ferg to sidestep in the hall-way to escape being run over. "First stall in the men's room; I told him that if he stirred, I'd kneecap him."

I glanced over at the Ferg, who shrugged. "Sounds like the perimeter's secure."

I pointed to his previous spot on the bench. "Sit." He smiled and hurried by as I went for the supply closet and ran the door into Lucian, who had already manned his post.

"Jesus H. Christ!"

"Damn it, Lucian. Move over."

"I am over!"

I squeezed past the door and sat on half my chair. "Shhh . . ."

"I ain't the one talkin', goddamn it." I turned and gave him the proverbial dirty look.

It was quiet in the hallway, so Vic must have stayed with Saizarbitoria.

I could hear the hospital heating system and Lucian's aggravated breathing, which had subsided into a regular pattern. I waited and strained my ears, but there was nothing to hear. I went back over the plan and ran through the usual litany of doubts. What were the chances that Leo Gaskell would come straight to the room? Would he be smart enough to check the clipboard we had casually left on the counter at the nurse's station with Anna Walks Over Ice's name listed for Room 216? Or, had he asked Ruby what room Anna was in? If he did, there would be an older gentleman seated in one of the hallway chairs with a shopping bag between his legs seemingly falling asleep. At the end of the hall would be a small, dark-haired general practitioner assisting a patient to his room and, if he looked close enough, a supply closet door barely ajar.

I waited twenty minutes and then started thinking about my options. I could continue to wait, or I could blow the whole operation and go do a little clear and hold. For some reason, Leo had decided to take his time and, for my money, that made him infinitely more dangerous. Leo was developing tactics. He owed the state at least two lives; I doubted he was keeping score. That was okay, I was.

Lucian had fallen asleep.

I stood, and he stirred. "What?"

I smiled at my old mentor as he craned his wrinkled neck, the one I had thought of wringing on and off for quite some time. "Nothing. I'm going out for a little walk."

He watched me and nodded. "Lasted longer than I would have."

Praise from Caesar. "You want a gun?"

Silly question. He put a hand out as I unsnapped the .45 and handed it to him. "You got one in the pipe."

"What are you gonna use, harsh language?"

I glanced out the crack in the doorway. "I'll get the shotgun from Ferg." I looked back into the darkness at the old sheriff and my gun. "Don't shoot me if I come back."

It was blinding in the hallway, but it felt good to stretch my back. I looked down the hall at Vic and Saizarbitoria; they looked competent and questioning as I held a finger to my lips. I pointed at them and looped a forefinger and thumb into an okay. They nodded, and I stepped across the hall. I knocked twice and opened the door a little. I waited a second then spoke into the black. "Henry?"

"What are you doing?" It was a scolding tone.

"I've got a feeling."

"Oh, goodie." There was a deep sigh.

I closed the door and started for Ferg's position. He checked in both directions as I stopped just short of the intersecting corridor. I took a look for myself, stepped across, and knelt down beside him. "Got your sidearm?"

"Yeah."

"Cock it and put it in the bag, I'm going to borrow your shotgun."

"Going huntin'?"

"Yep."

"What do you want to do about Joe Lesky?"

I glanced over in the direction of the bathroom. "He made any noise?"

"Not a peep."

"You reckon Vic gave him a heart attack?"

"She does me."

As I checked the short-barreled shotgun, the Ferg went over to the bathroom door and reassured Joe. When he came back, I slipped down the opposite direction and checked the only other wing on the second floor. There were no doors ajar, so unless I was going to do a room-to-room search, all that was left was the stairwell at the end of this hallway. There were heavy metal doors with thick, wire-reinforced windows set on a diagonal. I peered through as I passed, casually swung the door open, and held the shotgun ready.

Nobody.

I could go down and check the short entryway that led to the elevators, or I could continue from here to the first floor. The entry corridor would have been easily visible from Ferg's location, so I decided to drop down through the stairwell. I eased the door shut and glanced through the four runs of stairs to the concrete floor of the basement below. I hated basements.

When I got to the first floor there was a set of tracks leading down the steps. I placed my foot next to the prints and knelt down to look at them. The prints were of a different brand than the ones that had been left in the snow at the home, but they were larger than mine. Different shoes, but it was the same foot.

I decided to forgo the conversation with Ruby that I had planned and continued down the stairs to the next security door, which was labeled, in large red letters, HOSPITAL PERSONNEL ONLY. I eased open the heavy door and looked down the corridor toward a steel screen-encaged bulb that hung about halfway down and that gave off a weak yellowish light. The footprints feathered away on the smooth sheen of the chemically coated concrete, and my only clue abandoned me.

I quietly closed the stairwell door and moved along the wall to the first door on the right. I reached across and turned the knob. Locked.

I glanced into the darkness between the next bulb and myself, another twenty feet away. The second door was on my side and an equal distance from the first. I moved along the wall and tried the knob. It was stiff but turned and opened. I glanced in, but the room was dark. I felt along the wall and flipped a switch. It was a storage room with cut-down trays and medical cabinets. There were sterile dressings, bandages, and utility carts, but no Leo Gaskell, so I flipped off the light and quietly closed the door.

I thought I might have heard a noise, but I couldn't be sure. I stood there for a moment, listening to the constant thrum of the building as it continued to go about its business of life and death. Join the club.

The next door was locked as well, but I could see from here where the hallways joined at the center, just as they did on the two main floors. There were large pipes sticking from the wall that returned and disappeared into the concrete, and there was a little more light coming from the adjoining hallway. An old metal desk, crowded with papers and folders, was shoved against the wall. There was a chair kicked out to the side, and a faint set of boot prints where whoever had come down the stairwell had sat and waited.

Waited for what? Waited for whom?

It had been a while since I'd checked in, so I plucked the walkie-talkie from my belt. It was a calculated move, but I felt pretty sure about it. I switched the transceiver to silent so the only indicator would be the LED gain that hopefully one of my staff would notice. I hit the button. I hit the button again, clicking it off and on. Still nothing. I hit it one more time and got a response. "Where the fuck are you?" Good thing I had turned the volume down. "See anything?"

"Footprints, you?"

"Nothing. Do you need backup?"

"No."

It was silent for a moment. "You suck."

The bottom drawer on the right-hand side was slightly ajar. I stooped and pulled out an impressive ring of keys, each one numbered and color coded with small plastic edges indicating the floor and wing of each. Why would someone leave an entire set of master keys in an unlocked drawer in the basement? I quickly flipped through the sequential numbers to Anna's supposed room, each key clicking like an abacus. Key number 216 was missing. I entertained a dark series of thoughts as ice water flooded my bowels, and I turned the keys to the 100 series and found that key 132 was also gone.

The initial response must have been that my left hand pulled the fore grip back, moving the action bar and bolt assembly of the Remington Model 870 back into a cocked position. This same hand must have then come forward as I dropped the keys and slammed a plastic shell with slightly imperfect and deformed buckshot into the action and locked it for fire. Then my right forefinger must have punched the safety through the mechanism, because it did not fire as I lurched forward, pushed the desk back, and ran into the darkness.

I must have chosen the far passageway because it would give me a clear shot from the stairwell to the end of the corridor. I know it took no longer than a few seconds for me to make it down the hall, through the door, and up the stairs, but in the adrenalin-induced state it had all shifted into a hazed torpor. All I remember was yanking the door open to the first floor with the shotgun ready.

My father had trained me; he was a precise and persistent shooting instructor who started teaching me when I was five. Most people are self-taught; they don't shoot enough to acquire skill or even become used to handling guns. They stand wrong, hold their heads wrong, and even close one eye when they sight, thus cutting down vision and handicapping themselves in their ability to judge distance.

Thirty-five yards.

I clicked the safety off. "Sheriff's Department. Freeze!"

Only his head turned to me; his hands remained on the knob. He smiled with horrible teeth, and drew his shoulder back.

I knew that I would make the shot, just as I was sure that there was a .38 caliber revolver waiting on the other side of that door that was being held in a two-handed, standing position by a steady hand with a set of beautifully manicured nails. At thirty-five yards the 12-gauge would more than hurt him, but at eight feet the .38 would kill him. It wasn't that I minded Leo dead all that much, but I didn't want Cady to do it.

As his shoulder came forward so did mine, and I fired.

Contrary to popular belief, even the most powerful of modern loads and weapons only cause the target to slump and fall; Leo's attempt to push the door open was converted into an assisted collapse into the doorjamb where his knees buckled for a moment. He straightened as he turned to glare at me.

"Sheriff's Department, don't move!"

He did, of course, and transferred his weight into a galloping retreat down the corridor. One foot slightly dragged behind the other in his attempt to get away. I pushed off and started to pursue him. He was moving fast, especially for a man with a couple of extra ounces of lead in him. There were fire exits at the end of the hallways at Durant

Memorial, but he turned the corner leading to the front entrance and disappeared in the direction of the desk and Ruby.

I am not the fastest man in Absaroka County; I knew I wasn't even the fastest man in the hospital right now, but I was going to have to do. I tried to make the corner at the entryway and bounced off the far wall in time to see the pneumatic doors at the front of the hospital slowly close. Ruby was standing at the reception desk waving me on as I approached. "Go! Go!"

I slammed through the two sets of doors and onto the sidewalk. Surely they had heard the shotgun up on the second floor; I was going to need backup. He had changed direction and was running the length of the hospital toward the snow-covered golf course and the town park that were located beyond the drifts that had been plowed against the parking lot's chain-link fence.

Sixty yards, and I was keeping pace.

The air was cold, and each step felt as if I were pushing a car. I cursed my laziness at not running for the last few weeks but watched with satisfaction as Leo slipped on the man-size mountains of plowed snow and crashed into the fence. I started to bring the shotgun up but, incredibly, his hands clutched the twisted top of the railing, and he threw himself over and into the darkness beyond; I was convinced he wasn't human.

I knew I had to gain all the momentum I could between here and there, so I lengthened my stride and pushed the car harder. The frozen crust held just long enough for me to use it as a ramp. I calculated my options, threw the Remington over the fence, and hit the top rail at about my hips. The continued momentum carried me over head first, flipping me and depositing me flat on my back onto the cushioning snow below. I forced the air into my lungs, lurched up into a sitting position, and searched for the shotgun; I couldn't find it. I looked up to see Leo Gaskell making time as I scrambled onto my knees and looked for any disturbance in the snow that might indicate where my only weapon might be.

Nothing.

It was a dreadful decision, but the only one that made sense if I was going to catch him. I rolled to one side, pushed off with my back leg, and started after him unarmed. I could still see him in the distance as the moon struggled through the cloud cover and the branches of the huge conifers that surrounded the ninth green and the Clear Creek reservoir where an awful lot of golfers lost their balls. The snow was almost to our knees, but his long legs made progress like some crazy posthole tamper.

Methamphetamines, had to be.

There was a gradual decline, which led to a flat and a few deciduous trees before you got to what looked like a break in the fence and the creek beyond. He just didn't seem to be slowing, whereas my second and third wind seemed to be going the way of the first. My lungs felt like they were going to explode, but I could hear something coming up on my left. It was Saizarbitoria, and he passed me. His knees pumped above the snow like Leo's, and I could see the Baretta 9mm in his left hand and the bare soles of his feet flashing back at me as he pulled away. It didn't take long for him to get far ahead of me but, after a few more strides, I discovered that I could keep pace by running in Sancho's naked footprints. His stride was only a little shorter than mine, and I gained speed going down the hill. Just as he got to the flat area, Leo disappeared through the sagging part of the fence.

In the spears of moonlight, I could see where the bank dropped off down to another level area where the wind had pushed the snow pack from the reflective surface of the ice on Clear Creek. I saw Saizarbitoria charge through the fence, through the trees, and he too was gone.

By the time I got to the flat, lumbered through the fence, and bounced off one of the trees, I could see them struggling at the creek bank. The elongated, stalklike shadow of Leo Gaskell struck Saizarbitoria with a hammering, roundhouse blow, and I watched as my deputy slumped, and Leo lifted him to slug him again.

Up until this moment my size and weight had worked against me but, with only thirty feet to go, I put everything I had into Leo. He was just turning as I hit him with all the accumulated speed of the last five minutes; we carried Saizarbitoria with us as we went. I felt the breath go out of Leo as we flew over and out onto the middle of the creek. The three of us landed with a shuddering thud as the surface of the ice indented with a resonating sound that carried vibrations across the surface, through Leo Gaskell, Sancho, and into me. Almost immediately, the ice shattered and dropped us into the freezing water that traveled swiftly beneath the surface. Sancho wasn't moving, and I could feel he was under us and was dropping faster as the edge of the ice crumbled from underneath.

I closed one hand around Leo's struggling shoulders and clasped the hood of his insulated coveralls with the other, the quick popping noise telling me it had detached from the rest of him. He lurched sideways in an attempt to free himself of me, but I held on with one hand and dragged him back to the black water behind us. I threw the hood away and slapped a hand on Sancho as the current yanked at his legs.

I could feel Leo wrench away from me again. He was a monster; his huge shoulders and chest were disproportionate in comparison with his lean waist and limbs, and his head seemed like some block teetering out on the end of his stem-like neck. If my suspicions were correct, Leo Gaskell suffered from lack of appetite, insomnia, exceedingly high blood pressure, palpitations, and cyanosis with cerebral hemorrhage next on the list but, right now, he was just strong as an ox.

There were fissures in the surrounding ice, and the thumping of the trapped air and water was as loud as our struggling. I could see large chunks of the ice breaking apart where Sancho was sinking. I tightened my grip and tried to drag him toward me, but Leo took advantage of my brief distraction to twist sideways again and bring his booted foot up and into my face. I heard the surprising crack and grinding of broken bone. I tried to stretch my facial muscles to check the damage, but nothing felt as if it were moving.

I couldn't hang on to Sancho and Leo; Leo slipped my grasp, getting half his body onto the thicker ice at the edge of the creek, and he watched as the ice surrounding Saizarbitoria and me broke off with the sound of pistol shots.

The last thing I saw of Leo Gaskell, with my one eye, he was smiling, showing those twisted and rotting teeth.

There wasn't a lot of time to prepare for the effects of the water, and maybe that was a blessing. There's a tingling and a high itch that shrieks in the back of your head when you hit water this cold, probably some kind of alarm that's telling your body that this is a really bad idea. All I could think to do was keep a hold on Sancho's jacket as I felt him slip down with me. I couldn't feel the bottom, and the ridge of ice around us was breaking away in handfuls. My legs went along with the current, pushing against the undersurface and giving me just enough leverage to shove Sancho's chest up and onto the ice.

I turned my head sideways, trying to get the rest of Saizarbitoria's unconscious body out of the water, and it was then that the ledge I was hanging on to completely let go. I released Sancho so that he would not be dragged under with me and scrambled with both hands to get another grip on the broken lip of the ice, but it was too late. I was cognizant enough to draw a deep breath as the ice broke beneath me.

The sweeping current of Clear Creek yanked me below as my one eye looked for the surface by following the bubbles as they swirled away from me and began a stately rise to the air above. Paisleys of plum and electric green and the stark white of the moon reflected in the world I had come from. I hoped that I had gotten Saizarbitoria far enough up so that he would not be pulled under as well.

I was bleeding adrenaline, and the areas of unprotected skin were now absolutely numb. There were shadowy, echoing sounds that approached from all directions. With a sudden exertion, I slapped my hands against the smooth facade of the underside of the ice as part of my remaining air escaped with a faint rumbling noise that matched the thumping of my hands against the hard surface.

The one eye was still functioning, so I strained to see the bubbles, but the view was distorted and confusing and I continued to feel as if I were falling backward. The weight of my head pivoted me to the side and my arms trailed out behind me. I frantically tried to right myself and turn back, but my arms wouldn't move, and my fingers felt motionless.

The dull glow of the surface didn't appear from above but seemed to radiate all around me. Somehow it was lighter now, and I could just see that the bottom of the creek was scattered with broken tree limbs and large stones. Everything seemed to glow with a pale light with no shadow, and grand sweeps of bubbles stood still in the frozen water with deep cracks that shone like knife blades.

The back of my head hit something hard as I moved along, and a little more air escaped. I could taste a small amount of blood in my mouth, and my head was yanked down with the current and a sharp pain lingered in my side. There was a continuous thumping, but it was more rhythmical than before and was now accompanied by a continuous baritone that pressed painfully against my ears.

The vertigo caused by the current had subsided to a dull ache of inverted velocity. The uniform horizon had shifted from green to an almost impenetrable black, and the only thing I could hear was the sound of the drums that pounded my skull against what felt like solid rock.

With all the energy I had left, I pivoted to one side and tried to break free from whatever was holding me. I tried to drive my elbow into the ice above as the current knocked me back and forth. I shifted, this time keeping the movement more compact and not allowing the water to rob me of momentum: a resounding thump and then nothing. The bleeding adrenalin staunched, and air was now the issue. I slammed my hand against the ice this time, and the sound reverberated along with the drums. Shadows moved in the dull glow of the surface as I flailed against it with wooden fingers. I stretched my arms out in an attempt to widen my hunt and searched for any opening, but there was none. I almost laughed when the shadows appeared above me, and there was a strident sound, a shrieking din that sounded like the warbling pitch of Cheyenne plainsong, and I must have been hallucinating because it seemed as if a huge blade had knifed through the thickness of the ice. I fumbled a hand toward it, but it disappeared, and the pressure in my lungs built to the point of explosion. I felt my diaphragm tense as it prepared to blow my lungs clear of my last breath. I held it for a few seconds more, just as the broad blade of something like an axe appeared again.

They say that your life passes before your eyes, but that's not what happens. What happens is that you think of all the things you didn't get done, big things, small things, all the things that are left.

I exhaled and immediately drew in two lungs full of frozen water. There were still sounds, the echoing thump of the drums and the shrieking din of the discordant song, but they slowly faded as I wavered there in the current. The pressure pulled my chin down to my chest, and I noticed a white round speck lodged against the dark mud at the banks of Clear Creek just before the rushing eddies rocked me into the black.

"How is my English?"

Her voice came from the right and was slightly behind me. I dipped my head and looked under my arm to see a beautiful pair of naked suntanned feet. She was standing in the same swales of buffalo grass as she had before. I turned to look at her. "Good, better than my Basque." She was gorgeous and was wearing what she always wore in my dreams, a flowing summer dress with small white dots on a dark background. A breeze drifted from the mountains and pushed the chiffon against her legs, and the sun glowed warm against the Big Horns. She was petite, and my first instinct was to place my hand at the small of her back and lift her up so that I could get a closer look at the perfect face hidden in the swirl of dark hair. She reached a hand out, then let it drop in resignation, and glanced toward the ridges of the canyon above. I followed her eyes and noticed that clouds had gathered where

the mountains and sky met. There was a long line of Cheyenne warriors on horseback pressed in formation to the horizon at the break of
the canyon. "Friends of yours?"

She laughed. "Yours."

I looked back at the feathered headdresses, the beads, the fringe,
and the weapons. The horsemen were painted, along with their
horses, and their power stopped my breathing. One of them stood in
the saddle and looked down at me, the hair a different color than the
rest. "Is that somebody I know?"

She gestured with a slight incline of her head. "Yes." I looked up,
but as soon as I smiled, the warriors and their horses and the woman
standing in the saddle disappeared.

Mari laughed, and it was stunning. It lingered in a luxurious moment, and I studied the little laugh lines at the corners of her mouth;
they were like friends I had forgotten. I watched her talk and felt like I
was being towed backward through heavy water.

She stepped forward and took my hand in hers. She was so beautiful, I could not breathe. "I'm sorry, I don't know what's the matter."
Her free hand rested on my shoulder. Her fingers were warm, and a
fingernail flicked across the hairs at the back of my neck.

She pulled my face down. "It's okay."

I suddenly felt off balance. Her head had tilted to the side to escape the brim of my hat, and I could feel her breath against my chest
as she went up on tiptoe. "Sorry, I've got something in my throat or
something."

"It's okay."

Her face came closer, and all I could see were those huge brown
eyes that made me feel as if I were walking in mud that squeezed up
between my toes. I was still falling, and the background slid away from
me as she made tentative contact with my lower lip. There was still
something caught in my throat. "This is getting embarrassing."

"It's okay." She smothered my mouth with hers and blinked. Her
hands were now on either side of my face and were holding me as I
looked into gold bottle rockets shooting into the darkness of her

pupils with contrails of iridescence, but the colors changed suddenly and tarnished, and I felt very cold. My back bent, and I felt it arch against a hard surface.

I still felt her lips on mine. I felt the warmth and the desperation as her hands covered the rest of my face and refused to let go. I rolled to the side, and the pressure in my head lessened as I coughed and breathed with a ferocious intake of air. I felt as though I was being beaten with a hundred broom handles. I blinked, but my left eye didn't seem to cooperate, and my right one felt like it was about to fall out.

She was still there in my blurred vision; she sat on her knees and held on to the lapels of my jacket. Somebody was there with her, just to the side, some kind of monk with a hood pulled up around his face, and another person I couldn't make out. I could almost swear the monk had a hatchet. He shook almost as badly as I did, and I was afraid he might drop it on me.

She pulled me up by my collar, held me there, and I could feel her sobbing against me. Her grip was strong, and she pulled my head into the crook of her neck and rocked me. I could feel her pulse as she pressed me against her throat. The trembling in my own body refused to subside. I tried to move, and my head rolled back just enough to see her face. Her fingers slipped, and my head bounced on her warm, soft lap.

There was a time, a time I remember when people would show up and sit on the hillsides, and the professional diver would come to town from Casper. I was a child and sat on my mother's lap and watched in wonder as he put on his cumbersome diver's suit with the military-surplus, two-hose regulator. He would disappear into one of the small ponds to retrieve the little white balls. Every time he would reappear with a rush of bubbles, the assembled crowd would cheer and whistle. I asked my mother why it was that everyone applauded whenever the diver reemerged with the basket of ten-cent golf balls. I looked up at her blond hair and the translucent blue of her eyes where the angle of the sun shone through her pupils, and she smiled and squeezed my hand. "Small mysteries solved."

I took another breath, and the tremors became so great that my teeth felt like they were going to break off in my mouth. I started to rise, but her other hand held me against her lap. I tried to smile, but instead bit my lip and breathed out a liquid belch.

My hands fell to the side, and I must have loosened my grip because the golf ball that I had been holding slipped from my grasp and rolled across the ice.

She reached out and pounded my chest in a fury with her fist. There wasn't much feeling there, and the only reason I could tell she was striking me was that my head jarred a little with each blow. She beat on me until I feebly raised my hands in surrender. Her tears struck my face. "You stupid fucking son of a bitch!"

14

"We think it was the extra layer of fat that saved you." We were seated on the table in one of the examination rooms and were still waiting for the report from the eye doctor. Henry was sitting on my right because he knew it would irritate me. "A man with a normal amount of fat would have perished." I sighed, trying not to think about how bad my face hurt and instead fingered the little plastic band they had attached to my wrist. The band had my name, age, blood type, and two bar codes, one for my meds and one for my lab, but I wasn't planning on being here in another fifteen minutes so the whole system would become academic.

"You are lucky your coat snagged on the tree branch, or we would have never found you." I fingered the tender spot at my side and stared at the floor with my one eye. "We argued over who had to give you mouth-to-mouth, but since I was the one who pulled you out, Vic did it." He nudged me with an elbow. "I think she enjoyed it, or would have under different circumstances." I felt him shift his weight and then hold something far out in front of me so that I could see it. "I thought you would like a souvenir from the briny deep." He dropped a golf ball into my outstretched hand.

"Thank you."

"You are welcome." Simple and honest; no one accepted praise with the grace of the Cheyenne.

"How's Sancho?"

"I think he was more ashamed than hurt and is up and walking around even though his feet are sore." He watched me. "I think he is embarrassed that you had to save him." He was still smiling. "I told him you have saved lots of people."

I nodded, and it was quiet for a moment, so I changed the subject. "How deep is Clear Creek?"

He slid off the table and walked around to where I could see him. He still had the Vietnam Special Forces tomahawk in an oxblood sheath at his belt. "Usually three to four feet."

"Then why is it we have the Challenger Deep of the Marianas Trench out there?"

He was trying not to smile. "You picked the part that used to be the old reservoir."

"I didn't pick it, Leo Gaskell did." I looked up through my one eyebrow. "How deep is that damn thing?"

"Twelve feet where you went in."

I looked up at the clock in the examination room: 11:23 A.M. "I have to get out of here, where the hell is the damn doctor?" I started to reach up to my ear, but he slapped my hand.

His eyes stayed steady with mine as he slowly shook his head. "You are a horrible patient."

I bounced the golf ball off the floor. "How are Lana and Cady?"

"Still asleep. They had a late night after we brought you in. Their door is locked, and Jim Ferguson is sitting in a chair outside it." He dipped his head for a better look at my one eye. "Is that Cady's Chief's Special?"

I bounced the ball again. "I loaned it to her."

He nodded. "There were a lot of guns being scattered about last night."

"Anybody find the shotgun?"

He stood up straight and flipped his hair back. "I did. I also found Saizarbitoria's Beretta and your hat." He gestured toward the offending article on the chair beside the door. "I like him."

"Who?"

"Saizarbitoria." He thought about it. "He is tough. He outran me last night, barefoot."

It was as good a scale as any. "He's also half our age." I waited a mo-ment. "How the hell did Leo Gaskell get away?"

"Perhaps Leo Gaskell is tougher." Henry's turn to sigh. "That, and Joe Lesky's car has been stolen."

I waited a second to make sure I had heard him right. "What?"

"He must have doubled back to the hospital parking lot and taken the car which, lucky for Leo Gaskell, was unlocked and had the keys in it."

I shook my head and reached up to scratch my eye; he slapped my hand again. "I wasn't going to touch my ear, damn it." I rested my head against the pinched fingers that now held the bridge of my nose in an attempt to snatch the pain from my head. I bumped my eye patch and immediately regretted it. "Have we got an APB out on Lesky's car?"

"Yes."

"No signs of a Mack truck with a house trailer connected to it, I suppose?"

"No."

I released my nose. "Where's the staff?"

"All back at the office; we did not think there was any reason to con-tinue the stakeout."

I thought about Leo. I sat there like a typewriter with the carriage jammed. "Something's not adding up." I waited a while longer but, predictably, it was hovering, my usual itch just out of reach. "If you were going to kill somebody, would you walk there?" I looked down at my clean clothes, a gift from the hospital laundry, and turned my head so that my good eye was toward him. "Something else that's been bothering me . . ." I scratched that little itch in the back of my mind and started making connections. "Why didn't Leo kill Lana at the bakery?"

He took a deep breath of his own, and I marveled at how easily it went in and came out. "Any chance you might have chased him off?"

I summoned up the images from that morning. "There were tracks but no vehicle."

"Taking into consideration Leo's laissez-faire attitude toward transport, do you think it possible that he was still there?"

I thought about the one set of Lana's prints going into the bakery and none coming out. "He must have been."

The door opened, and Andy Hall was the first through it, just the man I wanted to see, even if it was only with one eye. Behind Dr. Hall were Isaac and Bill McDermott, who had decided to stick around in case we turned up some more bodies. It was three against two, but I had the Indian and that always evened things out.

Dr. Andy was the opthamologist from Sheridan and was a kind-hearted soul with an intelligent and quiet demeanor. He reached out with long-fingered hands, raising the eye patch and tilting my head back. It was funny how doctors handled people like luggage. "How do you feel?"

"Great."

He looked at me doubtfully. "Nonpenetrating fracture of the left orbital with lacerations to the retina." He half turned to the attending gaggle, and they all nodded in agreement. "I sutured the damage to the epicanthic fold; any cosmetic alterations can be done after the eye has stabilized." He released my head and looked at me. "How's your vision?"

"Before or after the eye patch?"

He looked back to Isaac for some assistance. The old doctor stepped forward with his hands clasped together. "The cold water was enough to slow your metabolic rate, but just so you do not underestimate the seriousness of the situation, you drowned last night."

I glanced over at the coroner. "If it was all that serious, I'd be talking to him."

McDermott was quick. "You wouldn't be talking at all."

Isaac started in again. "Pulmonary edema carries a progressive bacterial infection which we are preventively treating with antibiotics, but your shortness of breath, poor color, and general weakness . . ."

"Walking pneumonia." I smiled at them, and it hurt. He hadn't stayed in his hospital, so why should I? I snapped the little plastic wristband off and handed it to Isaac, who already had his hand out. I stood and picked up my hat. "All right, we've discussed the pneumonia; let's do some walking." I put my hat on; it felt funny, and I'm sure it looked worse. "I'll take the drugs if you want me to." He handed me a small plastic bottle. I steered Isaac out of the room and moved down the hall a little ways. "Is there a ring of master keys to the hospital that is kept in the basement?"

He thought. "A custodian might have left a set there, because it is easier for him to get to them, but he shouldn't have. It is a breach of security."

"Could you check that for me?"

"Yes, I believe I can do that."

I put my hand on his shoulder and looked back to the Bear. "Are those keys still on the floor beside that desk?"

"Vic took them for fingerprinting."

I looked back to Isaac. "I'll return those to you when we're through."

Bill McDermott stopped us as we passed him. "I'll need written permission to release the body of Mrs. Baroja to the next of kin. They've requested her about four times now."

"I don't suppose anybody's asked about Anna Walks Over Ice?"

He glanced at Henry. "Actually, somebody has."

I looked back to the Cheyenne Nation with my good eye and tried my half smile. "Of course they have."

It was a short drive over to the bakery from the hospital; I almost hit three other cars on the way. "Maybe I should drive?"

"This eye patch thing takes a little getting used to." It had warmed up, but there were still extended icebergs lining the roadsides and median. It had been a humid snow, and the coated trees looked as if they had been vacuum sealed for next year's use. I looked out at Main Street, at the three-quarter inch, exterior plywood cutouts of bells, wreaths, reindeer, and the like. Twelve years running, and I was sure they were the most unattractive decorations in Wyoming; exterior ply holds ugly a long time. I remembered Ruby's promise to take care of my Christmas shopping. I would have to check.

I parked in front, cut the motor, and unlocked my Remington long-barreled 870 from the dash. "I wonder if she has a hide-a-key."

"What's the fun of that?" We crossed the sidewalk, stepped in front of the door, and looked at the jamb surrounding the entrance to Baroja's Baked Goods. Henry pressed himself against the facing and placed both hands around the knob, carefully but forcefully shifting the lock mechanism to the right and away from the catch. The door kicked forward as the bolt slid past the jamb with a mechanical clunk.

The shop smelled just as good as it had earlier in the week. "I assume you've already been here, as a customer, I mean."

"Numerous times."

"Figures." I walked down the hardwood floor and listened to the hum of the big, white ceramic coolers. He went behind the counter and began filling the espresso machine. "What are you doing?"

"Making espresso."

I was sure there were entire folders of contact prints, photographs, pathology reports, DNA procedures, serology, and trace evidence on my desk about Lana's supposed attempted murder, but sometimes it's important to see the scene, to see the blood. I crouched down. There was the origin target on the floor, but the wave castoff and cast-off bloodstains were what I was looking for, the follow-through and the drawback of the weapon that had struck Lana Baroja. They were there, along the nearest table, on the floor and the baseboard of the back wall. He had stood beside the doorway and hit her as she came up from the basement.

"Walt?" I turned back because his voice had changed. "Someone has cut a loaf of bread on the butcher block, has taken some provolone and buffalo mozzarella from one of the coolers, and has chased the meal with a couple of jugs of Wheatland microbrew." He looked up. "Lately."

I was glad I had taken the 12-gauge from my truck.

There were three doors on the landing: one to the bathroom, one that went to the basement, and one that continued upstairs. The steps to the second floor were warped and swayed in the middle. Tongue-and-groove boards paneled the stairwell, and a tiny grime-covered window provided the only illumination on the second landing where the stairs turned and went the other way.

I jacked a shell into the shotgun, flipped off the safety, and started the second flight. I didn't figure I was going to surprise anybody, so I decided to introduce myself. Henry called from the front, "Ha-ho?"

"Broadcasting."

It was quiet for a moment. "Careful, I do not want to have to drink two espressos."

There were three rooms on the upper level: a small one for storage with a few windows that overlooked the alley in the back; another with a two-by-four table pushed against the wall; and the front room with a couple of windows overlooking the street. This was the room where Leo Gaskell had been living.

There was a ragged and torn polyester sleeping bag piled against one of the corners with a child's bucking bronco blanket and a dirty pillow. The remains of downstairs' repast lay on the floor nearby. There was a flashlight, which had been stolen from Northern Rockies Energy Exploration, and the coat I had seen him in last night. There was no Leo.

I coaxed the coat from its crumpled position with the barrel of the shotgun and flipped it open. It was a bloody mess. You could see where two of the pellets had done the most damage, one in the arm and the blood on the sleeping bag showed where the other had hit his foot. As bad as I was feeling this morning, somewhere out there, Leo Gaskell was feeling worse.

I nudged the jacket again and examined the inside pocket where two crystal-meth vials had exploded and thought that maybe Leo wasn't feeling much of anything after all. I put my gloves on and fingered the shattered glass containers. A full 65 percent of the Wyoming division of criminal investigation's cases concerned clandestine lab activity. It was a scourge. From Leo's dental situation, I had assumed meth-mouth and was right.

"Espresso?" We all had our addictions. I sat against the wall and clicked the safety back on the shotgun before placing it in my lap. I took off my gloves. My fingers hurt. He sat beside me and sipped. "Well, at least we know where Leo has been keeping himself."

"As the possible illegitimate grandson of Charlie Nurburn, I also ask myself where Leo's daddy might be, if anywhere."

"We are looking for a white male."

"With an Indian mother; a half-breed."

"Bicultural."

I glanced over at him. "Are you aware of the damage you are causing with all this political correctness to the language of the mythic American West?"

"You bet'cher boots." He studied the grim surroundings. "Age?"

"Ours, according to Doc Bloomfield. Anybody come to mind?"

"I always thought you might be a half-breed."

I ignored him. "All right, he may have been here when I found Lana, but he's definitely been here since." I stretched my legs out. "I'm also wondering where Leo might have hidden an 18-wheel truck and a mobile home." I took a sip, which tasted pretty good.

"And what is your answer?"

"Well, there's too much activity at Four Brothers Ranch, and Vic and I were just there and didn't see any evidence of Leo, but what about the 260 acres that Mari and Charlie lived on that is adjacent to the ranch? If I were looking for a place to hide something as big as a house, I'd go there."

Ruby was talking on the phone with Dog's head in her lap, and Lucian was asleep and snoring loudly on the wooden bench in the reception area with my .45, cocked and locked, lying on his chest. "How do you get any work done around here with all the noise?"

Her head dropped, and she raised an eyebrow over a particularly cold blue eye. "I understand you went swimming last night?"

"Technically, I think it was struggling and sinking."

She continued to shake her head. "You have Post-its, that woman from the state dropped off a love note and, lucky for you, Vic is delivering a summons to the bookstore for nonpayment on a newspaper ad. They don't feel they should have to pay for an advertisement that misspelled the word literature."

"I can see their point."

"Saizarbitoria is in the basement. He said he was going to look through Mari Baroja's effects. I think you should go see him first."

I plucked my sidearm off Lucian's chest as Henry and I went by.

When we got to the basement, Saizarbitoria was seated in the middle of the open floor with all of Mari Baroja's correspondence carefully arranged around him in a semicircle. The whole side of his face was dark and bruised, and he was wearing slippers. He stood when we came in and stuck out his hand. "Thank you."

I shook it. "You're welcome." I wasn't as good as the Cheyenne, but I was learning. We looked around at the amount of paper stacked on the floor around us.

"She wrote poetry."

"I'm sorry." Some of the piles were close to a foot high.

He studied the letter in his hand. "No, it's actually pretty good." He pointed to one of the larger stacks. "This is personal communication." He gestured to another pile. "Business correspondence, and this one is the poetry." I looked around at the neatly ordered mess. "You don't want to hear some of it?"

He was definitely spending too much time with Vic. "Maybe later."

We sat down, and he carefully placed the poetry back in its place and looked at the largest pile in front of him. "She was a savvy businesswoman. She bought up all the surrounding leases adjacent to Four Brothers including Jolie Baroja's, so she was not only getting the methane money from Four Brothers but also from about a quarter of the valley."

"Maybe Lana should open up a chain of Basque bakeries?"

Saizarbitoria ignored us and went on. "Mrs. Baroja was probably one of the richest women in the state, but she lived like a pauper." He glanced around and then back up to me. "I've been trying to establish some patterns, but it's difficult." He pulled a few bank statements out and a few letters from the personal pile. "She had established a trust fund for Father Baroja that he doesn't seem to know anything about. I remember he said that they didn't get along, but she must have felt sorry for him when his grip on reality began to slip. It isn't administered in Wyoming but set up in . . ."

"Florida?"

His eyes widened. "How did you know that?"

"A little bird told me, a little southern bird." I thought back to what Carol Baroja had said in the hospital waiting room when she tried to tie Lana with the ETA. I suspected that no money had gone to Father Baroja or the ETA. I figured that the money went to Carol Baroja's private charity, herself, but didn't think that that particular malfeasance had any relevance to the murders. "What about the personal stuff?"

He leaned in a little, and his voice dropped. "Mrs. Baroja may have had a long-term affair with Sheriff Connally."

The Bear and I looked at each other and back to Saizarbitoria; it was Academy Award stuff but lost on the Basquo. "Ancient history. Anything else?"

He paused for a moment and then went on. "The relationship between her and her daughters was a little strained."

"Uh huh." I turned to the side and stretched my sore legs again: Indian style wasn't working for me. "Any mention of Charlie Nurburn?"

"Old, numerous, and not kind."

"Any mention of the financial relationship between Mari and him?"

"Some, early on, but he seems to be cut out of the picture by the early fifties."

Henry and I looked at each other again, but he was quicker. "You can say that again."

Saizarbitoria's eyes were shifting back and forth between us. "Are you two going to keep looking at each other or are you going to let me in on this?"

"What's the story on Leo Gaskell? You knew him in Rawlins, didn't you?"

He grunted. "We were in the infirmary. He had sliced his hand open in a fight with some dealer from Cheyenne over what they were going to watch on television." His eyes narrowed, and he was looking back into a place he wasn't sure he wanted to go to again. "He was secured to a gurney but kept flexing his fingers, so I asked him if he was all right. He doesn't even look at me and says, 'I'm just wonderin' how long you'd cry like a bitch if I was to get my hands around your throat.' "

I listened to the heat kick on in the jail and resisted the temptation to look at the Bear again. "All right, Troop. You in or out?"

He propped an elbow on his knee and placed the pointy end of his Vandyke in the palm of his hand. "You're not going to tell me about Mari Baroja unless I stay?"

I leveled with him. "A lot of this stuff is local history. If you're going back to Rawlins then you don't need to know it."

He looked at both of us, his black eyes glittering like the backs of trout rolling in dark water. "I'm in."

We shook on it; the median age of our department was now securely under the age of fifty. "Mari Baroja cut Charlie Nurburn's throat in 1951."

He leaned back against the bars of the cell behind him and let out a long slow whistle. "Some of the poetry is a little dark."

The plows had been doing their job, and the highway was clear as I set off south to the old homestead, but we had to hurry because it didn't look like the weather would hold. Henry had made a few calls while I had gathered up some cold weather gear and called the Busy Bee for a few club sandwiches and a couple of coffees. Dorothy had met us at the curb with two paper bags. She hadn't waited for a response but just waved, turned, and disappeared back into the café. We kept the food in the front, away from Dog, who was still sulking about having to leave the office, but Ruby was going out with her granddaughter that evening and couldn't watch him.

About three miles out of town, we saw an HP headed in the other direction. He waved, flipped across the median, and pulled up behind us after I'd slowed and stopped. I wondered how Leo had escaped being detected.

"You were not speeding, were you?"

I didn't acknowledge him but rolled the window down and leaned an elbow on the ledge as the light bar on the highway patrol cruiser began revolving and the door popped open. It was Wes again, and I watched as he straightened his Smoky the Bear hat and strolled up with the gigantic Colt .357 banging at his leg. "License and registration." He folded his arms and leaned against my door. He pushed the hat back, and a strong dollop of gray flopped down on his forehead.

"Are you the only one working out here?"

"We've got our two, three more from the Casper detachment, and another three from over in Sheridan." He looked at my eye patch. "Jesus, what the hell happened to you?"

I gestured over to Henry. "The Indian beat me up."

Wes tipped his hat. "Hey, Henry."

"Wes."

"You know, all I'm looking for is a Mack truck with a mobile home attached to it."

Wes nodded. "Seems like we'd be able to find that, doesn't it?"

I pushed my own hat back. "I thought you were retired."

"Next week." He smiled an easy smile. "Why, you gonna have a party for me?"

"No, I was just wondering when we were gonna get some younger HPs around here with better eyesight."

He shook his head. "Where you guys headed?"

"Down to Mari Baroja's for a little look around."

"You want me to tag along?"

"No, but if you or your boys wouldn't mind swinging through Durant, Leo had been staying over Lana's little bakery next to Evans's Chainsaw." I turned to Henry. "What kind of car does Joe Lesky drive?"

The Bear looked up from a small notebook. "Tan, '87 Jeep Wagoneer, County 25, Plate 3461."

Wes nodded and reaffirmed that Ruby had already taken care of the car's ID. I smiled the half smile I'd perfected and turned toward him. "If I don't see you? You be careful down there in Arizona."

He smiled a smile of his own. "You bet."

"Do you want to hear about Ellen Runs Horse?"

I negotiated around a slow-moving 18-wheeler, neither black nor Mack. "Sure."

The dark wave of hair fell alongside his face as one eye studied me. "As we suspected she is Crow."

I continued to stare at the road through my one eye. "Anyone hint about her having an illegitimate child with Charlie Nurburn?"

He nodded. "Better than that." He shifted his weight and leaned against the door. "She registered a child, Garnet Runs Horse, in the tribal rolls, but gave the child up for adoption in 1950."

"Lucian said Ellen told him that the child died. I guess she lied. Where did he go?"

"Wind River."

"Name still Runs Horse?"

"I do not know."

I thought about it. "That would figure, since Leo's been living over near Lander, but where did he get the name Gaskell?"

"Maybe his father took the adoptive family's name?"

"Maybe so." I pulled my mic from the dash. "Base, this is Unit One, come in?"

After a moment of static, a cool voice responded, and it wasn't Ruby; I had forgotten that she wasn't there. "What the fuck do you want now?"

I glanced at Henry, keyed the mic, and quickly composed myself. "How was the bookstore?"

Static. "I bought you the *Idiot's Guide to Swimming*." The Bear snorted.

"Thanks." I listened to the static for a moment, since it was more comforting than her voice. "Can you do me a favor?"

Static. "Seems like I've done you an awful lot of them lately." Static. "What?"

"Can you run a check on any Gaskells who might be living over near the Wind River Reservation, Lander, or Riverton?"

Static. "I know what towns are near Wind River." I nodded at the LED display on the radio, trying to get it to be nice to me. Static. "Have you signed the release papers on Mari Baroja? The Wicked Witches of the West are here."

I wondered if they were in the same room and quickly figured yes they were. "I signed the papers and gave them to Bill McDermott who should still be over at the hospital."

Static. "I'll send them there."

"Get a hold of Bill Wiltse and see if Fremont's got anything on the Gaskells."

Static. "Got it." Static. "Just in case we need to get in touch with you while you are traipsing around the southern part of the county, how should we reach you?"

I thought about it. "Try the methane foreman."

Static. "Double Tough?"

I smiled. "Is that what you're calling him?"

Static. "Fuckin' A. Over and out."

Speak of the devil. As I headed down the ramp off the highway, I saw Jess Aliff with a couple of his roughnecks. They were on their way to Four Brothers, but he made the time to come over and answer a few questions. I asked him about the gunshot wound, to which he replied,

"What gunshot wound?" I liked Double Tough more every time I saw him. I also asked him if he would direct us to the old homestead where Mari Baroja had lived with Charlie Nurburn and whether the road would support the Mack and a house trailer to which he had responded maybe.

We followed the ridge that he had told us about, moving diagonally southeast toward the north fork of Crazy Woman toward the Nurburn place. With the wind blowing, it was impossible to see if there were any tracks; our own would be invisible in a matter of moments. I stopped the truck after a mile and a quarter where the ridge divided and split off into two directions. "Now what?"

He looked at me. "If I were a creek, I would be where the ground slopes."

"Right." Sometimes it was good to have an Indian scout.

We topped the ridge cap and looked down the small valley. The road, or what we assumed to be the road, hung to the right side of the flat. The north fork of Crazy Woman turned right, around a curve, about a half a mile away. The blowing snow had filled in the small canyon, and it was difficult to see where the road might be.

"Would you drive a Mack truck down here with a mobile home attached to it?"

He took a deep breath and looked at the missing road. "No, but there are a number of things Leo Gaskell would do that I would not."

I slipped the three-quarter ton into granny gear, it was already in 4-wheel, and committed. Most of the fill was powder, and the truck settled even as we idled the big V-10 down the canyon to the apex of the undersized ranch. At the far end of the stretch, I edged the truck against the coulee wall and glanced up at the meadow that opened to the flat at the bottom of the canyon. It was a beautiful spot but, if you spent the first part of the winter here, you spent the last part of the winter here, too.

The house was just as I had pictured it in my dream, weathered and leaning at an acute angle away from the predominant wind. Part of it had collapsed, and it looked like a cottonwood had leaned against it for a moment of support that had turned into forever.

I stopped the truck at the edge of the meadow, cut the engine, and decided to get out and check the ground before driving across. I had done enough swimming for one holiday season. I let the dog out and walked around to the front of the truck where Henry met me. The gusts had increased, channeling their force through the ravine, and hit us full in the face. It wasn't actually snowing, but the wind was strong enough to take a percentage from the ground and make it airborne. The wind was the only sound. We squinted toward the little house as Dog arched out, dipping his head in the snow and rooting for who knew what. Henry flipped his collar up to protect part of his face; his hair trailed back and swirled above the hood.

I squinted and watched an underlying cloud cover approach from the mountains. You could vaguely see the snow-covered peaks. I thought about a damaged woman, bareback on a horse, racing through a rainy night, and three small children huddled in a back bedroom forbidden to move. It seemed sacrilegious to speak in the face of all the tragedy that had unfolded here.

"What are you thinking?"

I was startled by his voice and took a moment to allow the words to form in my head. "I am thinking about how complicated this case has become."

He nodded. "It just got worse." His hand came up and pointed past the dilapidated house where, just visible through the blowing ground snow, was the back corner of a mobile home attached to a black Mack truck.

15

We stood there at the apex of the meadow, with the Big Horn Mountains strung across the far horizon like some painted backdrop in the theatre of our lives. I always felt things that Henry could better describe. "I know it is the earth that is moving, but at this moment it is as if the clouds are in motion, and the world is still and waiting."

His black leather duster was flapping in the wind, and I noticed the Special Forces tomahawk in his hand. "I'm getting the shotgun."

I unlocked the Remington and a handheld radio from the cab. Henry spoke to Dog. *"Hinananjin."* Dog went over and sat beside him. It had already been established that the furry brute was conversant in Cheyenne, Shoshone, Arapaho, Crow, and Lakota; English was the language he chose to sometimes ignore.

I flipped on the radio and listened to the static. I didn't expect to get any reception in the canyon, but it never hurt to try. I punched the transceiver button. "Come in Base, this is Unit One?" I looked over at the mountains and felt a familiar sinking feeling.

"Nothing?"

I blinked my one eye at him, dialed the frequency up a few clicks, and tried again. "Base, this is Unit One. Anybody there, come in?"

More static. Then a faint reply. "BR75115, come again?"

I smiled at the radio, keyed the mic, and deferred to the foreman. "Hey Jess, this is Walt Longmire. We made it down here to the old Nurburn place on Crazy Woman. We found your truck."

Static. "The Mack?"

"Roger that. How long are you guys going to be on it today?"

Static. "Weather's supposed'ta get bad, but we're gonna try'n' stick. I got a meetin' at 4:30."

"What's the meeting about?" It was quiet.

Static. "Firin' me, I'd imagine."

You had to love the guy. "I might need you to relay messages back up to my office. This canyon is causing too much interference, and I can't get through."

Static. "We can try, but if it gets bad, reception's kind of touch and go. How you wanna do it?"

"How about I give you a call every hour on the hour?"

Static. "This mean I'm officially deputized?"

I smiled. "I'll talk to you about that." I pulled out my pocket watch and rekeyed the mic. "In ten minutes it will be 3:00. Call me at 4:00."

Static. "Roger that." If I hired him, at least he already knew radio procedures.

Henry had kept an eye on the homestead while the foreman and I had finished our conversation. I clipped the radio to my belt as he turned to look at me. "We are walking from here?"

I stared at the corner of the mobile home. "Yep, after I put Dog in the truck." He wasn't happy about it, but I figured Henry and I were aware of what we were getting ourselves into, so we deserved whatever we got. I told Dog not to play with the radio.

There was a level area to our right where the banks of Crazy Woman shallowed, but it seemed assailable by an 18-wheeler and a house trailer. We crossed the frozen creek and moved within fifty yards of the house. There were a few dormers and a lean-to addition on the near side, and a screen door continually slapped in the wind, a brittle noise that grew louder as we approached. The broken trunks of the cottonwood were bleached out and whitened by the sun and the unending wind.

There was nothing at the house itself to indicate that Leo might have been in there. The Mack truck and the mobile home were buried axle deep in the powdery snow about twenty-five yards west of the homestead. The house trailer was fairly new and was small by white man standards, but it was still almost twice the size of the cabin. I could see where the folding steps had been pulled down at the front door; they were covered with snow and appeared undisturbed.

I glanced over at Henry. "You see anything?" He had stopped about thirty feet from the cabin; I could imagine his nostrils twitching. We had unconsciously fanned out from each other as we had approached; both of us had won hard lessons on what could happen when individuals bunched up in situations like this.

"No."

"One of the things I don't see is an '87 Wagoneer, not that I thought I would have. I don't think he could've gotten a car down in here with all this fresh snow."

I thought about the dark stories I knew and started forward. It was three steps up to the front door where the screen door beat its arhythmical response to the wind. I placed my hand on it and felt some of the paint crack and fall away like sheet music. The wind had stopped for a moment, and it was quiet. I looked into the house, and you could plainly see it was empty; the only thing that moved were the drifts of some tattered, faded, once-white lace curtains that rolled and fell back against the broken window glass. The curtains, shredded and billowing with the wind's persistent caress, reminded me that Mari had been here. I hoped she still was, because I needed all the support I could get, but I doubted it. She had lived the majority of her life in the house in Powder Junction. As I saw her, she only came here in the spring or summer, and she never entered the house itself. Her presence was there, though, along with the faded pieces of wallpaper. The house had contained her spirit but had paid the terrible price of purposeful neglect and had died a slow and inevitable death with no songs ever to be heard again.

His voice was soft and, if you weren't listening, it would have drifted quietly along playing a variation with the wind. "There is a cellar."

I clicked the flashlight on and cast a beam across the stairs; they looked as if they might hold me. Not much of the snow had blown into the basement, and you could see the hard-pack dirt floor, but not much else. I handed the shotgun to Henry and pulled out my .45. We looked at each other for a moment, and then I stepped onto the first tread, which squealed but held. I hated basements. I ducked my head under the jamb and continued down, casting the light from the flashlight across the small room. The stairs were centered, so I checked underneath and on either side first. There were a few broken nail kegs and floor parts from the room above. The flashlight illuminated the heavy beams and supports that stood centered on raised stone that had been chiseled from the bedrock of the canyon floor. I stepped down onto the smooth surface of the dirt, turned the flashlight back into the darkness, and I heard something move.

It was a muted sound, almost like the one that a feather duster would make. I stepped to the side and flashed my light to the center of the basement; it illuminated chains that hung there and the glowing golden eyes of a thirty-pound great gray owl. He screeched at me, dipped his head, and then exploded in a flurry of powerful wings that must have been six feet in wingspan to the collapsed wall of the broken foundation. His heavily feathered talons clawed at the rubble and found purchase. His huge head slowly turned to regard me: messenger from the dead indeed.

"What is going on?"

"I just flushed an owl from the other side."

It was quiet for a moment, but then his voice rumbled. "Messenger from the dead."

"I had that comforting thought all on my own." I played the light back to the support beam at the chains that hung there. "Wait a minute." I uncocked my side arm, slipped it back into my holster, resnapped the thumb strap, and walked over to the foot-wide support beam.

They were heavier than tire chains and old. I pulled one up and looked at the metal clasp hanging from the end, checking to see another at the end of the other chain. I held one of the manacles up to my wrist for comparison; these had been custom built for someone with a wrist half the size of mine. The heavy chains were through-bolted, and they had been there for a long time. The clasps were unlocked and hung like gaping jaws. I dropped them and watched as they slapped against the wood, bumping there like a child worrying a pant leg. The corners of the timber were worn from the repeated strikes against them. Horsewhip or quirt marks. I stared and felt the blows, felt the cries, felt that it was good that the man who had put these things here was dead.

"Anything?"

I passed the beam of the flashlight around the cellar for one more look, but all there was to see here, I had seen. I checked the owl one more time, but he hadn't moved. He continued to watch me as I made my way back up the steps. "Just more evidence to convince me that it's a good thing Charlie Nurburn is dead."

He glanced over his shoulder. "I think I just heard something in the trailer."

I was out and standing beside him when we heard it again. We looked at each other. "Did that sound like somebody moaning?" He nodded his head, and we headed for the trailer and the fold-down steps. I pulled my .45 out again and leaned against the trailer's aluminum skin, just to the right of the door, and cocked the hammer back. The Bear pulled up to the left; anything bad that was going to happen in the next moment would likely happen in the framework of the doorway we now stood beside.

I took a deep breath and reached for the knob, slowly turning it to the left and the right: locked. I pointed at Henry and the ground, indicating that he should stay there. He nodded, and I started around to look for another way in. I kept an eye to the windows, but the shades were all pulled down. When I got to the back, I could see another door about three-quarters of the way down. I slowly worked along the side of the mobile home, stopping just this side of that door. There were no steps here but, if I stretched, I could just reach the knob. With my fingertips, I pressed it and turned. It was tough at first, but then it clicked, far too loudly, and sprang open about an inch.

I ducked down a little and pulled the door open about a foot and looked down a hallway that seemed to run the length of the thing. Cheap paneling and some sort of indoor-outdoor threadbare carpeting with a few window screens leaning against the interior wall was all that was visible. No Leo Gaskell. I looked down the hallway in the other direction, but all I could make out was the textured ceiling and a cheap light fixture; at least I could be sure that Leo wasn't going to jump on me from above. I stood back up, took another deep breath, and casually opened the door the rest of the way.

Nothing.

I stood still for a moment, then leaned in about two inches and checked both sides, did it again, and then again. Still nothing, so I shot the works and stuck my head all the way in along with the .45. There was a closed door to my right and another at the end of the hallway that was partially open and led to a living room in which, sitting on an imitation leather sofa and swathed in about four Hudson Bay and buffalo blankets, was, who I assumed to be, Ellen Runs Horse.

I cleared my throat. "Hello." The condensation from my breath stayed in front of my face; it was probably colder in the trailer than it was outside.

She didn't move, just kept looking at me from beneath the blankets; after a bit she finally said, *"Eeh."* Crow. She said yes as a statement that held neither question nor interest. The small cloud from her breath collected there in the gloom.

"I'm Sheriff Walt Longmire, Absaroka County." I felt foolish saying it, but it was procedure. "Ellen Runs Horse?"

"Eeh."

Same inflection. "Are you alone?"

A moment passed. *"Eeh."*

I was feeling a little more secure but decided to test the theory using Vic's litmus test for sanity. "Ellen, did you know that I was a Chinese fighter pilot?"

"Eeh."

It was a fleeting security.

I stretched up, got the majority of my girth in the doorstep, and

wriggled inside. I was relatively sure that Leo wasn't in the mobile
home; if he had been, he would have most certainly bludgeoned me to
death as I wallowed on the floor. I pushed off the questionable carpet
and slumped against the wall. I looked back down the hallway where
Ellen Runs Horse was fumbling with something in the blankets; she
was probably trying to get up. I waved a hand at her. "That's okay,
Ellen."

It was then that I saw the barrel of a chrome-plated, pearl-handled
.32 rise up from the blankets like a howitzer and tremble as she en-
deavored to pull the trigger.

"Ellen . . . ?" That was about all I got out before the .32 belched fire
and the ceiling above me blew apart with a smart sound. The crack of
the automatic in the confined space was tremendous and my ears rang
so loudly that I could barely hear myself yelling. I staggered against
the interior wall and could feel my hand tightening around the grip of
the .45 in spite of myself. I coughed it out in a yell. "Jesus, Ellen!"

The automatic wavered but rose again as I dodged into the room to
my right. The next bullet went through the first wall into a mattress
that was leaning against it. I'm not sure how much protection I
thought the thin walls of the mobile home were going to be, but the
structure was falling below my expectations. I looked at the hole in the
wall; she was getting closer. "Ellen?" Silence.

I waited, but the next shot didn't come. There was another shuffling noise, so I ventured toward the door and slowly peeked around
the jamb. Henry was there, kneeling before her, with the tiny automatic cradled in his hands. "I think it is safe now."

"Jesus!" I turned the corner and looked at the two of them.

"Are you all right?"

"Jesus!"

He was doing his best not to laugh. "You take a little walk down the
hallway and come back when your vocabulary increases."

I stood there and took a few deep breaths as they continued a very
low conversation in Crow, a language that, like Cheyenne, seemed to

catch in the throat of the speaker. I could feel my heart rate beginning to slow to normal.

I picked up a few words, but they didn't make much sense to me. Her face was broad, and she had thick brows that seemed to gather at the center and curve up, giving her a sad and questioning look. The outside corners of her eyes folded within themselves, hiding the edges of the baking chocolate pupils. Strong creases at the corners of her mouth, cascading from the cheekbones, made it difficult to tell if she had ever smiled. The movement of her lips was slight, and her voice barely carried.

After she finished talking, Henry took a plastic cup from a television tray to her right, glanced inside, and reached to her feet for what looked like a half-frozen gallon jug of water. He shook it to make sure some of the water was still liquid, refilled the cup, and placed the straw at her lips. While she drank, I took a look around. There was a Christmas tree in the corner, a motley bottlebrush type, which was decorated with homemade ornaments constructed of Mason jar lids and old photographs. Standing beside the blind television set, the holiday enthusiasm of the scraggly tree gave the room the most depressing appearance of any I'd been in, never mind the opened and emptied cans of creamed corn, the mushroom soup with a single spoon sticking up, the heel ends of a loaf of white bread, and another jug of water that had frozen solid.

He closed her tiny hands around the cup, and she held it. Her eyes followed Henry when he stood; he quietly spoke to her again and then stepped toward me. "She is touched." He glanced back over to Ellen who seemed content to suck from the straw of the plastic cup. "She says that none of her friends have come to visit her for a long time."

"What's the story on the pistol?"

"Evidently Leo told her to shoot anybody that came in."

"What'd she say about him?"

"She thinks I am Leo."

I nodded a tight nod. "How did you get in?"

"Just forced it with the tomahawk."

"Noticeable?"

He handed me the automatic, which still had a round left. "Not that much." His eyes came back up to mine. "Why?"

"You've got to get her out of here." He looked at me. "I don't see any other option. We've got to get her some attention, but he might come back and, if he does, I want someone here to meet him."

"You are in no condition . . ."

I looked back over to Ellen Runs Horse. "You speak the language, and she trusts you. Chances are he's still in town somewhere, but I can get Double Tough on the radio and get Vic or Saizarbitoria down here later." I crossed back down the hallway and looked out the window. "We've only got about an hour till it's really dark." The wind was blowing again, and my boot prints were almost gone. I turned back to Henry. "You better get out of here."

We had tucked Ellen into the passenger side of the Bullet and allowed Dog to share the front, since he seemed to make her more at ease. I looked through my one eye at the Cheyenne Nation. "When you get out of here, call ahead and get them to throw together some supplies and bring a little backup."

He pulled the heavy leather coat aside and climbed in, fastening his seatbelt and pulling the Special Forces tomahawk from behind him. The carbon steel surface absorbed light like a black hole. "Here."

I shook my head. "I don't want that thing; I wouldn't know what to do with it." I patted the chrome handle of the tiny automatic, which was sticking out from my belt, balanced the Remington on my shoulder, and felt the .45 in the holster. "I have every gun we've got." He nodded and glanced toward the ridge. "Radio Double Tough and have him call in. I'll be here." He nodded and kept looking at me. "Aren't you going to turn on the lights?" I reached in and hit the switch he was looking for as the blue and red reflectors bled ghosts of light across the late afternoon snow.

He watched them for a moment. "This is the best part of your job." He placed a hand against the driver's side window as he passed, the large dark fingers unraveling against the glass like hemp rope.

I watched as the truck struggled to stay alongside the canyon wall, disappearing in the snow as the darker gray of its outline grew lighter with the distance, and the sound of the big Detroit motor planed, muffled, and vanished. I stood there for a while longer, wondering, like I always did, if this was the right thing to do. It looked like it was going to be a long night, so I turned and started the trudge back to the trailer. I was interrupted by a weak call on the radio.

Static. "Hey Sheriff, this is BR75115. The weather is comin' in, just like . . ." I pulled the radio from my belt. "Absaroka County Sheriff Unit One, come in?" After a moment, a very faint signal came through.

Static. "Hey, Sheriff, how you . . ."

I smiled. "I'm good, how about you?"

Static. "I'm fired."

The signal faded out completely, and I readjusted the gain. "Hello? Jess?" Nothing. I dropped my head a little and then keyed the mic again. "Jess, if you can hear me?" At least Henry had gotten out. I tried the radio again. Static. I looked at the radio, thought about my luck, and keyed the mic one final time.

Static. Damn.

I walked around to the back of the trailer so that Leo wouldn't notice any more of my tracks. I closed the door behind me and decided to check the other rooms. There was a back bedroom at the end of the hall with another mattress squatting in the corner, a particleboard dresser that had seen better days, and a vintage console television. There was nothing in the closet but old clothes and well-worn shoes, giving me an indication of the frugal life that Ellen Runs Horse must live. The next room was a lot more interesting; there was a card table with Sterno burners and all the products used to produce meth on a clandestine laboratory scale. The floorboards were lined with plastic gallon jugs containing the toxic castoff of the operation, and it was evident that Leo's drug venture was still a going concern.

I walked into the living room and looked at the beat-to-shit fake tree and wished it a Merry Christmas. The ornaments were made out of Mason jar lids with glue around the threaded edges to hold on the glitter, and there were bows of knitting yarn and ribbons to make the tiny ornaments brave; some of them used photographs that were old enough to be in Henry's Mennonite collection. There was a sepia one that carried the bruised image of a young girl with braids playing marbles. She had on a cap and an old jacket and a face of utmost concentration. I turned the ornament in my hand and read on the back, printed in block letters, ELLEN WALKS OVER ICE. There was another of a young man in a Thermopolis varsity football uniform doing the old chuck and duck; I could see that it was Leo. I turned it over to confirm my guess; the block letters said simply LEO, with no surname.

There were others, but the one that next caught my attention was one toward the back; I guess I noticed it because its face was turned toward the wall. It twisted gently as I watched, revealing a very young Leo with the man who must be his father. He had on a hat, a broad-brim, flattop like the Powder River cowboys wore, and his head was tilted down to the young Leo, the hat hiding the eyes. The jawline was discernible, along with the lips. The connection to Ellen was there, but the black-and-white photo did nothing to tell me whether his skin was white or red; he didn't look particularly Indian nor did he look particularly like Charlie. It was like doing a lineup with jigsaw puzzles. I turned the ornament over, but all it said was LEO & FATHER. He was her son, and she hadn't even written down his name, but she had cared enough to keep track.

I had the sandwiches that Dorothy had made and the coffee, so I had something to eat and drink. I went over and retrieved one of the jugs of water as well, the one that was only half frozen. I might need it and, if I didn't keep it with me, chances are it wasn't going to stay thawed. I gathered the blankets that were left and the buffalo robe, dragging them to a chair so as to sit as far away from the creamed corn as the furniture would allow. I pulled the Mag Lite from my belt for future use, placed the ornament on one knee, and pulled the little automatic out and rested it on my other knee. I placed the shotgun between my legs and pulled the .45 from my holster and checked it again. I felt like Zapata.

I studied the ornament and stared at the partial face, knowing that I had seen this man, knowing that he was out there, knowing that he and Leo were in cahoots, cahoots being a legal term in Wyoming, see cahooting in the first degree, intent to cahoot, and so on.

I sat there and thought about what a long wait this might turn into and about the course of things and looked around again. I noticed a strap sticking out from under the couch Ellen had been sitting on that was made from the kind of tubular webbing that is used for backpacks. I sat the gun on the floor along with the ornament, flipped back the buffalo robe, and moved across the small room to kneel by the sofa. The strap was followed by a grimy daypack. The zipper to the main compartment was broken, but it had been fastened together with large safety pins. I unhooked the pins and had a look inside: dozens of small glass bottles and a small bundle wrapped in the *Durant Courant* containing close to what looked like about $40,000 in mixed currency.

Leo, you bad boy. Whether he would slog his way through a blizzard to the middle fork of Crazy Woman to a trailer and his loopy grandmother was suddenly academic. Leo might leave his grandmother to starve to death, but he would come back for the drugs and the money.

I put the bundle back in the knapsack and stuffed the bag under the sofa when I noticed a battered cooler in the kitchen. I wondered what Leo might have put in there. The kitchen reminded me of my grumbling stomach, but my curiosity was stronger than my appetite. If I had been hungry, I wasn't anymore. I pulled the aged skull of an adult male from the cooler. I leaned against the counter and held it in my hand. "Alas, poor Charlie." The prominent gold tooth was there, central incisor, right. I guess Double Tough hadn't looked at the head; I didn't blame him. "You got off easy, you son of a bitch."

I carefully placed the skull back in the cooler and walked over to the window where I raised the blind just far enough to see a fog bank beginning to form along the shadowed canyon wall. The creek water must have been warmer than the air and, if the low cloud cover held, this was going to be a very foggy, as well as dark, place in about thirty minutes. Now all I had to do was relax and watch what little light there was at the bottom of the windows die.

Static. "Unit One, this is BR75115, come in?"

The blankets slipped and the ornament fell to the floor, but at least I didn't shoot the door. I had forgotten to turn off the radio. I struggled through the folds in the blanket and pulled it out, the small glow of the channel display providing a comforting light. "Hey Jess. You got through. Over?"

Static. "Sheriff, I'm at the base radio at equipment storage. I've got your dog here, and he's been shot."

I stared at the radio as a million and one things ran through my mind, all of them bad. "Are you sure?"

Static. "Yeah, I'm sure. It looks like a small caliber. I'm doing all I can for him."

"How did he get there?"

Static. "He must'a drug himself. I went out and followed the blood trail as far as I could, but you can't see a damn thing with all this fog."

I thought about Henry. If Dog was shot . . . "I'm going to need you to call my office, tell them that I think we've got a man down and that we need all the help we can get. Then get the HPs out here."

Static. "Roger that, out."

Here I sat with every weapon that we had, and my closest friend and blood brother was probably dead out there in the snow somewhere. It was a solid three miles back to the methane wells and that was if I could find him. That's if Leo left him, and what were the chances that Leo would have left him alive?

I'm lousy at ignoring first instincts and mine told me to gather the weapons and head out. I stuffed the little automatic back in my belt, holstered the .45 cocked and locked along with the Mag Lite, pulled the buffalo robe around me, and flipped the shotgun up on my shoulder. I stuffed the ornament into my duty jacket and started for the door, opened it, and sidestepped. I pulled my hat down tight and raised my head slowly to look into the vaporous white. Barely visible in the fog were blue and red lights that blinked across the blurred canyon walls.

My truck.

The headlights were shining at an odd angle and the blue and red ones were simply revolving in place, so I was pretty sure Leo had misjudged the width of the trail and had planted the three-quarter ton over the edge. He was lucky he had done it near the bottom, or the truck would have flipped and killed him. The headlights cast to the left, away from the homestead and the trailer. I stepped down and pulled the door closed quietly behind me.

It was only about 150 yards, but the fog made it seem like miles. I started the slow trudge, staying to the right and keeping my one eye on the slightly illuminated portion of the white distance. If he was coming to the trailer, he was going to have to cross that bit of diffused light and, when he did, I would be there.

I lowered the Remington from my shoulder and allowed it to swing forward; with all my training, here I was shooting with one eye. There was a movement to my left, just out of the headlight beams. I unfocused as always, allowing my eye to become a motion detector, and waited until whatever it was out there moved again. It did, and it was large. Not only tall but wide. I stood there, watching as it lumbered into view, in no way the outline of a man. It was at least four feet across and as tall as I am. I was thinking that it was a cow, confused and trying to find some relief from the storm or a horse trying to do the same. It was a blur in the fog. It swayed there for a moment, and it seemed as though a wing extended outward and then folded back.

After a few seconds, the wing extended again and caught a small movement of the air, then flipped sideways only to fall. It shifted its weight and then both wings caught the breeze, and I was sure the thing would take flight. My mouth fell open, and my mind was jarred to the image of Henry at the Busy Bee when he had spread the wings on his duster, his battle cry shaking the windows of the café.

The fog froze the inside of my mouth. "Bear?"

The blast was instantaneous. Leo had been waiting, hoping that I would say something in recognition, and I had.

It was as if someone had tied a rope around my leg and tied it to a galloping stallion. I couldn't move. Leg, left, and I thought of bone and the artery as the immediate shock sparked and then subsided. The reason his shadow had been so deformed was that he was carrying Ellen, which meant my shot had to be low. He wasn't expecting a return volley and was probably as surprised as I had been when he pitched backward with the flame of the Remington still in my hands.

I fell with the recoil, and the barrel of the shotgun buried itself in the snow and frozen ground below, useless. I rolled to the left, trying to keep him in view, but all I could see was the freezing fog that reflected in the dimness of the truck's lights. The pain in my leg clinched my guts and pulled my knees forward even as I tried to negotiate my left arm up for leverage. He was down too, but I couldn't be sure which of us would be able to get up first; the smart money would be on the man hyped on crystal meth.

My hat rolled from my head and rested there in the snow as I looked up. He seemed to be growing from the crusted surface. Henry's coat tried to hold him against the ground for me and, along with the burden of Ellen Runs Horse, did pin him just long enough for me to get the .32 up and out, the .45 still buried at my side.

I attempted to time the squeeze on the .32, waiting until a lull in the pain allowed my aim to stay steady long enough to fire off my only round, the chrome pistol extended into the fog. I felt like one of those near frozen buffalo in imminent danger of being torn apart by a pack of wolves, just waiting for one of those wolves to get close enough.

I pulled the trigger, and the little semiautomatic roared and bucked in my hand.

The air left his body as the impact of the slug carried his teetering momentum back. Center shot, or close enough. He fell with an angry, gargling sound, and the report of his pistol smacked like a bullwhip. His shot went off harmlessly into the frosted air.

I slumped down against my side and breathed again, the cold flood of oxygen inflating my chest as well as causing the searing pain in my thigh to start up again. I took a few more breaths and rolled my head back to look at him. He had collapsed backward on his shattered legs, doubled back as though he had been playing some perverse game of limbo. I stayed steady, looking at him, and tried to reassemble my mind so that I could begin making assessments on how badly I was hurt, how soon I could reach Ellen Runs Horse, and how long it would take me to get us both to cover.

Then he moved.

It was a feeble gesture at first, almost an involuntary one, but it was a movement nonetheless. I felt my single eye widen as his hand, still holding a very large stainless revolver, scrambled up from the snow like an antiaircraft battery. A shoulder surged forward as the other arm fought to push him up; like his grandfather, Leo would not stay in the grave.

His head lolled to one side as the trunk of his body approached upright, and the arm with the gun dragged across the snow. Our breaths billowed out to join the fog like two locomotives on a collision course.

I yanked on the .45 and freed it from the robe, feeling it swing forward, but he was already there, the endless, stainless barrel of a Colt .357 pointed at my face. I felt the surge of cold air in my teeth as I tried to bring the .45 around, but it was too late.

There was silence. He had paused for a moment, and all I could think was that this was the last thing I would see. Time froze then, and it was as if the air had died and the snowflakes just hung there like some ethereal mobile as I looked into the darkness of his face.

I waited as he wavered in the silence. The Colt toppled from his hand, and he stood there looking at me before falling forward, a Special Forces Vietnam issue tomahawk driven deep into the base of his skull.

The voice in the distance was garbled but still discernible. *"Nesh-sha-nun Na-woo-hes-sten Nah-kohe Ve-ne-hoo-way-hoost Ne-hut-may-au-tow."* Tell your ancestors Standing Bear has sent you.

16

I was pretty sure that the two of us looked like a human junkyard. We were sitting at the veterinarian's office. Henry struggled out the next sentence with the good side of his mouth, "How is your leg?"

"It hurts, but only when I walk. It's not so bad when I talk." He nodded, and we both looked at the carpet. "DCI is going to want to talk to you." He didn't move, so I continued. "How about I go through the story, and you can make corrections and additions as we go?"

"Hmm."

"What?" He turned to look at me, and I could see the bulge of the bandage at his jawline. "Just kidding. So, you found the highway patrol cruiser buried in the snow up on the flat?"

"Hmm."

"And you stopped the truck and got out to take a look, and the driver didn't move. So, you opened the door." I nodded my head for a moment. "What kind of rookie move was that?" He didn't respond, but I could see his jaw flex. "So he raised the glorified .22 and shoots you in the face right off the bat?"

"Hmm."

I nodded some more. "You're lucky it was a .32, the .357 would've deviated your septum. You don't have to answer that." He didn't. "All right, you fell backward, and then Leo rolls you over, takes you for dead, and strips your coat off of you?"

"Hmm."

"Because of this, Dog tries to eat Leo alive, and he shoots Dog twice and drives off with my truck?"

"Hmm."

I shook my head and looked at the operating room door. "Then you got up, sprinted after the truck, and followed Leo back to the canyon with half your face tied on with a bandana? You ran a half a mile with a subcutaneous bullet trail running from the cleft of your chin to the back of your neck?"

He held the bloody fragment of lead that Isaac had pulled out and handed it to me. "Hmm."

The door to the operating room was opening and, from the corner of my good eye, I could see Mike Pilch coming out to give us the prognosis on Dog. Mike was a vet who was something of an oddity in Absaroka County in that he actually tried to save domestic animals as opposed to giving up and putting them down. He stopped short. "Wow, you guys look like eight kinds of hell."

I held a finger to my lips to silence him. "We escaped from the hospital." I glanced over at Henry to see him wave a feeble hand at the veterinarian and readjust the leather duster over his knee. "The Indian's not talking today." He nodded and studied the Bear's face a little more closely. "How's Dog?"

He pulled his eyes away from the spectacle of Henry to look at me; I don't guess the view improved. "It's pretty bad, but he's tough whatever he is." He moved over and sat in the chair beside me. "The first bullet just grazed his skull. It was the second bullet that did the most damage, entering the abdomen and lodging in the muscle near the spine. I did an exploratory and found a section of the intestinal tract was perforated and had to remove eleven inches. I flushed the stomach with sterile saline and placed several drains. With the bullet so close to the spine, we'd probably do more harm than good if I tried to take it out, but the body will wall it off and it shouldn't cause any future problems. He's still dopey from surgery but seems to be doing well. I'll need to keep a close watch on him for the next few days."

As we left Mike's office, I finished questioning the Bear. He was buttoning his leather duster. "Did you put the axe in the base of Leo's skull just to save your coat?"

He gathered it up as he wearily climbed in the truck. "Hmm."

"Wow . . ." I glanced back at the Bear. "You could've missed. What kind of rookie move was that?"

It had been a long night. We had staunched our bleedings and had huddled in the cab of my truck with Ellen Runs Horse until Double Tough showed up in a D9 Caterpillar and pulled my three-quarter ton out of the creek bed like it was a Flexible Flyer. He had rendezvoused with the HPs so that Dog could be brought to Durant for more professional care and had drunk about a half a bottle of Wild Turkey in the meantime, but he seemed as impervious to liquor as he had been to bullets. He pulled us up and out of the canyon, angling the blade so that a slow-motion wall of snow cascaded away from the dozer and cleared a way for us as we were pulled along. By the time we had gotten to the flat above, revolving blue and red lights joined with our own, telling me that the rest of the cavalry had arrived.

Vic's unit was the only one that could make it this far. Before we had come to a stop she was there, yanking the door open and applying a more professional pressure bandage to my leg; Saizarbitoria helped Henry on the other side of the cab. We left the Bear in my truck, thinking it might help maintain the quiet Ellen Runs Horse had surrendered to. Saizarbitoria would drive it to the hospital with them, while I would ride along with Vic. As I leaned against her, she tipped her head around to give me a look. "You get him?"

My smile couldn't help but fade. "The Bear did." I glanced into the truck bed. So did Vic. The half-frozen body of Leo Gaskell was buried into the cradle of snow that had accumulated there. The black alloy tomahawk still stuck up from the back of his head like a pump lever.

She blew a brief breath from pursed lips. "Fuck."

There were four HPs parked at the underpass.

Wes was dead, only one week away from guarding those golf course ponds. They found him where he must have pulled Leo over.

He was a veteran cop with more than thirty-five years on the job, and he had known that Leo was armed and highly dangerous, but something had gone terribly wrong.

There was a buzz of activity at the hospital emergency room, one that I had grown used to as of late. Out of the three of us, triage speaking, I was third. I waited on a gurney as they stabilized Henry. Bill McDermott had cut off my jeans above the wound, irrigated the hole in my leg, and was now bandaging me up; Ferg leaned against the wall and watched the process. I glanced at him, trying to ignore the pain in my leg. "Cady and Lana?"

He smiled. "Christmas shopping over in Sheridan." He shrugged. "They weren't going to stay in that room any longer, and they don't know about all of this." He waited a few moments before asking. "Leo Gaskell dead?" I nodded, as we both stared at my leg. "You do it?"

"Henry."

After a while he spoke again. "Good."

It was a strange remark for the Ferg to make. "Why good?"

"He's better at living with it."

I felt the dull throb through the anesthetic and wondered where I could get a pair of pants that would fit around the bandage. I looked down at the coroner as he finished. "Does it bother you if I talk to you while you're working?"

He smiled. "Most of my patients don't, but go ahead."

"How's Ellen Runs Horse?"

"For a dehydrated old woman, who is suffering from exposure and malnutrition, she's doing quite well."

There was a nurse at the desk outside the Intensive Care Unit, but she was committing a copy of *Redbook* to memory and so only raised her head briefly as we passed. Ellen was in the curtained-off section to the far right with no one else in the room. They had cleaned her up, and she looked a lot better. I only felt marginally shitty about what we were doing, but when I thought about Mari Baroja, Anna Walks

Over Ice, and Wes Rogers, I felt better about it. Too many people had died.

I dug into my pocket and handed Henry the ornament that I had taken from the tree in her trailer, and her eyes followed it from my hand to his. He held it there between them; the Mason jar lid that dangled from the yarn turned slowly revealing the photo on one side and the name on the other. She stared at me long enough to convince me that I was interfering with the investigative process, so I went to the other side of the curtain. I could hear her whispering.

The next thing I knew, Henry was standing next to me. "Anything we can use?"

It pained him as he spoke. "She keeps repeating a phrase that means 'give up'."

"She's throwing in the towel after all this?" He shrugged as I glanced back and saw that she was watching us. I smiled and to my surprise she smiled back. She didn't look like somebody who was calling it quits.

"She is apologetic about it." I noticed that he was able to talk softly from the right side of his mouth.

She was still holding the Mason jar lid. "I'm going to need that ornament."

He looked back, and she smiled at us some more. "We will have to wait until she is asleep."

Vic had yelled at me last night, and I was thinking there wasn't anybody left to yell at me when I saw Ruby's car. It was a Sunday, but Lucian must not have felt well enough to come to work. Henry quietly closed the door behind us, and I felt like we were sneaking in after an all night drunk. We stood there on the landing as a set of ferocious blues looked down on us.

"How is Dog?"

I tried a weak smile. "He's going to be all right. We can visit him in a couple of days." The eyes disappeared.

We struggled our way up the steps with Henry assisting by allowing me a hand on his shoulder. My leg was throbbing, so we stopped at the top, and I caught my breath. I looked at the bench by the door; someone was sleeping, covered with one of our PROPERTY OF ABSAROKA COUNTY JAIL wool blankets. The place was like a boarding house. "Who is that?"

She didn't look up from the computer screen. "The methane foreman."

I looked over at Henry, who was risking injury by smiling. "Let's go to my office, shall we?"

My chair felt good, and I thought about spending the rest of the day there, but the obligations of duty called my attention to a large tan envelope that read Sheriff Sweetie Pie; I had forgotten that she had dropped off an envelope what seemed like an eternity ago.

There was a crisp piece of legal paper clipped to a photocopy. I started with the note, a gracefully looping script in red that sprawled across the rigid lines of light blue on yellow. "Mon Amour, I've left you a little present I found in one of my investigations of Durant National Bank's safe-deposit boxes. The manager found an old registration for box number 283, a Mr. Charles Joseph Nurburn. It hadn't been opened since 1950 but someone had paid the rental fee until around ten years ago when the bill came back with addressee unknown." I thought about the timing and that was when Lucian had taken up residence at the Durant Home for Assisted Living. I guess he had forgotten about the rental.

I looked up at Henry, but he was looking out the window, so I continued reading to myself. "I'm here for another day and a half, but then I've got to be in Denver on the 24th at 9 A.M. Call me."

I looked up at the old Seth Thomas clock, figuring maybe I could just catch up with her and convince her to stay another day but then wondered how Cady would feel about that. I hadn't seen her in almost two days and she'd be gone before I knew it. I flipped the note over and looked at the photocopy. It was Charlie Nurburn's Will and Testament or a copy thereof. It was pretty cut and dried and left all Charlie's assets to Joseph Walks Over Ice.

Joseph.

We had a name. I handed the copy to Henry and called for Ruby. Even with the limp, I met her at the door. "Get the NCIC and ask about a Joseph Walks Over Ice, male, about fifty-five years of age, born in Sheridan County. See if anything pops up." She disappeared around the corner as I turned back to the Bear. "Ring any bells?" He shook his head as I went around the desk and sat back down. "I've got an idea . . ." His eyes stayed steady with mine. I stared at the surface of my desk. "Whoever killed Mari Baroja did it to get her money. Since illegitimate or stepchildren cannot inherit directly, the only way to do that was to have Mari predecease Charlie so that he could collect his elective share. Then you kill off the already dead Charlie and inherit the money he left you."

The Bear's eyes widened, and I continued. "Leo Gaskell and, more importantly, Joseph Walks Over Ice found it suddenly financially beneficial to keep Lucian's ruse going after the methane started producing. I think it snowballed on them. I don't think they thought that that many people knew Charlie was dead. Even Lana would have to be on the list. She told me that Lucian had killed her grandfather the day I met her. Everyone who knew Charlie was dead has been either attacked or killed." I slumped back in my chair and yelled into the other room. "Have you got anything?"

The reply was curt. "Hold your horses!"

"There's something else that's bothering me." Henry handed me back the Will, and I laid the photocopy on the desk. "I'm sure they killed Anna because she was trying to tell Doc Bloomfield about Leo's plans or Joseph's, but how did Leo kill Wes Rogers?" It was quiet in the room. "Wes would have known . . . unless Leo Gaskell was not driving the car."

Ruby's voice called from the other room. "I've got something."

We rushed in, as best we could, and crowded around the computer screen as Ruby summoned forth Joseph Walks Over Ice. "The name came up in the Department of Child Services in Cheyenne. A child was given up for adoption to a Catholic orphanage, a Saint Anthony's in Casper, back in 1951."

Henry and I locked eyes. It wasn't that Ellen was giving up; it was what she had given up. "What else?"

"The child had numerous altercations and was described as emotionally disturbed. He was never adopted and left the orphanage at age sixteen." She looked up at me. "That's as far as it goes."

Henry spoke softly through his bandage. "At that period in time, a lot of Indian children took the surname of the priest who ran the orphanage."

Ruby's fingers started dancing again. She turned to me. "The priest who signed off on Joseph's papers was a Father Mark Lesky."

Lesky, Joseph.

Joe Lesky.

I grabbed the phone from Ruby's desk and punched in the number for the home. Jennifer Felson answered, and I asked her if Joe was on duty. "He was here a little while ago, but he got off at 8:00. Is there a problem?"

"Is he still around?"

"I'll check." I stood there with the phone in my hand. "Shelly saw Joe walk out of here with Lucian about twenty minutes ago."

"If they show up, call me. Thanks, Jennifer." I hung up and looked at Henry. Double Tough had woken up with all the commotion and was now standing with us. "He has been everywhere in this case." I looked down at Ruby. "Where are Vic and Saizarbitoria?"

She stuttered. "There was a fender bender on the highway bypass."

"Radio them and get them in here now. Joe Lesky's out with Lucian." I took a deep breath, trying to clear my head. "Where would they go?" I took another breath and thought out loud. "Where would Joe take him?"

It was the clearest I'd heard him speak since he had been shot. "Breakfast?"

I turned to Ruby on our way out. "Tell Vic and Saizarbitoria to meet us at the Bee." As we started down the steps, I noticed that the methane foreman was accompanying us. I turned my head toward him so that I could see him with my uncovered eye. "Where the hell do you think you're going?"

He smiled as he caught the door and allowed Henry to go through first. "I thought ya might need somebody who could both walk and talk."

He had a point.

We pulled up alongside the Busy Bee, just as Vic's unit slid to a stop beside us, only missing the front of my truck by inches. Her window was rolled down. "Joe Fucking Lesky?"

The place was packed as we flooded in, all the patrons freezing at the sight of an armed sheriff, two deputies, an Indian, and a construction worker; we probably looked like the Village People.

I caught Dorothy's eye from behind the counter. "Lucian and Joe Lesky?"

You couldn't ruffle her feathers with a brick. "Haven't seen them."

We regrouped on the sidewalk, and I started breaking it down. "Vic, you and Double Tough go to the home and wait. If they show up, just tell Joe that we've got some papers for him at the office. Try not to tip him off but bring him in no matter what." They left in Vic's unit as I turned to Saizarbitoria. "Santiago, get Ferg and do a perimeter. Radio the HPs and tell them to stop anything heading south on I-25 and that we're looking for Lucian and Joe Lesky." I tossed him the keys to the Bullet, and he was gone.

I turned to look down Main Street and then back at the Bear. I thought for a long moment. "I've got a question for you." He didn't say anything. "What makes us think that Joe took Lucian?" I looked back down the street at the Euskadi Hotel sign. "What if Lucian took Joe?"

"Mornin' Lucian. Joe . . ."

I limped the twenty feet to the table; Lucian was facing me as I came in, the old gunfighter to the end. Joe had his back to the door but turned and lightly smiled as I entered. There were two cups of coffee on the table, but it looked like Joe was the only one drinking. Lucian's hat was off and placed on the chair beside him with the brim down, which struck me as strange. The old sheriff looked relaxed, leaning back in his chair with his hands folded in his lap. Joe had his elbows resting on the table. Neither of them had their coats on, both were hanging from their chairs, and the jukebox was playing Fred Waring and the Pennsylvanian's "Ring Those Christmas Bells."

I hobbled past them to the bar back and poured myself a cup of coffee and gently placed it on a saucer. Coffee bought ten minutes. I raised a cup to Henry, who had stayed back by the door. He shook his head no. As I stalled at the bar, trying to think how I was going to play this, I thought of the mixture of excitements the next few minutes could unleash.

"What happened to your leg?" Joe was looking at me, but he was also glancing at Henry and his bandaged face. "And what happened to you?"

I shuffled back over to their table, turned one of the bentwood chairs around, and sat, giving me ready access to my sidearm and Joe. "Oh . . . we got shot."

They were both staring at us now. Lucian the first to ask. "Who the hell shot ya?"

I studied the little vase on our table with its decorative plastic sprigs of holly and mistletoe, then trailed an arm over the back of the chair and took a sip of my coffee, my sore hand hardly fitting the delicate dinnerware of the Euskadi. "Leo Gaskell." I kept my eyes on the old sheriff. "We've got him up at the hospital, and they're patching him up." Another Lazarus on the pile.

It was quiet for a moment, but then the music swelled with the false vibrancy and good humor of the season. "Who's Leo Gaskell?"

I turned and looked at Joe Lesky. You had to give him credit; he was good. "Drug dealer from over in Fremont County; looks like he's the one that hurt Anna Walks Over Ice." May as well keep everybody alive. "He's up there talking to the investigators now."

Joe's head nodded. He too was trying to buy time but in an establishment where nobody was selling. "Well, it's good you got the guy that did it."

"Yep." The old sheriff was watching me very closely as I turned back to him and tried to get a read. "What're you up to?"

"Doin' some Christmas shoppin'."

"The stores aren't open yet."

He looked back at Joe. "I got plenty a time." He adjusted his hat on the seat of the chair beside him. Now I knew where the gun was.

Joe started to push off from the table. "Well, it sounds like you fellas have a lot to . . ." Out of the corner of my good eye, I could see Henry's hands move from his pockets.

"Sit." It was the soft voice he used when he would ask me if I really wanted to make a move in our chess games, the warning voice that sounded like the guttural vibration in the back of a cougar's throat. Joe eased back into his chair, and I turned to Lucian.

We looked at each other like we had for decades, a blind man talking to a deaf one. There was a line that neither of us was able to cross: his sneering at my supposed weakness and my righteous indignation at his immorality. I was sure that the chasm between us was a generational one. Lucian's world was simpler, and he was unable to see that law enforcement had become complicated in the modern era; or was it that he was so close, so much of a part of the whole mess, that he had lost perspective on it long ago? Charlie Nurburn hung out there like a reoccurring nightmare and in Charlie's child and his child's child.

I guess the heat was getting to Joe, because he felt compelled to interrupt. "We were just having a little conversation somewhere quiet." His voice was a little unsteady. "I came across some information I thought might interest Lucian."

I glanced back as Lucian pulled his pipe from one jacket pocket and the beaded leather pouch from the other. The tension eased but only a little. "I got some information, too." Lucian filled his pipe and struck a match on the side of his chair. "I, um . . ." He sucked on his pipe until he got it going, the thick plume of smoke roiling from the corner of his mouth. "Beebee Banks was visitin' her mother over at the home. Walt, she told me to tell you she found out who had that little Baroja girl's bakery building before she did." The smile played on his face like a reflection on moving water. "Why, it was Joe here."

Like the motor drive on an automatic shutter, I counted six different stills as my head rotated to Joe, like six separate heartbeats. "Don't move."

The weight of it was in the room with us now like a cold cloudburst had suddenly let loose; the rain of recognition was dripping from all of us and, as I saw Joe's hand slip from the table, I was positive that of the four men in the room, three had guns. I saw the Bear move, but I was closer.

The bones in his wrist crunched with a nauseating give, and I finally got a look at the Joe Lesky that had been so carefully hidden from me as, with a snarl of rage, he tried to twist and pull away. My left held, but I wasn't going to trust it to do the job alone. His expression changed as the cold barrel of the .45 pressed up under his jaw, forcing his head back to where he had to look over the contours of his face to see me.

I took a deep breath. "I said, don't move."

I watched as his nostrils spread, and he pulled air in like a bellows. "Let go of my wrist!"

"I don't hardly think so." I eased the pressure of the .45 and allowed his head to lower enough so that I could see his expression. I thought of an old drill sergeant who had told me that a professional is the one who always has his gun. I risked a glimpse to the right, around the damn eye patch, and saw the long-barreled .38 of Lucian's duty revolver extended across the table eight inches from Joe's face.

I looked back at Joe, who was glancing at his coat and thinking about trying the reach with his left. "You do, and I will splatter your brains all over the pressed tin ceiling." His eyes came back to mine.

"Now I'm going to place your hands back on this table, and you are not going to move them, do you understand?"

I swept my hand behind him, lifting his coat and throwing it to Henry. I pulled my cuffs from my belt. "Put those on."

"You broke my wrist."

"Put those on." He pressed the one loop through and delicately placed it around his damaged wrist, only partially locking it as I counted only three notches that clicked. "All the way."

He looked at me. "It hurts."

"So will the .45." He clicked it again and then did the other hand as specified. I leaned back and took another deep breath as I pulled the Colt away from the underside of Joe's chin. I turned my head, so that I could see Lucian with the inside of my good eye. "You all right?"

"I ain't the one without a gun, if that's what ya mean."

I looked back at Joe. His eyes shifted from me, to Lucian, and then back to me. "I don't know what's going on here, but I'm not saying anything until I talk to a lawyer."

Lucian snorted. "What makes you think that you're gonna see a lawyer?"

My voice sounded a long way away, like it was coming from the land of reason. "Lucian."

The old sheriff's hand didn't move, and the extended barrel of the Smith and Wesson stayed even with Joe's eyes. "I aim to kill this son of a bitch, right here and right now." He pulled the pipe from his mouth and blew a strong lungful of smoke away from us. The pounding of "Ring Those Christmas Bells" continued as the jukebox charged on.

I cleared my throat and swallowed. "Lucian, I'm going to need you to lower your weapon."

He gestured toward Joe with the stem of his pipe. "You killed my wife."

I needed to buy some more time. I studied Joe. "When did you find out that Charlie Nurburn was dead?" He didn't move, but his eyes switched from Lucian to me. "I'm betting that you knew he was dead by the time you contacted Leo. I guess you figured that Lucian here had kept Charlie alive for fifty-odd years and there was no reason why you couldn't keep him alive for a little while longer or at least until you could get a share of Mari's money."

He didn't move. "I don't know what you're talking about." His tongue flicked across his lips. "Walt, you've known me . . ."

"No I don't." I leaned in on the back of my chair. "Did you kill Mari Baroja before you got Leo over here? You knew you could get him to kill Lana and Lucian, certainly Anna, but he didn't kill them all, did he? And you didn't do so well with Isaac."

I was tired, and I wanted it all over with, but there was so much more to tell. "Leo tried to save his grandmother; he was hurt and was going to run for it but you knew we were down on the old Nurburn place. You were the one that shot Wes Rogers, and then you sent Leo down there in the cruiser even though you knew we were waiting and either way, you figured this problem would solve itself." I kept the .45 leveled between Joe's eyes. "What were you going to do, Joe? Blame it all on Leo?"

His voice was strained. "I want a lawyer."

Lucian exhaled, his arm still extended. "Best you can hope for is a priest, and that right soon."

"You can't prove any of this."

I looked into Joe's eyes, trying to see some common ground between us, but there was nothing there. I glanced back at his rumpled coat, hanging from Henry's hand. "If I go over there and pull a .32 automatic from your coat pocket, and it makes a ballistic match with the gun that shot Wes Rogers, I can start proving a lot."

I reached into the pocket of my jacket and laid the Christmas ornament on the table, face up. I slowly pushed it toward Joe, where the visible part of the man's face in the photograph matched the man in front of me. "Never mind all the others . . . he was your son, Joe. How could you do that to your child?"

The old sheriff cocked the revolver.

I could see the lanyard ring at the base of the pistol's butt, the loop that used to attach Lucian's old service revolver to his belt in the style of the cavalry riders so that they wouldn't lose their sidearms while mounted. Like Lucian, this morning it was untethered, out there in the wind where bad things could and would happen. "Lucian, you know what it is Joe here was getting ready to tell you. Whether it was as a bartering chip or leverage, you can't do what you were planning to do because you're not alone in this anymore." He blinked, and I could see the welling in his eyes as Fred Waring and the Pennsylvanians took the Christmas train home amid four-part harmony.

I saw his trigger finger tighten, and the legendary grip squeeze the wooden handle like a lifeline. The best I could hope for was to knock it away with my own gun, flip the table, or throw myself sideways into him. In the split second I was thinking this, Lucian swung the revolver around and emptied it with five thundering reports into the shuddering and now forever silent jukebox. He tossed the empty .38 back onto the table where it clattered and spun with its barrel pointed at an absolutely immobile Joe Lesky. Lucian's voice was low and weak in the silence. "Jesus H. Christ . . . I always hated that damn thing."

EPILOGUE

The sounds the piano made were soft and just a little melancholy, with a poetic lyricism that matched the surroundings. Henry was planted behind the bar; Bill McDermott was dancing with Lana Baroja; Saizarbitoria was dancing with his wife, Marie; and Cady was dancing with our newest Powder Junction deputy, Double Tough. Dog was curled up by the piano; he had already called it a night, the shaved portion of his middle and the bandages on his head and abdomen making him look like a stuffed animal.

I made the musical bridge and cut in with an improvisational riff that paused the dancers but held my attention for a while longer. My fingers felt stiff, but I was loosening up. My eye patch was gone, and there was no serious damage to the cornea; my vision was a little blurred on the right, but Vic was to my left. I kept sneaking glances at her, still a little startled by her civilian clothes. She was wearing a short black dress and black cowboy boots with embroidered red roses and blue leaves. With the turquoise and silver chandelier earrings, it was western, with just a touch of gypsy insouciance thrown in for good measure.

There was brief applause as I reached for my beer and nodded in acknowledgment toward the dance floor alongside the pool table. I shifted my weight and leaned against the wall, looking over at Henry and signaling the jukebox. I had only played a half dozen songs, but my fingers hurt, and I needed a little relief.

Vic took a sip of her dirty martini and shrugged as the wind continued to batter the outside of the bar. Another storm had come in from the Arctic Circle and had dropped about eight inches of snow.

The Ferg had volunteered for duty, but so far there hadn't been any phone calls; it was the kind of holiday we liked, where the weather was so bad that the populace stayed in, including Ruby and Isaac, who had elected to stay home to avoid the amateurs who might have decided to drive.

"How's your leg?"

"Still not up to dancing."

"Nobody asked." She glanced over her shoulder at my daughter. "Cady flying out tomorrow?"

"If the weather's decent."

"Air Omar?"

I nodded and took the opportunity to watch her for a moment, like I always did when she wasn't aware. "You got two new deputies for Christmas." She stayed turned to the dance floor, watching Saizarbitoria, and tipped the delicate stem of her glass for another sip. "He's a dark horse, but he's sharp and he works hard."

I took another sip of my beer. "The wife is nice."

"Whatever."

I smiled behind her back. "What about the hillbilly?"

Her head pivoted a little as she watched Double Tough, who was still dancing with Cady. "He's durable."

"That he is."

She turned back around. "All right, so Joe got his name from the priest in Casper. Where did Leo get his?"

"Foster parents in Fremont County."

She nodded. "Joe brought Leo over for the job after he laid the groundwork by keeping Charlie Nurburn alive?"

"Basically continuing Lucian's efforts in hopes of getting a percentage for himself, but who knows? It looks like he was ready to kill half of Absaroka County to get what he thought he deserved."

"What about Anna Walks Over Ice?"

"We found an unfinished letter at her house, in Crow." I glanced toward Henry. "She outlined the whole situation; she had seen Joe add something to Mari Baroja's Metamucil that night." I took another sip of my beer. "I guess she just wasn't sure enough, at the time, to accuse him, and then with Leo it was too late."

She stared at the piano and tentatively reached out for a key. "Very understanding of you."

I looked at my friend with the bandaged face; he was still mixing drinks behind the bar. "I didn't have to kill him."

In the dim glow of the stained glass of the billiard's light and the Rainier beer advertisements, my chief deputy looked like some courtly renaissance woman, the kind that would poison your wine. "It's Tuesday night. He's probably got the board out."

I waited for more, but there wasn't any. She just sat there, with her finger resting beside the keys, her eyes far away. She had looked like this at the hospital the night she handed me Lucian's love letters from Mari. She waited there for a moment, then got up and straightened her skirt in an action that seemed both symmetric and disquieting. "Where are you going?"

She didn't turn when she said it but downed the martini in one gulp. "Dancing."

As I watched her approach the stilled dancers to choose a victim, Lana came over and occupied the bench seat next to me. "I'm leaving."

"I seem to be having that effect on people."

She glanced back at the Yellowstone County coroner. "Bill says he'll give me a ride back into town."

"You should take advantage." She placed a hand on mine and ducked her head to catch my eye. She kept looking at me with those familiar dark eyes, so I diverted her thoughts. "What are you going to do with all your money?"

She didn't pause. "Hire someone to work at the bakery." She smiled the jaunty smile that always seemed to put the world off kilter. "What would you do if you had a million dollars?"

"I don't have a million dollars."

She tipped my hat back as she rose and planted a gentle kiss on my bared forehead. "You never know." I watched with great unease as she turned to Bill, who assisted her in putting on her coat, the same purple, quilted teepee as before. "I left you something on the bar. Merry Christmas." The teepee swirled out with the coroner, and they were gone through the glass door with a flurry of flakes blowing in to take their place.

I drained the last of my beer and gingerly got up, keeping the weight off my left leg and trying to negotiate between the bench and the piano with the blurred vision of my right eye. I decided that the next time, I would make a concentrated effort to get wounded all on one side; it might make post-adventure life a little easier. I limped my way across the makeshift dance floor as Dog followed and threaded my way between Saizarbitoria and Marie and Double Tough and Vic, who ignored me as I passed.

Henry and Cady were congregated at the bar when I finally got there. We all studied the white box, tied with twine and resting on the worn surface of the counter. Cady laid her forearms along the bar and rested her chin on them, eye to eye with the box, her butt stuck out and her ankles crossed. She was wearing those fancy jeans with the sequins outlining the pockets. "Whatever happened to Charlie Nurburn?"

"Oh, like a bad penny, he'll probably turn up."

The lawyer reached down to pet Dog, careful to avoid the patched-up parts. "What do you think happened to him?"

I shrugged. "Who knows if the bones Leo found belonged to Charlie or not?"

"You don't seem overly concerned."

I glanced at her. "This case has had enough skeletons in the closet; I don't think I need to go looking for any more."

Cady's smile was brief. "What about Mari Baroja?"

I waited a moment, and then said what I was trying to hold back. "She's still dead." They all looked at me. "Mari Baroja is dead, Anna Walks Over Ice is dead, Wes Rogers is dead, and Leo Gaskell is dead . . . All for nothing."

Henry wasn't going to let it rest. "What does Lucian have to say in this?"

"He doesn't have anything to say in this, the law is the law and whatever DCI finds, they find. Whatever Charlie Nurburn was ended with Mari Baroja. She stopped him from hurting her children, and in a way she stopped him from hurting her children's children. Wherever she is, she can take a certain amount of satisfaction in that." Except for the jukebox, it was quiet in the bar. "I'm sorry. I'm tired, and I should take Dog and go home."

Cady protested. "Daddy, it's not even midnight."

"I'm sorry, Sweet Pea. I'm just worn out."

She straightened the collar of my new Christmas corduroy shirt. "Who am I gonna kiss?"

I glanced around the room at all the possibilities. "I bet you find somebody."

The Bear changed the subject, giving me an out. "We're supposed to visit Wes's family on Thursday?"

"Yep." I pulled on my heavy sheepskin coat from the adjacent bar stool and put on my hat.

He stuck out his hand. "Happy New Year, Walt." I took the hand, and he pulled me in for a hug, slapping me on the back with his other. "It has to be better than this one."

When I turned to Cady, she reached up and clasped her hands behind my neck. "What if I don't let you go?" I slowly stood up straight and felt her feet leave the floor as she trailed up after me, a ritual we had practiced since she could stand, even though I didn't lift her anywhere near as high as I used to. She frowned the frown that always got her what she wanted but let me go. "I'll be home, but it might be late. I love you."

I scooped the small box off the bar and slowly made for the door, Dog in tow. I paused by the dancers and reminded Saizarbitoria that he was on duty tomorrow. He smiled, being the last man on the totem pole of Absaroka County Sheriff's Department had its disadvantages. I reminded Double Tough to come in on Thursday to get measured for a uniform, and he said he would.

I started to step around Vic but, when I did, she turned and slipped my left hand into a reverse wristlock that suddenly brought my head down to her level. I could smell the alcohol on her breath. The big, tarnished gold eyes blinked as she reached out and nibbled my lower lip, gently sliding into a long, slow vacuum.

She kissed like she was pulling venom.

Her hand glided down the back of my neck, the nails leaving scorched earth as they went. She pulled her face back, and I wasn't sure if I could stand. She studied me for the effect, lessening the pressure on my left hand as I rose away from her, willing my injured leg to stop trembling. I stood there for a moment and didn't say anything. There was nothing to say. I remembered to breathe, and the moment passed when she turned to Double Tough, pulling him back to the center of the dance floor, her eyes away from me.

It was dismal outside, with the wind blowing the snow in all directions. I closed my right eye, since it was still a little tender, and opened the door for Dog. I gently lifted him onto the new seat cover, a Christmas gift from Cady, and he traversed to the passenger side, sitting and looking out the windshield in anticipation. I crawled in after him and fired up the Bullet; the small bakery box sat between us.

I adjusted the defroster on the truck to high, backed away from the Red Pony, and turned the wheel, slowly making my way from the border of the Rez toward the quiet of my little cabin.

When we got inside, Dog stopped by the door and looked at me. I looked back at him, then unbuttoned my coat and stood in the middle of the room. "What?" He didn't say anything back, just sat by the door and waited. "What? We're not going anywhere, that's it for the night."

Red Road Contracting had finished installing my wood-burning stove for Christmas and had left a card on the flat black surface that read, MERRY CHRISTMAS, NO CHARGE.

Dog still waited by the door.

I shrugged and walked toward the bedroom. I was trying to convince Dog of the strength of my convictions. It was Cady's room for the moment, and the amount of clothing splayed across the floor gave little hope to our meeting Omar at the appointed time tomorrow morning.

The little red light on the answering machine blinked 2 at me; I hit the button. "Hey good-lookin', I was just hoping I'd catch you home alone, but I guess you're out playing in the snow. I understand the Wyoming Attorney General has requested your appearance here in Cheyenne." It was silent for a moment, long enough for me to see dash light reflecting golden curls and a ferocious and devouring set of blues. "I read about you in the papers again. I think I'll start a scrapbook."

I stood there, punching my hat back on my head with a forefinger, and looked at the machine. "Anyway, it looks like I'm moving back to Virginia. Louis and I are going to give it another go." Silence again. "Well, I hope you have a Happy New Year." I looked at the machine, expecting there to be more, but there wasn't. Those echoes were still reverberating through me, but I had made the smallest investment and had gotten the smallest return.

The next message played for only a moment with a barely discernable sound. I bit my lip and punched the replay button. "Hey good-lookin' . . ." I forwarded to the next message and listened more carefully, barely hearing the word. "Horseshit."

Dog was waiting for me when I opened the door and walked gingerly out to the truck. I helped him up, and he climbed over the little white box on the seat and happily sat on the other side of the cab. I ducked in out of the wind, straightened my hat as I started the truck again, and glanced at the smiling dog. "You don't have to look so satisfied."

There wasn't much parking at the Durant Home for Assisted Living, and it looked like there was a subdued celebration going on in the main lobby. I wasn't really looking forward to running the gauntlet. The end doors were locked this late at night, so I walked toward the small stand of pines outside Room 32.

There was a light on, and the hide lampshade cast a warm glow. I stepped off the plowed parking lot and into the midshin depth of the snow, Dog staying in my tracks. As I got nearer, I could see more clearly.

He was seated in his usual chair, his head resting a little forward with his hands on his knees, both real and artificial. The chess set lay before him on the folding table, white toward me as it always was, along with a bottle of Pappy Van Winkle's Family Reserve, which was adorned with a green ribbon.

The door opened smoothly with a barely perceptible sound. I shook my head and stepped in, allowing Dog to go over to the sofa as I closed the door behind me. I stood there for a moment to let the room still again. He must have been awfully tired, because he didn't move, and the gentle whiffing of his snoring filled the room. I wondered how often he must have slept in the chair and figured it was more times than were good for him. I wondered if he was really asleep, if this was his way of welcoming me back. I wondered about the sad-eyed lieutenant and about how much Lucian knew about the baby who had been born perhaps not so prematurely to Mari Baroja, about the child that Charlie Nurburn had tried so hard to kill, and about the man who was fortunate enough to father a child of his own before a senseless war took from him all that he had left to give.

I reached a hand out and once again began the Queen's Indian Defense, Petrosian Variation, by advancing my pawn to F4 and moving his knight to F6; I approached chess the way I approached life, way over my head.

I smiled and took a step back; when I looked up, I saw a different set of dark eyes. It wouldn't have been surprising if they had risen from the old man in front of me, but they stared up from the sofa. Dog's head was lying on top of a chief's blanket that covered her. Lana smiled and started to speak, but there wasn't any need; she was holding the tattered letters that had been bound together with a thin ribbon, and they told the tale.

The letters from Lucian to Mari; the ones that told Lana how her grandfather had loved her, why her father and brothers were so quick to get Mari married after they had separated her from him, why Charlie Nurburn had done so well for himself at her expense. The old man had finally told it all to the person to whom it mattered the most. The rush of information came running in like a waterfall, filling me with the thought that hatred has a poor shelf life but that hope and love can limp along together forever. The water beneath Lana's dark eyes ran deep, resonating far into the last century.

I held an extended finger to my mouth and smiled again, as she watched me carefully back from the room to the door and silently pat my leg for Dog to follow. He was reluctant to leave the warmth of Lucian's room and Lana, but finally deigned to follow me as I picked up the bourbon and slid the double-paned glass shut behind us.

Dog looked puzzled as I collected a couple of the wood bundles and stacked them on top of the battered cooler that I had put in the corner of the cabin, along with the fifth of Pappy Van Winkle's Family Reserve and a book of matches. I opened the backdoor and walked off the edge of my deck another thirty yards. I sat the cooler down and unwrapped the firewood, stacking the pieces in the snow. I opened the bourbon. I looked back at the open door of the cabin and could see Dog watching me.

I took a swig and looked up at the starless sky. It had finally stopped snowing. I thought about what I was doing, then poured a strong draught of the whiskey onto the logs and lit them with one of the windproof matches. The fire took with a tremendous swoosh, and I stepped back to avoid burning my beard off. I watched it for a while and then headed back to the house. I shut the door behind me and took the bourbon to the bathroom. I sat it on the back of the sink and looked at myself in the mirror, started running the hot water, and dug out the shaving cream and razors that I hadn't used in quite a while. It took longer than I would have thought, but Dog watched with head resting on his paws as I slowly became myself again.

I studied the reflection and considered if I really was me. I was about to do something that I never would have done before, but then I remembered and a small cold feeling overtook my breath and I took another sip of the twenty-year-old bourbon.

I went out to the truck and collected three items from the center console of the Bullet and a shovel I'd stolen from Henry. This time Dog accompanied me out to the fire, and we watched it for a long time. I sat on the cooler with the three items resting beside me, the flickering orange, yellow, and red reflecting in Dog's eyes and mine.

The fire died down, and it didn't take long to dig the hole. I took another swig of the bourbon, then took the three items from the surface of the cooler and stuffed them under my arm. I opened the cooler and pulled out a long bone, probably a femur. I looked at Dog but tossed it back. Dramatic moments call for dramatic bones, and it only took a moment for me to find the skull.

I palmed it in my hand; it seemed smaller than it should have. I studied the skull, trying to see something in its structure that would explain the man's malevolence, but all I saw was the ghostly reflection of the gold tooth. It is said that the evil men do lives on, and the good is oft interred with their bones; I hoped with all my heart that this was not the case here and that what I was doing was the right thing.

I tossed the skull into the hole and eventually added the other bones until the cooler was empty. I pulled the tiny chrome-plated, pearl-handled .32 from under my arm and threw the empty pistol in as well, and then pulled the manila envelope out, undid the clasp, sat and looked at each of the photographs of the tortured and dead woman, returning them to the envelope as I went. When I was finished, I took the shovel and filled in the hole, making a raised area. When the rains came in the spring, I would tamp the area flat. It was amazing, the things you learned loitering in graveyards.

I sat on the cooler again and opened the small white box. Dog and I sat there, munching ruggelach, and I stared at the humped up earth and thought about how, perhaps, the old sheriff and I weren't that different after all.

Craig Johnson's third novel featuring
Sheriff Walt Longmire is now available
as a Viking hardcover.
Read on for the first chapter of

KINDNESS
GOES
UNPUNISHED

1

I didn't wear my gun. They had said that it was going to be easy and, like the fool I am, I believed them. They said that if things got rough to make sure I showed the pictures, of which there were only twenty-three; I had already shown all of them twice. "'Long, long ago, there lived a king and queen . . .'"

I looked around the room for a little backup, but there wasn't anyone there. They had said that I didn't have to worry, that they wouldn't leave me alone, but they had. "'. . . who didn't have any children. One day, the queen was visited by a wise fairy, who told her, "You will have a lovely baby girl." The king was so overjoyed when he heard the news that he immediately made plans for a great feast. He invited not only his relatives, but also the twelve fairies who lived in the kingdom.'"

"Where's your gun?"

My thought exactly. "I didn't think I was going to need it." They all nodded, but I wasn't particularly sure they agreed.

"How long have you been a sheriff?"

"Twenty-three years." It just seemed like a million.

"Do you know Buffalo Bill?"

Maybe it was a million. "No, he was a little before my time."

"My daddy says you're a butt hole."

I looked down at the battered book in my hands. "Okay, maybe we should concentrate on today's story . . ."

"He says you used to drive around drunk all the time . . ."

The instigator in the front row looked like a little angel but had a mouth like a stevedore. He was getting ready to say something else, so I cut him off by holding up *Grimm's Fairy Tales* open to the page where the young princess had been enchanted and put to sleep for a hundred years. "Why do you think the fairy visited the queen?" A dark-haired girl with enormous eyes who sat in the third row slowly raised her hand. "You?"

She cocked her head in disgust. "I told you, my name is Anne."

I nodded mine in contrition. "Right. Anne, why do you think the fairy visited the queen?"

"Because their daughter is going to fall asleep." She said it slowly, with the hearty contempt even young people have for civil servants who can't get it right.

"Well, yep, but that happens later on because one of the fairies gets angry, right?" Anne raised her hand again, but I ignored her for a slight redheaded boy in the back. His name was Rusty, and I quietly thanked the powers that be for word association. "Rusty?"

"My dad says that my Uncle Paul is a fairy."

I'm not sure when it was that my storytelling abilities began to atrophy, but it must have been somewhere between *Sesame Street* and *The Electric Company*. I think I used to be pretty good at it, but that was a long time ago. I was going to have to ask my daughter if that really was the case; she was now "The Greatest Legal Mind of Our Time" and a Philadelphia lawyer. When I had spoken to Cady last night, she had still been at the office library in the basement. I felt sorry for her till she told

me the basement was on the twenty-eighth floor. My friend
Henry Standing Bear said that the law library was where all the
lawyers went to sleep at about $250 an hour.

"You are the worstest storyteller we ever had."

I looked down at another would-be literary critic who had
been silent up till now and wondered if maybe I had made a
mistake with "Brier Rose." Cady had loved the story dearly at
an earlier age, but the current enrollment appeared to be a little
sophisticated for the material.

"My daddy hides his medicine whenever anybody knocks
on our door."

I tried not to concentrate on this child's name. I propped
the book back up on my knee and looked at all of them, the
future of Absaroka County, Wyoming.

"He says he doesn't have a prescription."

I was supposed to make the drive to Philadelphia tomorrow with Henry. He had received an invitation to lecture at
the Pennsylvania Academy of the Fine Arts with his Mennonite
photograph collection in tow. I thought it would be an opportunity to visit my daughter and meet the lawyer who was the
latest of her conquests. The relationship had lasted about four
months, a personal record for her, so I decided that it was time
I met the prospective son-in-law.

"His medicine makes him fall down."

Henry was planning on driving Lola. I had tried to talk him
into flying, but it had been a while since he had driven across the
country and he said he wanted to check things out. The real reason was he wanted to make an entrance with the powder blue
1959 Thunderbird convertible; the Bear was big on entrances.

"He smokes his medicine."

We were going for only a week, but Cady was very excited
about introducing us to Devon Conliffe, who sounded like a

character from *The Philadelphia Story*. I had warned her that lawyers shouldn't marry other lawyers, that it only led to imbecile paralegals.

"My mommy says the only thing his medicine does is keep him from getting a job."

Patti with an "i," my daughter's secretary, agreed with me about lawyer interbreeding. We had talked about the relationship, and I could just make out a little reservation in Patti's voice when she mentioned him.

"He's my third daddy."

We were supposed to have dinner with the elder Conliffes at their palatial home in Bryn Mawr, an event I was looking forward to like a subcutaneous wound.

"I liked my second daddy best."

It would be interesting to see their response to the Indian and his faithful sidekick, the sheriff of Absaroka County. They probably wouldn't open the gate.

"I don't remember my first daddy."

I looked up at the kid and reopened the book. " 'Long, long ago, there lived a king and queen who didn't have any children . . .' "

Dorothy Caldwell turned toward the patties on the griddle behind her, lifted the press, and turned them. "What'd you read?"

I pulled Cady's personal copy from the stool beside me and sat it on the counter. *Grimm's Fairy Tales*. "Brier Rose"— "Sleeping Beauty" before Hollywood got hold of it.

She gave me a sideways look and then leaned over to glance at the love-worn cover. "Kindergarten?" She shrugged a shoulder as she placed the meat press aside. "Kids have gotten a little jaded since Cady's generation, Walter."

I set my glass down. "Well, I don't have to do it again until after the election." She slipped the hamburger, lettuce, tomato, and bacon onto a toasted bun and slid the plate toward me. "The usual?"

She nodded at the old joke, sipped at her own tea, and peeked at me over the rim. "I hear Kyle Straub is going to run."

I nodded and put mayonnaise on my burger, a practice she hated. "Yep, I've seen the signs." The prosecuting attorney had jumped the gun this morning and placed his red-white-and-blue signs in all the strategic spots around town before finding out for sure if I was really going to run again. So far, it had been the strongest motivation that I had had to continue my tenure.

"Prosecuting attorney / sheriff." She paused for effect. "Kind of gives you an indication as to what his administration would be like."

I thought about my original plan, to run for sheriff, put in half a term, and then hand the reigns over to Vic, allowing her to prove herself for two years before having to face a general election. I chewed a chunk of burger. "You think Vic would make a good sheriff?"

Dorothy slipped a wayward lock behind her ear and looked past me. Her hair was getting longer, and I wondered if she was growing it out. The answer to my question about Vic, like everything else about Dorothy, was definitive. "Why don't we ask her?"

I fought the urge to turn and look out onto Main Street, where I'm sure a handsome, dark-haired woman was parking a ten-year-old unit in front of the Busy Bee Cafe. Wyoming had never elected a female sheriff and the chances of their electing an Italian from Philadelphia with a mouth like a saltwater crocodile were relatively slim.

"She's got the Basquo with her." There was a pause as I continued eating my lunch. "Those two are quite the pair."

Santiago Saizarbitoria had joined our little contingency three months ago and, with the exception of trying to put out a chimney fire single-handedly on an ice-slicked roof, had proven himself indispensable. I listened as the door opened and closed, the laden April air drifting through the brief opening. They sat on the stools beside me and threw their elbows onto the counter. In identical uniforms and service jackets, they could have been twins, except that the Basquo was bigger, with wrists like bundled cables, and a goatee, and he didn't have the tarnished gold eyes that Vic had.

I kept eating as Dorothy pulled two mugs from under the counter, poured them full, and pushed the cream dispenser and the sugar toward the old world pair. They both drank coffee all day. Vic slipped her finger through the handle of her cup. "How was this afternoon's premiere at Durant Elementary?"

I took another sip of my iced tea. "I don't think we'll make the long run."

She tore open five sugars and dumped them in her mug. "I been here two years. How come they never fucking asked me?"

I set my glass back down. "It's hard to read nursery rhymes with a tape delay."

She stirred the coffee into the sugar and spoke into the mug. "That monkey pud Kyle Straub's got signs up all over town."

"Yep, I heard."

Saizarbitoria leaned in and joined the conversation. "Vern Selby was talking very highly about Mr. Straub in the paper yesterday."

"Yep, I read it."

All our radios blared for a second. Static. "Unit two, 10-54 at 16, mile marker four."

We looked at one another. Ruby had made a crusade of using the ten code in the last few weeks, and it was turning out to be a royal pain in the ass for all of us. I was the first one to guess. "Intoxicated driver?"

Vic was next. "Road blocked . . ."

Saizarbitoria took one last sip of his coffee and slipped off his stool; he knew the chain of command. He clicked the mic on his radio. "Ten fifty-four, roger." He looked at the two of us and shook his head. "Livestock on the road."

Vic and I shrugged at each other as she tossed him the keys. She sipped her sugar as he hurried out. "Do let us know."

Vic hitched a ride with me. As we walked up the steps of the old Carnegie Library that housed the Absaroka County Jail and offices, I could smell her shampoo and the crab apple blossoms. We were about halfway up the steps when she stopped me with a hand on my arm. I turned to look at her as she leaned against the iron railing and slid that same hand up the black-painted steel bar. I waited, but she just looked off toward Clear Creek, where the cottonwoods were already starting to leaf. She glanced back at me, irritated. "You still planning on leaving tomorrow morning?"

I adjusted the book of poetry under my arm. "That's the plan, at least mine."

She nodded. "I have a favor to ask."

"Okay."

She sniffed, and I watched as the wrinkles receded from the sides of her nose like cat whiskers. "My mother wants to have lunch with you and Cady."

I waited a moment, thinking there must be more. "Okay."

She continued to look off toward the creek. "Super Cop might be too busy, but my mother is feeling negligent in her attentions toward your daughter." I watched as the muscles of her jaw flexed like they always did when she mentioned her father.

"Okay."

"I mean . . . It's not a big deal. She just wants to have lunch."

I nodded again. "Okay."

"You can go to my Uncle Alphonse's pizzeria—it's nothing special."

I smiled and dipped my head to block her view. "I said okay."

She looked at me. "It's a family thing, and like most of the family things concerning my family, it's fucked up." She sighed. "I mean . . . they should have gotten in touch with her a long time before this, but in their usual, fucked-up way . . ."

"We'll have lunch." I watched as she studied her Browning tactical boots. Her dark hair stood up in tufts of dissatisfaction. "I would love to meet any of your family."

"Uh huh." Nothing was ever easy with Vic; it was one of her charms. She started up the steps without me. "Just don't expect too much."

I shook my head, followed her, and caught the beveled-glass door as it swung back into my face. I gently closed it and walked by the photographs of the five previous Absaroka County sheriffs. I saluted the painting of Andrew Carnegie as I mounted the final steps to the dispatcher's desk where Ruby sat reading the last series of updates from the Division of Criminal Investigation down in Cheyenne. "What the hell is a 10-54?"

She raised her blue eyes and gazed at me through her salt-with-no-pepper bangs. "Ferg says that he's 10-6 today if he's got to work the next week and a half solid, and I'm 10-42 as of five forty-five for my church's ice-cream social."

I decided to ignore the flurry of tens. "Did he go up to Tongue River Canyon?" She nodded. The Ferg was my part-time deputy who made a full-time habit of harassing the local aquatic life with his hand-tied flies. He was going to have to take up some of the slack while I was gone, so I didn't begrudge him a day casting bits of fur and feather upon the waters. "Any Post-its?"

"Two, and that young man who is supposed to come in this afternoon."

"What young man?"

She shook her head. "The young man from Sheridan who applied for the other deputy position in Powder Junction. He said he'd be here before five."

I sat on the corner of her desk, looked at the time on her computer, and reached down to pet Dog. "Then he's got twenty minutes."

The beast's head rose, and Ruby examined the scar that a bullet had left near his ear; a tongue the size of a dishwashing rag lapped my hand. "Lucian called to see if you'd forgotten it's chess night."

"Damn." I was going to have to go over to the Durant Home for Assisted Living to see the old sheriff.

"Cady called."

"She's changed her mind, and doesn't want us to come after all?"

Ruby wadded up the second Post-it and dispatched it with the first. "Not likely. She says for you to bring along your gun because she wants to take you to her shooting club on Thursday." We looked at each other for a moment, and then she raised an eyebrow. "Shooting club?"

I scratched the corner of my eye, where the scar tissue had healed. "It's this thing that Devon Conliffe's got her involved with."

She smiled. "Devon Conliffe again?"

"Yep . . ." I didn't sound all that thrilled, even to myself.

"This kid's got you worried."

She watched me scratch my eye for a moment longer, then reached up and pulled my hand away. I thought about it. "Methinks she doth protest too much."

Ruby shook her head. "She's scared you're not going to like him." She carefully released my hand. "He's young, handsome, accomplished, and makes about six times what you do on an annual basis. He has wooed and infatuated the most beautiful, intelligent, and precious woman that you know." She watched me with a smile. "It's perfectly reasonable for you to hate him." She batted her eyelashes. "Ten twenty-four?"

I looked at her for a moment, then trailed off to my office and wondered if anybody would notice if I slipped out the back. I sat at my desk and thought about calling the Bear to see if he didn't want to get going early. He wouldn't. I hit the second automatic dial button and listened as the phone rang at Henry's going concern at the edge of the Northern Cheyenne Reservation, free parking, no minimum.

He snatched it up on the second ring; it was his signature. "It's another beautiful day at the Red Pony Bar and continual soiree."

"Can we leave early?"

"No."

I hung up. There wasn't any reason to argue; I'd lose. I stared at the old Seth Thomas clock on the wall, thought of my packed bags by the door of my cabin, and sighed.

I punched the first number on my automatic dialing system and listened to the phone ring one thousand nine hundred thirty-six and one quarter miles away, to the place where my heart was on sabbatical.

"Schomberg, Calder, Dallin, and Rhind. Cady Longmire's office; can I help you?"

Patti with an "i." "Hi, Patti, you guys are working late."

"Yo, Sheriff. We've got a brief that has to be filed by tomorrow. How's things out in the Wild West?"

I leaned back in my chair and set my hat on my desk. "Uninteresting." I threw my feet up, something I rarely did, and almost flipped over backward. I grabbed the edge of the desk to steady myself. "Is 'The Greatest Legal Mind of Our Time' available?"

There was a clicking noise and the phone rang half a ring before she picked up. Near as I could figure, Schomberg, Calder, Dallin, and Rhind were getting their collective money's worth. "Cady Longmire."

I smiled in spite of myself; she sounded so grown up. "You're a punk."

There was silence on the line for a moment, then a slightly plaintive voice. "Have you left yet?"

"No, the Indian isn't packed."

Another short silence. "Is he still carrying the photographic find of the century around in hatboxes?"

"Probably. What's this stuff about bringing my sidearm?"

A quick sigh of exasperation. "I told you about it. Devon and I go to this shooting club over on Spring Garden on Thursday nights."

I was bored and decided to use up a little time arguing. "Why?"

Another, longer, silence. "It's something to do, Daddy. Don't start making judgments."

"I'm not. I just don't understand why you and a bunch of lawyers feel compelled to go out and shoot things on Thursday nights."

"We don't 'feel compelled' and we don't 'shoot things.' We go to a registered firing range, where we take out our secured weapons from the locked trunks of our cars, apply for our assigned ammunition, and shoot paper targets under the careful eye of a licensed instructor. He's an old fart, an Army guy like you."

"Marines."

"Whatever." She sniffed and got soft again. "I just thought you could meet him. It would be nice."

"Is this a Devon thing?"

Her voice turned sharp. "Bring your gun or don't. You're being impossible, and I have to go."

I looked at the phone. "I'll bring it."

"Whatever."

The phone went dead in my hand. I put my feet back down, placed the receiver on the cradle, and thought about how I was making friends and influencing people. I thought about closing my door and taking a nap but, when I looked up, a tall, slim young man with sandy hair was looking at me through the doorway. "Sheriff Longmire?"

"Yep."

"I'm Chuck Frymyer." I stared at him. "About the job in Powder Junction?"

I motioned for him to sit down and pulled his file from the pile on my desk. Only a month earlier, we couldn't get two deputies to rub together, but now we'd had over a dozen applications for the job. Frymyer had the most experience, with two years in Sheridan County.

I looked at the young man's application; he was way over-qualified. I glanced back up at him. "You do realize that this job is our equivalent of the French Foreign Legion?"

"Sir?"

I tossed the file back on my desk. "You're going to be out in the middle of nowhere. Have you ever been to Powder Junction?"

"I've driven through it, on the highway."

"Under the best of weather conditions, it takes me forty-five minutes to get down there, so I need deputies who can take care of themselves and the southern part of this county."

"Yes, sir."

"Don't call me sir." I looked at him a while longer and figured that, like "Beau" Geste, he must have his own reasons for wanting to go off to the end of the world; it probably had to do with a woman, but maybe that was the romantic in me. With his two years of patrol duty, he'd be a nice addition to Double Tough, the other deputy I had down there. "You're sure you want to do this?"

He smiled. "Yes."

I stood up and stuck out a hand. "You may curse me for it later, but you've got the job. Get your stuff together and report here on Monday morning, eight o'clock, and we'll get you sworn in. Sheridan's uniforms aren't that much different from ours, but you can wear blue jeans in Absaroka County. Get a badge and a patch set from Ruby at the front desk; we'll order up the rest. No black hats—we're the good guys."

I leaned back in my chair as he smiled. Ruby appeared in the doorway and cleared her throat. "I have some bad news."

I leaned forward, and rested my chin on my fingers, which spread across the surface of my desk. "I'm on my way out."

"It's Omar and Myra. They're shooting at each other again." I raised my head and looked at her. "It's a 10-16, technically." She smiled. "I'm going to my ice-cream social. Have a good time in Philadelphia and give Cady a kiss for me"

And she, too, was gone.

I yelled after her. "Who called it in?"

I heard her stop in the hallway. She came back and picked up my hat, carefully dusting it off and placing it on my head. "Go out there, make sure they don't kill each other, then go over to the Home for Assisted Living and play chess." I looked up at her. "I'll take Dog with me, and if you decide to take him with you, just stop by on your way out of town."

I drafted Vic before she could get out of the office and told her it was a chance for us to say goodbye before I left; of course, we could also be shot by the matching set of .308s with which Omar and Myra usually held their domestic disputes.

Omar Rhoades was the big dog of international outfitters; if you wanted to kill anything, anywhere, Omar was your man. He led big-game hunts on all seven continents, but the most dangerous game he had ever faced was his ex-wife, Myra. They had been divorced for about a year now, but Myra had left her belongings at the Rhoades ancestral manse, and it was like a ticking time bomb as to when Myra was going to be back. The home they had built together was on the northern border of our county, about halfway up the mountain; if they were serious about killing each other, then they were already dead.

I banked the next turn and gunned the Bullet into the long straightaway.

Vic unlocked the Remington 12-gauge from the center hump. "The gate's open."

It was about a hundred-yard shot to the circular turnaround at the main entrance, and I missed the fountain by less than a foot. We slid to a stop, and I jammed the truck into park and unbuckled my seatbelt. Vic was already up the front steps before

I could get out. "Hold up! It's one thing if Omar wants to shoot us, but I'll be damned if I'm going to be shot by accident."

I pulled my .45 and looked across the heavy, cherry-paneled door that hung open. Vic jacked a shell into the Wingmaster and looked at me. You could hear music, and I'm pretty sure it was Edith Piaf.

I took a deep breath and, after a second, stepped over the threshold.

Vic's voice lashed at me from behind. "Well?"

It was dark in the main hall, the gallery windows affording only a flat, yellow light from the dying afternoon. There was no one on the landing and no one in the entryway. "C'mon." I aimed at the stairway to the left, following the wall with a foot along the baseboard and kicked a broken bottle of Absolut raspberry vodka. There was no liquor on the floor, so the bottle had been empty when it hit. Great.

I looked past the mounted heads that led down the main hall toward the kitchen and passed under the cape mount of a particularly large buffalo. "Omar!"

Omar was a friend, having gone so far as to haul my ass up onto the mountain in a blizzard and fly my daughter, who had been caught in another, from Denver for Christmas, but drunk and full of rage he was capable of accidentally shooting either of us.

Vic moved along the wall next to me. "You want me to check the back?"

"No, we'll go upstairs; that's where the music is coming from." I took another deep breath and peered over the foot of the landing. "Omar?"

The furniture was toppled into the middle of the passage like a makeshift barricade. There were holes in the sideboard and the Chippendale chair, with splintered wood and up-holstery stuffing scattered on the oriental runner. I slumped against the wall and looked at my deputy. "Either they're dead, or they can't hear us over Edith Piaf."

I started back up the steps; at least the barricade afforded some defense. At the top railing, I made the turn, thought about the layout of the second floor, and remembered that the master bedroom was at the end of the hallway. It was about forty feet to the door, which was closed, but even at this distance I could see where match-grade loads had traveled through it; ten rounds, maybe, at three thousand feet per second. Since Myra was the one who had been in Paris for the better part of the last year and since the music was French, I assumed it was she who was in the bedroom.

I was looking at the door when I ran my leg into the edge of the sideboard, causing the mirror to flip on its pivot and crash to the floor. Even with Piaf, it was a loud noise. I looked at the shards of mirror scattered across the expensive Turkish rug and thought about seven years of bad luck. Edith took a breath, and I made out the distinctive sound of a modular bolt action slamming home.

I dove behind the barricade and flattened myself against the floor as the first round splintered through the wood of the upturned edge of the sideboard. Less than two seconds later, the next round caromed off the door facing and dug into the floor just short of my outstretched right hand. I was attempting to scramble toward the stairway when Vic leaned out from the railing and snapped off two 12-gauge rounds into the ceiling, the salvo allowing me a rather ignoble retreat. I ran into Vic, and we both fell down the remaining steps.

I was lucky enough to have landed on the bottom; she was sprawled across my chest. We looked at each other, and she grinned. "That was close." We stayed like that for a moment, then she rolled off me and I slid against the wall. We were sitting there on the landing a full ten seconds before we saw Omar. He was standing in the foyer, eating a ham and cheese sandwich and drinking a bottle of beer.

"What the hell?" He lowered the longneck bottle and cocked his head. "What're you guys doing? You could get killed up there." He started up the steps, and I noticed he had a .44 hunting sidearm in a holster at his leg. "I brought you guys a beer." We continued to look at him. "If you want a sandwich, the stuff's still out." He took another sip, and I thought about throwing him over the railing. He motioned for Vic to take the bottles, which she did after shuttling the shotgun under her arm.

"What's the story?"

He rolled his eyes and pushed his 50X Silver Belly hat back from his forehead, the long curls of gold reaching to the collar of his white dress shirt. "She started drinking this morning, after we had a little talk." He took another bite of his sandwich—I have to admit, it was looking pretty good. "She said she had traded me in on two twenty-year-olds, and I told her she wasn't wired for 220. The conversation kind of deteriorated from there." He finished off the beer and threw the bottle so that it shattered against the hand-patterned drywall. He put his hand to the side of his mouth to direct the volume: "Bitch!"

Two more .308s slammed through the door above. Vic and I simultaneously ducked as the rounds sped harmlessly down the empty hallway above us.

Omar took both of the beers from Vic, opened them on his belt buckle, handed her one back, and took a swig from the other as the cap fell to the carpeted landing and rolled down the stairs. "You didn't, by chance, happen to count how many holes were in the door?" He continued to look after the bottle cap. "There's only one box of shells for that thing, sixteen in a box . . ."

I knew that there was an abundance of weapons in the Rhoades household. "What about all the other guns in the safe?"

"No ammunition. I moved it all downstairs."

They both took sips and looked at me. "Twelve." I nodded back to the landing. "And two more makes fourteen."

Omar nodded. "She's got two left." We all nodded, as he casually drew the big .44 from his holster, aimed it straight up, and fired two shots; the long-barreled Smith and Wesson bucked in his hand. A few pieces of the entryway, elk horn chandelier, and plaster ceiling fell down on us. "Cunt!" The .308 thundered in response, but this time only once. Omar took another swallow. "Wisin' up, conserving ammo."

I looked at Vic, who looked at Omar. "Any chance of talking to her?"

Omar laughed, and I looked at him. "Is there a phone in the bedroom?"

"Yeah." We traipsed down to the entryway table where an old-fashioned Belgian dial phone sat. Omar picked up the receiver, dialed the number for the bedroom, and handed the phone to me. "She's not going to talk to me."

The phone rang three times before Myra answered. "Bastard!"

"Myra, it's Walter . . ." She slammed the receiver down with an ear-shattering crack. I asked Omar to dial the number again. She didn't answer this time, but the thunderous report of the .308 and the brief squall and whine of the line informed us that Myra had shot the bedroom phone.

I hung up and looked at the two of them. Vic looked back at the landing. "She's out?"

Omar agreed. "Yeah."

I wasn't convinced. "How drunk is she?"

"Pretty damn, but she hasn't missed the door yet."

I crossed the landing, staying to the right, where I knew I could dive into the guest bedroom if she had ammunition left after all. The problem was that the closed door seemed a very dangerous twenty feet away. Credit the carpenters that built the Rhoades mansion—the floor didn't creak as I carefully made my way around the barricade.

I had holstered my .45; I had no intention of shooting Myra.

With the volume of the music, it was impossible to hear any movement in the bedroom. As Edith Piaf continued singing, I looked at what the 150-grain softpoints had done to three inches of solid wood and felt that familiar weightlessness in the trunk of my body.

I counted the holes in the door again, but the damage caused by the large-caliber rifle made it difficult to be sure how many shots had really been fired. I wasn't betting the farm. It did look as if the shot closest to the knob had taken most of the mechanism with it, and the door itself stood ajar about a quarter of an inch, so I opted for nudging the base of it with my boot; it opened four inches. I waited, but nothing happened. I nudged further, gently sweeping it back about halfway before my leverage gave out.

I took a deep breath to clear my head and stepped through the doorway into the outstretched barrel of the big .308. She had been waiting, but my left arm was still to my right so, with a sweeping gesture, I carried the barrel down and away from me in a backhanded pull that exploded a round into the floor. The sound in the room was just short of deafening.

I was going to kill Omar.

I made a grab for the front stock but missed as she stepped back, and the seemingly endless length of the bolt action swung up.

I had forgotten how good-looking Myra was, and the year-long sabbatical in France with close to forty-eight million dollars had done her no harm. She had long, blond hair, the kind you see on the covers of magazines, and perfectly tanned skin that I'm sure had been kissed by the French Riviera. She was wearing a pink mohair cowl-neck sweater that barely reached the top of her thighs, and that was all. She was tall and lean, with strong, capable hands. The honking diamond that Omar had married her with was still on the left hand that pointed the rifle at my face. Above the scope was the palest blue eye, and as my lungs froze, the barrel dipped a little, and the sweater-matching pink lips smiled as slowly as glacial encroachment. I listened to Piaf singing "Le Chevalier de Paris" or "Mon Legionnaire," I wasn't sure which, and thought about how this wasn't the worst way to go.

The powder blue blinked, and I settled on "Le Chevalier de Paris" as the little bird trilled and softly breathed out her lovingly aching words.

Myra sagged a little, almost as if someone had punched her, and tossed the rifle aside. She stepped forward, her arms outstretched around my neck as the sharp fragrance of raspberry vodka scoured the inside of my nose and her sweater bottom rose higher. "Walter . . ."

"Good thing she likes ya." He brought his queen out. It was the second game, and my plans for an early evening had gone the way of my three pawns, two rooks, and a knight. I went with the other knight and felt a shadow of impending doom as his bishop slithered along diagonally. The stem of his pipe swung around and pointed at me like the barrel of a gun, the second of the evening. "You get 'er outta the house?" The pipe returned to his mouth.

I leaned back in the horsehide wingback chair and placed my hat on my knee. The old sheriff wasn't ready to end the evening and skimmed the other bishop across the board for a completely different attack on my king. "She's at the End of the Trail Motel over in Sheridan; flies out tomorrow."

It was quiet in the room as the old sheriff looked at me. Lucian's mahogany eyes flickered in the half-light of the kitchenette behind us. He shook his head. "Well, ya know how my marriage experience ended."

I did, and we sat there in silence for a while before I admitted a prejudice. "I hate the domestic stuff."

He nodded and watched me. "Like the third man in a hockey fight, ya get the blame and get the shit kicked out of you for yer troubles." He waited as I made another inane move. "I hear Kyle Straub's got signs up all over town."

I took a sip and crunched one of the cubes. "I heard that too."

"You gonna stand?"

"I don't think I've got any choice if I want to get Vic in."

He shrugged. "I'd vote for her, but I've got the weakness." Lucian was referring to his habit of addressing Vic's chest as if it had an identity of its own. "The rest of Absaroka County is another question. Now, you can make sure she's the next sheriff, but it's gonna cost you a year or two of your life." I made a face. "But then, I didn't know yer life in office was so damn bad." His gaze dropped back to the board. "Check."

I looked at the assembly of courtly pieces and placed a finger on my king, casually toppling him over to premature death. "Yep, well . . . no act of kindness goes unpunished."

A PENGUIN READERS GUIDE TO

DEATH
WITHOUT
COMPANY

Craig Johnson

AN INTRODUCTION TO
Death Without Company

Featuring the remarkable Sheriff Walt Longmire, the hero of Craig Johnson's acclaimed first novel, *The Cold Dish, Death Without Company* takes readers back into the rugged terrain and colorful social milieu of Absaroka County, Wyoming.

When Mari Baroja, a beautiful Basque woman, is found dead in the Durant Home for Assisted Living, it is assumed she died of natural causes. She is an old woman, after all. But Lucian Connally, the former sheriff, thinks otherwise. He had been married to Mari for three hours many years before, until Mari's father and uncles hunted the couple down, gave Lucian a beating, had the marriage annulled, and married Mari off to an abusive Basque husband. Lucian suspects that Mari's death is a result of foul play. An autopsy reveals poisoning as the cause of death, and Sheriff Longmire suddenly has a murder to solve. But who would kill an elderly woman in a nursing home? And for what reason? These questions prove baffling enough, but soon Longmire is confronted with a rash of crimes that would seem more likely in New York City than in this sparsely populated patch of rural Wyoming. Mari's granddaughter is brutally attacked; Lucian himself is nearly strangled in his bathtub; Mari's doctor, Isaac Bloomfield, finds the brakes of his car have been tampered with; and Anna Walks Over Ice, an Indian woman who works at the nursing home, is found stuffed in a trash can, victim of a ghastly killing. Now Longmire, aided by his friend Henry Standing Bear, Deputy Victoria Moretti, and rookie officer Santiago Saizarbitoria, must find a killer who is as relentless as he is remorseless. In trying to do so, Longmire almost sees his own life go down the river.

And while these crimes tear at the heart of Sheriff Longmire and the community he lives in, he knows that "hatred has a poor shelf life but that hope and love can limp along forever." And indeed *Death Without Company* is a novel of great warmth, great friendship, great humor, and great love, written with all the wit and narrative drive that have made Craig Johnson one of the strongest new voices in literary mystery.

A CONVERSATION WITH CRAIG JOHNSON

1. What prompted you to write Death Without Company? *Did the novel grow out of a specific experience or intention?*

I've described Walt as a detective for the disenfranchised. In *The Cold Dish,* he was concerned with a teenage woman with fetal alcohol syndrome, Indians, and some young men whom a lot of people in the community would just as soon have seen dead. In *Death Without Company,* I was interested in the contrasts between Walt and Lucian Connally, the previous sheriff; interested in how the job was different, how the times were different. That led me to think about the aged, another group that is greatly marginalized in our society. I wanted to travel back and forth in these people's lives and show how they were different.

2. In what ways are you like Walt Longmire?

When I was young, I made the mistakes that a lot of young people make: I was judgmental, stubborn, and puritanical. I hope I'm that sadder but wiser person now. I would hate to think all those scars and memories were for nothing. I identify with a lot of the sadness Walt carries with him, and the humor.

3. In an interview conducted for the guide to your first novel, The Cold Dish, *you said: "Writing is a solitary pursuit and I think you have to be partially at peace with yourself, but it's the other part that's usually producing the stuff worth reading." Could you elaborate on that statement? Do you feel that a certain restlessness or anxiety or resistance to things as they are is a necessary spur to creative activity?*

I generally start with some injustice, something that's going to put a burr under my saddle blanket. I like dealing with large issues on a personal and passionate level and know myself well enough to know I write best when I write disgruntled.

4. You live pretty far from the literary centers of America. Do you have much contact with other writers?

A lot more in the last year. I was doing a reading at the Great Salt Lake Book Festival and they put us up in this fancy hotel. I had just started to eat breakfast and saw a man come in and look around. I waved and said, "Mark Spragg?" I think he thought about running, but I reassured him that he didn't know me or owe me money. We had breakfast. I don't think very many authors are used to being recognized; it makes them nervous. I sat on a panel between James Lee Burke and James Crumley at the Montana Festival of the Book, talk about nervous.

5. Walt Longmire says that he "hates mysteries," though he clearly thinks like a detective. Why are you drawn to the mystery genre? What satisfactions do mysteries offer that other kinds of fiction don't?

Walt hates mysteries in the sense that he doesn't like not knowing the answers; for him it's not an avocation or a distraction, it's his job and his nature. For me, there are structural elements to mysteries that I find appealing, the cipher; writing and reading with purpose. I also enjoy writing within a genre while trying to be outside of it. Then there is the inherent stake of life and death; it doesn't get any higher.

6. Indians and whites get along remarkably well in Death Without Company. *Is this generally true in Wyoming? What is life like for Indians in contemporary Wyoming?*

It would be foolish for me to speak for all Wyoming, and I can only address the subject from my own experiences. I have numerous friends from both the Northern Cheyenne and Crow reservations who are very important to me. Once again, I would warn against categorizing Indians as a group; each tribe is different, each band is different, each clan is different, and each person is different. The relationships and lifestyles of each are too numerous and it would be a disservice to attempt qualifying them here.

7. There is a horribly violent scene in Death Without Company. *Does that violence come from within you or from what you have experienced?*

That scene was a tough one to write. I wanted Lucian to tell the story, but I wanted Walt and the reader to feel it. I wanted to create a sense of helplessness, an inability to do something. I have experienced some tough situations in my life, and the thing it provided for the writing was a desire to make it real. I feel that brutality is glamorized in our society, prepackaged into something it's not. I wanted to display violence as it is: desperate, frightening, ugly, and with long-lasting consequences.

5

8. Your book deals with serious societal issues yet it also contains a great deal of humor. What role do you think humor plays in conveying your serious messages?

"I am my most serious when I am humorous, and my most humorous when I am serious." Not mine, Oscar Wilde's. It's the sugar coating on the medicine of the truth, or at least my truth. Without humor, the writing can get pretty pedantic, and then I'd find myself insufferable.

9. Your books are very unlike traditional mysteries. How would you characterize what your novels are or what you intend them to be?

I hope they're whodunits for people who get to the end and don't give a damn about who done it. I'm interested in the structural aspects of the mystery, but I'm more concerned with the societal issues and the people. I'm a great fan of the golden era of mystery writers—Hammett, Christie, Sayers, and Chandler— but I don't want to write what they wrote. The mystery genre speaks to a much larger audience these days and with that goes a certain responsibility for the author. To ignore the complexities of the reader is to ignore the complexities of society, and that would be criminal.

QUESTIONS FOR DISCUSSION

1. The title of the novel comes from a Basque proverb, "A life without friends means death without company" (p. 23). Why has Craig Johnson chosen this phrase for his title? What role does friendship play in the novel? How would you describe Walt Longmire's friendships with Lucian and Henry Standing Bear?

2. Rural Wyoming is not the typical setting for a mystery. What role does the setting—the landscape, weather, history, and culture of Wyoming—play in *Death Without Company*? What are the most distinctive features of the people and country in which the novel is set?

3. After Walt tells Henry Standing Bear about a dream he'd had about Mari in which he heard Indian drumming, Bear tells Walt: "It would appear that you now have an advocate in the Camp of the Dead" (p. 82). What does he mean? In what instances does this supernatural "advocate" help Walt?

4. When Walt tells Henry that Leo is a "half-breed," Henry corrects him by suggesting "bicultural" as a more apt term. Walt responds: "Are you aware of the damage you are causing with all this political correctness to the language of the mythic American West?" To which Henry replies, "You bet'cher boots" (p. 221). In what ways does the novel itself either challenge or confirm stereotypes of the "mythic American West"? How are Indians portrayed in the novel?

5. How does Craig Johnson build and sustain suspense over the course of the novel? What is most surprising about the way the plot unfolds and the mystery is solved?

6. What makes Leo Gaskell such a frightening antagonist in *Death Without Company*?

7. Walt Longmire describes himself: "It wasn't a bad face other than needing about eight hours of uninterrupted sleep, a haircut, the loss of about twenty pounds and ten years. My chin was too big, along with my ears, and my eyes were too deep set. . . . I still wasn't sure about the beard, but it hid a lot" (p. 81). What does this

passage suggest about how Longmire regards himself? Why is his self-deprecating humor so appealing? What are his most admirable qualities? What makes him such a good sheriff?

8. Near the end of *Death Without Company*, Walt is filled with the thought that "hatred has a poor shelf life but that hope and love can limp along forever" (p. 270). Why does he feel this way? What evidence of the enduring quality of love, and the transitory nature of hate, can one find in the novel? Is Walt an idealist?

9. Johnson assembles a lively cast of female characters—Vic, Ruby, Lana, Maggie, and even Mari, who exerts a powerful posthumous influence on Walt Longmire. What is most notable about these women? How do they interact with Walt?

10. *Death Without Company* is a story about passion, greed, family, and friendship. What does the novel tell us about these grand themes of human existence?

For more information about or to order other Penguin Readers Guides, please e-mail the Penguin Marketing Department at reading@us.penguingroup.com or write to us at:

Penguin Books Marketing Dept.
Readers Guides
375 Hudson Street
New York, NY 10014-3657

Please allow 4–6 weeks for delivery.
To access Penguin Readers Guides online, visit the Penguin Group (USA) Web site at www.penguin.com or vpbookclub.com.

AVAILABLE FROM PENGUIN
AS EBOOK SPECIALS ONLY

Divorce Horse

Sheriff Walt Longmire and his soon-to-be-married daughter Cady hit the Indian Relay races at the county fairgrounds that includes the first chapter from *As the Crow Flies*.

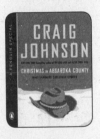

Christmas in Absaroka County

A delightful collection of four short stories from *New York Times* bestselling author Craig Johnson that includes the first chapter of *The Cold Dish*.

Messenger

Sheriff Walt Longmire comes face to face with an otherworldly messenger in a hilarious tale that also includes a teaser chapter from Johnson's novel *A Serpent's Tooth*.

**PENGUIN
BOOKS**

Depth of Winter

A Longmire Mystery

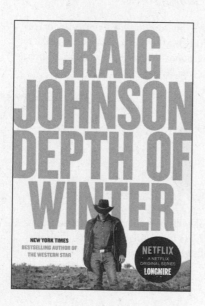

In Craig Johnson's latest mystery, *Depth of Winter*, an international hit man and the head of one of the most vicious drug cartels in Mexico has kidnapped Walt's beloved daughter, Cady. The American government is of limited help and the Mexican one even less. Walt heads into the heat of the Northern Mexican desert alone, one man against an army.

VIKING

 PENGUIN BOOKS